The Blood of Heaven

Kent Wascom

Grove Press
New York

Published simultaneously in Canada
Printed in the United States of America

FIRST EDITION

ISBN-13: 978-0-8021-2118-9

Grove Press
an imprint of Grove/Atlantic, Inc.
841 Broadway
New York, NY 10003

Distributed by Publishers Group West

www.groveatlantic.com

13 14 15 16   10 9 8 7 6 5 4 3 2 1

For if their purpose or activity is of human origin, it will fail. But if it comes from God, you cannot defeat these men; you will only find yourselves fighting against God.

ACTS 5:39–40

PROLOGUE

A Prayer for the City

New Orleans, January 26, 1861

Tonight I went from my wife's bed to the open window and pissed down blood on Royal Street. She shrieked for me to stop and use the pot, but below I swear the secession revelers, packed to the street-corners, were giving up their voices, cheering me on. They're still out there, flying high on nationhood. Suddenly gifted with a new country, they are like children at Christmas. I saw their numbers swelling all the way to Canal, and in this corner of the crammed streets the celebrants were caught and couldn't escape my red blessing. A herd of broadcloth boys passed under my stream while a whore howled as I further wilted the flowers in her hair and drove her customers off; and yawping steve-dores, too drunk to mind, were themselves bloodied even as they tried to shove others in. And if I could I would've written out a blessing on all their faces, anointed them with the red, red water from my Holy Sprinkler, and had them pray with me.

1

Pray for the children of this city drowned in sin, plague, and muddy water. We breach the filmy surface but can only manage whiskey-choked howls. Where bed sheets stained with bile and bloody flux normally fly from the iron railings of our balconies, now upstart banners are unfurled, the flags of the newly independent state and a people claiming to be free—of Washington, of tyranny, of our gangle-bones president. And we are free, in this place where I sell whip-scored flesh pound-by-pound. I have made speculation on the price of slaves my living for some fifty years, and have been blessed with an octoroon wife and a son further whitened by my blood. My wife and boy are free the same way the South is now free. Free for folly and disaster; free to go to hell—The hell I've made in the long and wicked years of my life, wherein I had another son, another wife, both lost to time, abandoned by me.

Pray for us who are annually subjected to those tropical atrocities: hellish heat, disease, and hurricane; who live along the fertile nethers of the South on the country's purest coast. Our corner of the Gulf is soaked in blood, brothers and sisters, and I have given my fair share to the tide. From the heel of latter-day Louisiana to Mobile Bay lies the Holy Land I wished to make with my brother, Samuel Kemper. We fought our revolution in 1804, in what was then called West Florida. We failed, through foolishness and gall and losing sight of God's true path; afterwards I'd try once more to take that country, through scheming and plotting and following the dreams of great men, but all for nothing. In 1810 a gaggle of planters would have their revolution and they were too respectable to call on Angel Woolsack. They had a country, so they called it, for but a few months. No matter—at that time I was wringing the first of my fortune from black flesh. And the half century since has passed like hang-fire and I'm glad my brother or any of the rest didn't live to see what's coming now.

Pray for those who scream for war.

This afternoon was a rage of flags, as every man whose wife knew how to stitch poured through the square with his idea of a new nation's standard trailing behind him like a cape. A madness of stripes and stars, of bloody-breasted pelicans, of crosses, of crowns, of snakes, of skulls—all dragged, tossed, raised, and trampled by the crowd. And it was in this chaos of colors that this prayer was fixed in me, which grew like a seed to bursting and blossomed into the gospel I now set down to write. The moment came while I watched some boys who'd fought through the tumult climb General Jackson's statue and tie their flag to the hat he holds at the end of an outstretched arm. The flag hung limp at first, just dangling blue-colored cloth, until a gust of wind blew in from off the river and unfurled it to roars and cheers and church bells; and in that instant, like a vision breaking over my head, I saw it was the planters' flag, the emblem of their starched and lacy revolution, the one the Texans stole some years later—a field of blue shot through with a single white star. So the failed are forgotten and the South now attaches its rebellious hopes to the dusty victories of the horsed and booted. Our blood-red banner of '04 bore the inscription THY WILL BE DONE beneath a pair of gold stars for me and Samuel—the fists of God punching holes through the sky. Now our flag is only known in its dismemberment by the brandy-soaked gentry, who used its holy design to make their own.

Still, I would've hurrahed with the rest, but I was disgusted at the sight of that resurrected banner, which they now call the Bonnie Blue. Soon the ringleaders had the people caught in song; I listened hard for a word about West Florida, about anything of mine, and finding there was none, I wept. Southern rights, Lincoln, niggers, and cotton were all I heard from them. My war and my country were a lifetime ago for these children of the steam engine. I wept at that great fool multitude. I wept to be forgotten; for my brother, whose name I adopted and forsook; for my first wife, my Red Kate; I wept for the child we put in the grave, and for a lifetime spent at the hands of God.

Pray for the planter boys like the one who saw me weeping and, amid the song and celebration, took me by the arm and said, Don't squall now, old man, we've won!

He didn't know that winning's not the prize. No, you have to win and win again. That is the American way of war: you have to win forever.

Besides, the only planter who wants to fight a war is bored so crazy with whipping his slaves that he'd like to try his hand at whipping something greater, so that he can see if it cows. I have fought alongside their kind and I know their stomachs for it. Atop lovely thoroughbreds and in fine outfit they will ride out to fools' deaths, drawing scores of poorer others behind them. And there will be enough dead to pack the mouth of Hell with bodies, like the doors of an opera house on fire. And afterwards those left alive will be in tatters and in rags, defeated, riding to the cinders of their houses on stolen nags.

Pray for the soon-dead gentlemen and for the crackers who will follow them. Pray for all the wild rovers, for the night-girls and the resurrection-men, for the wine-bibbers and the riotous eaters, for the Kaintucks and duellists, for free blacks and slavish whites, for virtuous whores and whorish virgins. Pray for the false prophets and the true.

Pray for me. I am one of them.

I am a victim of the Shepherd's Curse, that of the raised-up shepherd who ate the flesh of the fat and tore their claws to pieces, only to become the idle. So my right eye is utterly darkened, blinded in a skirmish all those years ago, and my arm is clean dried up, made a stump by the love of axe-wielding Kate, who suffered those years of killing and madness as long as she could.

I am too far gone to fight again, though my hand still better fits the pistol grip than the walking stick or cane. I have been the hand that does the will of His divinity. I have been the instrument: killer and conduit elite. I have rendered man, woman, and child unto the Lord with shot, stick, knife, hanging rope, and broken glass, but I have delivered many more with the voice I keep coiled down deep in my withered throat, and with such expedience as would make the crashing bullet weep and the knife blade, imperceptible in its sharpness, strike dull.

And if there are none in these Disunited States who will pray for us, they had better start clapping their soft hands together soon because I can talk to bones; and like Ezekiel I will call them up; and the soggy bones buried in our loam will do as good as the dry bones of the wasteland Hebrews; and I will enkindle them with the breath of life and they will march with me and light the streets with phosphorescence on our way to swallow up the world.

Brothers and sisters, we will never be the shining city on the hill, but with the grace of God we can become the rot-glowing hand that will pull the bastards down.

I see everything, past and now, like targets over the nip of a bead. There goes my father; there goes my brother and the wars we fought; there go all the souls that I've outlived.

Last night, as the prayer slipped out of this tomb-ready body, I was made again a vessel of their voices and the Word of the Lord. The eggs of corruption were cast out of my skin and the hatchling worms pulled forth by heavenly fingers. I am wounded and made whole. All my friends and enemies are back again. I see the face of Red Kate in the visage of my octoroon, my first child's eyes peering at me in bemusement from the skull of the living boy. The Resurrection of the Dead is commencing, and I hope my single wrinkled hand can let them out.

My wife was frightened of my prayer just as she is frightened of the prospect of me dying, so I save what may upset her for the page and soothe her once again this morning with the fact that if I die there will be coin enough to keep her and the boy. Sweet Elise was no wife at first, and isn't even now because she has a dropper's worth of Negroe blood in her. For us to be legal and wed I'd be forced to swear that I had some black blood in me.

Now, I thank God daily that I've mixed my blood with hers and made a son, but there are things this world won't bear; I couldn't stand it in the weeks before she birthed our son the way she undertook with a gaggle of old Creole women—her creamy forebears who survived St. Domingue—twenty-five prayers and passes of the rosary each day so that our child's eyes would be born as blue as mine. They were, but only for a week. At birth he wore a crown of golden hair like mine, which he retains to the age of ten. He's grown up bathing in milk and lotions, receipts Elise learned from those same Creole ghouls. She gives thanks each day for his color and keeps him in wide hats when she takes him out into the city.

I cherish her, even though she came to me like a parcel, in response to a notice my friend Billy Walker placed for me in the *Picayune* for an octoroon woman to come and share my bed. But young Walker also wanted me to teach him a few things concerning being a filibuster, which is what the Spanish Pukes called me in my day and surely their descendants Walker in his. We would walk the riverfront and there he listened to me tell how our first West Floridian rebellion went down; and I hoped that he might gain from it and learn. I don't know if he listened, but all he had to do was look at me to know that nation-making is a bitch who chews you up. As it stands, he took whatever knowledge I gave him to his grave somewhere in Central America. Still, he brought me my Elise and I am grateful.

The boy was bad to pull at her tit, bad at tooth-cutting time, but that didn't ruin her bodily for me. I am an admirer of the pendulous in women. Seems a swaying judgment when she is astride me, like the cantered weights of human justice when she dips her shoulder to lower left or right to my mouth, and I see the scales tipping always in this sinner's favor.

The round-heels are nowhere near her. Whiteness is all they have going for them, and in this land of every son of a bitch with enough coin having his pick of African concubines that is enough for them to charge a price to slip beneath their skin. I'm fair haired enough to be considered of exemplary whiteness, the purest of the pure. The New Orleans people give me that credit; no one wants to smirch the stainless in this city where all has swirled together. And even having added to the mix myself, I am still given the ranging benefits of my snowy bloodline. Money makes a fine shield, but I must always assure Elise that she and the boy will be protected when I die.

And what kind of father do I make? One who strops and shaves each morning, dresses in businessman's suit and beaver, has his high boots slipped on by black hands, then goes out from our muddy way to the pavers where the gutters run full from the rain, through people huddled next to coffee stands manned by clucking German boys whose hands are welted from tending their brass pots and dropping in cloves and ground chicory which tang the air and open the lungs of ones like me cutting through the chambered palisade of the market where early morning butchery has spilt enough blood and fat to lacquer the floor so that it squeaks beneath my boots and I leave a trail of red prints on my stride across the square towards the St. Louis Hotel, and up the steps of the rotunda to the nigger-seller's yawn, where I am surrounded by bedizened society whores and toasted by sugar-rich boys in high hats and school colors accompanied by their fathers' clerks. There I am the father who speculates on human prices, listening to the other sellers sing today of being Southern Gentlemen and newly free while they prod their niggers to dance and show muscle. What else for this father of lies to do but swig champagne served cold and complimentary to all us men of business and wait till out of the watchers and buyers comes Dr. Sabatier, my agent and physician, who tells me how the niggers looked this week in their pens, the great gaols where we keep our living wares behind brick and bar; he shoots glances to the youths when he's not scribbling in his ledger our daily losses and gains, the monetary measure of my iniquities. I am the father who hears the music and witnesses the great exchange, thinking that the barkers would make fine preachers and may yet be, so muddied is the face of this world and so lacking in steel.

My father was so godly that he wouldn't even let me call him *Father,* always *Preacher.* And Preacher-father was a hard thing to have. No whiskey tits for your fevers or teething and no fairy-tale reading, as I give my own son. There were no such things as tales when I was a boy—I was read to from but one book and all of it was true.

Bad word or bad deed Preacher-father punished with charcoal slivers pulled from the campfires we built beside baptismal rivers and from the stoves and fireplaces of believers from the northern neck of Virginia to the Missouri Territory. So it was his way not to holler me down the way he did his endless congregations on the mud fares of the border towns, or even to strike me, which was common in his preaching also, but rather to tell me to go to the fire and stir it with a stick, or an iron if we were in the house of a good family, to find a coal guttering there and pull it aside, then to wait beside it while it cooled such to be handled. I was then to pray upon my transgressions, an hour or so, testing the coal with small hands getting welted and red worse than any ass could from belt or switch. Finally he would have me take the coal and stuff it into my mouth and go to chewing. My lips would at first rebel, growing fat and cracked as the coal passed between them and the fire jumped up my teeth and into their roots so that my brain was burning. I always chewed lightly, huffing breaths, or sucked it like a rare sweet, because I knew at the middle was a hotter heart that still burned live. And while I chewed he would say his first words since he ordered me to the fire:

Do you taste the Hell in there?

And the coal would squeal between my teeth and he would ask if I could hear the cries of the sinners it held. Seeing me clench and grit when I came to the kernel of Hell at the white of the coal, he would say, And that's but a taste there on your tongue. Now swallow it down.

I've likened that I was born in 1776, just to be a completist in this country's birth and dissolution, but it was Samuel Kemper, my brother not of blood but of love and war, who was born in the year of rebellion, and he always said that he had a good ten years on me. It doesn't matter. Preacher-father never told me more than my name, which is Angel Woolsack: Angel for my golden hair and our last name which means Death in Scots talk, or so I've been told—Death what comes stalking the country to gather souls into his brimming black bag. The verses of our family history revealed only that I was the final issue of a wrecked line, Hell-bound, as my gospel will prove. My mother's expiration came from a disease that ate her up from womb to gifted rib. The public sick-house where she died Preacher-father burnt as her pyre, an act of anger he often repented, saying that it smelled like cooking years of rotten meat, but not as awful as it had smelled unburnt.

So I came from nothing, from damn-near nowhere, and moved piecemeal across this nation before it ever was. And now that it's no more I am further unencumbered of origins. Our seeds were scattered to the corners of the new country by breath passed through the anger-clenched teeth of God. And if the earth did have a face for darkness and light and water to fall upon, then we were the blue-tailed flies who crept across that countenance from place to pockmarked place, never lighting on one pus-drip for long.

My hand is not as strong as the one that brought me up, but I doubt such strength could survive these times. I have become weak out of kindness to my child, as I know he'd never survive that flinty education. Some days I see the boy off to his Jesuit minders or let him wander close to home in his wide-brimmed hat. His youth has none of the punishment of my own, but he may yet come to know the fire. And so for now and whatever days of mine remain I have a son to teach what I know: riflery, the ride, and the Word of the Lord. He will learn his delineation, of our preacherly race, as I learned it at the foot of a howler for Christ, from an early life led by Preacher-father's hand into worlds of our own making.

And so it seems to me correct that the death columns always list a man's children as having survived him. This wording makes some sense of fathers to me. For mine was never so cruel in punishment or trial that I did not endure him. But neither was he so weak either as to not make my life an act of survival.

Book One

IN THE BEGINNING

I

The Wild Country

Upper Louisiana, 1799

Into the Land of Milk and Honey

They would later say that the day we came into Chit Valley all the children's fevers broke and everybody's bowels were righted. But from the way we first arrived in that place, you would never think that Preacher-father would become their fighting prophet, their bloody savior. As it stood, we almost didn't make it there.

Some miles below the falls at Louisville the captain of the flatboat we'd taken grew tired of Preacher-father and his talk of baptism, and so had us flung over the side along with what baggage fellow passengers felt like tossing after us, our horses, kit, and feed left behind—or flowing on ahead of us, as it may be. This was before the western territories had been redeemed or given any settled name and the country we passed into was then known as Upper Louisiana, though so was much of the world. Now it's called Missouri, a dangling fragment of the carved-up Union.

It was a hard time to be a Baptist. The tar was always bubbling then and there were many who had no love for preaching. We were used to rough treatments, and if the boatmen and their passengers hadn't caught us mid-sermon, by surprise and from behind, we might've shown them something of a fight, rather than being sent tumbling into the swirling cold of the river. The laughter of the flatboat riders passed away with the splashes of our bags, then the voice of Preacher-father called out my name. I whirled enough to see him bobbing some distance behind me. He thrashed ahead until he was near enough to catch me by the hand, and so I held fast to my father and together we fought across the current to a stand of limbs lying partway in the water.

So there came days of wandering through marshes, being eaten by insects till we were scabbed and shivering in our soaked leathers. Though by guesswork I was thirteen, I was still shorter than the grass, and the deeper we went into the marsh the taller it grew until I was swallowed up entirely and spent days without the sun. My skin grew gray and wrinkled and I kept my eyes to his footprints in the slough— those that weren't immediately swallowed up by water and mud—so that I could follow on the good ground. We flattened reeds to sleep dry, but still I would sink into the earth and by morning would be half-drowned. I lay those nights with my head on my hands so that my ears would not fill with mud while Preacher-father wandered, calling on God and on the river, shouting, Hey, miss! Hey, miss! like it was a woman out there waiting, and he suffered to find it the same fool way most men hunt for women.

When at last he found the river, Preacher-father mistook it for more of the Ohio. We crossed that dark and swirling parallel on a raft we hewed and poled ourselves, not knowing until we came upon some other travelers, heading north to Cape Girardeau, that we had made the river and were now into the west.

For days more we followed ruts and traces in the grasslands, daily thanking God for our deliverance, through forests and up a rise of hills where the trees ended at the lip. Among the scrabble-scratch of branches we stumbled upon a squat of Indians all laid up in a grove. They were covered in sores and too sick to move or talk, nor give us more than a roll of flyspecked eyes. Preacher-father kept his hand on the handle of his hatchet all the same as we moved through their camp, which looked as though it had been set there forever, and we passed nearest to a squaw whose cheeks were so eaten away that I could see her teeth, though she was still breathing. After we'd left them and were heading down into the valley, my father said to me, That's how you know you're on the track to Christians, son. The heathen withers and dies even in their proximity.

The Chitites

In those wild and thinly populated reaches we found sullen Christians living at peril of soul and fearful of the avarice of the Indian. These beleaguered whites lived in holes dug underground; the only watch kept over the endless plain was by their meager stock. A homestead would only be marked by the lonesome beasts in their pens and the stovepipes trailing smoke from the fires stoked below.

Here were the very seeds of forsaken civilization, scattered along the prairie and waiting for us to sow them into a promised land. Or so much as Preacher-father said. The place was settled by no more worthless a pack of dirt-daubers than you will find in all this awful world. They were ten or so families, with names like Shoelick and Backscratch and Auger, and we were met at the door of each one's hole, which opened like a cellar, by bewildered and mistrustful faces. Their thin, dirt-caked children slept in biers carved into the mud walls of the dugouts and watched like rats as I stood beside my father at their family tables, if they had any. It wasn't rare for me to sit upon the floor and look up to see insects struggling in the ceiling or for an earthworm to drop into your coffee cup.

They had become like moles or rabbits and would hear our footfalls on the sod before our voices. When Preacher-father spoke, they came out, if they did at all, holding guns or farm tools, and their voices rasped with wonder for having gone so long speaking to no one but their own poor blood. When he asked them about Jesus or being saved, they stared and grew more awestruck with whatever next he said. Poverty of soul, he called it, but God knows we were bizarre, this growling man and little blond-haired boy, traveling with supplies so lacking that the holediggers all said we should have been dead. Maybe that was what first made them all believe in him.

They warned against pitching camp aboveground for the wind and the Indian to level. When they were made aware of the disease which had recently befallen the savages, the Chitites shook their heads and said that nothing could kill the devils. Dig, they said, and bury yourself for the empty horror of this land. But Preacher-father refused to huddle in the dark, hiding from the eye of the Lord and increasing his proximity to Hell. He said this was the place and these were the people he would lead to Heaven.

They were, he said, sore in need of his preaching.

The Fladeboes

Once we visited a dugout that was viciously armed. Sharpened branches stuck like pikes from around its door and there were holes cut in the boards for gun-barrels. It was early yet in our ministry of Chit, and our first time at this particular hole. I couldn't know that what awaited me within that dank burrow was my first great sin.

When a man's voice called for our names my father answered for us both. Leather hinges creaked and the door cracked open but an inch.

Come here, said the man. Show me your hand.

Preacher-father went and did as he'd been asked, then through the door-crack shot a hand that took his up and felt it, as if to see that he was real.

I'm a man of God, he said, and white.

So you are, said the holedigger, and let go his hand.

Inside the smell was not of dirt as you'd expect, but of people close and filthy. I was used to life in the open air and the dugouts seemed an awful, grave-like thing. They were the Fladeboes: father Conny, mother Fay, and—God forgive me—daughter Emily sitting there in the dark in a dingy sackcloth dress. The father led us to a short table with seats only on one side, already occupied by mother and daughter hunching over steaming bowls.

You can eat, the mother said, if you don't mind to share bowls and spoons with us. All we got is three.

They could eat off knives, the daughter offered, with a glance that in the tallow-light looked wild.

Good girl, said her mother. Go and get them.

The daughter huffed up from her place and disappeared into a darkened corner of the hole, returning, after a brief scratch and scrabble, with a pair of smooth-edged knives.

Emily, you'll share your bowl with this boy, said her mother.

Preacher-father waited till the man had set himself down at one end of the bench, then went and stood beside him, dipping now and then from the bowl with his knife, talking between swallows of our mission in this place.

I couldn't be as deft, crouching next to Emily and examining her hard enough to lose my food a dozen times down the front of my shirt. She had an eye that wandered: her left, a mud-colored marble rolling untethered in her skull. And she might have been ugly, my little starveling girl, but she was of age and I grew in her presence then, counting the ringworms in her neck and numbering them like pearls. She was gaunt as me and greedily we watched each other eat. So while Preacherfather awed the Fladeboes with our plans for ministry, I went slopping up the corn-shuck gruel and lurching after Emily in my mind.

The mother and father kept still and silent for his talk, and it was Emily who finally spoke, leaning over to whisper in her mother's ear and rocking back and forth a little on her end of the bench. The mother frowned and gave her husband, who was rapt, a good jab with a crooked finger.

She's got to pass, said the mother.

She can wait, he said.

At that, Emily gave a little whine.

Dirt or water? asked her father.

Just let her bring the gun, the mother said. She'll be all right.

Damn it, said the man. Boy, why don't you take that rifle from the door and go watch for her out there.

It hadn't struck me yet full on what he was asking. And before it did, Preacher-father was pointing me to the steps and I was taking up the rifle when Emily came hustling by, pushing out the door. I followed after her and let the door come closed. She was clutching at her lap with both hands. Wincing, she hurried off saying, Come on, it's over here.

I followed her past a pen of sickly-looking hogs, over to a patch of high grass which, when she parted herself a place to squat, I saw hid a trough of shit and piss. Soldierly I clutched the rifle to me as she got down on her heels, flipped up the backside of her dress, and started singing. I glimpsed her squatting, skirts bundled up and the grass-stalks blooming all around the white of her knees. Before I could turn, with a gyre of her wild eye Emily caught me in a glance.

I'm not looking, I said.

Good, she sang. Or else you might find that you've gone blind.

Devil-worms lit into me like magpies to a lamb's eyes as I stood out there with Emily and kept watch over her corruption. She sang on, whatever song it was, and I was busily recomposing Solomon's for her: Who is this that cometh out of the wilderness like a pillar of blond smoke, perfumed with black powder and campfire ash? We have a little sister who is mousy and flat-chested, she is covered in dirt and the blades of her hips show through her dresses; what shall we do for our little sister?

The answer in my young and foolish mind was *Anything*. A multitude of sins rose up but I could tell her none and only manage to hide the shame which grew prodigious in my lap when she hitched up, left the ditch, and, whistling, passed me by.

The Conversion of the Chitites

My father preferred solitude for the preparation of his sermons. He'd go off, sometimes late Friday or even early Saturday, carrying only his hatchet and Bible—a copy scarred and bitten as any barroom brawler—and return sometime before Sunday morning when he would gather me up in the dark and we would head to meeting. He always left me with a good fire going while I slept beneath the lean-to we'd built against the foot of the ridge that marked the eastward end of the valley. Really, I can't say whether it was even Sundays when he preached, for all the holediggers had forgotten days, dates, and names. It didn't matter; he made whatever day he wished the Sabbath.

Going to preach those horseless fall days when the grass turned golden and the world had not yet gone dim and brittle, you learned like the wind to go on winding ways from dugout hole to hole, gathering the flock, which at first was no more than a few women and their children.

Midday we would arrive at a bow in a stream that bisected several of the homesteads, unique only in the two large stones set there and the pool of calm water below, which was good for baptizing. It was also used for the holediggers' washing, so soap-fat clung at the reeds and the rocks were draped with drying clothes even on Meeting days. No one could tell where the stones came from, there being no mountains near enough or hills of worthwhile size to yield them. They were storm gray and always warm to the touch on their sunward side, where if you climbed you would catch a rain-dog whiff of sopping clothes. The biggest of the stones Preacher-father would mount and from the top deliver the service.

The first and only regular congregation of his life began with just that smattering of women and children, the men preferring for a while to stay behind to guard their meager holdings. Never mind, he'd say, it's always Eves who come quickest to the call and bring their wailing broods along.

From his perch my father howled against sin with such vehemence that the ears of the frontier women burned red. He danced on his stone and bid them do the same, sang songs self-composed and of the same vigorous roughness in condemnation of the evils of the world and so exultant of the Lord that, though harsh of lyric, they could never be profane. Before long those women caught the fire and danced and sang as best they could to keep up with his furious inventions. And from my place in the lee of the stones my heart went to raunch— to see Emily filled suddenly with the spirit, wheeling and shaking and stomping down the grass with the rest of them. More and more I was called up to preach, but only briefly; and even in those moments I was on her. My words were all for her.

Then, O God, the baptisms. Reveal to me the body of woman in all its shapes and ranges. She may be hard and underfed but a temple nonetheless.

I sorrowed at being put to dunking the little children downstream, and I watched Preacher-father drawing Rachels, Ruths, and Hagars from the water, a miracle of dripping jenny and hind. I'd seen many baptized before and have baptized many since, but to see it then at the worst of my youthful urges was a revelation of clinging wool and sackcloth, of hair to be wrung out on the bank as converts were exhorted into the drink. Emily Fladeboe went, dress ballooning as she stepped down into the water, and was received.

Heavenly father, he said, take this girl close to your heart and keep her, for she has forsaken sin and wickedness. This ewe is washed in the blood of the lamb.

And so she was dipped and came up gasping slick and beautiful, reaching out her hands for someone on the bank to take. My own hand was on a small one's head, holding him under while I lifted my voice to praise when she waded smiling to the bank. And because I was forgetful and forever sneaking looks to where she sat sodden in the cane-break, humming piously with the other women, I more than once withdrew a half-drowned child from the water.

We sent the sisters off full of the spirit, and soon the husbands gave up their guards and followed. By late fall the faithful were wearing out traces in the grass on their way to be cleansed of sin.

The Plague

The locusts appeared first in singles, clumps, and clusters, then in hordes, and your every step sent up clouds of them playing dinnertime fiddles while they chewed, the sound of which was like a thousand-toothed mouth gnawing on and on.

We're thankful, Lord! said Preacher-father to his flock on the first Sunday of the plague while the assembled Chitites swatted at the horde that would soon drive them down into their underground homes. We're thankful even for this!

By nightfall we'd draped ourselves in sheets and blankets, sat that way for the locusts to make us mounds of their scratching bodies. For days tiny legs marched over me from sole to scalp and my brain was driven off course by them and I went about administering to myself a good and thorough daylong beating, without even time to wipe the still-twitching mush away before the open patch was filled by the kith and kin of the recently deceased. So it went one night that I was still slapping at myself, peeking out from underneath my sheet, watching how the towering fire Preacher-father had built just outside was doing no more to drive them off with smoke than our coverings did to keep them out, when he cast his sheet away and was a-swarmed. They rode the ends of his hair and were mitts over his hands, they swole up from the ground and made crawling trunks of his legs, swallowed him so fully that the only way I knew he'd not been eaten all away was that he still retained some human shape and moved. My father's steps as he left the lean-to were foreshortened like he was afraid to crush too many of his multitudinous clingers; he reached into the mass of them at his chest and brought out his Bible, which they immediately covered, and I swear that in the firelight I saw them nibbling at the leafs, eating pages clean of ink or messing passages with juice when they found one not to their liking. He spread the Book wide and stared out from his locust cloak at me, and above their ever-present drone came his voice screaming how he was thankful. They streamed around his words, poured in and out his throat.

He went on like that for the remainder of the night.

II

The Pilgrims

1800

The Arrival of the Kempers

They came with the first thaw marking the end of a miserable winter, a damp and clammy millennial dawn which had as yet brought no portents of Apocalypse. My skin still crawled with locust legs though the things had long since departed the world, when Preacher-father woke me of a morning to look and see a pair of wagons tottering down the lip of the hill, coming into Chit. He told me to stay, then gave a pat to his hip-slung hatchet and went out to meet them.

I itched the phantom legfalls, which I now think weren't ghost-bugs at all but sinning angels pocking pecks at me while I stirred the ashes of our fire with a stick and watched his progress across the field. How he must have looked to them on his approach: gape-eyed and

23

barbarous, still bearing the marks of mandible nibs; yet it did seem that when he left me there his senses had returned somewhat. He'd smiled when his hand was on the hatchet. Perhaps he knew what he would find; perhaps that was the locusts' answer.

The first wagon was close enough for me to see its driver, a dark blob before the tarp, whip the reins and turn his team towards us. The second followed and they made a wide circle of the field before they were aimed head-on at my father. I thought he might be ridden down, but he side-stepped the oncoming beasts and ran along the sideboards of the lead wagon, waving at the driver, who waved in answer. I stepped out of the draping of the lean-to and scratched at my bites and watched Preacher-father walking alongside, every now and again pulling himself up onto the footboard to shout something in the driver's ear. When the horses were near to trampling our fire, Preacher-father called out to me, Up! Help the man unhitch his horses! and I came barefoot through the soggy chilling grass to the snorting beasts presided over by him and this clean-shaven man in good outfit, making me suddenly aware of my own mean clothes, only for the man to holler, Boy, get down! And then from the second wagon there was a rattle of kit and binds and from around the side came this great bleary-eyed bastard—Samuel Kemper—who, once he had his feet, proceeded to shove me aside and do the task himself, eyeing me as he did from two heads taller height but still a young man's face.

To be out from under this glaring behemoth I went around to the open back of the first wagon and saw another smaller boy within, laid on his back amid the provisions, groaning and swathed in sheets. The boy rose up, revealing burns rippling from his neck to fingertips, and looked for a moment at me before squeezing shut his eyes and letting out a long high keening wail that sent me scrambling back around to be knocked aside by the big one on his way to help the smaller.

The fathers came to attend him also and I followed mine, watched the bandages be changed and the salve applied to the wailer, whose name was Nathan.

These were the Kempers: the father, who mine called Deacon, styled himself a student of the Lord, having given up meager but regular holdings in the Cincinnati port and leaving behind other sons at the family merchantry; the two remaining were the one with hambone knuckles and the glare, Samuel, and the screamer, Nathan, who now had the wagon rocking with jolts of struggle impressive for one so young and infirmed.

They were Virginians all, by birth; true Christians, it seemed; and were joined immediately to us as providence, prophecy, and the Will of the Lord. At least that was how Preacher-father saw it, and I couldn't help but see it also what with the boys being of similar age and motherlessness as me. I would have embraced them right off if it wasn't for Samuel eyeing me so.

Once the boy Nathan had been doctored, Deacon Kemper carried him out of the wagon, laid him on the ground, then brought us around to the back of the second wagon. Inside were the goods he planned to sell the Chitites, though he ignored the pewters and spindles and lamps and bolts of cloths, and showed us his arsenal instead. Firearms for Preacher-father were no different from hammer or spade, but this Deacon Kemper gathered them unto him like best-loved blood relations. It would be his sons who taught me to appreciate the other kind of fire, the kind kept in muzzle and in bore, as something more than a means to bring down meat or man. For the Kempers, firing a gun was to shout up a prayer so loud as to hear the echoes of God's answer reverberating in all the corners of His mouth. Deacon Kemper explained all of this while he showed us his pieces, finishing by saying, How could we not be like those first and greatest preachers and go well-armed?

My father heard all this with eyes alight, saying, Yes! Amen! Yes!

I braved the secretly stabbing elbows of the elder son to get a better look. Not even bruises to my ribbage like a spurred-on horse could stop me from gaping wonderstruck at that collection. I could see that Preacher-father was ashamed of our lost rifle when he asked how much a worthwhile hunting piece might be.

Forty dollars, Deacon Kemper said.

How if we worked it out in trade?

My friend, Deacon Kemper smiled, I would be delighted to make a gift to a fellow man of God. He reached into the wagon and drew out a long Kentucky rifle and handed it to Preacher-father, who held it close and accepted it without even a look.

Bless you, he said. There's not much tithes about out here.

Not another word, my friend.

My father clutched his gift and Deacon Kemper grew more excited in showing off his bestiary: two more Kentucky rifles, a brace of shotguns—some plain and some ornate—and short-stocked busses which could be loaded with slugs or pebbles or Indian corn and fired to wound and scare, muskets, short-arms, and finally a pair of pistols in a pine box lined with velvet. All supplied with kegs of powder and crates of shot packed in straw.

How'd you come by those dandies? Preacher-father asked.

There are stories to them all, said Deacon Kemper.

I mean the boxed pistols. They look like a dueling set.

Ah, said the Deacon. Don't we sons of Virginia know them well?

I never fought any, myself.

Only once, for my part. Deacon Kemper shut the box. I was at seminary in Richmond.

So that's what they teach at seminaries, eh? my father laughed, a miracle in and of itself.

Deacon Kemper grinned and said, Not so much as that.

How'd you end up a Baptist—escaped the Church?

The duel and my conversion are all of a piece the same story. I was, as I said, at seminary. It was a high-minded place, with nigger footmen for our rooms, and Greek and Latin always on our tongues. This was six years before the Revolution. I was drunk on the plushness of my surroundings and went roughly with my fellows into town, raising rich boys' hell among the populace. I was a model sinner, yes. Going to chapel reeking of sick. A port-wine swiller and a brandied fool. So I had some reputation when I first met Ruth, my wife and their mother, who is now gone, snatched from this world while I was away with General Clay in Pennsylvania. Were you in the war?

Yes, said Preacher-father. But not for long.

Well, her father had some misgivings about my character, which we settled one day on the field with these very pistols. Of course I was expelled, but still I absconded with enough books to continue my education. On that, does your boy read?

He can.

Well, I have a few saved by if he'd like to.

I marveled at this offer while Samuel stealthily mashed my foot under his boot.

You won't read shit, he whispered.

My thoughts were of shooting fathers down for the sake of love, looking warily at my own, who presently gasped and said, That's a hell of a parable you got there. If you said you didn't preach for the Lord I'd call you a liar.

I appreciate it, said the Deacon. Particularly coming from a man like yourself.

I have to say, though—Preacher-father bowed his head—that the people hereabouts are poor and, if you don't mind me saying, I can't see you selling much to them.

It's nothing, said the Deacon. Though I hope you don't think we came here just to sell.

Lord, no. I only wanted to warn you.

My friend, that's precisely the reason we're here. To warn. I've given up a steady trade to ride the outlands and tell the people of the coming wickedness.

My father looked bemused and asked which wickedness it was.

Wickedness, brother, like you've never seen. A whole slew of people, blinded, man, woman, and child. They've been traveling since Cincinnati, where I met them and knew their evils from the start. They follow a prophet of falsehoods and there's not a girl they wouldn't steal or barter off you to make a bride of her. And they do try desperately to draw others in.

But what are they? I said.

The fathers both glared at me and Samuel took me by the shoulder as they returned to talking.

They're the vilest, like the Gips, he said. And they come after little shits like you in the night.

Enough of that, said his father over one shoulder. They are a religion unto themselves. Their prophet styles himself as having written a latter-day testament. They've been driven out of every corner of the eastward country and they'll soon be heading here. Last I knew they were at the Cape, but I did my work there and they'll be harried here for sure.

But, brother, what if you miss them?

I trust in the grace of God to deliver them to me.

My father drove him on for more and my ears prickled at the talk of child brides, thinking of the Fladeboe girl huddled out in her hole.

With no one until Sunday to give witness to, they evangelized each other. Deacon Kemper had a good soft voice, a learned voice, and through storm-gray days and howling nights it played counter-point

28

to that voice I'd known all my life. Gentle enough to make you at first distrust him, any man attuned to the rhythms of the Lord could soon discern that his words were lit the same. In this man Preacher-father found, as he'd say, a same-such prophet of the course of John's baptism with water and Christ's baptism with fire, and at last we could truly walk the path to righteousness and glory.

Samuel

While the fathers were busy shoring up the particulars of their religion and going off most days to scout for the arrival of the aforementioned pilgrims, Samuel Kemper kept sneaking me blows and waiting me out. I did not give in to his baiting. I tended to my tasks, even fetching water for Nathan, who was something of a salvation for me, as Samuel maintained a prayerful vigil over him, and at such times would be too busy to go jabbing at me. Kneeling, hands clasped at the back-boards of Nathan's wagon, Samuel would lay graces on his poor scalded brother's head, only to turn and spit curses at me. He was a masterly cusser, and I was alternately a fuckero, shitbird, cunnytwist and rag, a bullockflap, scroter, piss-leg, cockswill and turd.

When we'd drive out their wagon to make rounds of the Chitites' holes, Samuel selling what he could for his father or taking food in trade, he liked to run me down all the way to the doorways.

How old are you? he asked once.

I don't rightly know, I said. Seventeen?

Jesus Christ. I'm twenty-three—I know for sure—and you're nothing but a new-born spit.

It's not that much difference.

It Christing sure is for me to be out here with my pa, and damned if I'll play your caretaker.

Fine enough. I've made it this far.

You haven't made it anywhere, he said even as some holediggers came topside. This place is nothing. I'll bet you've never even seen a town. God knows I should've stayed with Reuben in Cincinnati.

Samuel cracked the reins. What ho, neighbors! We've got some wares for you to see!

Truth be told, I did try to give him back his prods and gouging as much I could, swiftly secret where I placed my retributions, and with vicious intent. I made sure to hide it from the fathers, for the coals were still on my mind if not my tongue.

We caught each other first in quick and bloody skirmishes on the boards of the wagon, or when we were sent out to the scrub forest for kindling and lengths to expand our shelter, while the fathers worked their voices by the fire. These instances never bore any real satisfaction and we would return to camp only to resume our tormenting of each other.

Sundays Samuel would use being full of the spirit to thrash at me when we were all in the melee of worship. These were good days, though, before the pilgrims came and set the Chit in uproar, because it was at meeting that I could have the upper hand; for on occasion the mood would strike Preacher-father to call me out of the crowd and have me step up on the stone he now shared with Deacon Kemper and wail at the congregation. That time was mine, by God, and I could lead the people to holler and yowl, look out on those pitiful creatures and hold my eyes on Emily, say it all to her directly without a soul knowing, or so I thought.

Sure enough one Sabbath evening, on our way back home, Samuel announced himself with an elbow to my side and said, What's that puny girl you're always eyeing? She looks like she'd blow over in a breeze.

The fathers were walking up ahead, Nathan draped over the back of his and watching us.

It's no business of yours, I said.

Maybe not, said Samuel. If she wasn't so damn ugly I might try for her myself. But then, I could just tell your precious daddy that you're lusting.

Do it and you're dead.

Samuel laughed and clapped me on the back. So you've got some fire in you after all, you little shitwaller.

Pilgrims and Backsliders

They arrived behind a late blizzard, so they were either desperate or fools. I liken maybe both. The pilgrims settled in a dip at the northern edge of the woods and, so we heard, were clearing the trees after the Indian fashion, burning them out at the stumps and marking their presence by the tower of smoke always hovering above their camp, and constructing standing houses from the hewed wood. All this was reported by some of the curious holediggers who were already making visits to their place. The people of Chit backslid and it seemed that Deacon Kemper's warnings were confirmed.

Where'd you come by the pickled egg I see you chewing, Brother Magee? Preacher-father asked a Chitite the Sabbath not a week after the pilgrims' arrival.

Brother Magee took nervous and gulped his egg down. The folks at the woods, he said. Same place Sister Auger got that cloth for her dress.

That's a damn lie, cried a woman in paisley. I got this from the Deacon's boy. You ask him!

Brother Magee, said Preacher-father, you're ready to vouch for these people?

They're nearby, he said, and they got things. I don't mean anything by trading.

He sat in on one of their services! Conny Fladeboe called out.

31

Magee turned. You been taking their feed for those hogs, haven't you?

Now understand, Preacher-father said, there's nothing wrong with being Christian to others. With making trade with fellow new-comers. After all, my boy and I were once new to this blessed place and you all showed yourselves to be the milk of kindness, taking us both in and preserving us through the harsh times, allowing me to be your shepherd. But good brothers and sisters, why not keep your trade with the ones who've followed after us, the Kempers. Won't you open your arms just as wide to them, and not shirk them off for what-ever's come next? Of course you would treat these people Christian. But ask yourselves: How can you treat them so if they aren't Christian themselves?

Some holediggers by then were nodding, thinking they'd avoided his admonishment and wrath, and so began to grin and cut their eyes at neighbors who were impugned and downcast out of shame. Emily sat beside her mother, cross-legged in the beaten grass, wild eye doing whips in her skull.

But they've got milk cows! called one woman. The mother Flade-boe shut her up with a thwack to the back of her bonnet.

We don't need any milk from wrong cows, she said.

Then what about feed? the bonneted woman hissed.

Our hogs have been sick and that feed only made them worse. Now they act devilish, try and bite each other. I tell you, it's a curse.

Amen, sister, said Preacher-father. Now you've learned, and so should all of you learn not to stray from the path nor backslide into the snares of this world. We'd be happy to come and see the hogs, sister.

Bless you, Preacher.

Now, he said. If we need to be refreshed in our understanding of these people, then let me ask Deacon Kemper to step up and witness again.

Brotherhood

Next night found Samuel, Nathan, and me alone when the dead man's wife came calling. The fathers had left that morning, one toting pistols and the other with a hatchet, with purpose unspoken and heading north along the hillside. I imagined they were off hashing plans and would be gone till the following day; what they were doing was putting a plan into its first bloody motion. So it went that I had my wellspring knockaround with Samuel.

Rawboned at fist and shoulder but otherwise heavyset, he was hell to grapple with.

Ass-kissing midget! he called me. Fucksaken squirt!

There was plenty room to move, to dig our feet into the dirt. The dark came on with Samuel's fists falling on my head, my own fists knocking at his briskets and his chin. My eyes began to boil shut and I thought his did also, because his swings grew glancing. But after some time of blind fighting we seemed granted second sight, and soon both our fists were finding their marks and we were renewed in our violence—he leveled his blows at my arms and they became dead weight; I used my head to try and knock the breath from him. And when neither of us could throw knuckles anymore, we wrestled. I could see the firelight through my swole-shut lids as we went on, grabbing with swollen hands to force each other to the ground, only to get the false hope of a bent knee, blading my shins at his to cut him down. In bloody dance, we misted each other with the red breath from our busted noses, cussed through split lips. It was only when Nathan gathered up the strength to grab at us, crying that there was someone coming and how we'd all be punished, that we collapsed to the dirt, heaving and sending numb fingers to search our loosened teeth.

Little brother danced around us, clarion call in our blindness—no eyes to see what approached, no sure hearing over the roar planted there by knuckle and thumb, feeling out the sharp and aching world with broken pieces unrendered of their touch.

I heard Nathan only dimly, and not for my fist-struck audition, but also that there were more resonant rhythms working in my head. He was making worried trips from me to Samuel, and having his hands slapped away, lamenting the future striping of his legs and ass and reporting on the progress of the lantern-holding figure, when I spoke.

Samuel, can you see?

Not a bitching bit, he said. You hit mean for such a scrawny shit.

Nathan saying all the while, We'll get whipped, whipped, whipped.

Samuel said for him to shut up so loud I felt the bloodspray from his words.

I feel like old Jacob after he wrestled the angel.

You don't miss a chance to sermon, do you? said Samuel.

It's coming, Nathan said.

Damn me if it doesn't seem that way, said Samuel. I feel more godly than I ever did.

This place is our Pineal, I said.

Brothers, Nathan whined. It's on down the rise. A woman.

What's that? Samuel asked.

It's in Ephesians, I said.

Samuel sagged and winced. I've got to do better about the Book, he said.

Nathan whimpered and fussed as we went on driving each other into a scripturous drunk.

It's like the Lord had us lay into each other so we could tear off our old names. No more Woolsack, no more Kemper. We are Israel.

God damn, Samuel said, sucking and sputtering with fat-lipped reverence. Israel. You hear that, little sucker?

For a moment I thought that little sucker was me until Nathan answered yes. But there's still someone coming, he said.

God damn yes, I said. And yes we vained and blasphemed until Nathan hushed us; and I was not ashamed, understanding that if a man can't blaspheme when he is on the raw edge of revelation, then when? If you can hear the thunder of the holy heartbeat, where the conscience rests that burns holes in the sky and calls up pits of spiders to swallow the weak, do what comes natural and your actions will be smiled upon.

The Widow's Oil

With strength in our legs, buoyed with a newfound righteousness of purpose, we wobbled there awaiting the arrival of the wife Magee, who came as a hip-thin fuzz in my vision. She carried her infant child in a bundle in her arms.

You boys shouldn't fight that way, she said.

It's settled now, Sister Magee, I said.

Sister Magee set down her lantern, hugging the child bundle to her. She grunted, Where's your fathers?

Out praying, I said, still gogging blind to see her.

Whenabouts might they be coming back?

Before dawn, I believe. Right, Sam?

Then I'll wait, she said, and plopped herself down beside our fire, in the dirt just now settled from our struggle.

What's the trouble, Sister? Samuel said. If you don't mind me asking.

Well, she said. My husband's dead yonder in the woods with his head split open and I was wanting your fathers' help.

Half a day and into the night she'd spent going to find her husband, discovering him at last in the lonesome woods between their homestead and the pilgrims'. We couldn't find a thing to say for comfort, and she was so cold about it that comfort seemed a foolish thing to try.

Nathan shut right up and was horrified, but Sister Magee, after clucking a few minutes over the state of our faces, handed off her child for me and Samuel to take turns holding, rose, and went around our camp, gathering up roots and grasses which she ground into a poultice between two of the creek-bed rocks from the lip of our pit. This accomplished, she bent between us and rubbed the poultice on our swollen eyes. We didn't even think to thank her, for she was so quiet and the only thing to do was be silent yourself. So we passed the child back and forth, cooed it psalms, and the swelling abated and our sight returned, revealing to us each other's busted faces and the child's sunburnt head lolling in our arms.

The fathers came talking out of the morning light and didn't stop or take notice of Sister Magee and her baby, much less our wounded faces. They were concerned with their own, which were scored and cut with red slashes.

Wake up, you boys! Preacher-father called, stumbling into camp, supporting Deacon Kemper with an arm. What a rotten stinking day it's been.

The disciples didn't fare any better at the hands of the heathens, said Deacon Kemper.

They both fell beside the fire and my father held up his arms to the light, examining his clothes. They ran us out with sticks and switches, he said.

Whipped us like mules, said Deacon Kemper, holding out the flaps of his coat, which were indeed shredded.

What happened? Nathan asked.

Pilgrims, said Preacher-Father.

Sons of bitches—how? said Samuel.

Watch your tongue, his father said. Sister Magee? What brings you here so early? No trouble, I trust, though there seems to be so much in this sorry world.

Sister Magee had stood when the fathers first appeared, and now she swayed between them and the dying fire. Say you saw the pilgrims, Preacher Woolsack? she said.

Yes, Sister, he said. More than saw them. Endured them.

You take the way through the woods?

Yes, Sister, we did.

You see my husband?

Preacher-father's look soured.

Why, no, we didn't, said the Deacon.

What's the matter, Sister? My father asked with kindness in his voice, though that look in his eyes was the same as when he'd give me the coal.

He's dead—had his head stoved in the woods.

Well, said Deacon Kemper, I believe we know the culprits now.

Sister Magee looked unmoved. In my arms her child whined and I muffled it in my coat. I would carry it on our silent way winding across Chit to gather up the holediggers for the funeral service. I bore the tiny burden, for its mother never asked it back, and I watched Preacher-father, striding at the front of his marching congregation, the head of his hatchet slapping time against his leg, Deacon Kemper alongside and both of them barely able to contain their gladness. What they tried to mask in holy sorrow I knew even then was foul design. They'd been no more beaten by the pilgrims than me or Samuel. Their wounds, like ours, were by their own hands. The hatchet clapped and tolled; I'd seen him do worse than split a man's skull.

When we came to the Fladeboes' hole I edged through the haggard crowd and went to Emily and suddenly the child was like a great weight on me. I reached the child out to her and she took it, smiling, drawing it close, and with her good eye she stared at the pitiful thing and with the wild eye she looked at me. Emily held it only for a moment before her mother scuttled by and swept it from her arms. Mother Fladeboe took the child and Emily both, one tucked under an arm like a gourd and the other pulled by the wrist to walk with her at the back of our procession with the other chittering women all the way to the Magees' tract.

The days of the wife's journey and ours back with her weren't kind to the body of the husband. She had soaked his shroud in lye soap, thinking it would preserve him from the insects and the elements and abate the smell. She was about half right. The stink of rot was there but different, and when Deacon Kemper lifted the sheet from the body, besides that it had swollen and blackened, the flesh was welted and melted in places and came through his clothes. The husband's face was a runny mess, but the maggots that had nested in the split in his skull were all dead. I don't know how Sister Magee bore to look on all that, even as her red-faced child was passed between the women of Chit.

Preacher-father asked whether she wanted her man buried or burnt and Sister Magee couldn't suffer the idea of fire—perhaps lit by the very wood her husband had been cutting when he himself was felled. So Samuel and I were put to digging while the fathers sermonized the Chitites.

That's about the worst thing I've ever seen, I said, pointing with my shovel-blade to the shrouded corpse.

Samuel turned some dirt and scoffed. The worst I've ever seen, he said, is General George Washington ride a man down and club his head with a Powhatan war hammer.

Washington?

The man himself. This was when I was little and we were in Pennsylvania. The general put down an insurrection single-handed. Rode

189

on a horse slung with all kinds of murderous things he'd collected on his travels: clubs, swords, French pickaxes. Sometimes he swung an iron ball on a chain. That got his men going, I'll tell you.

I never imagined him being like that, I said.

Gospel damn truth, Samuel said, voice choking a bit, whether out of emotion or having caught a whiff of Magee. And you know, when I saw him, I knew that's what I wanted to be.

Why aren't you then? I said, chucking a shovelful past his shoulder.

Samuel stuck his blade into the earth and considered me. We were but a few feet down and our hole was as yet shapeless. I thought we were brothers now, and friends, he said.

We are.

Samuel put one great foot to the head of his shovel and turned up a clod of prairie dirt. Then I don't expect to hear such things again, he said.

We dug the grave up to Samuel's shoulders, taking breaks on occasion to sit at the lip of our hole and spy the Chitites sitting at our fathers' feet, listening like children to the story of their scourging at the hands of the pilgrims. Finished, Samuel called to Nathan, who was laid out on the ground between us and the congregation, for him to go and tell them the service could begin. I pulled myself up out of the grave and attained the higher ground beside Magee's body. The wind had blown the sheet from his head and his face was boiled into a mask that gaped with empty eyeholes and a wide-grinning smile with lips skinned back over teeth that had gone translucent and lost their divisions; and I wanted nothing more than Emily to be beside me, even if she had to look on the tortured form of the corpse, just so long as I could look on her while she did. Spit out a word or two to soothe her for the horror. Samuel bent quickly to cover up Magee before the others arrived at the grave. And horrors seemed to be the order of the day, with all us hoisting the body up on its wrappings, only to have it tear through and spill onto the graveside in a revolting jumble. Samuel and I had to push him in with our shovels while my father gave the burial verses.

During the sermon Sister Magee stayed far aside, and did not weep as the other women. I edged towards them, and while they were mostly busy dabbing hems to their eyes I stood beside Emily, who remained quiet and tearless, hands at her sides. And so amid the lamentations I let my fingertips brush against her palm, once, and seeing that she didn't move or pull away I did the same again and she closed her hand tightly around mine for but an instant, then let me go and began to sob after the fashion of her elders. I was too shook to know what it meant, and made my way back to Samuel, who gave me a sly look.

Afterwards, the grave covered over and the burial service done, the Chitites built a fire up and stayed there into the night. One man, after a custom, poured a few necks of whiskey from a cask into the earth. A cup was being passed and Preacher-father and Deacon Kemper drank of it grimly but with some satisfaction on their faces as they heard their teachings working in the people.

They seemed so clean, said one Chitite.

Well, they aren't, said another. Tell about the prophet again, Preacher.

He is a wicked fool in black sugarloaf, their Prophet Thomas. When we came upon them he was reading aloud from his ridiculous apings of the true gospel. Said this was their promised land and an angel had told him so.

It sounded like Gospel, said Deacon Kemper, it did. But I knew his tricks and asked about all the other promised lands his angel had told him about, all the ones they've been run out of.

It might as well have been written on the skins of unrepentant whores and child diddlers, said Preacher-father.

The Chitites laughed uneasily and passed their whiskey, which came now to me and Samuel.

And that's what you told them, wasn't it, brother? said the Deacon.

Yes, indeed. And that's what set them on us like wolves.

Y'all should've shot the lot of them, said Conny Fladeboe.

If we'd known about Brother Magee, said the Deacon, things would've been different.

Amens circulated amongst the Chitites.

We can have them now, said one holedigger. Tonight!

Samuel, smiling, nudged me with an elbow and I imagined him as his terrible Washington, the heads of his enemies pulped by ancient weaponry.

My father held up his hands and said, Not yet, brothers and sisters. Not yet, but soon.

But if it wasn't them? said still another.

That don't mean a thing, said Conny Fladeboe. They're still rotten. Who here doesn't have animals sick and crazed since they came along? Even the good Deacon's medicine's don't help. The beasts grow worse day by day.

I shouldn't eat them, said his wife. Lest I'm struck down by the same devils.

My plow-horse chewed off his own leg.

My chickens already pecked each other to death.

Had to shoot two of my oxes. Gored each other even with sawed-down horns.

My friends, said Deacon Kemper, you know as well as I do that there are demons in this world; the Book tells us of them slipping into beasts of the field and sowing trouble for their masters. And we will clear them out from your stock even as we banish these pilgrims from our land.

Amen, said Preacher-father.

Amen, said Sister Magee. And so all eyes were upon her where she sat, shrouded in a skin blanket. Get them all out, she said.

Casting Out Demons

Despite his punishments, my father's love for me was such that he thought I could turn the tongue of any serpent, that I could be brought to the mountaintop and made to look down upon the cities of the world and say I didn't want them. He was a man of faith, and like all men of faith he was blind.

I was faithful too, you see, and took it on their word that we dearly needed to go out amongst the Chitites and minister to their demonized beasts. And so I rode with Samuel the unhitched Kemper horses out to the northernmost family plots: the Augers, the Braenecks, the Scruts, even Sister Magee, who cared little for her animals nowadays, but did send us off with a draught a-piece of whiskey, her bereavement gifts. We carried with us a skin of water from Baptist Creek to sling purification upon the possessed and drive their demons out. Nathan was left at camp, now healed so much that he was doing small chores about the place; and for their part the fathers had taken the homesteads of the south and western corners of the valley as their exorcising territory. And maybe it was that Preacher-father did distrust me, for those tracts were the ones which housed the girls of age. Still, the path of our return would lead us along the edge of the hole where lived the only one I cared to know.

We had left the Augers and were heading south, done for the day and having accomplished little but Samuel getting bit on the wrist by a Satan-struck horse, which, when the Augers' backs were turned, he punched in the eye. My brother's swing had about as much effect upon the demon as our verses. But we weren't dejected on the ride back, despite the drizzle, still bearing winter cold, and our failures; the sky cleared long enough for the sun to show a moment before it fell, warming our sides and reawakening the whiskey. The holediggers had done their best to keep the beasts corralled and separated, but some of the meaner ones had broken through their rickety yards and were said to be marauding around the countryside. Before full sundown a crazed ox had come thrashing out of a patch of soft-corn; frothing and red-eyed, the ox made for our horses before lumbering off towards the hills with the pair of shots we'd fired in its side. My brother looked to me, waving his rifle to dispel the smoke, and laughed loud and long. And so did I; but as we neared the Fladeboes' my mind took dark and the worms were turning in me. Samuel mistook my shifty glances and silence for caution.

Don't worry, he said. That big fuckerall's in the woods by now. Probably troubling the damned pilgrims.

It's not that, I said.

Samuel never was quick, but when he did come to understand a thing, he latched to it. Taking a squeeze from the water-skin, he said, So you're aching for it?

Like Satan's hooves are dancing on my bollocks.

You little letch—you're struck hard, aren't you.

Don't pick.

O, just suffer and take it. There's nothing for it here. Samuel flourished eastward with a great hand. Now, if we were in a city, things would be different. You could sneak with her in an alley or a privy.

Damn it, I said not to pick.

And I said I'm not. That's how I dipped for the first time, and for several more thereafter.

I know, I said. You're old and wise of the world.

Samuel slapped the neck of his horse and laughed again. Now you're the one who's picking, he said.

In the distance ahead smoke pinwheeled from where the Fladeboes' crooked stovepipe stuck out the turf. And I heard faintly,

43

above the whistle of wind in the tall grasses and my brother's huff and chuckle, the squeals of the hogs. Homeward seemed a sorry course to take.

Sounds like they didn't get any demons out either, I said.

You are a clever one, said Samuel.

I only want to do what's right by the Lord and bless the beasts.

Naturally, he said.

By the time we'd come to the Fladeboe hole the sun was down and we took our bearings from the fire, where husband and wife stood turning a spitted hog that was blackened and already missing a fair chunk of throat. We passed those that remained, in their pen set against the ditch where I'd stood guard over Emily that first day. The hogs' squeals were loud and awful, so that I couldn't see how the family stood it. The Fladeboes hailed us and I looked around balefully for Emily, imagining her hid away in the cruddy dark of the family hole, stoking the fire beneath a pot where more pork surely cooked. We got down from our horses and approached the fire.

Your fathers already came, said the wife.

Yes, sister, I said. They told us to follow after them.

In case their efforts didn't take, said Samuel.

Conny Fladeboe cranked the spit and the hog's skin hissed and bubbled. They hadn't scraped the hair from the hide and the smell was like a pyre. How's that? he said. The Preacher and the Deacon rode south, and it seems y'all two have come from the north.

They told us this morning, I said, before we all headed out.

Didn't tell us, said Conny.

Now, said his wife to hush him. Another try's better than them all being dead—right, boys?

Yes ma'am, I said.

Samuel handed me his reins, saying, Why don't you go tie the horses off and start with the casting.

I took them and, with a nod to my brother and the Fladeboes, headed for the pens.

I could hear him saying how I was really the one with the gift for the Word and he was mostly my helper. The Fladeboes agreed and said that when the hog was done he could go down with them and eat. After all, they said, it was late past supper.

The hogs had the horses jittery, and so I had to soothe them before I began, drawing out my Bible and not reading a bit from it, but hollering loud my own words and making a show of my godliness, hoping that the daughter would hear my voice through the ground and be moved.

Fly! Unclean come likewise out of the unclean. For there is not a place on this earth for you to take purchase that is good enough! Fly these hogs and trouble them no more!

I went on like that for some time, but the only answers given by the demons in the hogs were louder squealed appeals to their dark master. I leaned against the fence and hollered out, and the hogs gave me beady eyes lit by the fire, which cast my shadow and the shadows of the knobby bars of their pen down on them. Soon the fire was guttering and I looked back to see that the Fladeboes had retreated belowground and taken Samuel with them. It grew too dark to see and I preached to the shadows, out of which came on occasion snouts snatching bites from the toes of my boots. Pausing mid-cuss at the sound of the dugout door creaking open, I turned and saw amid the pikes a figure moving out, holding by the sharpest points and easing the door-trap shut behind.

I shouted more prayers for the casting out of demons, and I watched Emily—for it was plainly her, lit by the smoking fat of the betty-lamp—approaching me from the ditchward side. I guessed perhaps she'd told them that she had to pass, only when Emily came to the pens she set the lamp on a post and said they'd told her to bring me a light to read by.

I thanked her and tried to look loving even with the hogs' squeals and their eyes now lit red from the lamp.

Why do you talk like that? she asked.

Like what? I said. Girl, this is the Bible I'm reading.

You hadn't been reading and I know it's scripture. I heard you do scripture before. But you talk like you're chewing leather.

She was standing close enough to touch and I prayed on what she'd said, told her to come on over and I'd show her why I talked the way I did.

She did and both me and the hogs regarded her with our animal intents. And with the Word silent on the air one of them came to stick its snout under the gate and bite at her skirts. I swifted it a kick and the hog went squealing away.

Don't kick at her, said Emily.

But it's biting, I said.

They weren't like that before those people came. Sadie even ate up all her piglets. That's her was on the spit.

Well, I said, they won't be that way when I'm done.

She thought for a moment, swooped her wild eye around, and breathed deep of the stinking tallow smoke. Do you think it's God? she said.

Everything's because of God.

I think it must be He's mad at us.

Nothing's happened to me, I said.

You already talk funny. So maybe something worse'll happen to you.

You got the crazy eye, I said. Maybe you'll get something worse than that.

Emily grunted and tried to squint her eye still.

Sorry, I said.

She gave her bony shoulders a rise. I've seen you looking.

Fat dripped and hissed in the pan of the lamp. I said, You can come and look me right here and I'll show you why I talk funny.

She bent down to be in the light and I did the same, stuck out my chin as though to take a punch, let flap open my jaw and flop out my tongue.

God, she said, and screwed her good eye into my mouth. You're all burnt up.

She looked so hard and close that all I saw was the top of her head, wherefrom a nit jumped to ping off my face, making me flinch and catch her with my chin. I looked down again and she'd turned to see inside with her other eye and that eye was wonderful, like it had to be wild and spin and search to take in all of me. She let it go crazy and with the other she looked dead into mine and asked me could she touch it.

I gagged yes, but when she reached her fingers in I gave my tongue the snake's flicker and clamped shut and she giggled.

I can't be long, she said.

We went away from the pens, not for the smell, for it was worse near the long grass at the ditch's edge, where she made a cross of me, her opening to mine, plump line to my supine after she put me down in the grass and spread her legs to straddle my chest with the hems of her skirts tickling gentle at my nose, then squatted low above me and brought my face under that curtain, taking me by the hair, saying, I washed on it.

Scarcely could I catch a breath while in that wiry patch; my hands holding fast to her hips, the words I said into her were my first true sermon, a sermon on the furry, clefted mount. My burnt and sorrowful tongue was at that moment healed, and I tasted fully for the first time in my life; what now would surely cause my gorge to rise was then a revelation. She rocked and grabbed fistfuls of my hair and called it pretty, pretty, pretty, and I dug furrows in the prairie earth with my bootheels.

We were joined only for a few minutes; fear and noises which proved to be nothing forced us to tear away from each other. In the silence following what had sounded like the hole-door opening, she said that it was no sin to put the tongue in. And this made sense, my tongue being anointed and girded with hoary holy callous as the Archangel's loins.

Emily struck a flint to light the lamp again and I was smiling at her. She plucked a hair from my bared teeth and ducked away when I tried to kiss her.

No sin, I said.

She hurried back to the hole, softly singing:

There's a lily in the garden
For you, young man;
There's a lily in the garden,
Come pluck it if you can.

Dear God, said Samuel when I told him what we'd done.

What was it you expected? I asked, walking alongside my horse and leading it, for the rubbing of the saddle only made worse my painful engorgement.

For you to stick her, he said, not—not that!

Come now, brother, I said.

Brother me no brothers. Samuel shook his head. Then he looked down on me and said: With your mouth on it? I can tell you right here that I never heard of such a thing. I don't even know what you'd call a thing like that.

Whatever you call it, I said, it's wondrous.

It's against God as sodomy or bestiality.

There's worse things done by men beloved of Him in the Book.

Maybe, said Samuel, but she wouldn't let you at her true?

Not yet she says.

Then there you go. That blue ache's Him telling you you've done wrong.

Shit on you. You don't know about it.

Samuel whirled in his saddle. Don't you tell me what I know and what I don't, he said. When I was in Cincinnati I spent time with plenty fillies, but I never did a thing like that. And I'm old enough to have a woman and a baby or two by now, you ass—and you think I don't know? I'd done the deed before you even knew about it. And you know what I got for it? Buggywhipped by an Irish mother, that's what. My brother Reuben, God bless him, he had to knock the old bat off me and he pled my case that I didn't ruin her daughter. Staked his reputation on it. Saved me from having to work off the debt of her maidenhead. That's partly why my father brought us out here. He thought the town corrupting.

I didn't mean anything by it, I said.

Don't lie. You did. Samuel looked off eastward, as though peering for that same brother, of whom I'd only so far heard whispers and legends. Son of a bitch, he said, I got nothing out here but beating myself under a blanket. I tell you, I'm heading back there first chance I get.

We stopped at the Baptist and while the horses drank I tried to wash the smell of Emily from my face. It was a painful and stiff-legged amble home, with a prodigious ache from bearings to gut, as if all my weight had fallen there to collect like a supplicant who praised and begged for more. And we would need the lantern light to make our homeward way, and the time to figure on what lies and truths we'd tell the fathers—who wouldn't care, they were so fixed on their plans for the pilgrims—while they sat waiting out the morning at the fire.

A War Sermon

I was thinking of the demons I'd cast out and the accompaniment of devils and dark angels whose skeleton wings would shelter me on my way to Satan's bosom, when Preacher-father mounted his rock that meeting day. And I was only just laying out the way I'd take to get to Hell, with words dripping lies and with deeds much the same.

Emily's wild eye went gyring while the other, and those of the rest of the congregation, pored over the welts and scratches the fathers showed during the service. I looked along with them, wondering how, days later, their wounds seemed worse than the night they'd been received. For all I knew they'd been flogging each other to have the marks just right for the day they'd make their call to arms. I did notice that Nathan was watching me close—had his brother revealed my sins to him? It didn't matter; I was searching out the corner of my eye for any breasts budding in the rumpled front of Emily's dress.

I stared at her until Samuel gave me one of his correcting jabs to the ribs, and I straightened up to watch Preacher-father, high up on his rock, bear down upon the collected rabble of dirt-caked believers and give his barbed sermon:

Listen now closely and hear the voice of one crying in the wilderness. Prepare ye the way of the Lord, and make his paths straight. By his hand every valley shall be filled, and every hill and mountain shall be brought low. The crooked shall be made straight and the rough ways shall be made smooth. And now, the axe is laid unto the root of the trees, and every tree which bringeth not forth good fruit is cast into my fire. There it is, friends, to be found in your familial Bibles in the Book of Luke, chapter three. And so, brothers and sisters, there is also to be found, not a half day's ride from here, a valley dug and planted with such malignant growths. And

50

they are flourishing. O how they grow—in the sight of your good works, in sight of your hard lives, and your mercy they grow and grow. And I ask you: Do they suffer like you do? No. They laugh at all your toil and hurt; they've made a pact with Satan, and the gaming chip of this unholy deal is our own hard-scraped lands and our own people. But I'll say this—they are a generous people. They are that. They freely and without guilt make child-brides of their young girls to each other, and there isn't a man among them who doesn't have a quarter-dozen wives. Wives, I said. And don't think for a moment, brothers and sisters, that they won't extend this same generosity to your wives, and to your daughters. Maybe then they'll have themselves even finer stock to pacify their wicked urges with. But listen to me now, valley neighbors, Christian families: you know me, you know my boy, you know the Kempers, who've come to aid our ministry and first told us of the threat, and you've known us all through fertility and famine, through locust and snowstorm, through demonization and through flood. So then you know that all we've ever done is kept our humble duty of witnessing and baptizing, never trying to increase our stocks, often even refusing your own good-kindness because we've come to be your rock and we will not set ourselves up as usurers of our flock, with the Word and salvation as our Jew's Coin. We've asked you for no charity, nor do we now. We ask for the charity of your justice. The charity of bodies in the saddle—or afoot, as you can afford—to ride with us to this black encampment and cast out the vicious spirit there that's struck down one of our brothers. Now, I can't say that if you are kind, if you treat the blasphemers with sweetness, with mercy as your good hearts surely would, that your crops will wither in the earth, that when you come upon hard times they will use your children as loan currency, that you will watch more husbands' and wives' heads split by those who are given arm and reign over the land you've worked so hard to preserve. But I can promise you that your souls will shrivel, that your spirits will be cleaved and gutted, and your children will grow up as slaves in a godless country, all because these blasphemous roots are allowed purchase by your kindness. So put away mercy and kindness for a time, and unlatch your horse from the plow and bights, take your axe or rifle or scythe, and bring yourself some kindling fire and we shall burn out the tree and its roots.

And in the tumult that followed, amid the singing and the screaming for bloody vengeance, I made my way to Emily. The wildness of the people was our hiding place, and we took hold to one another. Smiling, she asked me how many would I kill. There was no answer I could give but that I loved her, nor can I now explain how in that moment I felt such damnable joy.

Righteous Fire

Pregnant women tottered belly-slung for the longhouses as we charged upon the pilgrim camp out of smoke and fire lit by the foolish hand of some holedigger who held his torch too high and caught the low-hanging limbs of brittle pines. There were maybe ten of us on horseback: the fathers, a few Chitites, myself, and Samuel sharing his with Nathan, who carried a long-handled shovel, bouncing and jostling behind his brother but for the first time looking well and clear in eyes and complexion. The rest followed on foot up the last lip of the hill into the clearing, armed with either ancient pieces bearing continental gravings or the marks of Deacon Kemper's generosity, a K notched into the grain for future reclamation. Others carried tools: axes, sickles, trammels, and flails, the spiny cradle-scythe. And so they put their tools to work and the chaff was cut down even as it begged and pleaded mercy, just as my father said.

I carried a buss tamped with grape, and with the first shots and screams like out of another world I emptied my bladder into the seat of my saddle. Soaked and shamed before I'd done a thing but ride into the slaughter, I kept close behind Samuel and Nathan and we circled round the camp and saw many things. A pilgrim impaled in the tines of a fork; others crowding in through the doors of the longhouses while Chitites hacked at their hands and tried to force the jamb, which was shut on the unfortunates, who tried climbing through the windows but were mostly brought down; a Chitite's head blown into the air by a volley from such a window—Samuel giving one back in return.

I remember his shot, for with it we came around the pens and corrals of the pilgrim's beasts, harried by bullets from those now-barricaded indoors, and saw Preacher-father and the Deacon riding circles around a man in a sugarloaf hat. All around them was battle, but they only rode and shouted at the man. The prophet held up high his hands and took the hat from his head and waved it, entreating. The fathers called for surrender and banishment, but the prophet didn't seem to understand. Samuel highed for them and I was close behind when the second volley came—I don't know from which direction, but the fathers toppled and were on the ground with the prophet, fallen also. And in the after-roar I threw myself down to the dirt and landed upon Nathan, whose throat was torn away. He whistled bloody breath at me and I tried to stop it with my hands but failed, and I crawled on those hands mixing blood in the hoof-churned earth to Samuel and he sat up and stared as though I wasn't there. The fathers both were up, the Deacon holding his leg and Preacher-father shouting he'd only been thrown. The prophet lay dead at their feet. Deacon Kemper shambled towards us, shoving both Samuel and me aside, and catching up his dead son from the ground, hurried down to the woods.

It was Samuel and me left there on the ground and we didn't hear the next shots, only the screams of both our horses, a gobbet of knee

53

landing between us on the ground. I shouted asking if he'd been hit; he gaped past me at the trees. To my left I saw a crescent of the woods on fire. I pawed at my brother and there was gunfire again but more-over the roar of flames and burning. A hand took my shoulder from behind and pulled me up. It was Conny Fladeboe, and he looked grim but pleased. He was still holding me up when another holedigger came around and grabbed at Samuel, but he shrugged him off and ran after his father. Fladeboe turned me loose and I fell again to ground and snatched up my buss; and when he tugged me up the second time I ran with him towards the nearest longhouse. I was screaming as I over-took him and threw my back flat against the hot boards and jabbed the short barrel of the buss in the flame-licked windowsill, which had cracked and crumpled brittle-black even as the barrel rested there but a moment before I fired. The only scream I heard was Fladeboe's; the gun had blown back out of my hand and struck him in the face. That was the only blood for sure I drew that day, and mine was among the last shots fired. Pilgrims poured out the doors, some on fire, being beaten by their fellows trying to put their burning clothes out, scream-ing peace and surrender; and they were received.

We made our way back through the place in the woods where the flames were lowest; and we passed through dying fires without caring; and was this what my father wanted? Was this the fulfillment of his lifelong preaching? I could judge nothing then but the smoke which rose from the burnt soles of my boots, slowly staunched in the grass of the hillside where three dead holediggers were laid out. Nathan was not among them, but down at the foot of the hill with his father and brother kneeling above him.

The surviving pilgrims were gathered in a bunch and Preacher-father presided over them. He hugged his rifle and faced them so that none could look away, even those attended with wounds. There were ten or twenty pilgrims, mostly women and children and young boys. Now he seemed to speak with one old lady at their front, whose hair was singed to her ears.

Downhill I went to join Samuel and his father, looking along with them at that pale and split neck. Deacon Kemper reached for Nathan's shut eyes and opened them, stared in, then smoothed them back closed. Wishing I still held the buss, so that I might take some strength from its weight, I did what I could with my hands and held them together as in prayer. But no prayer came.

Deacon Kemper kept opening and closing his dead son's eyes, and I tried to stop his hands and pull them back as gently as I could. Samuel took my wrists and shoved me back; and there was a moment of recognition in his face, and he slapped his father's hands back and held them.

How will we tell Reuben? asked the Deacon of his surviving son.

We can leave, said Samuel. Leave here.

His father turned to him. Leave?

You got what you wanted, Samuel said.

The Deacon fell back from his knees and sat. His hands now free, I expected them to head again for Nathan's eyes, but he let them rest in his lap and said, The Revolution wasn't like this.

Samuel didn't try to parse his father's words, nor did I. The Deacon would spend the next months out wandering the valley, leaving Samuel alone while he fired his dueling pistols at invisibles.

Eventually we rose and took up Nathan's body, and in a long line headed southward into Chit. The holediggers peeled away slowly from our train, back to their own houses. Some carried the dead to wives and families and we could hear the wailing from a ways off. Preacher-father promised he would comfort them in time, and that they would be provided for. For the moment, he said, there was the matter of leading these people out. And we did, when the guard of

Chitites had departed and we passed through our own camp, leaving the Kempers behind.

So it was Preacher-father at the head and I at the back, the last of our walks together. The pilgrims had no food, no tools, not a thing to bring into the wilderness. I thought they might turn upon us, but they never did. They knew when the hand of God was upon them in disfavor. And strangely there was little weeping or even talk among them. Once a girl of Emily's age in a frilled bonnet turned, looked at me, and spit. The woman beside her slapped her head back around.

We led them to the southern bend in the hills, at the termination of the Baptist into marsh, and there my father gave them a sermon, on forgiveness. I said nothing; and if this was what it meant to be an agent of the Lord, then I damned my station. Nathan, burnt in life, burnt in death, went writhing through my mind. If the Lord could take the weak and suffering, then I was also prey. But above it all, ringing in my soul, I felt the power of His will borne in me. I was alive and that was proof. We had won and that was proof. The Lord of Hosts and Battle smiled down on me with teeth of knives and powder-horns and firearms, and He blessed me with an awful glory in accomplishing His works.

Preacher-father sent the pilgrims off and together we watched them go.

Some die, he said, so that the Lord may live on stronger in the hearts of others.

When I did not respond, he asked me if I understood. I said that I did and we walked back side-by-side through the darkening valley. And when the light was gone, and we and all the world about was shapeless, I made to fall back from my father and see about Samuel, but from out the black his hand caught me up and he said, Stay alongside me. You are a blessing of a son.

III

Rebellious Sons

Fall 1800

Blessings of Christ's Kingdom

The days went bloodlessly by in the wake of the raid: the Chitites were again good congregants; Preacher-father strutted and showed them his teeth, barking bits of sermon in leftover anger; and I set out on the thorny course with Emily and so would make myself a crown of them.

Deacon Kemper went to collect the guns he'd lent, brought them back, and cleaned them solemnly. He still made his daily shooting walks and solitary dances with his pistols, no longer bothering even to load them—just made their noises with his voice. From our camp you could hear him start into it when he came upon his first assailant: *pah, pah, pah, pah,* he went, and without knowing it invented the repeating pistol in his lunatic's mind. And you knew he was keeping in step with the pistol-fire, using it for a metronome, the great dance master's hand on his shoulder and him blowing holes in the offending air. How Samuel would wince when he heard the mouthed shots.

I sat with Samuel those days and listened with him to his father's ghostly battles, even went once to see him making pirouettes. Thinking it would help him to hear about my yearnings, I spent them out to him in long fool streams of talk.

From what I saw at the service, it looks like she's filled out a bit.

You showed me then, Samuel said.

She's prettier when she's not so sickly-looking.

That doesn't take much.

I've put a sermon together for her, listen—

I don't want to hear it, he said.

Why not?

Because I don't want to hear about you trying to Christ your way into her cunny.

But my brother would hear it, just as I would hear him go on about leaving Chit. We traded these dreams while out working amongst the people, hewing logs or laying fences for the widowed. He would say that whenever he had the chance he was leaving to join his brother Reuben back east. But instead on those hired-out days he played lookout for me and Emily, now rejoined and freer because her father was laid up in the hole, healing his eye, which was infected. I would bring him medicines from Deacon Kemper's wagon, or what the widow Magee would grind, and the man's thanks and his wife's would still be upon me when I'd hurry off with their daughter to the bushes or the corn patch and we'd lay down right there at the feet of the stalks and in the bug-rustle and withered silk have a fast sin together.

Samuel endured it, listening hard for the door or for the father Fladeboe banging blindly about.

They can probably God damn hear you, he said one day. They can probably feel it in the ground, you humping.

We told Preacher-father and the Deacon that we'd been gifted with visions out in the valley, this to explain our usual lateness. Samuel rarely told his well, and so I'd tell enough visions for two.

But first I would test my Angelics and mystic sights unseen on Emily, when we were finished and she would recompose her clothes, or when I was still in her lap, something in me refusing to be out of her. Emily's ears were better than her eyes and I made my visions fit her. She'd feature in them along with the angels and the burning clouds.

Once, when I was done relating, she said for me to keep on talking.

That's the end, I said. There isn't any more.

I like to hear you talk. I don't care what you say.

I thought my voice was funny.

That don't mean I don't fancy it.

It's all lies anyway, I said.

I know that. So say some more.

And I would. I could lie for hours straight if we'd but had the time. And she would whisper to me, Lie on, Angel, my Angel.

We stunk of each other and that was one of the pleasures of those days. We washed on Sundays, maybe, but it was often weeks of adding on the anointment of our couplings. So much that I would go to dirt wallers and roll in them till I was covered in dust or mud. Neither of the fathers ever questioned any of it, especially Preacher-father, who rocked gleeful on his heels at our fire whenever I told him a new vision.

You could come and call on me with my folks, said Emily one day. They'll know it then.

They can know it. I don't care. They'd be happy to know you were loving me.

59

I'd have to tell my people, and my father, he'd go blind. A prophet has to keep pure until his time comes.

I'm your time. And he wouldn't be angry with you. You want to make a wife of me, seed me, seed the land. A preacher should love that.

I thought on what she said, prayed on it most days even when I was hustling off to meet her. Would I have been content to live out my days with her in our mud-hole or thatched cabin? With that girl who was thin and worn already at the age I knew her? I could be the shepherd of my father's flock and another generation of dirt-caked worshippers would follow me, knowing his legend by heart, trusting in me that I had the same fire that set their forefathers on the pilgrims. Or I could have taken her from that baleful valley and somewhere hacked out what life we could. But I was a boy, and fearful, as boys are—ground between desire and cowardice in this millstone of suffering.

The Vehemency of Love

There is no beauty in the thing when it is done by the young. The heat was on us and it was only rushing place to place and hustling quickly into Emily; and she was not delicate about it—lifting and parting for hasty work done out of need.

But she was no more a whore than I was a whoremaster, and it was a lovely thing she did to me. The world had lost its bearings and tilted under my feet. And between my made-up visions and Sunday work all I could take stock of was my next chance with her. The dead should walk if ever my sight were to right itself after that sweet laying down.

With Samuel I brought her to the pilgrims' burnt encampment to search for any usables that had escaped the retreating pilgrims or the fire. Samuel was being a good brother, hanging back at the scorched tree-line. Also it was that he couldn't bear to stay so near the place where Nathan had fallen. The place had been picked clean, not only of good wood and most supplies and beasts, but also of carrion. I wandered aimless while Emily went among the blackened timber piles, picking out buttons, needles, nails, and other trinkets, holding a pouch of her dress as a basket for her fired keepsakes, revealing flea-bit thigh and scabby knee, beautiful to me. But before I could snatch her up, Emily returned to her work and when she was done stirring the ash piles her arms were black to the elbows.

On our way back she said to Samuel, I would've put a flower on your brother's grave. But there's no mark.

He's not buried there.

O, she said. I just heard this was where he died.

Samuel's mouth bit into itself. We don't bury people wherever they fall.

Nathan's at our place, I said to her. And Emily nodded gravely and whipped her wild eye.

She couldn't bring her treasures home, so she hid them in the knot of a tree, telling Samuel to turn his back when she picked the one, for only she and I were to know.

We would visit them those weeks and she would take out her play-pretties and arrange them for me around her, talk about me calling on her manure-caked parents, and about their suspicions. Emily taught me her body and I learned from her when comes the blood, when the blood staves off and what it means. In late September she told me her condition, in the plainest way, saying that she hadn't bled in two months.

You bastarding fool, said Samuel. You've ruined yourself.

I was snuffing like a child and gave no response.

God damn it, he said. You're stuck now. You'll stay and that's it. If your daddy doesn't kill you.

I was chewing my tongue when he hit me, sending me to the ground.

Answer, damn it! I'm in this, too! I helped your sorry ass!

Samuel kicked me in the stomach and I retched empty.

Answer! he cried.

But it all seemed signs and wonders, and in this way my sins would be revealed.

My Heart Is Sore

I put her pregnancy away, kept myself from Emily for weeks, and she thinned in my memory while she thickened round the middle in life. All my thoughts of love gave way to sorry prayers for fire or Indian attack or sudden disease to sweep through the dugouts, wicked fancies of nighttime forays with a shovel to bury over the Fladeboes' door and seal her and my shame underground, or that she might trip and fall gut-first upon a doorway pike. So I skulked, a rotten, fearful boy, who would not own his works.

Keep hiding from it and see what you get, said Samuel.

But I would hide, just as I couldn't muster any more angelic visions for Preacher-father, and gave him a child's vision of apocalypse instead. Skies of blood, roads of blood; if blood could be smeared with blood it was in my prophecy—a lazy red vision of the end. Paul's scorpions made appearances, and so did that famous quartet: the skin and bones, the pox-house man, the soldier armored in plates of dried flesh, and the long-haired grinning harrier of souls. It was all another lie, for my true vision was this:

Shrouded in steam, Emily Fladeboe held in her bare arms a child bloody and slick with afterbirth and all around her were pale, raw-headed women working great scalding pots, and into them they dropped squalling infants; the women cooed in sweet voices to the vats and drew the reddened babes from out the boil, setting them, steamed and rendered for the scraper, on butchers' tables. Not yet the color of a person, our child mewled viciously. I was there with Emily and together we cleaned the child and I swaddled it in towels until the blood was gone. We handed the thing over to one of the ghouls, ourselves cooing as she dropped our baby in.

Along with such horrors and the awful prayers already detailed, there were the thoughts of marriage. Bizarre ceremonies came to me often those days: Emily covered in milkweed flowers, the only white bloom on the prairie, amid the morning sunlight attendance of the entire muddy population, Preacher-father performing the deed with a smile on his face. Another: fire-lit and shadowy; the holediggers there as an accompaniment of freaks and Samuel standing in judgment. My father is there again and in his hands he holds a needle threaded from a long spool. We betrothed stand naked before him and the entire congregation. I say my vows with my mouth moving like a nightmare scream. In the vision my father starts with his needle at our heels and sews me and Emily together up our legs and backs and skulls, unwinding his spool and twining us down the front. When it's done and we are bound, bride and groom can only shuffle our feet to turn and face the cheering crowd.

I know I tortured Samuel, telling him things like that. He would listen like a disciple, then cuss me half-heartedly, say he hoped they found me out soon; that he couldn't stand waiting anymore and would threaten to tell them. Behind it all there was the older brother, the long pull of the Ohio River, and at last Cincinnati.

We could go, he said. If you mean to deny her.

That's what you always say. You can go.

Come with me and we'll be rid of it all.

But my brother was as bound to his father as I was to mine. Or it was that he was bound to me and would wait for judgment at my side. I like to believe this; that his truer sight let Samuel know that we would be delivered, though in such a way that all our future courses and endeavors were the Devil's own.

No. There is no power greater than God's. And if I deny His purpose and His workings in my life, then I deny my life entire. And whether I have suffered for it or gained, the pain and glory are not mine. What happened was His will.

Israel a Wretched Infant

By September Emily's belly had risen like a boil from her ribs to her mound—not enough to truly show, but I still could not believe that her parents didn't know.

Pa's blind and Momma thinks I've got the worms, she said. But she suspects.

Emily was sitting back against a tree, sullenly enduring as I went longingly at one breast she'd let out from her dress, when I pulled away to find my mouth still full as though I had her still enlipped and, choking down what was there, I saw the yellow early milk on the beads of her paps, sliding down the hairs that had so often tickled my tongue.

I scrambled away as Emily hitched the top of her dress back, regarding me with such a look that said I was the worst thing in the world, but she would take me on like a burden.

And while her eyes burned into me, two more eyes soaked through the front of her dress.

I knew it'd come, she said.

You brought the milk too soon, she said, and, eye spinning, lifted up her dress to show the veined belly split down the middle by a rippling long dark line. Bared like that it was an awful revelation.

Samuel had come thrashing through the bushes at her sound, and now he stood beside me panting, unwittingly faced with her house of conception. He threw down his rifle, averting his eyes from the hurriedly fastening and covering Emily, and stormed off.

I tried to help her up but she tossed me off and we followed Samuel silently like children back towards the Fladeboes' hole. She didn't hang on me as we walked; I hung on her. But she was hard as her belly and gave me no smiles or sign of love. Samuel turned when we were at the edge of her family tract. God damn it, he said. Will you look at her! She's wet at the tits! We'll have to wait for her to dry off.

Shut the hell up, I said.

He ignored me and told Emily to get in the sun.

They'll know soon enough, she said.

I don't care, he said. They won't yet.

I told her to do what Samuel said, that we should wait till she was dry.

And Emily nodded, found herself a place full of sun, and sat, hunched in a way which showed her belly even more and sent my mind lurching to know that the little thing I'd made was turning over in her. She rested in the light, and perhaps it was the sunlight warmth but she wore a smile of inexplicable contentment, radiant and alive even as the world around her began to die and chill.

The Lord's Punishment

Trudging to that Sunday's meeting, I lagged back from the fathers, from Samuel even, as we gathered up the congregation. My cowardice howled loud enough to shake the plates of my skull, and yet I heard the voices saying, What will your father preach today? And will we have a word from you? The Chitites dimmed and the land was wavering, for I gave nothing my full sight until we reached the Fladeboes' tract.

I might have hidden in the dirt, dug myself a hole, so as not to be seen by her. As it stood, I slunk behind the bodies of the chattering faithful, hoping to prolong the time before I would come under

Emily's eye. But, so it went, the only soul about that bitter patch could not have seen me if he tried. It was Conny Fladeboe's voice, calling as he came from out their hole: Brothers? Preacher? Is it you?

Samuel by then was shouldering back through the congregation, bearing down on me; the fathers were at the dugout's mouth to help the wobbling, reaching Fladeboe out. Wife and daughter had gone at sunrise to do some washing in the creek and hadn't yet returned. It was, he jabbered, not like them at all to dally.

Perhaps they're waiting for the service to come, said Deacon Kemper.

Save themselves a trip, said Preacher-father.

No, no, there's dinner to be put to cook—

Preacher-father took up the man's arm, wound it with his, and led him into the crowd. Don't worry yourself, brother. We'll meet them on the way.

Yes, yes, said Deacon Kemper. Or they'll be there waiting.

Samuel, before me now, waited until they had started off again to speak. Looks like you've got yourself a little time to cower.

I shook my head and my brother had me like I was the one blind. Come on, he said, and hauled me away from the pens emptied of hogs, away from the hole with its door lolling open in the first cold wind of the fall, which blew now with increasing fury as we trailed the congregation snaking through the hillsides of shriveled grass. It was a gallows-way march that September day, the sky hemming in all us fools, cupped within the leaden hands of God. Samuel let me go, but now I followed close on him, hiding behind his back for the sight of the smiling Chitites: youngsters capered round women who clucked about fevers and bowel-trouble, men gave each other shrugs over hoof rot, and from out this din of commonplace misery a pair of daughters, young as ten, together started up a hymn. Gruel-fed voices made a song of thankfulness and grace that such a glorious day the Lord had made. That our lives were so blessed.

Faltering again, I strayed from them, wandered upon a high hillside, and, turning, looked back upon the Fladeboes' cut of the valley rendered small; their works—home, crops, ditching—faded into earth as will a corpse left afield too long.

Not far from Baptist Creek, my father broke from his place at the front, fell back through his people, and sought me out. Samuel picked up his stride and gave space for him to walk beside me, smiling.

You've been so quiet lately, he said. It's been a long time since you were this way. Then, with a laugh of recollection: Remember how you'd get after a coaling? You wouldn't speak for days.

I was afraid, I said.

Ah, you learned well by it, I'd say. Left the imprint of the Word on your mouth.

Yes, it did.

That's why I hate to see you not speaking. You're a fine preacher. Better than I was at your age. He took my hand, gripped it hard as he continued. And that is why the sermon today will be all yours. No one else will take the rock.

I matched my father's smile with a false one and bowed my head as though grateful, when really it was all I could do not to hang it low with the fear that I would, that day, speak before my Emily whatever lies of goodness I could muster. My voice would choke, wither within me, to stand before her and all the believers and tamp down the lies I held inside with the greater falsehood: that we are all beloved of God, and for us He wants only the best.

I prayed on it recently, said Preacher-father. I want to hear your voice lifted up again, so today is yours. He raised his head, surveying the horizon, as we ascended the hillock which would lead down into the meeting place. After all, he said, some day this will all be yours.

So he brought me with him to the head of the flock, telling each as we passed them that I was to give a ringing sermon this day. Blackbirds swept in peals across the sky, fluttering stormcloud formations, and as we came to the lip of the hill there could be heard the voice of a woman, talking, down below. With Preacher-father's hand at my shoulder, I strode foremost in descent.

My eyes at first refused the sight—a mad stitch-work of weeping mother, laundry enwebbed upon the rocks, and among the soap-fat foam the daughter lying prone. One of the Chitites screamed and the mother Fladeboe then raised up, where she knelt beside the body of her daughter, and answered wail for wail. Preacher-father's hand was gone and he rushed past me, the congregation trailing in growing frenzy and bewilderment, until I was borne by them, stumbling downhill. Samuel ahead of me muttering Jesuses, we came to the stones and he stopped, turned away with his eyes shut as the people huddled in a crush. I tore through them, their voices crying out, Drowned, drowned, drowned, and when I'd broken free it was to fall out of their midst and to the bankside, where I looked upon Emily.

Her clothes had been torn mostly from her, gooseflesh spread across her legs and even to her belly; and, dear God, her face—twisted and pale, teeth bared upon swollen tongue; eyes open, the left gaping heavenward and the wild right frozenly regarding me. I had not long to look before her mother, at the sight of me, came clawing across her daughter's corpse with such awful jerking speed that her hands were at my throat, her bony withers atop me, throttling, screaming that it was because of me she'd done it—You, you bastard boy! You made me!—before the others could pull her off. The father Fladeboe was yowling to know what was happening, and his answer came in pieces from the shrieking wife— that I had put a baby in her, I had ruined her and disowned her. And the people's hands were now upon me, but I was crawling for Emily, clawing at her breast where blood in livid patches rose to pallid flesh, and, weeping, tried to hold her up, sucking water from her sopping hair as I wept and pressed to her face; that awful face; against my cheek the cold purple bloat of the tongue which had only asked of me to love.

I was on hands and knees, spitting blood, when Preacher-father tossed the shovel to my side. Samuel had been sent to fetch it, and had returned a-horse, he said, for speed. He'd left, running for our camp, as the blows began to fall—from the Chitites, from my father until he grew exhausted, and I was lifted up and held in place so that even blind Conny Fladeboe could strike me; but that man was too far-gone with grief to deal much punishment, and the helpful Chitites took hold of his arms and swung them for him until the man doubled, gibbering, and was brought away by Deacon Kemper, who had the wife also apart; and I could hear as Preacher-father, wringing busted hands, approached me, the yelp from the mother Fladeboe as her husband went for her. With Deacon Kemper hollering, the commotion died even as my father said, Now speak. Tell it all.

By the time Samuel returned, I had. To the gasps and wails and lamentations of the people, I told it all. Confessed myself unto my father in halting sobs, all the while dead Emily bore gruesome silent witness.

The blade struck me at the hip, and with fingers clawing dirt, I pushed myself up as Preacher-father spoke.

You did this. No one else. Whatever demon is in you overtook Sister Fladeboe, just as you corrupted and overtook her daughter. You did this, he said. Now dig.

He sent the congregation, who cursed me softly, off a ways, so that, he said, he could counsel me in my evil. And so we were alone when I took up the shovel.

Where? I said.

Preacher-father shook his head. Right here where I preach and wrongly let you do the same. Right here, so you'll know it all the days of your life.

I went and stood not far from Emily, pale corpse in the corner of my eye, the patches of risen blood blossoming about her darkened paps. I let the shovel fall and slipped off my coat, with which I draped as much of her as I could.

No, said Preacher-father.

Let me cover her at least, I said, my hand at her forehead.

Your sin won't be covered till there's earth over it. Six feet.

Silently, I left my coat atop her and held the shovel. So Preacher-father did the job himself—a flutter of dark cloth cast amid the washing abandoned at the rocks. I bowed my head and split the earth. And as I dug, the awful hour of turning, shaping the hole, he would speak to me.

You must think you're some kind of great cocksman, eh? he said.

I was knee-deep and said nothing, worked the blade and tried not to see Emily as I went further down. In the distance, above the Chitites' gabble, I could hear Samuel and his father, shouting.

Well, you must think yourself one. You're grown enough to have that dead girl and that dead child, but you were supposed to be a man of God and wait for Him to show the way. Instead you gave her a belly-ful of maggots. And are you proud?

Another inch down, another inch closer to a Hell which seemed unreal, for all around me were the marks of damnation.

Answer me!

A split worm twisted in the dirt at my feet, hacked root-works flayed raw the air. I was quiet, my throat choked shut with the memory of coals.

You turned your back on God, he said.

I managed to say, I know.

You don't know a damned thing. You don't care what you've done. . . . You don't know your wickedness same as you don't know my love for you. Don't know or never did.

The sun, now in its full prominence, fought the clouds but couldn't staunch the chill. The burning eye of God, unblinking, regarded me in my labors: my arms afire but moving machine-like, turning shovelfuls out upon the growing mound. Shoulder-deep now, so Preacher-father had to bend.

There was a time, he said, when you had a mother. And together we lifted up our voices and sang you into the world each day. There was a time, I still believe it, when you walked in the ways of the Lord with me. . . . I should've known what you were made for. But I fought against it. I fought to keep you from the fire.

His boots ground at the edge of the grave, which was bent and poorly shaped in my haste and wrecked vision. It curved uneven so that, when he said for me to put her in, I had to bend my Emily to fit. I stepped down into the hole, her gooseflesh rough against my hands, as though on any chill day when I would touch her; only now it would not go away, no matter how long I held her.

Set her down, he said.

But I couldn't. I crouched with her and bore full-on the look of her twisted face until my eyes were closed and I was weeping.

Stop that, damn you, and put her down.

So I laid Emily in her grave, the weeping growing worse when my boot-heel took purchase in her thigh as I pulled myself out. When I stood, he pressed the shovel to me again, saying now I would cover her up.

And now I have to think of what's to be done with you, he said.

Nodding dumbly, I began. And this was worse than the digging, for whenever I emptied the blade there was the sight of her, slowly being covered over. What began as doleful work became a frenzy as I slashed at the mound and slung earth into her grave. My mind was on dirt-beads at her neck, her jewelry of ringworm—how I'd loved them all when first I saw her, glowing in the tallow-light. And that had been underground, in the dark of the earth. Shoveling faster, her song playing in my mind: *There's a lily in the garden, For you, young man; There's a lily in the garden, Come pluck it if you can.*

Now I wasn't even raising the blade, but scraping it across the ground. Preacher-father looked to the distant congregation—where Samuel leaned against the horse's side, his father close in his ear—and spat, his hands seeking something.

If I only had the strength in me, he said, you'd be down there with your whore.

As he spoke, I drug the blade, saw the dirt settle softly at Emily's face—those gaping eyes, that tortured mouth, saying, Love me. I held tight to the handle, hunching there, unable to look away from her or drive off Preacher-father's words, which hung in the bitter air even as I lifted up the shovel and, in one brutal instant, swung.

My father dropped, tottering on one knee, black blood running from the gash in his head. From the mark I'd made. All words, all the curses I sought, were caught within my throat as I stood over him. And neither could he speak, but mouthed his shock, gulping and blinking ever-widening eyes against the drip. My own blood, my sorry heart, now thundered in my skull. Shouts came from the Chitites, who, as did my father, saw me raise the shovel high. For a moment, as the shouts grew nearer, my arms refused to move; but this, as all the pain and love and fear which make up this wretched world, did pass and I brought the shovel down upon his head.

The Chitites were all around me, grabbing for my weapon, treading in their rage over my struck-down father. Deacon Kemper howled, the blind Fladeboe father reached for my eyes as I was lifted up and the mother with a screech flung herself at me, climbing the bodies of her fellows. And I tore at them all, thrashed against them, sure that I would die in pieces but glad for it—to hurt as many as I could. In their hands I was turned facing upwards, to see the same sky as faced Emily's dead eyes, and they were carrying me towards the grave when there came the sound of snorts and hoofbeats, and Samuel rode into them. I felt myself now falling as they stumbled back into the grave, but my brother's hand caught me up, hauling me as though I were weightless across the neck of the horse, which he wheeled and gave heel to run. I clung there, jolting, unable to look back.

Book Two

THESE ARE THE NAMES

I

The Journeys of Israel

Indiana–Northwest Territory, Winter 1800

Into America

For weeks I scarcely looked up from the ground and only when Samuel demanded it did I allow myself the horse's back, raising up my head to pursue the horizon and the Ohio tearing away at our right. Almost a month removed and my arms still ached from their work that day in Chit; my soul pained all the worse.

My brother would call behind to ask if I wanted to stop and I'd tell him to take back his horse, but he always refused. So I remained a-saddle, gathering sores while the sun and moon rolled overhead and the plains went beneath us like a carpet pulled away. All the crossings were too dear, and so we went amongst the tribes, who still held the territory north of the Ohio River. I recalled the pox-faced Indians, and in my trot-lolling head the cheekless squaw became Emily—a confluence of desiccation and bloat-tongued strain, as though I saw her rotting in her grave, the earth of which was surely as frozen as the brittle riverside woods we now traveled. From them came calls and whoops and the crackle of dead leaves, the smell of fires, dragging me for moments from out my delirium of guilt. I had no fear of the savages, no fear of dying, but rather of living on.

To keep his mind and maybe bring mine back, Samuel maintained a steady stream of talk, like I'd done for him after Nathan fell. He inventoried our belongings: the rifles he'd hurriedly lashed to the saddle; some twenty dollars in silver from his father's purse, which he would hold to for when we reached our destination; our food—bony blackened squirrels and hares we'd gathered on the way; the dueling pistols in their mahogany box, which were the last thing my brother grabbed in our frantic scouring of the camp; meager shot and a single horn; bear-cloaks for our bedrolls; our only clothes upon our backs; the Bibles we wore at our breasts.

By Shawnee-town the snow began. My brother cut his blanket down to wrap his boot-legs for the drifts. I'd grown used to the ache and throb of the boils on my thighs and ass—the only revenge our poor horse could have on me for being such a bastardly weight on his sloping back. The boils rose on my nethers and I accepted them, thinking, Let it rot. I didn't drink enough to piss nor eat enough to pass, so I had no cause to look upon my growing swarm of wounds. Instead I envisioned something like the syphilitic's fungal-looking bits or John's many-headed beast, all of them with eyes and pus-weeping mouths.

On the third day out from Shawnee the horse was crawling and Samuel, stepping high through the snow, fell back and gave a rub to the bent neck of the horse and I would not look at him, but rather to my legs, where I could see the boils bloating through my pants.

Not unlike the river itself, Samuel's talk would ever flow back to his brother Reuben. The eldest Kemper had thrashed fourteen men in an Ohio tavern with nothing but a busted chamberpot, sat on river-docks reading the philosophies of the Greeks in one hand and lifting sugar barrels with the other, had never married for there was no woman who could content him. Samuel bandied legends and dangled them out before me as my vision dimmed. We would find him, he said, in Cincinnati.

I was harried in my dreams by Preacher-father's face, the way he'd looked at me before I brought the shovel down the second time, waking with the question of whether he was dead, and knowing in my soul the answer. Sometimes instead it would be Emily I struck, beating her back into the pit. So I awoke one night from such visions in the chill of my snow-soaked cloak with the horse's chest throbbing for breath beside my head and Samuel looking down on us. The earth rocked under me like I was still riding, and it was hard to see my brother's face. I raised my head as much I could from the packed snow and saw that in my lap the jean was crusted with dried yellow pus.

When did I fall?

You didn't, said Samuel. I knocked you down.

Why? I croaked.

It's been long enough. Look at you. You need to lay the hell down.

You could've broken my neck.

It's better than you dying up there.

I nodded, or my head was just used to flopping by then. It's cold, I said.

Samuel took a rifle up and examined the flint; seeing that it sparked, he said, Sleep, you rot-crotched lunatic, and I'll start the fire.

Cloak bundled about my burning ears, I laid there in my soiled pants and wallowed.

The Village of Cincinnati

Our horse died that night in the snow, and so we butchered its haunches and shoulders and cooked what we could, and carrying a few pounds each, we made the rest of the way afoot, passing through patchy towns that had been attacked and burnt. Still we didn't fear the tribes. They surrounded us but we saw no feather of them. Samuel kept up his talk of Reuben and a house full of mulled wine and turkey while we chewed horse-steak and shuffled ever onwards through the white, preserved occasionally at the cabins of settlers outlying the village.

When at last we arrived it was dark and we were so tired that we snuck into a carriage house to spend the remainder of the night, stumbling out before dawn when the stallboy came to tend. A young black face above a lantern, staring at us in our huddle of warm dung-rolled straw—he didn't try to run us off, but watched with a sullen understanding of the madness of white men.

We went out into early morning streets deserted by the moon but still too dark for selling wares. Revived by the chill that blew between the ramshackle houses, we set off down what Samuel said was Main Street towards the river, where Reuben kept his house. I watched the lights from the landing at the foot of Main fade as Samuel gave me his description of the place. He changed with the growing light and was reborn a man of town, greeting people who didn't know him from any other frontier straggler, but he beamed as though he counseled them all.

That's the place where I was whipped, he said, pointing to a house which leaned heavy on its neighbor. And that is the church my father founded.

The church was set on wooden blocks, painted and windowed, and seemed too fine a place to leave; the sign told it was a Presbyterian meeting house, not Baptist. But I had no care for truth that morning, save for the fact that he did have a brother and that brother was here and somewhat moneyed and had a fire going in the grate.

At his brother's house, Samuel rapped the door and what came in answer were harsh shouts from a man's voice. He grinned at me and I noticed the hollowness of his cheeks, thinking also of my own. The door was presently flung open and a man still in nightclothes stood in the jamb.

What's this? said the man. It's too early to ask for work, boys.

Samuel bristled, said his name, and asked where was his brother.

The man in the doorway shook his head. I bought this house, he said, outright this April. You want to talk more, go wake the judge.

A woman's voice piped from within the house. I could smell fatback cooking, felt my knees go weak and was unable to parse what words Sam and the man exchanged before he slammed shut the door and left my brother standing ashen-faced on the step.

I know where to go, Samuel said. Don't worry.

So we broke off from the street and went along the bottom of a hill, slopping through muddy snow, slipping and falling so that we had to hold each other by the hands to stay upright. He said this was a short-cut to the house of a man who would have answers. Through a grove of dead and girded trees we came to the home of a lawyer named Van Nuys.

He's a Dutchman, but a good friend of my father's, Samuel said as we made yet another porch; only this one was finer and gabled and lights shone through the windows.

Samuel's knock was answered by an Irishwoman who squinted at him when he said his name.

You're not Mister Reuben, she said.

Samuel, said my brother. Please tell Mister Van Nuys that I need to see him and it's urgent.

The Irishwoman stuck her head out the doorframe and eyed me. And who's this?

Angel Woolsack, I said.

She shuddered and slipped back inside and soon produced Van Nuys, who, thankfully, smiled upon us both and took Samuel in his arms.

The mud fell from my boots upon the rug as I trailed Van Nuys and Samuel.

Take off your packs, Van Nuys called back, grabbing Samuel's shoulder strap. I let mine fall straight from my back to the floor, heard the butt of my rifle rap the boards and the Irishwoman cuss, and followed the pair of them to the family table, where sat the wife and three children eating breakfast. Samuel was given the only open chair, and I stood behind them wobbling now with the sight of their food until the Irishwoman hustled another chair to a corner of the table for me. Samuel told the lawyer his lie of our departure as brightly as though we hadn't but taken a walk down the valley. Meanwhile, plates were brought for us and heaped upon them were trout and chipped potatoes, eggs black from cooking in lard, boiled chicken, and broad swaths of bacon shining in the lamplight. I thought I would vomit, and when a cup of beer was set down for me I drank it quick to choke the bile back, sat holding the mug while the Irishwoman refilled it from an earthen pitcher.

Glad to hear that your father's well, said Van Nuys, spearing a cut of fish.

Samuel nodded and chewed over a mouthful. But Reuben—

He has gone south to make his fortune, said Van Nuys, which I have no doubt that he will. His contract with Mister John Smith is fair.

Not Pastor Smith? Samuel said.

The same. He's become something of a shipper. Your brother left last year for Philadelphia—said he met Thomas Jefferson, you know—and came back with a barge of goods to sell to the Spanish citizens of West Florida, and set for those parts on the same barge with Mister Smith.

I like the sound of it, my brother said, then turning to me: He's a Baptist and Virginian, too. He'll be treating Reuben right.

Yes, yes, so long as your brother does profitable business. And the country sounds worthwhile—Feliciana, it's called. Van Nuys looked to me down-table. Lovely, isn't it? he said.

I had at last begun to eat, forking lightly the potatoes, then the chicken, then both fish and bacon together. Glorious, I said.

Van Nuys laughed, and it spread through his children and wife. I meant the name of the place, my friend, he said. *Feliciana* has a good ring to it.

The small boy beside me gave me a nudge with his finger, giggling. I had forgotten laughter, and so I kept quiet for the rest of the meal and ate all I could while the talk wore on. I would have eaten more if my stomach hadn't shriveled into such a small thing. My plate was half-full with pot-scrapings when breakfast ended and Van Nuys rose to go up to his office and begin his lawyering of the day, leaving Samuel twitching with this new encumbrance of knowledge and myself gorged and drowsy.

My brother's promise was now across the continent, and even addled with food I could tell that he was melancholy at the thought. But by the time we were brought to the fire, where a pallet and blankets were laid out, he was mumbling to me his new designs before I was claimed by warmth and sleep.

That night Samuel showed me the village as gusts blew in from off the river and reduced the infrequent streetlamps to cold and darkness in their cages. There was mulled wine sold by vendors from kettles set on tripods over fires built in the streets, and we drank of it and headed for a place Samuel said was called the Licking River Tavern. It was situated near the landing, beneath the second of the town's seven hills and beside a lone elm tree, which for whatever reason had been left untouched by hewers and stood watch over the waterfront until, later in the month, it was struck by lightning. That night, though, we passed beneath its branches and to the open door of the Licking River.

When Samuel said his name was Kemper, some boatmen took up a cheer and we were bought spiced gin in pewter cups. And it was there that Samuel first said to someone else that I was his brother.

He don't quite have the Kemper look, said one.

Too small, said a second.

Naw, said still another, grabbing me by the head and pointing to my eyes. He's got the ferocity right there.

With the boatman's hand upon my head I grinned and glared at them all, trying ferociousness on like someone else's boots. Let my old Woolsack skin slip, slough off like the scabs of my boils, and be renewed in the hide of Kemper. I felt already like brass tacking to a legend in life.

See it plain as day, the boatman said. That's the same eye I saw old Reuben get before he put a Kaintuck man's head through yonder window.

I couldn't muster any words, but tried to maintain the look.

Samuel, hands hip-wise and nodding prideful, said, Damn right. You can tell a Kemper a mile away.

One of the dissenters leaned in, saying, And that's as close as some may want to get.

Unless you happen to be a girly, said the one still holding my skull, which presently he twisted so that I looked about the room. And here we got ample chance for you to prove that too.

And as he spoke I saw, fussing in darkened corners, leaning over table-lips, shouldering to the rail, women and girls who smiled and chattered, haggled, enduring the smacks and pinches of the patrons before leading those agreeable to the stairs, where lurked their sisters eyeing men as yet unclaimed.

Samuel clapped his coat pocket; his father's coin clinked. I suppose it's time we spent some, brother. I'll treat you.

Now the voices of the women drew upon me loud, a river-roar of bodily commerce. Amid the tales, Reuben's specter growing to the ceiling, some would come and join us, tapping at my shoulders and taking drinks from my cup. A gurgle of gin in one's bobbing throat, the sound of drowning. Fleshy, flush, and untiring in their efforts, the whores added inventions of their own to the makings of the family name. Hemmed by bodies, I worked to douse grief and weakness as both story and toast became slurred. A young fool drunk off his feet, unlimbering his new place in the world, casting foggier and foggier glances to the stairs. I did not want them, wouldn't have one that night or for all that followed while we waited for the thaw to begin our journey south. But I couldn't curse them either—they sought survival as best they could. So I endured their offers, and proffered false and heartless boasts. I was, after all, a Kemper.

II

A River into Eden

The Ohio–Mississippi River, Spring 1801

Aboard the Ark

We dangled our heads over the side of the barge to watch the muddy water roll with stars reflected near and warm, not distant and cold like they had been in Chit. The end of February brought the flood and the Ohio swelled and at the landings where we stopped to load and unload cargo the wharf-boats were bobbing at the treetops; and likewise the Father of Waters overran its banks and we passed above the tips of pines and willows where would be islands in the drier seasons. We would turn south at the Cape and pass forever by our fathers, and so were cast into Eden.

Still, my father hadn't left me; he visited day by day, sometimes brought guilt, sometimes avarice or wrath. If I had killed him, and I believed it to be so, he was now nothing more than rot. But I knew even then, laid out on our flatboat's deck, that if he had one follower yet he would not go into corruption; he would be burnt, taken by the wind and scattered in his ashy wisdom; or that same follower would scrape his ashes into the baptizing creek, and let Preacher-father silt the waters which would carry him through the wiry lattice-work of tributaries, slowly churning him with the mud until he reached an artery of the Mississippi and came into that muddy organ and lived in it, possessing all and watching me with the milky eyes of catfish, seeking land at the banks and islands with frog-legs and the claws of alligators.

Those nights we listened to the groan and creak of the flatboat's timbers, to the men fighting over tobacco or liquor or money, or just to fight: the sounds of something being slowly torn apart in the current. We learned to find good sounding by the color of the water, to read the currents, and to see bars and traps by the ripples in the water.

The boatmen gave us tastes of their drink and smoke when they were feeling good-natured. But they found that our appetites were fierce and these gifts were soon rescinded. We worked, shucking loads at pitiful landings all down both rivers, and before long we could afford our own drink and smoke—though we only had one broken clay pipe to split between us and it was often either tobacco or food. We passed our pipe while we toted casks and bales and sugar-sacks and the men of the wharfs would say, Some preachers! and go on making fun, singing bawdy hymns at us until our captain, a man named Finch, would holler them quiet. He carried with him at all times the biggest knife I ever saw, and would use the breadth of its flat sides to knock you awake or get you working at a faster clip.

The work on the river was bizarrely a thing of speed. We floated slowly, poling where it was shallow, sometimes lashing ropes to great live oaks to pull ourselves along, but so did our competitors, and if they survived our poles on the water we would be sidled up next to them at Big Bone Lick or Bear Grass or Clarksville, and there we would unload against them and whoever was clear first to get his stock ashore would get the market price of the day and the choice of contract and credit to move further downwards, with the loser gaining nothing but merchants' chop-change and some brawling. The shipping men would scoff and laugh amongst themselves about these river rats. Once, when I was sent to fetch contract papers from a merchant's office, the man snapped back from his desk and waved a hand before his face.

Christ, boy, tell your captain to send someone who doesn't smell like they floated down here in a privy.

I'd turned away to scowl, imagining how he would look with a gun-barrel leveled at his face. And such thoughts had visited me more and more, whenever we would pass into a town and see the sated and slothful. I wanted to take, but moreover I wanted someone else to hurt.

When work was through, Finch would let us go out into the docks and landings and preach if we felt the urge. The need to witness was in me and I considered it my repentance to weep and tell the people my sins and calamities, with Samuel standing like the God of Judgment behind me. And after I finished even those who had jeered and hissed me would straighten up when my brother lumbered forward to take my perch from me and deliver the moral. It was rare that any coin would sail into our hats, rarer less than the souls we turned to goodness; but what little off-chance money we did receive we gave an equal share to Captain Finch.

Lean as our provisions were, the captain was a good man, a teacher, and some miles below the falls at Louisville, not far from where Preacher-father and I were cast from our boat long before, and having dropped our pilot and proceeded downriver, the captain took Samuel and me both up by the scruff and made us look to a high, sloping bank of limestone marked with a great cave. About the cave, nailed to the trunks of a pair of trees in early bloom, were signs variously reading: WILSON'S LIKKER VALT, BILLYARDS, CARDS, & HOUSE OF ENTERTAINMENT. Cargo-laden boats like ours were docked below the mouth of the cave, and it was to them that Captain Finch pointed, saying, Those boats are manned by dead hands.

It looks a fine place, I said, thinking more of rows and bawds than the captain's words.

Captain Finch took a-hold of my nape and said, Boats land and the crews drunked, whored, and by the next day, killed. The cavers float down to New Orleans and sell the goods off, the bastards. Yes, it's a damned fine business.

He withdrew his hands from my neck and went to fiddling with his belted knife. And I didn't know why then that Samuel took quiet and looked afraid, only understanding later, in the night, when he told me that he worried if his brother Reuben might have met that kind of fate. I said that from the sound of him, he'd have bored the pirates' eyes from their skulls and painted their cave with gore, then writ a treatise about the process. Samuel laughed, but in the day, slowly passing Wilson's cave, we heard other laughter issuing within and the voices of barkers shouting to us, Come down, fellows! Don't float off now! Cheapest drink, ripest teats, fairest cards in the country! Don't float now! Come!

Captain Finch gave me a whap of his blade to drive the point home further, then raised his knife up between us so that the blade must have shined with the sun and struck the dim-eyed cave-lurkers with its brilliance, and hollered back at them, You want this scalp and money you'll have to come and get it, you cunt-lapping dogs! I hope the river rises twenty feet tonight and drowns your sorry asses! Then he turned to each of us, saying, They're good robbers but worthless on the river. I see their boats wrecked all along the way. Ain't that right, you rotten sons of scabby bitches!

Samuel's voice cracked a bit when he shouted along, Fuck to your souls and see you in Hell!

Right-o, said Finch, sheathing his blade and clapping him on the shoulder. That's the spirit, my boy!

Christ Comes as a Thief

And the spirit which came over me in the following days was one for preying. I'd grown sorely tired of seeing the merchants, stuffed into their waistcoats, stroll along the wharves and spit whatever change they so desired. Whereas our fellow crewmen were content with the occasional combat, I wanted my violence as I would later in life—swift, secret, by surprise. And to lift some coin from those hated purses had no small allure. My hunger grew more sharp, the ache of work more sore, and the thought of setting fear in the heart of some fool—not of Hell, not of God, but of me—became too sweet not to bring unto fruition. I could've lived on our provisions, on the fruits of our more honest labors, but I needed to right the balance of sorrow. So I sat one evening on the deck with my brother, our packs for pillows, fingers caked with dried flour-mud, and put it to him.

I'm tired, I said, of being on my knees. I'll bow down before the Lord any day, but not these fools, these money-counters.

You want to quit the ship?

Not that, brother. I want to take.

No point in getting killed before we ever get to Reuben.

There's no point in living hand-to-mouth until we find him either.

And how'd you go about it?

With your father's pistols.

They aren't his anymore, said Samuel.

That's right. Now they're for us to make our way. I reached for his pack and gave a rap to the box which held the dueling set, saying,

Toting these around and never putting them to use, you might as well carry a Bible and never crack the spine.

Samuel drew on our pipe, eagerness creeping at the corners of his eyes. This hasn't got much to do with money, does it?

The following night at a shabby landing the boatmen departed for the taverns and we followed after them. But while they carried razors or knives in their shirts, we wore each a pistol in our belts beneath our river-rotted overclothes.

Raw-eyed and fully loaded, we went out into the town past the houses where the boatmen drank and whored and battled, to the finer establishments up the way where the cozy imbibing of the merchants went on behind unbroken windows and the proprietors had both their ears; for the owners of the lower bawds were generally marked with the thief's punishment as was dealt in the territories those days— the cutting of the ear.

Tucked into an alleyway, watching groups too large to trifle with go by, we awaited our first transaction.

You're right, said Samuel. They're full of drink and money. They're laughers.

They eat money, I said. I can hear it jangling in their guts.

The wait was long and once our chance showed itself we had worked up a murderous righteousness. Stepping with a shout out of the alley's mouth with pistols extended mule-dick fashion we robbed a chance of dandies on their drunken nighttime way, one who puked on his boots as he fumbled for his purse. And when our marks would catch sight of us, come to understand their sorrowful position, I drank in their looks of fear and redeemed their money as I would a soul.

In this way I believed crime was spiritual, robbery an act of faith. Like saving a man's soul or healing the sick, the hand of the healer being as under as the robber's; in the process, both parties were

91

brought closer to God, one to gain and one to lose. I numbered that the prayers said during our nickings were more numerous than in any church. And they were prayers that saw us clawing back to the first man ever gave: let me survive, let me retain.

The City Under the Hill

We passed first the fine city on the hilltop, then eased round the banks to lower Natchez where the goods were put in and somehow the money would ascend that peak to tickle the fingers of merchants and planters. On the down-hill side of the finery and the respectable was where we'd make our home, where we'd come to find more than money or mission.

Time being, our eyes were softened slightly by the spoils of our recent robberies and we were bacon-fed and feeling easy the morning we moored at the landing.

The work that day went easy, chewing rind while I shouldered sacks of Kentucky flour and brought molasses in casks back to the boat, the whole time looking out to the town all filthy with hopes for gains ecclesiastical and profane. Thus were the prospects of the rougher places of the world, that they could satisfy both sinner and savior in us.

All down the great landing other crews worked the wharf-boats after we were done. Captain Finch was brandishing his knife on one, waving it in the face of a merchant's agent until he stormed off, hopping back onto our keel, red with anger.

Bastarding Pukes! he shouted at no one in particular. Dog-ass mothers!

What say, Cap? called the men. How's it?

Finch jerked the hilt of his knife and said, The God-damned bastards have raised the rates on American goods at New Orleans. And these shit-birds, he said, indicating the men on the wharf-boats, they think they might just be putting a halt to all the bitching American cargo coming. Damn-all!

So we can't load up when we get there? said one crewman.

Hell if I know! But I'll burn the place to the fucking ground if that's the case. We got orders upriver to fill, by God!

Hell yes, Cap!

Who's doing it? said Samuel.

The French-ass Spanish, who else? Finch said. Can't tell them apart anyhow.

Samuel understood the issue better than I did at the time. Meanwhile, Finch and the crew went on bemoaning and cussing until the high sun put them down; a few went and fell in with the workers, their foremen hollering out the journeyman wage, or shucked off through the piled goods to town. I swear there was steam coming off the river, and seeing all the toilers still working on the landing, the merchants' men and the loaders, slave and free, mechanics, boat-rights, and all the gathered souls teeming there for me to save, I swole with the Word and itched to preach a bit, told Samuel so, but he didn't hear. I said to him, Look out there and tell me there's a thing wrong with robbing.

That's honest labor you're seeing, he said.

True, they're Caesaring, I said. But half of them are niggers who can't help it besides.

Samuel rose, pointing to a stack of crates high above the toilers. All right. You want to preach? Let's do it there.

And so we set out armed with our Bibles and pistols, which were tucked beneath our shirts, onto the sun-beat boards of the wharf-boats and up the landing to the piled crates. Captain Finch, having his first dip of the day, perhaps to calm himself, raised his cup as we went by.

Go to it, my boys! Go to it!

We wove through the men and mounted the crates, where Samuel stood high and hollered out the name of the Lord.

Not a head turned.

Work on, men, I said. It's fine not to look on me—but don't you dare turn your eyes from God, for He won't ever turn His from you!

The workers said not a thing, but their overseers did glance at us suspicious.

Brothers, I went on, I turned my back on Him and cut my eyes from glory. I thought He couldn't see me if I wasn't looking at Him and I laid down with a girl and made her fill up with child.

Hoots and jeers issued amid the crack of crate and commerce. I continued:

But both that girl and my child were struck dead—dead sure as if I'd killed them with my own hands. That is the power of God's eyes.

One called out, What'd you kill her with, your prick?

Samuel put a hand to my shoulder and said: He knows what all you do. You do it in His sight, so don't turn your head from him. He'll love everything you do if you just look on Him and be cleaned.

Ask my ass! called another.

We're young! I cried, and I know we look fresh-faced, but we work this river same as you and we've packed a few hot Hells' worth of sinning into our short time.

Here Finch's crew whooped praises and now were black faces giving us swift glances over work-bent shoulders. I'd never seen so many in one place, long strings of slaves played out upon the landing, working alongside others that were free and cheaper.

I went on with my sermon in the swelter and some bedraggled whites hollered for me to shut my cotton-headed ass up. Samuel nudged me to see Finch's men sidle them with gaffs and razors and I preached on:

You work hard here on earth, but you're only paid in gold. And you've forgotten your Father's work. Do you Father's work in all your ways, do it all your days and you'll be paid by Him with a mountain of heavenly gold!

Now the overseers and the merchants' clerks grew restless and one came to us with his hand in the pocket of his waistcoat and said why didn't we just save it for the Sabbath. When he gave us his back, satisfied, Samuel let out a yawp and I went even harder into the Word. Soon men were dropping off from their work and came to listen and shout back in refrain.

You work, I said. You work hard!

Christ yes! they cried.

And your misdeeds on earth aren't but a fly speck in His drink if you are only washed in the blood of His son, Jesus Christ. Wash yourselves clean of work-sweat and whore-juices, everything! Under that eye of fire up there, make it clean. Make it joyous in His sight and if you're a sinner like me, get yourselves up now, and go to the end of these boards you walk with so many earthly burdens and cast off Satan's weight—and fly into that water! Fly into that muddy water! It may look dirty, but it'll make you clean in Jesus' eyes.

And they did fly, at first a few gathering at the edge of their wharf-boats, timid with their overseers screaming for them to stop, then joined by a press of more; and a few Negroes broke through and ran to their backs, howling, Jesus! And in the crush of bodies and out-stretched arms and whipping heads both black and white to search the sky for signs of Christ they all went tumbling over.

Samuel was beating me over the back with his Bible he was so happy, and from the men splashing in the froth there came much laughter and singing. The baptized beat the sides of the boats with joy, and their drivers tried to call them out of the water. The workers stood idle down the landing but for a few untouched by grace and the water was a tumult of goodness. The braver of the overseers laid out on the lips of the wharf-boats, reaching for necks and arms, only to be turned away by gouts of Mississippi.

High hats flew from heads as a dripping clutch of overseers hurtled down the docks towards us. Cursing, they mounted our makeshift pulpit and we scurried back the other side and went clattering along the wharfs to our boat with the cheers of the saved hailing our safe passage. And when we came to, merchants' men biting at our heels, there stood Captain Finch waving us by with his knife, giving me a slap with it across the backside and some steeling words before he whirled them each-by-each across their rage-puffed faces with the fat of his blade, shouting, Glory hallelujah! And we turned, feet beating the air from our bellows, back around to race again across the bobbing wharfs and onto the landing, up the frontage, and into town.

III

The City of Refuge

Natchez, 1801

The Wicked World

Mother Lowde would tell us whore-tales, of New Orleans line-ups and the boat game, of being sold for slave just because her nose was flat and her skin browned by the sun, of Natchez-Under-the-Hill and its environs: Rowder's, Clay's, Door-knock alley, The Church. Later she'd even tell of that brother we'd so long sought. She was our landlord from the first day, when we came scrambling into her tavern by chance, breathless and looking over our shoulders; and she was good to us boys, that lady who'd once been a whore of some repute, famous for her barrenness, but now in her dowager years she only took callers on occasion. She'd been a river rider in the early days of its commerce, hopping from barge to barge on the slow go south, taking advantage of the lonesome oarsmen and polers. It was said that if two boats were close enough she could stretch herself across their sides and pleasure a man on one craft mouth-wise while another on the adjoining had her from behind. Thus she was infamed. She ran no young fillies now and lived the life of any aged doting aunt, keeping her tavern and its rooms, which we left day and night to wander streets warped like wood-grain along the river-bend, and there were many places that looked good to preach, many places also good to hide and spring from. Mother Lowde sewed onto our hats flaps of cloth with eyeholes in them, to be pulled down over our faces before we robbed or tucked atop our heads when we weren't. We left our Bibles holstered and kept our voices low.

Our own Corinth; Natchez was hellish fine and chocked with sin and unrepentance. We watched the vendors' stalls change through the course of a day—bread to pies, the coffee urns going cold, liquor tinctures before the taverns opened their doors. There was even one who pushed what looked to be a tinker's cart but sold only weapons, knives mostly, but also cudgels and guns, a few all-nations pistols hanging on nail heads. He marched with his cart of deadlies up and down the rows of bawdy houses from mid-day through the night and when some under-armed man, a drunken sufferer of drunken insults, came storming out into the street, he would find the weapon-seller and lay down however much he had and would receive the tools corresponding. So the now-armed man would stride back into the house of his insult—sometimes the insulter followed right along with the aggrieved and waited behind him at the cart to buy his own piece—and then have out the fight in the streets, the seller dragging his jangling cart out of the way of combat.

We only shuffled by the whores, who cawed and mocked or offered of themselves. For all the good our thieving had done, how every fear-struck face had put Emily's and my father's further back, I still couldn't bear to take one on. They were different from the Licking River girls, often as not a head taller than me on their iron-point heels. We talked with some and came to know the houses and their legends. The alley girls spoke in awe of the rows of finer houses, each being differently owned and featuring ranging talents; some had Negroe girls in African garb of tiger skins and hoop-rings in the strangest of places, while others were more lacy and regular. And I do remember from their warty lips the warnings not to stray too near The Church, a sympathy also held by Lowde, for it was not church at all but a house of the most vicious whores, the mistress of which was a woman who cut the pricks from unlucky customers and kept a jar of them upon her bedroom mantelpiece. They called her Raw Liza, Bloody Lizzy, Miss-Chop-and-Swing Liz. This was our first hint of the woman of bones, when she was only stories and not yet real. And so we kept from that house of parapets and spires and windows of red-colored glass, set upon a foundation of tales of the horrors that waited within for the unwary, the unlucky, and unwise. At the time I tossed such rumors aside, for how could a business full of working girls operate if all they did was maim and steal? And even if they did slip the occasional razor to the pecker of some prick, or poison a rich traveler to get at his purse, it couldn't be so common as was said or they'd just be violent paupers, bloody waifs, and terrorful gamines.

I considered that the house's points reached higher in the sky than anything besides the boatmen's watchtower; and it was said that from the highest tower room, belonging to the mistress, you could see even down into the Devil's Pisspot—a vast sink in the woods northeast of town, alternately known as the Devil's Punchbowl by citizens with clean mouths or the Pisspot or Devil's Ass-hole by those most likely to frequent its depths. Regardless of who did the naming, the ownership of the aperture was always Lucifer's. And this was fitting, as the Pisspot was said to have been flat land once that had been struck millennia ago by a falling star.

Sundays were spent not at preaching, hearing the bells of the churches on the hill-top and the rusty whomp of iron drums beat with pans which sounded worship down our way, but waiting for night and robbery. I, more missable, would pull down the flap from my hat and, so masked, first corner the mark with my pistol poking from my coat.

Hold tight, whiskey bibber!

Then Samuel would appear from behind some shadowy overhang, saying, Stiff as a plank now. We'll have your money.

To some I'd slip a little evangelism. Your coin for tithings, I'd say, raising up my pistol so the barrel-mouth was square in the wretch's face, for the eye of the Lord is upon you.

Once it happened that while we were hunting ones with full pockets and empty heads, a voice called out from behind and we turned to see a fellow pistoleer holding on us. We both had ours drawn and when our assailant looked on this and to our masks he gaped for a moment before bursting into wild peals of laughter. And it must have been a contagious madness, for so did we, walking backwards watching him make the same awkward trek to the corner.

No ill feeling in robbing the heathen or the wicked man, said Samuel afterwards, but not too wicked.

And he was right. The place was full of bastards tougher yet than us.

The Iniquities of Our Elusive Brother

We'd but returned, loose-mouthed with excitement, from a night's work to find Mother Lowde lipping the nub of her pipe and seeming glum. The pre-dawn hours we generally spent listening to Lowde talk and drinking with her a mash of coffee grounds and rum, giving her a little gospel or singing in return, as well as her small cut of the night's take, which she often refused, saying that she loved just having us about the place. When one of us would speak, there was delight in every bed-rattled bone of her. That morning, though, she was guarded.

How many people have you told your names? she asked us, for we were both known to her as Kemper.

A few about town, said Samuel.

Just a few?

Not many, I said.

Lowde eyed us both and blew smoke from her nose while she drank her coffee. I never heard a preacher-man to talk the way y'all do, she said. And I've known quite a few. Some almost had it right, but you two surely do.

We were brought up for it, I said.

And did you have another brother that was raised that way? Like a preacher?

Yes, said Samuel, leaning forward in his chair.

I sat there and stared into my cup, somehow knowing what Mother Lowde would say next.

And you've come down here after him, she said.

Reuben Kemper. Samuel said it like it was a charm.

That's the man, said Lowde. His brothers, eh?

You know him?

Course I do. He visits Natchez on occasion, but not to such a place as mine. I've never seen him, only heard tell.

Can't put much stock in that, I said.

Your ass, my young pup, she said, angling her pipe at me. I'd think some preachers would know that tell and stories is how we come to know the world and all its people.

We heard he was in West Florida, Samuel said.

That's gospel. He takes his barge this way sometimes. Not so much anymore. There was a while, though, when you couldn't help but hear of him—great big man, smart, and with worthwhile money. He knows Governor Claiborne, who lives on the hill.

See, brother, said Samuel. I told you he was up there with the high and mighty.

I nodded, not answering for the look I saw on Lowde's face.

She said, He's told to be courting the mistress of The Church.

The cutter? Samuel said. Bloody Lizzy?

The same.

Good God, I said, suddenly fearful of the man we'd come so far to find.

Can't be, said Samuel.

O, it can. We're strange creatures. I didn't tell you sooner, not because I don't trust you boys, but I was awaiting similarities to crop up, and they did. And I figured you were seeking him. And, truthful, I don't much want you to leave me.

It's all right, Mother, I said.

She gave a shrug and downed more coffee-rum. Her pipe had gone out and she sucked at the dead embers, awaiting more questions.

But it could just be talk, said Samuel.

Sisters in trade, said Lowde, may often as not lie to the ones they lie with, but not to each other.

I thought you dealt no more in whores, Samuel said.

Just because I don't run them any longer doesn't mean I don't talk to some.

Well, hell, he said. What's it matter? He can have his fun. No skin off my ass.

She's given him labors, said Lowde. Things he's to do for her so she'll court him fully.

Like what? I said.

Lowde twirled her pipe between her teeth and looked to the corners of the tavern room. She knitted the short and stubby fingers which had made our masks and oftentimes I'd find stroking my head while I slept of an afternoon. You boys, she said, wouldn't happen to recall the story of King David?

So she means to have him kill a giant, said Samuel.

Don't sass, she said. How did David win his bride?

I don't bitching know, said Samuel, growing more bilesome with her every word.

God Almighty, I said. Not that.

See, said Lowde. He knows what I mean. He must be the real preacher in the family.

Samuel jerked in his chair. He is, he said, but I'm the thinker, so tell me.

Lowde wouldn't speak. Only cut her eyes at me as though we shared a conspiracy.

I said, He had to bring the king fifty Philistines' foreskins.

O, God damn it! Samuel said.

Lowde jabbed at him with her pipe. And King David brought back two hundred of them.

Samuel gave an ugly laugh. Who sold you this run of bullshit?

Some girls from her house, she said, who listen at her keyhole. The mistress Aliza doesn't deign to walk the streets much.

It's nonsense!

I don't believe it's near that many, said Lowde.

Christ, said Samuel, just one would be madness.

She went on to say that she couldn't recall the exact figure, but Samuel flung back his chair before she finished and stormed out the tavern, where his shape could be seen in the window with the growing light of day, pacing and waving his arms as though in argument with Reuben's shade.

Bloody Madam Aliza

Whether or not he let on to Lowde that he believed her story, Samuel gave it enough credence to spend some days working the town and asking about his brother. The first day he avoided The Church and came away with little more than Mother Lowde had given him; the second day he fixed on going there and talking to the mistress himself.

There must have been some hold-over fear of the razor-whores in him, for he was loud and boisterous that afternoon on our walk to The Church, laughing, shouting that maybe he would drop a few dollars there, not with the mistress, of course, who we knew by then lay with no man except, it seemed, Reuben, but with one of the other fillies in her stable. And I could come along—and why not; if Reuben was as rich as they say, we could afford to treat ourselves now and again.

I saw myself entangled with some girl, her turning chill as creek-water, her tongue swelling within my mouth until I choked; I declined him.

Suit yourself, said Samuel, and he mounted the steps of The Church.

The door was set with a peep-hole and three feet below that the latch-trap door where the guest would be asked to invest himself and be investigated. He gave the door a rap and, noticing a bell-handle hanging from a chain, he pulled the cord and sounded the bell and I imagined that the whores, now awake, thought briefly of their work. He looked back to reassure me at the foot of the steps, and there were murmurs of a voice behind the door, to which my brother spoke his name, and then was saying, Yes, all right.

They would have him examined—not like the attic-whores who used their long fingernails to pry the lice, ticks, and fleas from you, but with who knew what instruments: the magnifier and clamp for those too tiny, or the dreadful syringe full of mercury, its brazen tip jammed straight in and a press of a lady's delicate thumb creating a cleansing wash of pain so that you were clear of clap and buboes, but would end up paying not just for the shot but also for the extra time it would take for her to get you straight again. I imagined worse horrors than these while Samuel fussed with his waistcoat and then the buttons on his britches. Once this was accomplished and he'd freed himself, he stepped up to the latch-trap and there he stood, waiting like a Frenchman at his guillotine, or like the king old Cromwell had decapped. And likewise Samuel did not shake or shiver, though I'll say that I was full of fear, expecting every second his de-manning to commence. He stood stock still at the door; and they did not use pincers or give him the jet of mercury, but he would later say that it was just a hand that held him, one silkily gloved, and that it skillfully checked him through and through. My brother seized up for an instant and I was sure the blade had fallen. But it was only his release by the hand unseen, followed by his hurried fumblings to tuck himself away and be presentable again, and there was ample time to do so, for it was another few minutes before the bolts were broken and the door was opened and my brother went inside without a word.

I wonder now whether it was Aliza's hand that did the checking on him; making comparisons between the Kempers before she received him in her upstairs parlor. I spent my waiting time musing on the mistress. She was alternately the last duchess of a failed European line, the long-escaped daughter of an upcountry planter—having years before absconded with her father's gold and set herself up a bawdy house. And she would always be a mystery, and prey all her life to the madness which kept her shuttered in her Church.

Other men went in and out the door. By evening its windows were lit red with lamps and I looked into their glow for signs of movement. At full dark, the door to The Church opened as it had many times that day, only it was Samuel leaning out. He called my name and waved me over as a slender arm reached round him and slammed the door shut.

I would have to be inspected. And being the faithful brother, I slipped my pants and pressed against the cold metal of the trap, and let myself be fingered for disease, my examiner sharing jokes with Samuel as she worked, traipsing and unfolding until she was satisfied and I was received therein.

Not so bad, eh? said Samuel.

Righting my pants, I looked to the dark-haired girl who'd been holding me and said, There's plenty who'd pay for just that.

Aliza's upstairs, said Samuel, leading me into the grand receiving room of the place, which encompassed the entire first floor of the house and was filled with plush furniture, a long bar running across one side, and cords of golden rope hung from the corners, pulled by Negroe women to make billow a sheet-bellows at the ceiling—and everywhere such girls as to make you forget that there was even such a word as *whores*. They weren't languishing on couches in their stockings, but in short stays over loose white dresses which each had embellished with jewelry or ribbon-work, and they bustled about the room, humming and fixing drinks from the bar.

She watches for him, said Samuel, with a spyglass from her room.

So it's all true, I said.

She's an amazing creature.

I said, There's more than her, it seems.

She's no great beauty, but there is something—

Will she come down?

I doubt it, he said. She has a letter from Reuben that says he'll be coming up from New Orleans in July.

I thought he was in West Florida.

Of course he is, said Samuel. But he's got business in the city as well.

Presently a short girl with hair the color of fresh-spilt blood came by and handed me a cup of rum punch. Her features were broad and rough-hewn, her skin dark. She regarded me with a fierceness that sent a shudder in me as I hadn't felt in many months. The cup she handed me was cold, and in it floated chips of ice which burned in my hand and made my teeth ache such that I had to set it down on a nearby table, finding that she'd drifted away.

Who was that one? I asked, reaching again for the cup, which I could still only hold long enough to tip back a quick sip of sweet rum mashed with watermelon meat.

Which?

The girl who brought the drink.

That's your own task, brother. The mistress says we're to have a night on the house.

I took the burning cup up once again, swished the sweetness in my mouth, and thought of the feel of dirt-beads being rubbed from Emily's skin, knowing that this girl would be clean. My Bible felt a sullen weight at my breast.

Is the rest true, too? I asked.

Samuel acted as though he didn't understand.

Is he cutting foreskins for her?

Drink your drink, he said. She says she has a bride-price, and he's the only man who's come close to paying it. She's awaiting him.

Will we wait here for him too? Or can we go on down to find him?

We'll wait. It's ripe here and we've got work yet to do, he said. What're you, tired of it?

We've got a good bit of money now. And I thought you were eager to get to your brother.

Samuel swiped my drink from the table and downed it. I won't meet Reuben like some fuckerall with nothing to show for himself.

It's got to be more than fifty dollars—

Nothing to show but fifty piss-nicked shitty dollar bits. No, brother, I won't. Samuel surveyed the room. Now go, he said, and pick yours before she's claimed and get this business off your Doubting Thomas mind.

Secrets and a Sign of Future Promise

She was called Red Kate Collins. Her people were Irish, of the swarthy kind that are often compared in newspaper drawings to apes. She knew her age, which was fourteen, and shared her room and bed with three others, and gathered all about were scraps of muslin and calico, costume jewelry winking in tangles of old socks that smelled maybe of men but in their confluence gave up women like a ghost.

Your brother's a fine impressive man, she said.

I've never known him rightly, I said.

Neither have I, she laughed. Not that a-way. He means to marry the mistress.

So I hear.

The party'll be lovely, she said.

Beside her on the bed, I stopped her fiddling with her dress-front, saying, Can I tell you something?

A secret? she said, knowing me even then.

Of a kind, I said, tugging at the sheet she'd wrapped around herself. I'm no Kemper, I said.

How's that? You adopted?

Right, I said. My brother calls me brother. You call me Angel.

O, she said. That suits you more, with that hair. She reached out and smoothed some back behind my ear. That's all your secret is?

The girl I first laid with was murdered by her mother over me.

God, she said. Stranger and stranger you get.

She had a child in her.

I take my tinctures for that, she said. So don't be fearing.

And she looked on me like I was some thing dredged up from the river-bottom by a storm and washed ashore, but it seemed also that this strange thing was one she wished to pocket and keep even then. I told Red Kate the story of my time in Chit, of Emily's death and how I'd stuck my father down. It spilled from me, the first and only time I would give anyone the story full. And when I came to the sputtering end, I expected her to revile me, to turn and spit or send me out. But it was that her eyes had widened, her look grown even fiercer, as though I'd told her own life, which she, excitedly, proceeded to give. Her family had settled in the inner piney-woods of the Mississippi—a mother whose memory she bore only in the stings of whippings, a sullen silent father, and a brother who leered when he thought she was sleeping, his prick nudging her in the bed they shared—and were arrived and set up in their cabin but a month when a horde of Creeks descended on them. She didn't cry when they were cut down, lamented this fact even more than her time of captivity, weeks being hustled from camp to camp and living with a grubby Indian family until one night, when they were all asleep—husband, squaw, and four youngsters—she took up a hatchet and hacked them apart save for one of the children, who escaped screaming into the woods.

She supposed that she had killed two sets of parents, and that was worse even than me.

And her words were more sweet than any tumble in the sheets, though I was hunched over with desire for that also. Red Kate's hands had returned to her buttons and I felt my throat close up as each one was loosed by those hands which I envisioned tensed with the work of vengeance, awaiting blood-spray. You're a miracle, I said.

That's kind, she said, and flicked undone the last of her trusses. But I'll be damned for what I've done and what I do. Now you'd better be quick. All this talk's eaten up your time.

Red Kate squared into my vision and I wondered at her bareness, the fine line of reddish down extending from between her breasts and belly. I said, Every demon in Hell would hang their heads in shame.

You do talk, she said, and began tugging at my shirts even as I spoke.

God's grace is greatest on those of us who've got the fire, and you do. I can see it.

Nodding with a grin, Red Kate put me down. But before she could work off my pants, I took a-hold of her thighs, tugged her to my face, and tried feebly to give her what Emily had wanted on that night beside the demon-hogs. My nose had not but poked her, my tongue barely grazed what it sought, when she bucked from me with a curse.

I stared dumbly at this girl now riled and covering her cleft. Jesus, she said. What do you think you're doing? She thrashed her head. All that pretty talk—

And before I could do more than crumple and jabber, there came the fists of her sisters banging at the door, the grumbling of customers, calls to get out growing shriller as I gathered up my clothes and, giving one last look to her—eyes broad in shock, white tips of teeth bared but not a word escaping—stumbled out.

Downstairs, Samuel was waiting for me on one of the couches. While we shared a drink his whore returned, dressed in fresh and more resplendent finery, to bid him good night. When she left, we waited for mine, but Red Kate never came.

I suppose you weren't too good, Samuel said, grinning.

I was glaring at the empty staircase, where other men and their choices shuffled up. Piss on it, I said, let's go to work.

It was just after mid-night when we went out into the streets. I thought of those small hands wielding hatchet-handle, knew then that I could speak no more doubts or ill of Reuben's love of bloody Aliza. Tucked between smashed casks in a close alley, I told Samuel I was sorry for doubting and he said he knew that I'd be cured up there. Then he pulled down the flap from underneath his hat and I did the same.

The drunks who happened by were in vicious groups, and we figured this couldn't be for our sake alone, though it was something to consider that the bleary-eyed world had to arm itself against you.

We made no take that night, and I believe I would've dropped my pistol anyhow for the way my mind was wandering. The places it went were soft and the color of dark-burning flame. To clear my mind, on our way back to Lowde's that morning, I left Samuel and went to find some souls to save. He hollered for me to tuck my mask back and I realized that the flap was still down, the frayed edges of the eyeholes appearing now.

The early morning passersby were for the most part unmoved. Vendors doing far brisker business as the hour grew late and the sun came full up watched me from their stalls, sniggering. And my voice was worn to a rasp and my tongue grown thick and dry like the Word burnt there had gone bad. By noon only a pair of raggedy old men had come forward to be saved. They were both so filthy I didn't want to put my hands on their greasy heads when they took off their shredded hats to be touched, and I wouldn't go down to the river with just these two. I had them stand by while I resumed the call to Salvation so that they jabbered behind me a list of their own sins. My idiot chorus drew no further followers, only more scorn and derision, which harried the Word out of me. I was tearing at my hair, cursing them all, cursing in my heart the way my verses were cut off even as I spoke them. My old converts followed suit and I sprung up onto a store-front railing with every cuss I knew, found a rain barrel there, and clawed water from it to cast on my mumbling supplicants; and they lifted up their hands and sang praises. I was slapping them across their faces when a man going by said, Some preacher.

I flung myself at him and I was the good shepherd indeed; and the crowd that gathered parted for me when I got up from the battered heckler to go home. My followers didn't follow; they'd fled while I'd been clawing at the man on the ground, whose screams were still audible a street over. My fingers hurt for all the blood caked underneath my nails. I looked at them and all they did was remind me of her.

The Shining One Appears

I might have gone in straight-away and tossed my Bible in the fire if it weren't for the roomful of guests at Mother Lowde's. The lady herself was at the long table with them, as was Samuel, and they all hallooed me when I came in. The man at the far head of the table was bejeweled and shining as Lucifer himself. At his neck he wore a silver collar-guard; his hands—one holding a glass, the other hugging to him the bare shoulders of a mulattoe girl—were covered in rings.

Samuel rose, clapped a hand to my back, and escorted me table-side to be introduced to the Reverend Ivan Morrel.

The Reverend put out a gold-and-silver-decked hand and I forgot how battered mine was from the heckler's face and gave it to him with-out a thought. Knuckle splits barely dried on my walk were reopened by his grip.

So you're the other preacher boy, eh? He had a sweet voice that could lead you far places, and you knew he could do justice to a psalm. He'd not let go of my hand and proceeded to bring it close to his eyes and examine my cuts.

My, my, said the Reverend. You brained some poor body, didn't you?

I might've, I said to the titters of those seated at the table.

Did you kill him? asked the Reverend.

Not so much as that, I said.

More laughter all around, loudest from Mother Lowde, who seemed to know him.

Morrel had me put my hands out on the table and the others all leaned across and leered at my busted claws. He took my hand again and dug beneath the nail of my forefinger, picking out a peck of flesh, and letting me go again, rolled it into a ball between his fingers. Not taking his eyes away from the pearl of flesh, he said, You must be a fine preacher. Anyone willing to dig at a man's skin to get at his heart is a true Christian.

He was well-fed and tall, but in his words and face there was an aspect of my father, and this harrowed me. Before I knew it Lowde had a-hold of my hands and was wiping them clean as best she could with the damp of her apron, which was daubed and spotted with blood-stains older perhaps than me or even Samuel.

And I hear, said the Reverend while she wiped, that you boys even managed to bring Lady Lowde into the fold. I've known her for years and tried my best, but none of it ever stuck.

Mother Lowde let me go and I found a place at the table beside Samuel. The Reverend Morrel's fellows were raunchy-looking suckers, nowhere near as decked in finery as him who now called for Lowde to make us a round of coon-boxes.

I only got three eggs, she said.

Well, hell, said the Reverend. Then one coon-box for each preacher you see here.

There was no grumbling from any of the others, and I swelled a bit at being favored.

Behind the counter, Lowde had taken a pin from her hair and was presently twirling the point of it against the small of an egg until she made a tiny hole there; and pressing a finger on the opening she turned the egg delicately over and made another such hole at its base. With this accomplished, above, she pulled a glass in front of her and put her lips to the hole at the small end and blew into it so that the white and yolk began to flutter out the larger end and into the glass. When she'd emptied three shells, she set them beside the glass and went out into the street, returning with a handful of blue clay dug from the roadside. She took a pinch of the clay, put it in her mouth, and began chewing.

The Reverend said, I know from Sister Lowde that you're more than preachers, but also fellow chips.

Neither of us answered.

Don't fear, he said. I admire that just as much.

Then it's true, said Samuel.

And I bet you're too young to've been caught, said Morrel.

Not yet, I said.

Well. You've got yourself some hands there, but have a look at this. Morrel put out the hand I'd shook and turned it palm-up. I have been caught, he said.

There was a line of raised dark flesh in a slash across his palm. The others looked as though they'd heard of it many times, but still all eyes were on the scar.

The iron wasn't hot enough when they first tried it on me, said the Reverend. They did it right there in the God-damned courthouse— my sentence for stealing horses because no one wanted to take my ears. Horses! God knows I've done better than that.

His men laughed. His whore was as rapt as Samuel and me. Mother Lowde brought our coon-boxes, the eggs now filled with sweet rum and sealed at both ends with clay so that you had to tooth out a hole to suck at the liquor mixed with the remaining white which clung to the walls of the shell. I went baby-birdy at mine but Samuel's cracked on his first attempt at the juice and he plucked it into his mouth and licked the rum from his hands. The Reverend for his part was an expert at coon-boxes, feeding drops to his mulattoe while he continued.

Tennessee is a worthless country, he said. The people are cruel from plowman to judge. They caught me with the bridles in my hand—not even having taken the horses proper. I ask you, how could a man have a horse full-stolen if he's not even on its back and riding? So they dragged me into their ratty courthouse, rapped the gavel a few times, and then in came a man with a tin-worker's stove and an iron. The stove was smoking when he put the iron in, but they were too eager, had me put my hand on the rail even though I saw the iron wasn't red, and I said, It's not hot enough to burn me, brothers. But they wouldn't hear me. And I looked into the eyes of the judge and the man with the brand, and when he laid it on me there was no smoke, no sizzle. O, it burned, but no more than a pan-handle. The man's eyes bugged when

THE BLOOD OF HEAVEN

he took the iron from me and he went running to stoke his stove. They all looked at me like I'd ask some reprieve for already being punished once—but no, I wanted to see if they could burn me. The brand's end glowed red when the man returned and I said unto them, You can visit torments on me, but like Jesus I'll endure. And when he laid it to me I didn't give so much as a whimper for pain. I didn't even grit my teeth.

Egg slime rolling on my tongue, I wanted to spit it out and tell him about all the coals I'd eaten. My childhood of fire. But I kept quiet and swallowed down my words and drink.

They said they'd hang me, that I'd ride the horse that's sired by an acorn. But they wouldn't and it wasn't finished after my branding. Next they took me to the post and the townspeople gathered there to watch me get my lashes. Thirty of them with a whip as big around as your arm. They stripped me of the good clothes I'd worn to court figuring on them respecting respectability and they threw them in the dirt. I only asked for rest twice in the whipping. And if my whipping did anything—and I could even thank those Tennessee shits for it—it was to show me my calling was to liberate more than horses and white souls, but black bodies as well.

What do you do with them? I asked.

Sell them, of course, said the Reverend. You sell them to another man and have the black escape again, then the process is repeated.

Damn, said Samuel. That's a scheme if there ever was one.

It's good money, said Morrel. But more than that it's a balm to the soul and an investment in the future. Like the Book says, every day we inch nearer to the great battle. And, my God, when it happens, what kind of army will I have! It will come to pass, and I'm the one to make it so.

I was awed that he would tell us such a thing. It would get you hung just mentioning; or locked up for a madman. But the Reverend Morrel must have known the way his words and vision would strike

115

us, for we both nodded that we understood. It was the first time since the night before that Red Kate was off my mind. I thought only of a black army, swallowing the houses of the moneyed. And I could tell already that Morrel wasn't the sort to boast idly, but the kind of man who could make such things possible.

Move aside, split tail, said Lowde to the mulattoe as she squeezed herself onto the bench. The girl started cussing but the matron whore said nothing.

Now, said the Reverend. I've got the blood too hot in here.

The mulattoe was standing up, but Morrel put his eyes on her and she sat back down without even a hiss.

I got distracted, boys, said the Reverend. But keep the idea in mind, for when my story's through I've got a proposition for you both. Now, after I was whipped they put me in the stocks, and for three days of that torture I preached a sermon to the townsfolk. After a while of watching them I knew all their sins and wrongdoings and made sure they heard every bit of it. Hey there, chappy, your wife lays with your plow-mule when you're in town! Ha! So when the bastards finally took me down I'd turned the place into such a tumult of rage, revenging, and mistrust that they gave me a horse so I could ride away faster.

Morrel finished his coon-box and crushed the shell in his branded hand.

I'm on my way, he said, to preach some great revivals in the southern end of the territory, and here look how lucky I am, finding two young preachers in the house of my good friend. You boys have God's gift, I can see it already. Always been able to tell a good preacher. Drink another with me, sons, and we'll go down and do the work of salvation together. For the love of God, let's have full glasses!

IV

His Disciples

Lower Mississippi, Summer 1801

The Great Revivals

All the preaching I'd forsaken those weeks at Mother Lowde's was then visited back upon me in hundredfold measures of the fiercest religion I'd yet seen.

After we'd spend a few days preparing the site—building the stage and the pine-limb piles for his barrels of whiskey and rum, and stacking cords for the great bonfire—the Reverend Morrel's Most Glorious Camp Meeting and Christly Wonders would roar itself to life.

He convened his revivals on Thursdays and they would run like a battle into the next week with the tents of an army of frothing worshippers set all around whatever land he could procure for his purposes—usually by guilting some pious planter into letting him use his fallow fields.

We thought we'd seen things, but the Reverend put it all in the ditch.

Women would take men by the hand like picking a partner at a dance and lead them off into the bushes or a tent if he was lucky. When the drums got going and the singing started people fell flat to the dirt, stiff as boards. They were being overtaken by the spirit all around, and some just dropped with their partners to the ground and went at it. Like good Christians they kept their liquor well-hidden for the first few days, and we kept them well-supplied. But it never failed that by the first Sunday of a revival the lines at the limb-piles were long and bottles and cups were held out proudly, jumping to lips, changing hands, and striking heads rapt with Christ.

It was a legion of wild believers and even without the drink they would be struck mad by the spirit. You could look two ways and see one tossing his head and babbling, sending ropes of spittle like streamers flung in celebration of the Reverend's words, while another would have the shakes starting in her—a-quiver from her very insides. And when you looked back again the man would be nodding fiercely and slobbering long trains of strange words and sounds, and the woman would be quaking in full fit.

Morrel's dress would change considerably before a revival—gone were the jewels and dandies, the fine clothes. He wore the dusty black outfit of a preacher. A trim man, despite his libertine nature, in this kit he was a black skeleton dancing on the stage before an enormous painting of the horrors of Hell, which would be wheeled out behind him to the awe of the onlookers when he reached the point of damnation in his sermons. And his words were those of a man of Heaven who knew the pits of Hell enough to have it painted from life, with a great red face open-mawed and containing fire in its mouth and throat and the tiny tortured aspects of condemned souls clinging to its teeth or being dragged down by demons of the most horrible kind. Morrel could raise you up into ecstasy so high that you could almost kiss Christ's feet, and then he'd cast you down and point to the particulars of the painting, where you'd find yourself among the mass, maybe perched on a smoking bit of rock overlooking the lake of fire, all the while with him making note of how you burned.

And when it was that the worshippers were whipped to full froth there would be cripples sent onstage to beg and be healed. But our Reverend Morrel was no mean huckster or mere magician. He claimed no powers he didn't have. And why would he? The man was already so punishingly gifted.

Morrel would embrace the cripple and call out that he would be most blessed of all in Heaven, and the worshippers would scream louder than if he'd healed the poor bastard, which he'd done anyway with money. The Reverend was a patron of the odd and the afflicted and all who approached the stage were in his employ.

For Morrel they paraded on withered legs or no legs at all; a whole mess of harelips sputtered praises—forever speaking in tongues, those perfect Pentecostals; a man born with two heads called Look-Twice Philbert; the clutch of the regular lame with withered legs or crooked spines, or blindness; the Thorny Rose, who'd have been called just Rose if it hadn't been for the pants-leg-tearing thorn of an endowment, called the cliver, fixed on her womanly parts. It had to be handled delicately when she appeared onstage, only spoken of with maybe a flutter of skirt for a hint as though a propitious wind had blown through. Later she'd be in her wagon and charge fees for gawkers. And there was also one deformed who fast became our friend; this was Johnny Crabbe, who was red-skinned and walked on all fours, with his limbs cocked at weird angles in their joints.

For our part we worked odd jobs with Morrel's other trustees, had signed a contract to do so for the summer preaching season, staking our own fifty-dollar investment on a two hundred percent return. We dealt out whiskey from the woodpiles, marking far-gone drunks for pocket-picking in the night. Mornings we'd walk with the Reverend through the camp and he, great admirer of horseflesh that he was, would pass, let's say, a fine stallion some farmer had ridden there to hear preach the man who at that very moment would say, Brothers, that's a fine-looking horse.

Yes it is, Reverend, we'd say.

So Morrel would nod and say how he'd sure like to own a horse just like that one.

And that was all he need say, for we knew it meant we'd soon be slipping the reins from their post and leading off the beast under cover of evening down to Morrel's runners, who awaited enough horses that they could ride on into the next town with a market and sell them at half price.

On those dog-tired nights after we'd returned from revival to our camp and hid the day's take amongst Morrel's already impressive holdings, we would sit by the fire and share a brief nip of whiskey between Samuel, Crabbe, and me. We told him stories of the northern territories and our travels, and Crabbe would tell us what it was like to be an insect.

When I was small, he said, I was but a mite and was covered in a sheet to go out into town. I was always stepped on until the Reverend rode in one day and snatched me up, thank God.

And we were also thankful, for we were already earning our investment back, according to Samuel's calculations, by the fourth revival. And as summer wore on into June, there came times when the Reverend Morrel's voice would go or he needed us to buy him time for a drink and he'd have me come up and witness. Samuel would stand aside, for it had long been confirmed between us who cared most for the Word and who had the talent for it. By that time Morrel would have the crowd at a pitch of fervor, so that when I came out onto the stage they were biting and screaming and jumping for me. The man at the skin drums would beat out a rhythm for me to preach to as cruel words for Preacher-father went through my mind: Who is the hand of God now? You rotten old bastard, I am. And I could have gone on like that in my head but for the desperate, howling crowd.

I'd spread my arms wide and open my mouth as though to swallow all their moans and calls and wild tongues and spit salvation back at them.

When I finished with my witness I would fall to my knees for the feeling of being clean and clear of sin, and there would be arms at my shoulders and it never failed that the Reverend, returned and smelling of whiskey, would hold me up by the shoulders and lift me like a pelt to show the crowd now blistering the air with hallelujahs and grown mad with glory, letting out peals of concern for my hunched and shuddering person. And our routine went like this: that before he had me to the steps and off the stage I would grow full of the spirit and, renewed, throw off his hands, cast my coat aside, and come scrambling back to the stage-front and start it up again, my legs jittering and stomping as to splinter the boards, my voice like a thunderclap of Grace.

Before we left Natchez and Mother Lowde, drying her eyes when we rode off with Morrel on a pair of horses he'd procured for us and saddle-works scoured of the names of former owners, I'd gone to see Red Kate a second time. A paying customer, I didn't ask her why she hadn't seen me off the other night the way Samuel's whore had, for I knew in the moment I saw her again, hidden behind the others of the line-up, a blood-colored creature, short and snubbed of the patrons' affections for the tall and willowy, that she was not my whore but the cross of love upon which I'd be struck and raised. She said nothing of my try with the tongue, and instead took me more traditional.

There, she said afterwards. Isn't that a better way?

I found her sweetness unchanged, and loved most that behind it lay a past of violence. I called her Copperhead and she winced at the name, saying that she was no snaky thing. I kept her words with me the way most men keep a locket of their lover's hair. She said that this was not her life. She didn't mind it and liked the money and there were no cruelties visited upon her by the mistress or her sisters in the business, but she said that she could see far ahead and the paths of her life stretched out into the forests and the untilled land. And it might be that someone not unlike myself was there with her.

I said, We're children of desolation, meant for one another.

It's too wild to think, she said. But I do.

We were a knot of raw, afflicted youth; and before I'd leave her that day, she tried to put my words and hers away as foolish talk. But I took her hands and told her all of it was true, the Will of the Lord. Maybe I knew even then that if I had Red Kate for my own all I would bring her was sorrow. But that was my path, and if she saw it in her vision, she knew well enough what lay ahead. I soon took to inventing sermons and speeches to give her when I returned, whiling away the ash-smelling time before sleep with thoughts of her.

And it was at such times that Morrel would come and make his prophecies of me; take me out of one world and into another. The wording often changed, but the soul of it remained the same and I was always lost in faith and wonder and pride at what he said.

Who cares if we kick holes in something that's rotten, he said. Listen to them all crying and singing up there—we have a dominion of faith in our hands, and if we help them to Grace we can help ourselves to them when they deserve it. Listen to me and learn by me. I see you being known in all the land. And you'll have the sword so that the heathen may know you. And you will hew a nation from this rotten country. But you cannot fail God, nor me.

He'd go on, saying things that made me swell with willingness to live even more for God and gain. Once he was spent, the Reverend's face would be clenched in the sternness of his prophecy, and when he'd leave I'd lay awake a while prying apart his words and hunting them for truth.

I found them always utterly golden, and my purpose was nightly confirmed.

Slaves to Whomever We Obey

Morrel seemed to bring out of me things that had been there all along. I became surer at the pulpit; I hardened to the wildness of the revival days and by July, with a trail of scorched stages behind me, had the endurance for it down and had learned his kind of pity for the lot of blacks.

Black skin called out to the Reverend as much as horseflesh, or the gold that either would yield. Between revivals that season he couldn't restrain himself if he saw one or a few Negroes bent to some task at the lonesome edge of a plantation. These were generally older family retainers who could be trusted out of sight of master and seer. And with one falling under his eyes or the eyes of one of his scouts, Morrel would gather to him some of the friendlier-looking fellows and ride out to meet his quarry.

He bore a malicious pity for the nigger-man. And he was always prepared for such a dubious blessing as an unsupervised slave. If we came upon one such as that, we were to hush and hide the mis-shapens—who without fail would stick out their heads, legs, and claws to ask why we'd stopped—have them put away their offending limbs, hide our own armaments, and, as Morrel said it, put on our Christly faces.

When Brother Zach was first sighted we were just outside Wilkinson, a settlement named for the General of the Armies of the United States, of whom it was said even then among the rabble in Morrel's train that he was a rotten creature who'd put rebellious laborers to the sword in Natchez in '99, and that he presently plotted for the Spanish to take Mississippi in exchange for paltry silver. So I suppose it was a fitting place for graft and sin. Samuel rode back to Morrel and the others while I made my check of the Blessed in their carts. Johnny Crabbe reached out a claw, giggling, saying, It's nigger time! Yes, sir! Good old dirt-dumb nigger time! I told him to shut the hell up and went on to the next, where Thorny Rose was sitting spread-legged in the gunchair, hitching up her dress in mock temptation. I tried to keep my eyes from where her cleft and thorn were bared out to the sunlight. I told her to cover up.

The nigger's way out there, she said. And besides, it's you I want to look.

I've seen, I said.

No preacher should be scared of a bush, said Thorny Rose. And if you want to pick this flower, you'll have to catch a prick.

The harelips within the cart were sputtering laughter, when she said, Aw, now. Don't be scared.

I said I wasn't.

You might need be, she said. What I've got's like nothing you've ever seen.

I've been to Natchez, I said. I've known plenty.

Not like this, yellow-head. I might just curl that pretty hair of yours.

When I caught up to the outriders, Samuel was leaning in among them and the men were laughing and giving jokes about the Negroe's fate. All except Morrel, who seemed not to hear a thing and kept his eyes on the dark figure beneath the oak, offering a wave of the hand that the old black did not return. So we all got down from our horses and followed the Reverend across the field, for as Morrel said, often as not niggers would take off running at the sight of white men on horseback. As we approached, the old man kept looking over his shoulder at us, Morrel in the lead, waving and smiling all the way.

Nearing, the Reverend made for his prize with arms out as though to embrace him, which he did, wrapping the black bones tight and holding him close to his chest—for Morrel was a head taller than his quarry—while the slave remained immobile, watching us.

They exchanged names and Morrel talked as though he already knew him, saying, Brother Zach, I'd give you some good light clothes, rather than all that winter wool, but I know surely as you've got a master who'd send a man out to work this steaming day all weighted down by his Christmas suit, he'd also whoop you for bringing in new cotton clothes.

The old man's eyes were on us and he said, He do. He think I stole it.

And you wouldn't have—the clothes would be a gift from one friend to another; they don't even feel like you're wearing clothes. The cotton's from the islands. My suit's made of it and you don't see me sweating.

A nod of the black head. He says we not to take off shirts or pants. That it's wicked to do. Even if it's hot as thunder.

Your suffering in life will be rewarded in Heaven, my friend, said the Reverend, who'd yet to let him go.

I pray for it. I pray all day.

Good, said the Reverend. But that doesn't mean you can't help yourself here on earth.

Ain't no helping it, said Brother Zach.

Can I offer you the help of a little sweet rum? Morrel held out his silver flask, which, as was the case with most of his belongings, bore the name of another man, and began unscrewing the cap.

I can't.

I insist, said the Reverend, holding the flask gleaming even in the shadow of the oak before Brother Zach's face, now tucked up under the crook of Morrel's arm like a bosom barroom friend.

Brother Zach shook his head again, but Morrel held out the flask like a beacon to his eyes. It's an awful sweltering day, he said. And a touch of this will make you feel like it's first snow.

When Brother Zach took Morrel's offering, then tipped down his throat for so long that his gullet bobbed, the men all congratulated him and I did the same. Brother Zach's thanks were all raspy coughs while the Reverend made sure the black saw him take that same flask to his own white lips without wiping and drink.

I can't say whether it was this act of goodwill that did it or Morrel's words or his steady embrace or the course of rum now running in him, but Brother Zach suddenly looked on the Reverend Morrel with lovesome awe.

What keeps a good man like you here with such a wicked master? the Reverend asked.

He keeps me, said Brother Zach. They's nowhere else.

There is, though—up to the free and clear North. And I can take you there. I am a man of God, and we're going to be traveling up that way soon. Do you see the wagons yonder? We can take you in secret and spirit you away to freedom. No more work, no more toil, no more cruelty. Would you want that?

O, Rev, I want it. I want it terrible.

Morrel hugged him harder and both looked near to weeping. Good man, he said. You are a good man, Brother Zach. But listen. I've done this many times before with many of your brothers and sisters, and what you'll need when you get up there is money. A little something to set yourself up right. Free or not, money's the thing.

Money, said Brother Zach, the word itself falling from his blue gums like a silver coin dropped to a tabletop.

Yes, and the way you can have your money and your freedom is if you come with me—and as we go along I'll sell you a time or two, then come and rescue you from your new masters. Each time I'll give you half the money.

Brother Zach nodded so gravely deep that his head touched the Reverend's chest.

Now, said the Reverend. I haven't done my work so far south. So could you tell me, Brother, how far I'd have to go for you to be unknown? For your master to have no friends?

O, said Brother Zach. I only know the names of where he goes.

Of course, good man, said the Reverend. Tell me which those are.

Fort Adams, he said. Sometimes Natchez and New Orleans. Woodville, Sakeum.

All right, then we'll avoid those places, won't we. Now, do you have any family here? Anyone you'd want to bring?

No, Rev.

Is your house close enough to hear me fire a pistol on this road?

Plenty close. I'll hear it. I'd hear it if I was drowned.

Good man. But don't be overeager and make your dash for freedom before you hear my pistol speak. We don't want any of your fellows following and betraying you, or worse, your master or one of his men.

They won't hear me. Nobody's gonna even see me.

Good. Then wait for the pistol-shot and come to meet me out on the road where it faces the tree.

Jesus I'll be running.

And so went the Reverend Morrel's acquisitions. They were always easy on the front end and I never saw him fail. We'd ride on far enough and meanwhile the Reverend would wait alone at the road, and would sound off with his pistol and soon enough there would appear one like Brother Zach. Those black faces—wide-eyed and giddy with the freedom Morrel had given them—haunted our caravan all throughout our way south. God, could they take suffering with a smile. Standing up on the block in some little village in Mississippi, or even at the very border of the country where he would be sold to a West Florida planter, Brother Zach looked like he had not a care in the world, beaming white teeth while his fellow slaves, sold and unsold, sulked all around him.

When he escaped the first time, Morrel got Brother Zach drunk and let him palm half his worth in silver for a night, before taking it back for safekeeping. But while he had the money in his hands, old Zach held it like a talisman and wept. He talked about his woman and his children, who'd been sold off years before.

Morrel would occasion to take off his shirt and show him the scars from his lashing, saying, I know the sting of the whip, my friend. And Brother Zach would go on weeping.

It was on the third of Brother Zach's escapes that Morrel entrusted Samuel and me to hide in wait and give the signal. It took so long for old Zach to come that I thought he was caught, but he came loping out the trees and into the roadway, blessing us in whispers. He didn't know that if we were caught by militia or master we were instructed to tell them that we'd seen the slave escaping and had caught him, then to demand a reward. There were no other parties on the road, and we came to the first of the scouts, a man named Jasper, who was supposed to ride with us back to camp, but was bent over the corpse of a man who'd happened upon him earlier in the night. He was holding a plank up to the moonlight, trying to write his name in blood on it. Jasper dribbled at the wood with a switch which he dipped continuously at the well of the dead man's wound. It took us a moment to take stock of the situation, Brother Zach behind me going, Jesus, Jesus, while Jasper dabbed and scratched with his switch.

I'll smash that board over your God-damned head, said Samuel, if you don't get moving.

Jasper whipped his switch. Eat shit, preacher-boy. I got myself a name to make.

You'll have on with the Reverend for all this bullshit, I said.

Fuck you, said Jasper, switch a-popping. You know what? I'm putting my mark on you, boy! I'm putting my mark on you and him!

Jasper was pointing his switch back and forth from Samuel to me, and I don't know if it was that I felt the blood from its tip flecking me in the eyes and face, if it was that I was sick to death of nigger misery, or if it was something I had wanted to do always and deeply, but I drew my pistol from my coat and I shot him through the head. Jasper fell and red-washed his name from the plank. He was the first man I knew for sure I'd killed.

Jesus Christ our Lord, said Brother Zach from my horse.

God knows what Morrel'll do, said Samuel once we'd dragged Jasper and the man he'd killed from the road.

He won't do a thing when I tell him what that fool was doing, I said.

True, said Brother Zach. That boy'd gone wild.

Back at camp I told Morrel that Jasper had been gunning for posterity and I'd written his name in the Book of Life. The Reverend made no bones about it, said I'd done the proper thing. I knew it myself, for the feeling in me was one of awesome glory. I sat with the Reverend Morrel and he gave me a brief sermon on murder.

You can be the wine cup of God's fury, overfull and brimming. But don't let it spill on just anyone. Reserve yourself. Don't make this a habit.

Meanwhile, old Zach held his silver, wept some more, and was given rum. There would be no fourth escape. The Reverend sold him to the West Floridian planter and he may have spent out his years waiting for the sounds of pistol-fire from a distant roadway, mistaking the gunshots of hunting parties and running out to find an empty path.

You had to be drunk to bear it, and it remains that way for me. There were times when I wanted to squall along with Brother Zach or whoever we held that week. And it was harder than any killing or robbery. Kill a man and you don't carry his corpse along with you so that each day you witness his putrification; you dispatch him and your guilt with the same killing shot. Even if you have to fill up his belly with sand and sink him in a river—which we learned to do also in those days with Morrel—he is gone soon enough and stolen gold mixes in your pockets and is soon passed to pay for other sins. But this was to live with a breathing, talking, crying corpse that ate breakfast with you of a morning, beaming about being free.

V

Our Deliverance

Pinckneyville–Natchez, July 1801

The Brother and the Reverend

Morrel's men watched me more carefully after the killing, Thorny Rose gave me more twirls of her skirt, and I attained a somewhat higher station in the order of our band. Now I could give orders as we set up our revival between the Mississippi and the town of Pinckneyville, just over the border from West Florida. I'd have the pine limbs laid over the whiskey barrels, the wood cut to make the stage, the stage itself built, and the scrap timber hauled away, all by the male Blessed, who I'd decided should earn their keep by more than mere existence. The harelips sputtered and grumbled, the legless sat beside the casks and sullenly piled on the limbs, the blind cussed while I made them feel through the gathering branches for the spigot so that it could be found

131

even in the dark of night, the fat and the tiny both shrank and grew with their labors, but they all worked well and I worked alongside them—only not so much as them, which wouldn't befit an overseer. They rolled themselves in dirt to staunch the sap that had gathered in the crooks of their arms, their hands, and the dips of their necks. Others, digging the trench to fill with tar to burn for mosquitoes, were blackened at the legs and hands.

Maybe it'll stick your mouths back right! said Johnny Crabbe to a pair of harelips, scuttling by with a pile of limbs in one claw.

One came trying to kick him but saw me and went back to his task, fluttering his mouth-parts with soft curses. I'd remained wary that there would be reprisals for Jasper. But as yet there'd been nothing for me to watch but a few drunken grumblers going by no different from the billowing tent-flaps and wisps of spark from the campfires. So days I went about my work hustling the Blessed and nights I spent preparing my sermon for the coming Thursday. Samuel, though, seemed transfixed on the idea that we'd soon have to square up with some of Jasper's friends, and often scolded me for not making any preparations—leaving my pistol in the tent and not carrying any shot or powder beyond what was tamped into the barrel.

Monday evening, finished with work and swimming in drink, I sat with Samuel at our fire while he cast shot from ingots of lead. We had enough but this lately seemed to soothe his worries, and he relaxed watching the bubbling gray turn bright and almost milky in the dark iron ladle.

I feel good, brother, I said. Feel like I'm in my place at last.

Samuel withdrew the ladle and poured its contents into a clamp-mold he'd had Crabbe steal from one of the others. Bossing freaks is one thing, he said, but don't forget we've got higher things ahead. He put the ladle aside and waited a few moments before letting loose the clamp so that a ball of shot fell out and rested amongst the silvery dollops of lead which had spilled over onto the ground when he poured.

I don't know if sitting on my ass and selling buttons in your brother's store is higher, I said.

Samuel waited for the spattered leavings to cool, then scooped them back up into the ladle and set it in the fire, and we watched as the grass and dirt was purged from the lead and gathered in a film across the top.

You'd abandon me after all I've done, he said.

It wouldn't be abandoning.

It damn sure would. Samuel took the ladle out and poured again, and again a ball fell from the mold to the dirt and the sprinkling of silver was on the ground like a sign of future wealth. I wouldn't do that to you, he said.

Maybe I'm just caught up, I said.

Maybe you are, said my brother.

At that moment the Reverend Morrel rode through our end of the camp in his town-going clothes, passing us without a word, and disappeared towards the road into the dark. In the morning the Reverend was still gone, but we went straight-away to rigging and completed the preparations a day ahead of normal. When Morrel returned that evening, he seemed pleased as he made his inspection of the stage, the great painting of Hell at its center, half-covered by a tarp.

You're a worthy disciple, he said to me, getting down from his horse. You may just be my Peter and spread my church across the land when the time comes.

Samuel was beside me looking stony at this pronouncement as some of Morrel's lieutenants arrived, sidling us, and we listened all to what he said next.

But tonight, said the Reverend, we're hosting some gentlemen from town who don't favor the religious aspect but were kind enough to let us use this land. And they're rich enough to be of some . . . use. So we'll have a carnival atmosphere, eh? Then the Reverend Morrel went off to make his own preparations, and when he again appeared, that evening, he was dressed resplendent as I ever saw him in frock and jewels and polished boots, and he strode lordly through the arrangements.

The Blessed did a little frowning and grousing, but soon the place was all turned out, and though the gentlemen had yet to arrive, little revels had begun. There were targets set up for throwing knives or shooting, and a tub of fish gathered from the nearby creek and tied with ribbons bearing fortunes, which to obtain you would jab them with a long sewing needle. One of the lieutenants had his fiddle out and the drummer was told to beat soft. Just before the appointed hour the Reverend had us put the Blessed who weren't manning games away back in camp, which we did, and those of us who were unmangled and deemed worthwhile by him were told we could return—that is, as the Reverend said, if we wore our Christly faces when we came.

Despite their grumbling at being kept from the party, the Blessed proceeded to have their own at camp. Crabbe was making crazy-legged circles of us, laughing; someone plucked strings; a key-box groaned to life. Round the fires became a place of jigging and the singing of hymns modified to rough uses; skewers were rattled along the legs of spits, bells made from pots.

Neither Samuel nor I danced, but watched for a while the Blessed go about their fun until they had us backed close to the fire by their whirling circles. When my coat-tails began smoking my brother grabbed me by the collar and yanked me from the fire.

Christ, he said, patting out the flames. You're a prize fool.

Go fuck an anthill, Sam.

Tie your cock in a knot.

Laughter and shouts came from the Blessed:

Preacher's lit himself!

Better keep the whiskey from him!

Shit, keep the guns from him!

Amid all this, while Samuel was still slapping at the burnt ends of my coat, now more out of anger than kindness, there was a hitch in their dancing circle as an enormous figure broke their rhythm and the capering prodigies had to scatter from what might have been a new addition to their troop—a man half a foot taller and with the same shock of red hair as Samuel, who, clapping the ashes from his hands, ran to embrace him.

This was Reuben Kemper. And he took his smaller brother up in fistfuls of coat and raised him from the ground, smiling, but not so happy as Samuel. The older brother set the younger down and, having to holler for the noise of the Blessed, asked what had become of their father.

He ran us off, said Samuel.

And who in hell is us? said Reuben.

Samuel pointed with his thumb hooked and waved me over. Still smoking, I approached the long-sought Reuben. He wore his coat buttoned down the middle and I could see that there were bulges in the fabric at his chest and hip as my hand was taken up first in one of his then doubled over by the other—as though to show that he could swallow me whole with them.

Angel Woolsack, I said.

Damn that, said Samuel, punching his brother in the shoulder, he's a Kemper now.

Reuben narrowed his eyes at me. I'll take my brother's word for the moment. But now you need to come with me to see your Reverend.

We followed him from the party of freaks to the pleasures of human men. On the way Samuel told him something of our story,

135

pausing heavily on the death of their youngest brother. I couldn't see if Reuben wept, for the two giants were ahead of me and all I saw was backs that blocked out everything until we passed beneath a tent, stepped up onto the stage, and they stopped and stood apart, revealing the Reverend Morrel sitting with a pair of men at a table set with candelabra and bottles of wine.

So, said the Reverend, you've found my best two young fellows, Mister—

Kemper, said Reuben.

Samuel started to explain but his brother hushed him. The fiddler was working down below the stage and the whine of bow across gut-strings made me want to run before a thing had happened.

The other men at the table stared knowingly from under their brows at Reuben. These were Daniel Clark of New Orleans and Edward Randolph of Pinckneyville. Clark you could tell from the moment he spoke that he was a scion of Ireland, Randolph that he was a genius of a kind. They were merchants, speculators, and I would come to know both well, but this was my first sight of them. Someone had pulled aside the tarp from the painting of Hell, and the business of the night commenced beneath the grinning, fiery face of the Devil.

You're blood, said Morrel. How fine. Of course, there's a resemblance, if not as much in Angel.

Reuben said, That's because he's no Kemper and besides the point. Sam here tells me he's got a contract with you through September.

That's right, that's right. Pull up a chair and have a glass. Morrel waved a bottle of wine and in the candle-light I could see the dark drink sloshing in its bottle.

Reuben Kemper hauled an empty chair across the boards and sat, keeping one hand to Samuel's shoulder.

And what does my brother do in fulfillment of this contract?

Morrel poured wine for all at the table. Well, he said. I don't have the papers on me for specifics, but it's a bit of preaching at revival time, though that's mostly Angel, and otherwise just chore-work. I also tend a trading business, like you men, and he helps in that.

Chore-work, said Reuben.

I don't mean for it to sound menial, said Morrel. These are good young chaps. Maybe the best I've got.

With that in mind, said Reuben, how much would it cost me to assume my brother's contract?

The Reverend Morrel smiled, propping his thin arms on the table so that his rings glinted when he laced his fingers, affecting deep consideration. O, he said, we're not yet half-way through the season, work's been a bit slow, so I'd say about one hundred dollars.

No, sir, Samuel said, rasping surprise at the reverend's exaggeration. It's fifty a piece.

Not a bad wage for chore-work, Reuben said.

Well, the Reverend said, I'd be remiss to say the boy doesn't help in some of my other ventures.

Samuel leaned towards the Reverend, saying, But you said—

I believe I can swing a hundred, Reuben said, pulling his brother back.

Morrel's eyes lit like his rings. Then perhaps we can work something out.

Samuel bent to his brother's ear. I won't leave without Angel, he said. He's been my brother when I had none and he came this far looking for you.

I opened my mouth to say that I would stay and didn't need to be a Kemper anymore, but there was, stronger than the need to keep on preaching, stronger than the want to steal, flipping like a lock onto a flint, the thought of Red Kate. And if this Reuben was betrothed to the mistress, then I might have an in with her for my own future bargaining. So I shut my mouth and felt like an unwanted nigger on the block, not even asked to dance.

Has the other one signed the same contract? asked Reuben.

Roundabouts or maybe even more, said the Reverend. But I don't think I could spare both, and not Angel here, who's the best young preacher I've ever seen.

Reuben shifted in his seat and creaked the table, jangling glassware, when he put his elbow down to lean forward and say, You know, I believe actually I'll have the pair. Two hundred even, is it? Grinning, he reached into his coat as though for a billfold, but the Reverend, sensing quarry, now put up his hands.

Like I said, one I can spare. But two? No, Mister Kemper, that may just be impossible; Randolph and Clark here can vouch, Reuben said, or make up the difference if you care to.

Indeed, said Clark.

Randolph nodded thoughtfully, eyes shut, as he drained his glass.

See, said Reuben. I'm well-respected here and below the line. Have you been to West Florida, Reverend?

Can't say that I have.

O, it's a fine place. A little freer than the American side of the line, if you'll take my meaning. That is, if you don't mind some oily Spanish dealings and machinations on occasion.

Clark bleated a laugh and Randolph put fist to mouth to smother his.

All right, Reuben said, clapping the tabletop so hard I thought the glass would shatter. The pair it is.

No, Mister Kemper. Now that I've prayed on it a bit more, I don't think I can spare either till September. Come see me then.

Not for two hundred?

Sorry, no. The Reverend twirled his glass and shined bright.

Nor for two hundred and, say, ten?

My apologies, but that's just not sufficient. I foresee a good end to the summer's trade and I need my hands.

Two hundred and twenty-five, said Reuben. The glee in his voice as he leaned his bulk further across the table seemed without reason and worried me.

The Reverend Morrel put up his hands together to show that they were tied by circumstance.

Well, my friend, said Reuben. How about if I told you I wanted them both, and you were to pay me what they've earned.

Morrel stiffened and his voice grew soft. I'd say you were a fool, he said.

Reuben clapped his leg. Maybe I am, Reverend. Maybe I am. The kind of fool who hears in Natchez that his little brother's fallen in with the likes of you and comes all this way into the country to find him. But I'm also the kind of fool who knows Lieutenant Wilson of the Army of the United States, who's presently marching troops down from Fort Adams and gathering up militia to raid your camp.

You're lying, said the Reverend.

I'm afraid Reuben's being true, said Clark. When I lent you my land I didn't know your history.

Like hell you didn't, said the Reverend. You believe you can frighten me with untruths!

We know an awful lot of truths, Reuben continued. Like that you've got one pistol in your pocket and a skinny knife in your boot. And maybe five or six men with shotguns roaming. And we know if you accost any of us three, you'll have every Mississippi man here and the whole damn territory on your ass worse than it already is. And I know you've done your share of murders so you may just get one or two, but hear this—my apologies, gentlemen—but you'd better pray you get me good, because even dead my hands'll be locked around your bedizened neck, and they won't let go until you're cold.

The Reverend Morrel was no longer the shining star but gray-faced, cowed eyes searching in the revels below for his men to call, finding nothing but music and the tumult of games.

So, said Reuben, Do you have any cash on hand?

No, said the Reverend.

Back at your camp, then?

Yes, said the Reverend, regaining his comportment some. If you'll come—

Pardon me if I don't go with you alone to some secret place where there could be an ambush laid. How about the six of us go. That way I'll feel better about the odds.

The Reverend stood up, stoop-shouldered, and the others rose as well. Still on the stage and before the face of Satan, Reuben unbuttoned his coat and revealed his bandolier of three pistols. He extended his arm as to direct the Reverend's progress. I was in blasted awe of him. Truly this was the brother foretold. Samuel said as much, needling me with his elbows as we followed the Reverend back to camp, where we passed through the still-gamboling Blessed, Johnny Crabbe giving looks to our procession, and then Morrel went off with Reuben, Clark, and Randolph to his tent while we gathered up our things in a daze of hurried movement and readied our horses. I was lashing my pack to the saddle when Crabbe appeared again, asking, Where're y'all going and who's that with the Reverend?

Crabbe, I said. You'd better haul your ass on out of here. There's an army coming for Morrel.

And you're leaving?

Damn right we're leaving, said Samuel, stepping with his things out the back of our tent. What did I tell you? Didn't I tell you! He's the best God-damned brother and hardest man in the son of a bitching country.

Who? said Crabbe.

I spoke the name of the man who was not yet my brother, praying a little then that it could one day be so. I listened hard for shots or shouts above the music and singing as we made the final lashes to our horses, but the Reverend returned with the other three and he sidled close to me as we made our way back to the stage.

He whispered, I'm damning you, you deceiver. Here and now.

Go ahead, I said. I already am.

Not so bad as this, hissed Morrel. You'll know my mark all the days of your short life.

Hey, now! called Reuben from up ahead. No cross words. You've got a fair bargain, Reverend.

Morrel was silent the rest of the way, occasionally giving me the eye, or tapping a now-jewelless finger to his temple when he saw me looking. Reuben wouldn't let the Reverend leave until we were in the saddle.

The army will be here tomorrow night, said Reuben. So I'd say leave by morning.

The Reverend raised his head up haughty and said, I will do as I damn well please and the good Lord dictates.

Well, said Reuben with a flick of his reins, you can't ask more than that of a man.

We were a ways off and going at a good gallop when Reuben Kemper reached into his coat pocket and took out the Reverend's silver-plated pistol and tossed it back over his head. I turned to watch it fall and saw Morrel as a small figure back-lit by fire.

We made the road and split, with Clark and Randolph, pistols out for fear of traps, riding east towards Pinckneyville and us heading west to Tunica Bayou, where Reuben had his barge. Before the pair left he thanked them and they both laughed, Clark saying that he always knew whenever he came upcountry there'd be some sort of fun, Randolph that there were ways out of any business, no matter how rotten. Reuben roared more thanks and gave a blessing on their souls that there were such good friends in the world.

A few miles below the mouth of the Tunica, Reuben held us up at a tree-walled bend and we slowed and went to the side of the road.

I asked why we were stopping, but he only held his hand up and I was answered by the rattle and march of soldiers and militia as they rounded. They were about fifteen, some on foot and some a-horse, and at their middle rode a man I judged to be the lieutenant. He wore the highest hat and the brocades of his dark blue uniform shone for an instant in the moonlight when he hallooed Reuben and broke ranks to ride over.

Reuben, admiring the troops, said he thought it was ten or so more miles to the encampment.

Should I expect much violence?

Well, said Reuben. I may've whipped his froth a bit.

Lieutenant Wilson clipped a quick smile. We have been eager for some . . . experience lately.

Then get yourselves down to the line, said Reuben, and drive out the damned Pukes.

Both men laughed and the lieutenant said, Still troubled, eh?

You know how it goes with me.

That's why none should ever leave the bosom of the United States. The lieutenant sighed and looked to his winded but antsy troops. But I'm afraid we'll have to talk more another day. Then he bid farewell to Reuben and cocked his hat to me and Samuel and rode off, harrying the men to their feet.

A River Ceremony

When the ground grew soft our horses were so blown that we had to get down and walk them the last two miles. Samuel followed his brother without question and I followed them into the swampy outskirts of the Tunica. There was little moonlight, but Reuben made his way in the dark, fixed on a pinpoint of light so tiny that I couldn't see it until we'd come almost to the upper landing, where his slave sat beside a lantern tied to a pole driven in the ground and below lay the barge. Reuben said this was the Cotton-Picker and I thought he meant the nigger, but he left his horse beside him and passed without a word and went instead to inspecting the riggings and keel, calling, Ferdinand, let's have her off!

So the black untied the lantern and with one hand pulled the pole from the ground, put the lantern-handle in the mouth of Reuben's horse, and led it onto the barge. Once we'd loaded ours and the horses wobbled uneasy on the boards, Reuben had us both get off and shove while he pushed with the pole until the Cotton-Picker broke free of the shore, drew water, and was floating down the bayou. The water was almost to my neck before I could make the boards of the turning barge, wary of the hooves being kicked at me as I tried to clamber aboard. Samuel and his brother's slave had already made it up, only half-soaked, and my brother stuck his hand out and I was brought dripping onboard to the laughter of Reuben.

The lantern was now at the fore and lit the forms of animals in the trees we passed beneath and the green scum at their bases which broke with our wake. This was easy water before we'd have to pole against the current when the bayou met the river, and so we spent the time resting, laid out on the deck while Ferdinand worked us round the cuts and bends. On occasion one of us would kick horseshit overboard. I was soaking my shape into the woodgrain when Reuben sat up and said, Don't just lay there and shiver—get bare.

I did and soon was stark in the chill just before morning, and sat back down, thinking I'd rest and gather myself a bit longer, but Reuben was up and had Samuel before him and they lit pipes and talked over his reasoning me being a brother of theirs. I wrung out my clothes and their talk wore on a while with Samuel telling more in detail our travels and sufferings and gains, never, of course telling the truth of what had happened in Chit: we had, he said, been banished for fooling with the girls. Even as lies I hated to hear it all again, for my brother couldn't falsify it right—the way I did when I preached. Rather than give my own version, I made my case to Reuben.

I know I'm not worth much, I said, but all I have I owe to my brother, and I am grateful for all that he has given me. And now I owe another brother, and pray he'll take me on, for I've had no family but a madman, no company but pale things in caves in Kentucky and the beasts of the field all my sorry youth until I found the Kempers.

The brothers both were moved; even Reuben's stony aspect had cracked a bit with my account of things. Samuel stayed silent and Reuben made a few circles, puffing smoke. When we came to a straight run of the bayou, I was fishing in what I dazedly thought was my saddlepack for shirt and pants, but found it was neither mine nor Samuel's but Reuben's. I knew this because of what I felt with my fingertips beneath the crumpled clothing and kit—the pocked surface of cork, then glass—stepping back to notice how the leather bulged in the shape of a small jar and was worn along its outlines, as though the jar had been kept there for some time. Reuben, passing by, said, Don't bother dressing yet. If you want to be a Kemper then we'll baptize you as one right here and now. Will you have it like that?

I said I would and followed him to the side of the barge, where both brothers took me by the arms and held me out over the water.

May the good Lord bless and keep this brother and bind him to us, said Reuben.

For good or ill, said Samuel.

Then they dropped me in and I was held beneath the water until I thought I'd drown, struggling against their hands, my head thrashed back against the gunnels. I'd kept my eyes jammed shut, thinking this was how Emily had felt in her last awful moments of life, but as the water overtook me I was becalmed and opened them to find the bayou-life illuminated by a heavenly light. The catfish and gar regarded me with glowing eyes, and the alligators brushed me with their scales; crabs and crawfish nipped and fingerling shrimp bristled my face with their legs. And I knew at that moment I was baptized by God not only into brotherhood but into this country as well. They hauled me gasping from the water, Ferdinand singing a hymn as he poled, and when I told them what I'd seen my brothers both agreed it was a good vision.

Reuben slung the water and scum from his arm, saying, What a damnation of a day. Ride thirty miles to face a wicked man, bring back my brother and a new one in tow. And with all that I'm to be married when we make Natchez. That's how I heard it, you know. My sweet Aliza told me who you'd fallen in with. And in a day's time I'll be joined to her. Christ Almighty life's a joy!

I dried again and dressed, finding my own saddle-pack this time, but not forgetting, even in the elation of brotherhood, Reuben's horrible bride-price. And like a fool, caught up in being brother to those two, I asked him if the stories were true.

Samuel looked as though he'd strangle me; but Reuben only smiled broad and called to his black, You hear that, Ferdie? The legend's spread!

Ferdinand sang back a song about a Caribbean king who had a hundred of the blackest wives and murdered and ate them all, then rolled in their heaped heads. And it may be that in the July night, amid the screech of owls and the chittering of coons and possums in the trees, as the song of murder and infamy went on, I felt embraced, accepted

145

into the arms of family as I'd never known, the cords of brotherhood binding together, and even then that knot was choking out the righteous purpose of my life, leaving room for foolish fealty, the dreams of others to which I'd attach myself for years, held there by the same unrelenting faith that made me such a fine servant of the Lord.

So, little brother, Reuben said when his slave had finished the last verse, don't take too much stock in legends. They're often embellished.

I told you, said Samuel.

Not to say there's not some truths in them, he said to me. You've unburdened yourself enough to make me feel at ease. Besides, you know I'd crack your neck like an errant twig across my path if you betrayed me ever.

So you did cut some, I said.

For a woman who I'll never share a bed with but for a few nights at a time, because she can't abide the backcountry, or even traveling to New Orleans. For a woman so terrible and beautiful that I'd do anything to have her. What's the skins of a few pricks to me when love's on the line?

I thought it was lies, said Samuel.

Reuben said, It's lies only in number. Aliza's had her share of suitors, but none were willing to pay the price. You understand?

I did and was glad of it. I decided then that I'd do for Red Kate everything I'd been unable to do for Emily. To have her would be like—as I'd often dreamed on our way to Cincinnati, or on the flatboat's boards, or laid out awake in the late morning in my pallet at Lowde's—pulling Emily from Baptist Creek and having her come out of the water not blue and wrinkled and dead with a dead child inside her but alive and with breasts heavy with milk to feed our child and a bowed hard belly to press against my own when we kissed.

Samuel said he understood too but sounded shaken, remaining so until we were drinking in Lowde's, where we'd convinced Reuben to stay that night. The old Mother would welcome our return with mixed feelings, knowing something had gone wrong with Morrel, but she decked the place to the best of her powers and Reuben received visitors until the early morning, sending notes to his betrothed by Negroe runner when he wasn't toasting all present.

By morning we'd become the wedding party, bleary-eyed all in a row at the counter, bending over shaving basins set amongst the empty cups and bottles. New suits of clothes arrived by courier; and into his satin jacket I saw Reuben slip the small jar. He cinched our collars, leveled the brims of our hats, and, satisfied with our appearance, led us out into the street, which he'd paid to have cleared of dung and layabouts and strewn with musicians and the flowers children had culled from the trees about town. So we set off like a row of black teeth towards The Church and I was already filled with a terrible resolve. My Copperhead would be awaiting me.

The Wedding of Reuben and Aliza

The moment I saw the mistress I understood my brother's madness. She was so thin in her purple dress and when she stood her body-bundle of angles unbunched and she became like a crack in stone. Aliza was a child born from sharp things—her mother a razor, her father a bayonet. She was veiled in red cloth and her hair, a high tangle of blond worked with the feathers of a red-tailed hawk, gave her the look of a scythe that had swung so hard through the field that it caught unwary birds along with the golden grain snatched up at its tip.

She stood at the far end of the receiving room, before a long table set with wine cups and flowers and candles, surrounded by her retinue of whores. Among them was Red Kate, off to one end, not so much in favor as to be close to the mistress. She smiled at me when we came in and I drew off my hat and bowed. And not only did I understand

Reuben, but through him came to understand myself. The mistress could shatter the world, but I wanted to go through the cataclysm with the short one off to the side: Red Kate, a butcher's grate caught with gobs of beauty.

All right, Reuben said to me, above the clapping of the gathered guests and the start of fiddle music. I wasn't for having a preacher, but how about you say a sermon when we get up there. That work, little brother?

I was dumbstruck and still staring at Red Kate, who cocked her head to the side as though to say, Come on. Samuel put a hand to my shoulder, saying, I told you, didn't I? and Reuben took the first step in our procession to the altar.

What followed and passed between him and his bride seemed rehearsed, like they had planned it their entire lives. Reuben stepped beside Aliza, pulling from the pocket of his new coat the jar, in which floated a single milky twist of flesh in a swirl of pickling. He held it out to her across the altar and the glass cast a blinding light on us all. Aliza, for her part, squinted at the shine but never took her eyes from my brother—though he would not yet look on her—as he set the jar down on the altar table beside a pair of rings on a sheet of black cloth, where it would give off a steady glow for the entire ceremony. When he did look up I saw behind her veil Aliza's mouth sheer open in a smile. And once he'd looked, his eyes refused to part from the sight of her.

Talk, brother, he said.

Give a good one, said Samuel.

So I went and stood between them, close enough to see the jagged lines of Aliza's bones threatening her wedding costume, and Reuben's great shoulders thrown out straight, dwarfing her. They had the look of a boulder being married to a wicked split in its side. I looked down the row of whores to Red Kate, and hoped she'd know what I said was meant for her, but all she gave me was a bustle and shift in her dress, strained by a frame about the size of mine. I faced the guests and tongued a broken tooth, worrying it until the skin split; and I felt my mouth fill not with blood but words, so I opened it and let them out.

Brothers and sisters in Christ, I said, all you here who live on the down-hill side and are sneered at by the booted and horsed, listen close. When Adam was alone at the creation of the world, he dreamt at night, and these were terrible dreams—of what he did not know, only that they were terrible, and he'd awake to the dumb eyes of the animals in the garden and could find no succor in them. So he began to wither and dream even while he was awake, but still he did not know what he dreamed for, what he wished, only that he needed and would give anything for it. And in those days the Lord walked in the Garden with his creatures, and foremost among them was this one He'd fashioned in His image, which was now withering for he would eat none of the plump fruits or berries the Lord had set a-blooming all around him, such was his melancholy. And when the Lord our God watched this man He'd made wither, watched His own image going pale, in a fit of wisdom and worry one night He found the man asleep under an ash tree; and the Lord knelt next to His creation and He knew the dream, and He prayed on it for a moment, for He knew that there are two answers to the question of need—either kill the wanting thing, or create for it. So the Lord, taking pity on this creature Adam, squinted at him lying there and knew that this thing wanted so much to have itself remade but in such a way as to receive himself into it utterly, and that Adam would not stand for any gift that came from dust, as he had, and it would put his soul in the ditch if he made no sacrifice to have what he wanted; and the Lord took a survey of Adam's parts, and saw him down to the veins and muscles, and deep into the marrow of his bones, so God found the part He could most easily take from His creation, so that he would know that what he'd been given was of him, but unlike him; and He slipped His hand to Adam's belly and pressed his fingers till he felt the line of rib and knew it was here. In an instant the flesh parted and the Lord slipped in his fingers and the rib-bone came away like it was from a long-dead corpse, easily plucked; and with the other rib He'd do the same. Adam dreamt that night of blood, though he did not know blood yet, never having spilled a drop of his own; still he tasted blood in his dream-mouth and he knew what it was, that the pulse and tang of it would let him know another; and when he awoke from the night's dream—the Lord had already departed, off to do some other work but always watching—Adam found that the taste was gone from his tongue and beside him slept a creature like unto himself—what he'd gleaned of his own form in reflection by the pools and gentle streams of Eden—but not alike entirely, and as the sleep passed from his eyes he saw that this creature was different, its face more round, lips of greater thickness; its shoulders, rising and falling with breath, seemed smaller, and between them were breasts; and a madness took his hands and he threw them to his own body and felt, and in that groping found that his sides were bowed wrong, and he felt down his ribbage, finding there that he was sore and his guts sat different; he felt of his endowments, which were then stirred to greatness, and he saw that she had no such things; now, full-fraught with awe and a fury going in his loins, he mustered up his courage and bent to touch this creature, thinking, Is this the truer form of God? And Adam's fingers felt and his mind knew; and if there were storms in Eden it would be like lightning shot through him, and a breath escaped his awe-opened lips and the sound the breath made was *her*.

This last sound came out like I was Adam, and all the wedding party, whose feet had been nailed to the floor by my words, sagged and shifted and looked to one another in a daze broken when next I spoke, saying, When man lays eyes on woman, he is back at the creation of the world; he was not there to see our God do His first work shaping the earth, but what man did witness was the creation of *his* world, and the world which would become his in inception and his habitation until the day of his birth into gore and violence and death, and the world to which he will and must return all the days of his life; for avenues of flesh are made thus, and human fittings exist to be joined, and with the Blessings of Almighty God, I here, in the spirit of that first union, do now join in Christian wedlock Reuben Kemper and his Aliza.

Presently I turned to her and before I could ask she said, I'll take him.

She said nothing else, but in those words was more than any speech, for as she spoke, Aliza extended her wiry arm to my brother and took his hand in hers. Reuben's eyes broke from her and he was staring at the ground.

When I saw he wouldn't speak, I took up the rings and they slipped them on each other's fingers. Then I put one hand on the crown of Aliza's head and, reaching with the other till Reuben bent, laid my hand upon him, saying, Through death and fire, lovers!

All assembled erupted and tears flowed freely. I didn't see them kiss, but they walked around me and took hands and stepped off the platform down into the surging crowd. Samuel had me by the arms and was shaking me, howling about glory; and it was that the eyes of Aliza's girls were upon me, and I struggled to pick my Copperhead out.

Someone later said that Reuben twirled Aliza two hundred times that night, one for every foreskin he would have brought if she'd asked. I couldn't see; the whole waking world was dancing in that whorehouse Church. Everything spun and whirled, corks shot through the air, and I tasted my first champagne from a bottle shared with Red Kate. We traded sips and capered and she said to me, O, I know now what your gift is.

Life swole up with light and I danced with her. When the hour grew late the bride and bridegroom made the stairs for her chambers to our uproarious yells; and the whores went about sending home the guests, who clambered for them even through the crack of the closing door, hollered love through the trap-latch. And it was that Samuel and I were the only men left in the place. And I watched Red Kate grow nervous when one whore, hands on her hips, addressed us, saying, Miss Aliza says you're both to have a wedding gift.

The others had followed behind her and now stood in a dazzle of eyes and shapes and hair.

You preached so pretty, said one. Can you say all that for me?

And you, said another to Samuel. Are you as good as your brother?

We stood there in our sockfeet, having kicked off our boots for dancing. I gave Samuel a nudge and told the gathered whores that they were lovely, but there was only one among them that I'd preach to. Then I went and held my arm out for my Copperhead to take; and she did, viciously, with the sharp glance, as we went upstairs, of a lesser sister in triumph.

It's all yours! I called to my brother, buoyed by the tightness of her grip.

Fucking hell, Samuel said, almost breathless. And I know that in his heart he said fourteen prayers that he might last the night.

My Copperhead had fangs and they were at me even before we'd found her door. Inside, we passed our own wedding night; and in the moments when we were unjoined, she'd have me tell her all I'd seen and done. All I meant to do. And so I told: I would go into another country, maybe for a time I'd deal with Reuben's store, do that work until I had foothold enough to take my place and stride into the world, ballasted with coin, and do the true work of the righteous, dispel my father's prophecies of fire and damnation, and in their place erect a throne of glory, though I didn't yet know for what cause, only that the Lord would show me.

And did you know, I said to her—could you tell that what I preached was meant for only you?

Yes, she said, jerking up, fists clenched in confirmation, so that her heat flooded out from wafted sheets. Hell yes I knew.

Late next morning, with my share of the money taken from Morrel, I bought her outright. And, unlike Aliza, who sat in her chaise and tried to refuse my money, Red Kate would come with me into the other country, West Florida, to bear the times ahead, to suffer me and suffer woman's fate, which is to hold in brood the savage hopes and dreams of men, to nurture husbands' desires until, like children, they burst forth to screaming bloody life and both parents believe they're shared; and then comes the bitter awful day when those hopes and dreams turn back upon their mother with a sneer and say, I was never yours at all.

Book Three

AND HE CALLED

I

Ferrying the Dead

West Florida, 1802

Happiness

As it would often be, we lived at the feet of planters. Our house and store were at the Bayou Sara landing, a small village some miles below St. Francisville, which sat on the hilltop and was home to the finer people of the country. The Spanish Pukes called it the District of Feliciana, and its name was claimed to mean the Land of Happiness. Meanwhile we lived between the swamp, named for a French whore, and a smaller offshoot called Bayou Gonorrhea, the name of which came from the sorry fate of the Indians who had lived there in the early days of the country, when a French explorer going upriver marooned the whore Sara among them, and she proceeded to lay down with every man from lowest warrior to chief, who then laid with their wives, so that when the explorer returned the next year there were no Indians left, only the whore, who lived out her days in those swampy places which bore both her name and the name of her curse. The place remained so-called even once the settlement was founded by John Mills, when the colony was briefly British; much aged by the time we arrived, Mills lived in St. Francisville, his presence serving as a doddering reminder of past days and of how the Pukes liked for all their beloved Anglo settlers to feel welcome. And this amicable farce needed to be maintained, for as it stood there were so few Spanish in our corner of West Florida—the majority of their government and forces, the decadent remains of their back-dealing and treacherous Catholic empire, were housed three hundred miles to the east in Pensacola—that the dons sold off much of their land to the Anglos, who they then set in places of minor office as alcaldes, though the true power in the Louisiana districts was still held by the Puke commandant in Baton Rouge. All such things we learned in time; and it was that when Mills told the story of the names to us one winter day at Reuben's store, he finished by stamping his cane and with eyes bright from having seen so much wonder and wilderness in his days said, And why shouldn't we call our town after happiness? If you live here you already are.

I told this to Red Kate before bed that night and she said it had the ring of truth, pressed her flat nose to my cheek, and hummed with gladness. For months I'd forgotten the itch to rob and even the need to preach. Instead, I stole my bought wife's love every night and whispered sermons in her ear. My pistol hung on a peg beside our bed, which was a grand brass frame with a mattress and its down stuffing taken from the unsold wares of the store, a gift given us by Reuben, who never stayed long enough in Bayou Sara to need more than a pallet in the foreroom, and I carried a weapon only to ride with Samuel out to Reuben's timber tracts and hunt.

We'd gut deer in the woods, then return with the carcass and proudly mount the steps to the house, which was raised on pilings eight feet high, and hang the beast by hooks on the beams for butchering. This duty was my Copperhead's, who would appear with her knife and basin and go straight to her red work. With the hides she made us leggings or covers for our powder-horns. Resting from the ride, I'd stand with Samuel and watch her arms grow covered with blood to the shoulder as she worked, then go to grab her and have the tang of it in our noses while we embraced, looking out to the bayou, the store and the land abounding, raised, as we were, above it all. Eight feet above the fetid swamp, above the fecund goings-on of the few hardscrabble people, but our heads were in the heavens.

She was born of the frontier and before the massacre of her parents had learned the backcountry arts. Within our first months in the Bayou Sara house she'd planted a truck patch of soft corn, cow cabbage, leeks, and potatoes. We ate well, miraculous to me then, as was my very presence by the hearth while she cooked; I was awestruck by domestic happenings, and amazed to find myself comforted by them. The slow assemblage of the trappings of home and family seemed stranger than my preaching-life; the everyday became a fascination when all you'd known was warped faces and rotten minds shrieking at God, mewling malformed grifters, or the skulk of alley-way ambushes. So home had my vision clouded, and I joyed in it for a time and made it mine as far as I could. But there were also Reuben's matters to attend, our keep to earn; so Samuel worked the store whenever customers happened by from St. Francisville, which was rare, and it was left to me to tend to upkeep and other duties, only helping my brother in mercantiles on occasion. By Reuben's orders we sold mostly on credit, in order, so he said, to cultivate friendship and avoid acrimony; and besides, he'd say, the goods were Smith's and he wanted them gone, had already claimed half lost in the shipping. Don't blot the ledgers with these deals; what isn't written can't be writ up by the law, eh?

When we first landed and came to the house, we'd found the door kicked in. I stood back with my wife while Reuben cussed and thrashed about the place, looking for missing valuables. Finding none, he decided that this was an act of what he called the damnable Puke cabal to ruin him. The store, down the way, was found to be locked and undisturbed.

Early on we came to find that Reuben held much, but none of it was his. Only Ferdinand and the Cotton-Picker, for the rest—our house in Bayou Sara, the store, its goods, and all his land—were either mortgaged by New Orleans usurers he took to be his friends or owed to his ex-partner, Smith. Samuel explained it to me this way: a man can have no wealth in this country if he doesn't risk, or try to slice his part from the fat sides of the wealthy. But we didn't mind and were content. The tiresome dealings and legal proceedings were at first left up to Reuben. He'd leave Bayou Sara each time almost as soon as he arrived, boarding his boat and floating back down the bayou for New Orleans or to see his Aliza in Natchez, leaving us in charge of the land and store. He would return on occasion, bearing goods he shipped for friends in West Florida and news such as the cession of Louisiana to France. I'd heard the name *Bonaparte* bandied by people in Natchez, but it was from Reuben that I learned truly who the man was; and I recall my ears perking at the sound of the word *conqueror*. It went that he'd bring Samuel along, so we kept store loosely and the ledger told of long stretches without money-sales, hosting there the friends we made like Mills, or Basil Abrams, who'd squat by the stove and drink whiskey with us in the cold months and talk over his anger with the wicked local leaders.

Scoundrels, he'd say. They carve away at my holdings like it's a flitch of bacon.

These men were the alcaldes, local magistrates, and arbiters, easily given over, like the petty and the small always are, to puny purchases of power. Some were Tories, escaped from the war and still bearing British accents, such as the indigo man Alexander Stirling. Others were American but running-boys for Spanish masters: the bastard Ira Kneeland. And there were also those who kept two masters but above all were ruled by the coin, like the Reverend John Smith and General Wilkinson. Slowly, through personal dealings or, more usually, Reuben's cusses whenever he was home, did we learn the names of the wicked and hateful. And there were also the Pukes themselves, like the surveyor Pintado, who I'd often see riding out with Kneeland, his deputy, and their strange instruments to take measurements of shadows thrown by the sun or to gauge the river's rise and fall. Pintado was the one, some months after we arrived, who gave us the oath of allegiance.

It was in February and early morning. Samuel and I were on our way back from riding our tracts to hunt, and to see if more timber had been poached, when we saw on the ridge above the bayou a pair of men with shining things like spyglasses aimed at the sky. The pair adjusted their gadgets and one would point his at the sun while the other scribbled in a notebook.

What do you think they're searching for? asked Samuel.

God, I said. Every fool for science, all he looks for is the face of the Lord, but they refuse to see.

They'll burn their damned eyes out doing that, said Samuel, shielding his from the light with his hand.

We left them and rode on home, and weren't half through our morning hoe-cakes when there came a rap at the door. It was the pair of surveyors, one very fair but dark of hair and in an unbuttoned uniform shirt of a Spanish officer, the other prim and powdered. The first was Pintado, the second Kneeland. We'd encountered them in passing and tell, but not face-to-face and proper. They addressed us, one in

Puke's quick clip and the other in the slow-rolling tones of American planters, taking so much time to let their words play out that in the yawn of stretching vowel you'd find plenty room to pack with hate.

You are the new brothers Kemper? said Pintado.

We answered that we were.

And do you gentlemen intend upon staying and becoming citizens? said Kneeland. Visitors are fine, mind you, but you are here doing business.

We were told, said Samuel, to take the oath whenever it was presented.

Excellent, said Pintado, and he gave the oath to us there on the porch, a quick affair and without the indignity of swearing loyalty to the Pope, only King Carlos. The Spanish were, after all, accommodating.

Well done, said Kneeland. I'll come by with the papers shortly.

Fine then, I said.

Kneeland cocked his shoulders and took on a biting look, contempt and greed hidden beneath all that syrup. I would tell you that we've surveyed out some thousand arpents to the north and east, he said, if you were interested in your own purchases. But with the matter of ongoing litigation between your brother and Mister Smith—

That matter's settled as far as I know, said Samuel, who knew rightly that it wasn't.

O, said Pintado, I am afraid it is not. Your brother, he is on land debted to Mister Smith, and the store is Smith's.

The goods were to be liquidated, said Kneeland. But we hear there's still a good bit there, and, shall we say, poor accounts?

Before I could speak Samuel bowed up, saying, Have you taken account of the God-damned people cutting our timber? We've sold some, but we can't keep on with every planter carving off pieces whenever he needs a twig to pick his teeth.

Are you impugning a particular character, sir? Kneeland said.

I am not, sir, said Samuel, mimicking the planter's diction.

May I say, sir, that it would be unwise to do so?

Samuel replied: And I'll say that it would be awfully unwise for any son of a bitch to poach our living from us.

Pintado had had enough and started between them, giving, as a bureaucrat will, a litany of terms. Gentlemen, he said. This is another matter and it will be addressed. I will order Captain Mills to take some militia out next week to your land. You may accompany him if you choose, but for the moment I must inform you that, while you are welcome as citizens of the domain as good subjects of King Carlos the Second, Mister Smith has asked Commandant Grand Pré in Baton Rouge to appoint arbiters to look into the accounts of the partnership with your brother and assess a judgment in the dispute. Smith is, as you say, making a terminus of the partnership—and you must inform your brother that he is, by Spanish law, bound to nominate his own arbiters, in order to do away with any hint of favoritism or prejudice.

There you have it, said Kneeland. A fair judgment assured.

Ask my ass, I said.

Kneeland reddened. What did you say? He stepped towards the doorway and tried to put his height to me, stretching so that my nose was at his collar. What did you say to me just now?

Gentlemen, said Pintado with his hands in the air.

You, sir, said Kneeland, are not only impudent but insolvent—as poor a combination as there ever was.

When they left, Samuel slammed the door so hard the window-panes shook. Red Kate, wrapping the last of the cakes in a molding cloth, turned and asked what was their business.

The business of trying to destroy ours, I said as I went to her.

My Copperhead folded the last of the cloth into place and put the cakes away in a dark iron pot, then sat another pot within it to flatten them. She smelled of cooking and ash and I remembered the sorrow of my burnt tongue and what a dream it was for it to have been dead for so long when such things were in the world. I put my arms around her waist once she was finished and held on to her hands.

To hell with them, she said, turning to look up at me with a glint of what could only be called murder in her eye. You'll have them soon enough and by the bollocks.

That's the truth, I said.

I see their wives, she said, in town sometimes. They're a lousy bunch of biddies and shrews. Thin-backed, never worked a day on their feet, or on their backs. Not a one came to Willy Cobb's funeral. Deemed him too common, I suppose.

I'll bet that Kneeland has a shrew for sure, I said.

No, said Kate, he's a bachelor I hear.

From who? I asked.

O, she said, the widow Cobb. You know how the man plagued her husband, what a woe, so I suppose she knows a great deal of him.

Samuel sat himself at the table, put his fists together, and sat his chin upon them, contemplating the wall with a look of fury. But I knew there were other things there working in him. The Cobbs were friends of ours; Arthur, the younger brother, lived several miles up the bayou, struggling to raise cattle, while his elder, William, had lived with his wife only a mile from the line of demarcation between West Florida and American Mississippi until he died of ague late our first September, leaving his widow alone at the borderlands with a farm to mind. Arthur and William had come to Feliciana for the cheapness of the land and the looseness of Spanish governance and found themselves betrayed by both. There were many times when one or the other would come knocking at the house to go and have a drink at the store and grouse over the foolishness of the surveyors, who drew their lines wrong and forced the brothers to come into town to rectify their mistakes. They both bore a serious hatred for Kneeland, and it was that

William even took a whip to the alcalde's back one day; though, when I asked him why he'd done it, he refused to say much more than it was all the same business of deceit and rascality. By the time we heard he was down with the ague, we had time only to say a night's worth of prayers before Arthur came with the news of his brother's death the following afternoon. He was rendered alone and brotherless and I hurt for him.

The widow Cobb, for her part, was still young, not more than nineteen, but she refused to leave her house, which overlooked the fifty-yard swath cut in the cane and bramble denoting the end of one country and the beginning of another. She'd come down in her buggy on occasion to Bayou Sara, take on provisions which we gave her free, and sit with Kate and do needlework, which neither preferred except that they could tell stories. Mostly it was Copperhead who talked, with the widow Cobb giggling at her ribalds and blushing at the stories of her former days. Her name was Ezmina, and when she was in our house, Samuel would hover about her, filling her cups of coffee and offering her tips of gin, lingering at the edge of the women's talk. He'd often ask her to stay the night, giving her his pallet in the sitting room while he slept on the floor of the store. By December our charity to the widow Cobb had grown to include him riding over the frost-covered country to bring her things from the store or cut her a week's worth of wood.

One morning I met Samuel by chance on the road down from Thompson's Creek, which was the eastern border of our timber tract, and he told me everything. It was no confession he gave, but a testament to the loveliness of the widow. He grinned as he spoke. After all, Will was dead and at the worst all he was doing was cutting short the mourning.

She's a miracle, said Samuel. Just for her height. And she's a smart woman, always thinking.

I haven't seen much indication of that, I said.

You wouldn't. She keeps it to herself and tells her mind just to me.

You're happy?

Like a damn glory, brother.

Marry her then, I said.

Samuel looked down the road, which up ahead descended from the higher ground into the swamp and there was cane which grew thirty feet high. Not until this business of mourning is settled, he said. I don't want to make her seem—

Like she doesn't honor the memory of her husband? I said.

Don't play with me, said Samuel. But, yes, that's the gist.

You'll need to tell Arthur.

We'll see when I tell anybody. Let me just have this for a time. I watched Reuben and you latch on with women—now I laid with plenty, don't get me wrong, but you two have more than an ache in your loins for your women. I believe I've got that same thing for Ezmina.

Amen, brother, I said.

We rode to where the cane swallowed up the sun and the sounds of creatures rustling in it was loud. Our horses nipped each other's necks, nervous, as a rat scuttled out from a break in the cane onto our path.

Mark him, I said.

He's yours, said Samuel. If you can hit him.

I drew my pistol, fired, and made the rat jump five feet in the air. And there would be a day when we'd make it our mission to clear the land of all its vermin. The Pukes and their alcaldes were as yet nuisance only. The culling time was later to come. I didn't know this was a sign.

We rode over the hole in the path left by my shot, and the rat had been flung back into the cane where we couldn't see. Samuel's horse had been startled by the shot and he rubbed its neck to calm it. Then he turned to me and said, She won't take off her veil, nor any of her black laces.

Ezmina? I said.

The same, replied my brother. She works her garden in her funeral clothes. She cooks in them and there's places where salt from her sweat is in white smudges, like at the small of her back and the pits of her arms. And the way the black looks on her skin is God-damned wonderful. It troubled me at first, but now some way I wish she'd never take them off.

The Dead

The blacks came one day pouring down from St. Francisville, ghastly and with dark skin dyed darker from working vats of indigo, past our house and to the Bayou Sara landing. I went outside and saw the tail of them heading to where the others were huddled at the bank, emptying their bowels where they stood and shivering though it was early summer and the heat was on. They were herded by a man on horseback who stopped at my porch and said he was one of Alexander Stirling's overseers. He asked had I got the contract for shipping them down to New Orleans.

I said I had, but couldn't take my eyes from them, counting twenty or more of the wretches, men and women and children dressed in clothes that had once been other colors but were now an awful shade of blue. The slaves were silent and some had fallen to the ground, unmindful or too weak to care what was expelled upon them by their brothers and sisters. Women holding bony children opened their mouths as if to speak, but only streams of purple vomit fell from between their lips and the held children didn't struggle. I thought of the Reverend Morrel, whose memory was not often absent, his injustices and also the wicked justice in him. And the urge was upon me to go inside, load every weapon I owned, and kill them all. Instead I went for the overseer.

God damn it, man, I said. You're bringing a plague down here!

Sir, said the overseer. It's only the niggers get it. From working the indigo.

I don't give a piss, I said. This wasn't in the blasted contract.

Your brother, Mister Reuben, knows well enough it is.

He's not even here yet. Are they supposed to stay here, fouling, until he comes?

I was told he'd be here today. And besides this is delicate.

The door opened behind me and I saw Samuel on the porch and my wife leaning out. My brother's face was hard and Kate was gaping down the bank, her hand over her mouth.

Get inside! I called to her.

But my Kate, my Copperhead, seemed to fall out the doorway and stumble onto the porch, still staring and now with both hands held over her mouth as if muffling a scream or the rising of her stomach.

It's a five-year cycle, said the overseer. Like planting the crop itself. They only last that long before—

I didn't want to hear him any longer, whipped back to face the porch, and howled, Get fucking back inside, you hear me!

Samuel was coming down the steps and my wife did as I said, her hands now covering her eyes.

Jesus Christ Almighty, said Samuel as he approached. This is what Reuben agreed to take?

Yes sir, it is, the overseer said.

What if he doesn't get the barge here until tomorrow? I said.

Then they'll stay there, said the overseer. You've got no other responsibility than to ship them down to New Orleans for sale.

Who'll buy such niggers? Samuel said.

That's not my concern or purview, sir. Once they're in New Orleans the pen-owners'll feed them cod-oil, fatten them back well enough to last another few months.

More of the blacks had lost their footing in the mess and were splayed out on the ground, heaving. It was darkness upon darkness and the hand of God saw fit for a wind to blow in from the bayou and carry the smell of their rot internal up to us. The overseer, Samuel, and I all batted our heads and huffed out breaths to try and expel the stench. I shut my eyes, held up my head, and faced the sky; and when I opened them I saw the breaking of a clear summer day and I damned the color of the horizon, which was such a sharp blue that it mocked the dread horror at the landing now suffering for the human need to approximate the work of the Lord.

Again I heard the door open and Red Kate came out with a bucket and ladle; and when I stormed over and met her on the steps I saw it was water.

They don't have any, she said. It's fifteen miles from—

I told you to go back inside, I said.

She glared at me, and the fire of her hair was put to shame by the fierceness of her look.

Go, I said. They're dead anyway. I hope they die on the way to New Orleans and the bastard doesn't make a penny.

Ma'am, called the overseer. Don't fret now. They can't hold much water anyway. It's got to be mixed in with the oil and feed and—

My wife moved to step around me but I stopped her. She stood there, knuckles paling at the ladle's handle.

Just go inside, ma'am, said the overseer.

I turned to him. You, I said. Say another word to my wife and I'll cut your bastard lips off.

Watch that tongue, sir, said the overseer, stiffening in his saddle.

Shut your mouth and go tend your niggers, said Samuel from close enough to have dragged the overseer from his horse and beat him into the ground.

The overseer shook his head, mumbling that he'd tell this whole event to Mister Stirling.

Tell that Tory whatever you want, said Samuel, but he damned sure better pay.

The overseer rode away and I took Red Kate by her arm, which was burning hot with anger, and led her back into the house. Before I shut the door I heard her begin to weep. It was a true Irish keen, high enough for some of the dazed black heads to turn and regard the house for the source of their lone-sung funeral wail, and I could hear her even in the yard with Samuel, who tried his best to ignore it. We could do nothing but survey the sorry scene.

If I were a true man of God, I said, I'd go and bless all the heads of the sick.

Or kill them, said Samuel.

I told him how I'd thought of that as well.

We both fell silent and went to sit on the steps; and the hours wore on and the afternoon came and the sun began to fall and its fires were merciful and bled the sky of the horrible blue and there was the comfort of the enveloping redness.

And is this what you want? I asked my brother. To be a planter and have that on your head?

I wouldn't grow indigo, Samuel said.

I said I wished Kate hadn't seen.

She's seen worse than this, said Samuel.

That doesn't mean I don't want to shield her eyes. Will you tell Ezmina?

O, said Samuel, I tell her everything.

And it was when the sky had turned the color of my wife's hair that Reuben's boat was sighted down the bayou and the overseer called to us that he was coming. When the Cotton-Picker neared, I saw that Reuben and his Ferdinand already had masks tied about their faces. Those slaves who could stand did, wobbling to see what would carry them down the river. I'd grown used to the sounds of their corruption, and when Ferdinand jumped from the boat into the water, to take the hogs-head and bank the boat while Reuben poled, the noise he made all splash and slosh was but a part of the horrible chorus of fluids and groans.

Reuben debarked while sopping Ferdinand lashed the boat to the foot of a small tree. Our brother, in his mask, made a wide circle of the slaves and went to talk with the overseer, who handed him a writ and packet before he remounted and hied away, passing by our house and giving us a pissy flip of the arm. Reuben and Ferdinand were calling for the slaves to board and, though I didn't wish to, I accompanied my brother down to see.

The last time he'd come to Bayou Sara, and the time before that, in March, we'd told Reuben of the Pukes' orders to appoint arbiters in his case against Smith. Both times he'd waved the thought of it off and said how we must only wait, for the country would be America soon and he'd have a proper judgment.

Reuben's towering stature and sun-browned features were as mocking as the daytime sky had been to the awful bunch now lurching for the boat and clambering aboard, dragging those that couldn't walk and leaving trails of filth as marks of their passage. When he came close to us, his mask, a paisley cloth, smelled strongly of oil of mint.

It's horrible, brother, said Samuel.

I know, but there's too many debts to be paid.

Swamp the boat, spill them into the river, I said. Say there was a storm.

I can't do such a thing, said Reuben. I'm paid on delivery.

God, I said.

You can be no judge, he said. This is life.

Will you stay a while when you're back from New Orleans? asked Samuel.

I believe, he said. I'm sure there's more business to discuss.

The arbiters? I said.

I told you both and I will tell you again—we wait. No matter who we appoint, the judgment will be Smith's. He has the dons all in his pocket. The damned commandant. Let him come down from Ohio and claim what he thinks his.

Ferdinand hollered that all were aboard; and we all looked down to the landing where before had been the blacks and now all that remained was a wide pool of sickness.

We'll discuss the matter further when I'm back, he said. This will be a quick trip.

I guess it will, I said. They can't last too damn long.

Long enough, Reuben said, then wiped his brow of sweat and started for his boat, where the cargo presently was dropping, wasting already. He called back that things would be better when he returned.

But my mind was on pagan lines and the figure of the boatman of the dead. And before me went the very image of the ferrier, great and broad, hoary and strong, to lead the damned to their place in Hell. I tried to fill my mind with the true God and His blessed scriptures rather than the earlier evils of the gentile peoples; but Reuben, now aboard, took up his pole and Ferdinand unlashed and shoved them off into the current and the boat spun, a dazzle of corpses gyring out on the water. The boat was righted and drifting towards the first bend in the bayou, where after they rounded it the horror would be gone. But only from our eyes, for by its nature, I knew, the trade must move throughout the arteries of the country, the scene so many times played out, so that even utmost horror becomes a common sight.

II

The Creation of Louisiana

Summer 1802–Spring 1803

Tidings of Joy

In the early days of our second August in West Florida, when the heat was monstrous and I was up on the roof with Samuel putting raking-boards on the house, my Copperhead came outside and watched us work—a small figure down below, taking the weather like a gift rather than a blasting sun and its swelter, which wilted lesser ladies and kept them indoors. From my perch on the low-slope of the roof, I waved to her with the wood-plane I'd been using to curve the boards. She didn't wave back, but cupped her hands at her mouth and called up that her blood was two months late. I leaned against the gable, the sun beating hell upon me, and I gaped down at her—stomach hidden in calico aproning, cloth hiding flesh, flesh hiding womb, womb hiding a pinprick of promise pulsing with life. Making for the ladder, I found I couldn't grip, and wobbled there on the edge of the roof before Samuel hauled me back. And with all the awe of Revelation, I asked if she was sure.

Sure as can be, said my wife. I've been a long time off the tinctures, and I believe the poison left and a child took.

Now I'd begun to weep, tried again to take the ladder but still my hands were wasted, and so I rose and scrabbled up the slope, my brother harrying behind so that I wouldn't fall as I capered at the peak and bayed in joy to the marshlands and waters all about. Twenty feet down, Red Kate had taken up my dance, slow twirls kicking dirt clouds at her feet. In all my wretched life I was never so unhitched from the world as on that day, when I swung from the chimney and swore for how I'd made myself a life. There would be no one to drown her, no father to make me dig her grave, no tribulation and no shame. I'd make sure of that.

The Time of Waiting

Our talk was often names and eyes and hair and sexes, making a child with our words even as it quickened in her. Reuben, when he came to Bayou Sara for one of his brief and angry exchanges with the alcaldes, congratulated me and seemed happy for the prospect of a child about the place.

It's a glory I won't ever know, he said. Aliza has it plotted out like a Papist woman's calendar.

We were sitting out on the porch steps, sipping gin from the store. Fall had come, the leaves gone brittle, and they blew in drifts across the bayou and were snatched up on occasion by great catfish whose backs broke the water in swells and slipped beneath in one mysterious motion.

I'm talking years, said Reuben. I've known her for more than five and there's been no sign of it in her.

There's always room for the miraculous.

It wouldn't be a virgin conception, I assure you.

I didn't mean that, I said.

I know, said Reuben. I think of miracles. I pray on their likelihood. Like for Smith to stay in Ohio a bit longer, and the Pukes to keep out of our business. For America to take the territory, double the price of our land.

Have you heard anything more from New Orleans?

I've heard in Natchez, I've heard in New Orleans. The country will be American soon.

But why not appoint our own men to the tribune? That way we'll have a hope of fairness.

Don't trouble yourself with that mess, he said. The Pukes are slow in law and I'm making money from hauling, enough to pay whatever they ask if they judge in his favor. And besides, it won't be for years. By that time I may be able to buy Smith out. Sue his ass.

I do worry on it, I said.

Don't. I took that old Reverend by the scruff, now didn't I? You doubt that I can do that with a bunch of frilled surveyors and politicians?

I don't.

Then let me worry. Reuben finished his cup of gin and after hissing out a breath asked me was his brother off with the widow in the woods.

I said he was.

Good. He seems happy enough.

He needs to tell Arthur, I said.

Give him time. That's what you should learn here. Give everything its time. Reuben stood and stretched, looked up to the house. Well done with the cornices, he said. The Pukes can tell Smith we aren't slothful. He drew a fattened billfold from his coat, saying, This is near a thousand dollars, and I want you to go to Pintado and buy as much land as you can with it, and the second you have it, lease it out, sell the timber. That way we'll be earning from it.

I took the billfold and told him we would. Will you go to Natchez next?

Most likely, he said. I haven't seen Aliza in two months. I'll bring her the good news.

Reuben held his arms out wide so that they stretched across the rails of the porch and breathed deep of the cooling air. Then he said, I wonder if she is to be the miracle of my life.

From that same lady, gifts were sent and arrived in November, not long after we bought the land and leased it off: a fine crib and swaddling clothes and toys of various kinds. We set them out on the billiard table in the fore-room and they were added to by our friends all the following months. Abrams and Cobb passed frequently, as did the Bradfords, the Silvers, and even Edward Randolph down from Pinckneyville, who spoke philosophically on the raising of children, himself desiring fatherhood, though he'd yet to be so blessed. Samuel rode the widow Cobb down to cook for Kate till the end of her term. Christmas came and we celebrated the birth of the Savior, with all songs and readings of the Book seeming like they pertained not to Christ but to the coming of our own child.

Widow Cobb in her mourning clothes brought us cups of hot spiced punch, first to Kate, then Samuel, then me, and finally to her brother-in-law, who was there that day. Arthur eyed Samuel a bit from over the lip of his cup. We drank and Ezmina, a fur of coon-tails about her shoulders for the cold, knelt beside my wife and spoke.

If only my Will had had time to give me one, she said.

There's hope yet, said Kate, cutting her eyes with a smile to Samuel.

He stiffened and Arthur stood, cursing.

It's nothing wrong here, said my brother, himself rising.

Cobb was at his chest and they glared at each other for a moment. Arthur cocked his head as though shaking water from his ear. I don't give a damn, he said, and turning to the widow Cobb with strains of broken hope aching in his voice: It ain't like she's my wife.

Samuel put his hand out and Arthur took it, sat back down, and resumed drinking, and the matter was left at that for a time; though later, when Arthur Cobb came to know the full extent of Ezmina's sins, he'd gnash his teeth and cuss and tear out most of his hair, going about for weeks in the tatters of the same clothes he wore the day he heard, and it was clear that he also loved her. But by that time we all had other things at hand; and Arthur Cobb, ragged and profane, joined in with Samuel and me without complaint.

As winter wore on and the child became apparent in my wife, I took to keeping all my pieces loaded and near me in our bedroom, where I didn't so much sleep as lay there with my eyes held shut. I thought again of Morrel, that he was still prowling the countryside, of his vengeance. And the firesides of the country held stranger rumors than him; there was talk of an enormous spider, the size of a man, seen roving the roads and at the edges of yards. Even such fantasies gave me pause. I'd never had anything to protect other than my sorry self, and I was happy that we were constantly beset by visitors those days.

It happened that one night I heard a rustling outside and put my hand to Kate's arm and told her to stay and listen hard. Then I took up my pistol and shotgun and went through the house, awakening the widow Cobb on her pallet, Samuel rising beside her to join me at the front window, seeing there in the moonlight a boy unlashing my horse from its post. I gave Samuel the shotgun and we took the bar from the door and the boy must have heard us, for he was skittering off into the dark when we came out onto the porch and I aimed my guns on him. He stopped, holding some livery in his hand.

Hold, now, boy! Samuel called out.

The boy was wormy, hatless, coatless, and with peeling moccasins; but he squared and held his ground under our guns, which pleased me despite my anger.

What's your name? I said.

The boy didn't answer and by then the horse was loose and wandering the yard, picking at the dry grass. I came down, took the lashings from him, and went to tie my horse back.

Do you have any friends in Feliciana? I asked.

He looked at me in confusion, as if to say, If I had friends I wouldn't be stealing your horse.

There's no man who'll hunt me down if I kill you?

No, he said.

You're trying to steal a damned horse? said Samuel.

I cinched the last knot in the tie and left the horse, moving out of Samuel's line of fire but still close enough to see the stony expression of this boy faced with double-death.

He's just looking, I said. Right?

No, he said. I meant to steal your damned horse.

Tell me your name, I said.

The boy chucked the livery down and said, Ransom O'Neil.

Samuel said, That's a thief's name if I ever heard one!

All right, brother Ransom, I said. Now I'm going to ask you one hell of an important question. Do you know where you're going?

Ain't going anywhere while you're holding that gun.

No, not now. Do you know where you're going to go when you die? When some man catches you filching his things and puts you down to eternity?

I'd go in the ground or in jail, he said.

I'm for the first suggestion, Samuel said.

I stepped closer with my pistol, trying to look stern.

Shoot and get it done, Samuel called.

Ransom O'Neil's eyes searched us out with fearful glances. I guess if I'm stealing then I'll go to Hell, he said.

Damn right, you'll go straight to Hell.

Are you to be the one who sends me?

Maybe so, said Samuel.

I smiled at him, saying, I don't want to be the one that does it. Though I could just as easy. No, I want to save you from it.

He stared at me unbelieving.

The Lord should hate me, but I've been saved by the grace of Jesus Christ and I'll never burn for what I do. No matter what it is, He knows I work for Him—

Jesus Christ, Angel, said my brother, are you evangelizing this turd-swill?

I said I was, never taking my eyes nor the barrel of my pistol from the boy.

What kind of scripture's that? asked Ransom O'Neil.

The Word of the Sword of the Lord, I said. And if you let yourself be baptized you'll have that same weapon, that same love. I'll throw down this gun and baptize you right now, and if you follow me you'll never want again. What say?

Shit, said Samuel, get it over with. I've heard you preach enough.

Ransom O'Neil brushed scraggly black hair grown overlong from his forehead and said, It sounds mad, but I'll go.

Samuel followed behind us with his shotgun trained, and I believe it wasn't the first gunpoint baptism in Christendom, but it was my first. I brought the boy to the edge of the water and, taking him by the collar, followed him in. Before I dunked him, he said, If you drown me, I swear I'll haunt you.

Amen, I said. And he went under easy and the water bubbled for a few moments while I said my prayers and invocations. Then I withdrew him from the murk and brought the new convert, gasping and sanctified, to the bank. He was cackling in bewilderment, though I'd like to think he was dumbstruck at the glory of God.

Before we put him in the store for the night, Ransom told of how he'd come up from New Orleans, where his people were indentures, and that his father and mother had been buried alive in the canals and he'd been left to tend to four brothers and sisters, who he'd abandoned when the fever came upon the city. He would be one for odd work, often hired out to the Bradfords or Cobb as the new year dawned and winter lagged to an end. That night he said he liked any work that wasn't knee-deep in mud and clay where sometimes digging you'd turn a shovel and find the pale corpse of another worker, perhaps the curled white hand of your own mother, like a mushroom disinterred.

When I came again into the bedroom, I found Red Kate sitting up with her lamp lit and belly piling the sheets.

I worried you were dead, she said.

I sat beside her and put a hand to her belly, wherefrom issued a kick of a tiny foot, and I was filled even more with grace and glory.

If I died, I said, you'd know because the very ground would split and there'd be a sound of thunder.

You're wild, she said.

The world will know when I pass out of it, I said. And the mark I leave will be great.

Red Kate pressed a finger to herself, where she thought was our child, and said, This is your mark. Nothing more. And don't forget it.

Creation

The widow Cobb's face was ashen when she drove me out of the house that night as the birth began. I didn't want to leave, for the last I'd seen of Red Kate was her face twisted in pain before the widow blew the lamp out, saying that there must be darkness or she might go into a fever for the oppressiveness of light. This was the last day of April, and Reuben happened to be there, and he along with Samuel hauled me outside to the store, waking Ransom, and put a cup of gin in my hand. It was before midnight, and I'd been awakened to a wet bed and shuddering wife; and her hair, darkened and matted down with sweat, looked so much like streams of blood that I was terrified.

My Copperhead would tell me next day, when she was rested, how it went; but in those hours amid my gin-soaked prayers and with the consoling words of the brothers rattling like a babble in my ears, I envisioned her suffering in the time of bringing forth. The widow would have her propped and legs bound apart with sheets in the darkness; how she worked without light I'll never know. There would be the pulse of Kate's body urging out the life she'd held these past months; and was it small or twisted and warped? Was it a breech? I saw the widow hunched above her in the bed, her hands down at Red Kate's lap, and the widow was shook for the force of the world was wracking the bed. I went outside to listen for screams and stare at the black window of the bedroom, but I heard none and was soon brought back in by my brothers. The widow's hands would feel the curve of a head without her and those hands were like the hands that held Emily under the water, for that was what I thought of when I felt the chill of Red Kate's flooding in the bed. I stared at the candle Ransom had set burning in the store once he was up, and that pinprick of light was in the bedroom now as the widow felt the small slope of shoulders and the light swelled to eat the darkness to the corners and beneath the trembling, creaking bed as in a final slip of flesh and blood the wrinkled form of the child came into her hands. And I rushed outside again and swear I saw the house explode with a light which burned for an instant like the sun, so that I had to hold my hand up to my eyes and shield them. A cry, a tiny shriek of infant life, issued out from the house and I ran to put my face to the bedroom pane. I pressed there and listened, and I heard the crying of the child but not his mother. Hands were upon me and my brothers dragged me fighting back to the store and had to hold me down for the time it took, an hour or more, for the widow to appear at the door and tell me that they were both alive, but I mustn't go inside until the dawn. I cursed her and my brothers tried to hand me more gin, which I knocked away, rising up with a furious strength and bowling the widow Cobb aside. I ran through the yard, busting my lip when I hit the steps, but still I clambered up and was inside the house, dripping blood I couldn't see.

When I came into the bedroom, Red Kate said my name. And in the dark I went to her, palmed my way across her through cord and the cold touch of a knife set aside, through afterbirth and blood and all the effluvium of life, feeling sweat-soaked sheets and her trembling beneath them until my hands came to the small form she held bundled in her arms. I cupped its head, her face where it started just above, and kissed them both, overwhelmed by the smell of more than blood, more than life. The child began to wail and she didn't try to muzzle it. Nor would I have had her quiet the cry of advent. The widow had begun cleaning, and I knelt beside them, put my hands to wife and son, touching the boundaries of a new and unfathomable country.

In another part of the world the imaginary boundaries of America were being redrawn: a little man, a diplomat, dashed from his desk and ran through town and hedge and forest down to dip his ink-pen in the bloody fields of Europe, in casks of gore sent back from St. Domingue; and cupping his hand beneath the dripping tip the way at that moment I held the head of my child, he scampered across the Atlantic to the shores of America before the blood had even dried; and there he waded to a beach and touched his pen-tip to the sand and everything was changed.

This is my vision of the purchase of Louisiana, which came into being the same day as my child, which I wouldn't know till morning was a boy, for Red Kate was silent until dawn and I would ask nothing of her that night but that she breathe and her heart beat and that the child do the same.

But in that span whole flocks of little men with pens were poised that instant to sign papers and sell a country, their pens daubed with the fresher blood from St. Domingue. And these men were so pleased and filled with their success that they were already hosting balls and banquets to celebrate their great feat of policy. They leaned out of their chairs, toasting, and each and every one felt a tightness in his back like a rash or boils; and their shoulders festered and swole up with sores and they hid them in their fine clothes, and when the sores began weeping they stuffed their shirts with documents to sop the pus, but still the sores grew to great size and profusion. When at last the boils burst, out of them poured clouds of mosquitoes which went in circling swarms about the diplomats' heads like pestilent crowns until they were chased away with candles waved by wives and consorts. The mosquitoes escaped through nearby windows, from which hung the triumphant spangled banner, through cracks in doors, through knotholes in the floorboards and out into the world, churning in a great cloud before the moon, then to the South and West, where they sucked deep at everyone they met. And in this way the contagion of the Purchase was spread.

We learned of it some weeks later, from Reuben, who heard it in Natchez. But I knew it already. There were many questions, uncertainties, alarms over the particulars of the sale. I had none; the boundaries of nations shifted and I read them in the soft pate of my son's skull as I sat with Kate while she nursed him. Here are America, Louisiana, West Florida—holding form only by the most tenuous coverings and connections. In time the soft will harden, demarcations fade, and all will be as God intended: One.

III

Judgments and Offerings

West Florida–New Orleans, July 1803–January 1804

Wicked Men

Senator John Smith stepped down from his barge onto the bank, attended by a retinue of slaves and their masters. He was a tall man, and his hair was whitened and swept back from a high forehead perhaps shielding—I judged—the remembrances of his own preaching days, before he became a man of business and a function of government. I watched his ascent with Reuben and Samuel, the elder brother pointing from our porch hissing, There he is, the bastard.

That morning had brought a gathering of putrid haughtery to the Bayou Sara landing. Pintado and Ira Kneeland, along with Alexander Stirling—who batted a handkerchief at his nose as though to ward off the lingering smell of the spilt bowels and emptied lives of his sold-off niggers—and others of the Feliciana planting class, stood there await-ing Smith while slaves waved frond fans at them. When at last the Senator arrived, they hurrahed and welcomed him, then had their blacks unload his trunks onto a carriage-back, accompanying him as he waved off the carriage and strode towards our house.

We'd learned a week before from the network of Reuben's debts and friendships—Edward Randolph from Clark, Clark from his deal-ings with the newly invested Governor Claiborne of the Territory of Orleans—that John Smith was elected a senator of the Territory of the Ohio, flush with federal money, and that now with the American sei-zure of Louisiana imminent and the fate of our Louisiana-bordering corner of West Florida uncertain, he was desirous to come and settle his affairs and buy off more land.

Reuben took this news the same way he'd taken Pintado's final request for him to appoint arbiters, which he refused. The result of his stubbornness was that in May Smith's tribunal, stocked with his bedfellows like Kneeland and Stirling, came and spent a week going over our ledgers, taking account of the holdings and comparing them to books sent by Smith from Cincinnati; Kneeland waved the old contracts at Reuben while Stirling, in his brogue, mumbled numbers. They grew stooped from being so long hunched over the accounts; and they had to bring their own tea and kettle to boil on the stove because none of us would give them a thing. The widow Cobb tried to bring them out a plate of food a time or two, setting plate and fork before Ira Kneeland, who eyed her with his gentlemanly acceptance of being served, until Samuel ran her out.

Each day Reuben would go to sit in the store and silently watch them. Sometimes Samuel or Ransom joined, but neither could keep up the vigil like the elder brother, who sat for hours in his chair like a colossal impediment to their aims. Myself, I was content to spend those days occupied with my wife and son, who we named Samuel

Aaron Kemper—Samuel for my brother, who'd brought me there; Aaron for Red Kate's Indian-slain father; and the Kemper name because I'd put mine long behind me, taken the oath of citizenship as a Kemper. Woolsack stank of death and the fanatic devotions of my father. Let the boy have a start without that awful heritage.

Red Kate had tried for weeks to have him christened by a priest, Father Burke, who came to our store one day while she was pregnant, asking credit which I intended to refuse him for his popery, but my heart was softened by my wife's insistence that we help this man of God who'd been run out of the stores across the river in Pointe Coupee. In return for my kindness, Father Burke tried to reawaken her Catholicism, murmuring blessings and always asking if she'd name the child for this or that blessed saint, and that after our son was born he'd be happy to preside over his christening. I wouldn't have it. My son's name would not go down in the records of their wretched parishes, added to the butcher's bill of souls sold to Rome. My Copperhead was insistent, though, and I had to put it to her same as I would to Elise many years later, that if she wished to burn in Hell with all the other papists, that was her business, but my child wouldn't be among them.

That's a wicked thing to say of me, Kate said, almost in tears. A bastard mean thing.

Would you rather I smiled like a fool while you consigned our son to damnation?

It's not just that, she said. You believe I'm for Hell and you don't care a nit.

No, I said. I've saved you from it, so long as you stay away from the popelings.

That's not what matters.

If you were in Hell I'd go down and bring you up.

Red Kate sighed and went from me to tend the pan in the fire, which hissed and spit like the bile between us. The flames held her in their glow and I could see damnation there before her face. She said, You talk like you already have.

That's right, I said.

Then don't talk to me like I've got horns and a forked tail, said my wife; and the matter was left at that, though it cropped up now and again in our growing shortness with one another, in the cries of the child when it wasn't at her breast, in the way she never seemed to notice the smell when he fouled himself. And it went that if the boy was in the bedroom and let out one of his wails for milk and mother, I'd see the eyes soak into the front of Red Kate's dress the same as they had all too soon with Emily. So I let Reuben and Samuel deal with the alcaldes and tried to be a father, in the time of infant life when fathers are unnecessary.

When the alcaldes declared an eight-thousand-peso discrepancy in Smith's favor, Reuben told them to both go to hell, howling that he'd take the matter to the commandant in Baton Rouge, to Governor Folch in Pensacola, and all the way to the damned king in Madrid. The recourse of Puke law allowed for such things, and he did them all. I remember his furious nights spent scribbling the letters, and how, upon receiving each reply, he damned each one in turn, from clerk to king. The judgment was made at Baton Rouge by Commandant Grand Pré, the debts set and money bound to be paid.

So Senator Smith, in rosy silk waistcoat, came to the porch like he expected to be welcomed with cheers. When he stopped before the first step, his followers stopped also and stayed back but within earshot. I noticed now how Smith's hair was powdered and worn curled at the sides. He was the image of the affable country parson, only clothed so well that you knew he had more to him than the Lord's work. A specu- lator, a money-grubber, the Senator—and Reuben along with him— was a fool to have thought that a store in the wilderness might make any fortune. But then again, it was said—by Randolph, Clark, and the others—that Smith's designs were on grander things: to continue acquiring land in West Florida and await the inevitable American tide, then parse the holdings out and when the speculators drove prices to a worthy height, sell it all and roll in cash. The Senator presently produced a writ, signed by Grand Pré and ordering Reuben and all of us to vacate and render the property, not only the store and house but Reuben's three hundred acres of timber land, to Smith as payment in part.

Reuben came down the steps and took the paper from him.

I know, said the Senator, that you don't have the money. So it's only fair that I'm awarded this and the passel to the north.

Is that what it says? Samuel tried to grab the writ from Reuben, but the elder brother snatched it away and read it over and again.

The commandant can't order me to pay anything more than two hundred pesos, he said.

That's the law.

Laws change, said Smith, placing a hand in the pocket of his coat with the air of a man out for a stroll and happening upon a friend.

They change for the lawmakers, Reuben said, then balled the writ up and threw it to the ground. Pintado stepped forward, hand on the hilt of his sword. I leaned against the railing and saw Kneeland grinning his crooked teeth at me.

I've written the governor, written to the damned king! Reuben said.

I'm quite sure, ventured Pintado, that they will both agree with the commandant's justice.

We'll see about that, said Reuben.

Smith took the first step so that he stood now at Reuben's collar. My brother brought up his hands and I thought for a moment he'd smash the Senator's skull, but he only set them on his hips.

Reuben, said the Senator, I want you to know that none of this is false dealing. I've only ever been straight with you. I hired you when you were nothing more than a mechanic. The store was simply a poor venture. An experiment—though maybe poorly executed or poorly kept.

I kept it, he said.

I'm not here to lay blame or pass judgment. That's the purview of the Lord and Him alone. We signed an agreement.

We changed it too.

And you stand in forfeiture of both, said Smith, his patience waning and his soft parson's voice cracking a bit. It's as you agreed: half the cost of shipping down from Cincinnati, half the cost of the goods, and the mortgage on the land. I don't intend to ruin you, he said.

You damn well have, said Reuben.

It's your own fault, Smith said. You neglected my affairs, gave away more goods than I can tell, did God knows what with the money from what few goods you did sell. I am the one who took the risk, paid for everything, so it is also my fault to an extent, for putting so much trust in you. We must all bear our share of culpability, in this world or the next.

I may let you find out just what the next one's like, said Reuben, quaking with rage at the foot of the steps, a giant tied down with spider's webs.

Senator! called a man from the crowd of followers. You'll be late for your own party, sir!

Smith gave them a wave of his hand, saying he'd be not a moment longer. Then he bent and picked the crumpled writ up from the ground and unfolded it, thumbing the red seal of Spain, and handed it to Reuben, saying, You have eight months to vacate.

The afternoon brought a rain that quickly turned to flood. As Smith's party started off onto the road through St. Francisville the first drops were falling and Reuben looked to the approaching clouds and said, I hope it drowns the lot.

When we came inside, going to the table to sit, the widow Cobb and Red Kate gave us one look and retreated to the back room.

He's bribed them all, said Reuben. All the Puke officials are in his pocket.

I looked at this enormous man, now leaning his full bulk against the table in dejection while his brother sat beside him like a terrier and nodded along with his words. And what Reuben said might have been true, but with Reuben it always seemed more that he was making speeches for himself.

And what are we to do? I said. I've got a wife and child to care for. I've got my parcel and it's not in this judgment. Should I go there and start splitting logs for a cabin in the God-damned woods?

Calm yourself, said Reuben. We're not had yet.

We aren't? I said. Won't we be run out of here in eight months because you were too damn stubborn and I was too stupid not to call you on it?

Everything you have, everything you both have, is because of my stubbornness.

Then tell me what we're to do. Wait?

Reuben sat upright and glowered at me. You'd be running niggers and whiskey for that Reverend, or be dead, if it weren't for me.

Fine enough. What are we going to do besides let you worry about it?

The rain was coming hard and we turned at the sound of yipping and clattering up the steps. The voices belonged to Ransom and Ferdinand, who danced about outside to try and stamp the soak from their clothes.

Now, he said. I will explain it to you again. They've made their own noose with the eight months. Louisiana will be American and I have it on good authority that the government will honor no Spanish judgments.

Even when the man you owe money to is a senator in the blasted American government?

Then we'll fight him again and it'll take another three years.

This is too much intrigue, I said. I can't cipher any of it.

Reuben clapped the table. If we hold here and now until the flag flies over the whole territory, then the price of the land will double, triple even, and we sell everything we have except the house and landing ground.

We just have to hold out, Samuel said to me.

It's all for nothing, I said.

Ransom and Ferdinand came into the house, laughing and sopping and shaking off like dogs. They eyed us, then went and stood before the fire. The river's rising up, said Ferdinand.

Did you mind the boat? Reuben said.

She's fine, said his slave. It gets any worsen I'll ride it out on her.

What's the trouble? Ransom asked, wringing out his pants-leg.

The kind we just have to wait on and it's fixed, I said.

Reuben gave the table another thwack. Don't you doubt me, he said. I won't have it.

Go and kill the bastards then, I said. Hell, I'll help you.

I just might, he said, laughing, sounding now as he had when he'd told us that the foreskins legend was false. But it's not time for that yet. If we hold and make them act, what Americans will help them drive us out? They won't follow Britishers like Stirling or a rich bastard like Kneeland to run off one of their own countrymen.

I think you've got too much faith in Americans, I said.

Reuben frowned. And I think you haven't got enough.

With that I left them and went out onto the porch, where Ferdinand and Ransom had brought the horses, which now stood snorting at one corner; and the wind was bearing down upon the river and driving the water over its banks. I watched the Cotton-Picker rise with the flood and in my time out there alone the water swallowed up Red Kate's truck-patch and drowned the first steps. I leaned over the railing, letting my head be battered and soaked, and saw the water was at the two-foot mark on the pilings. The door opened and Samuel stepped outside.

This is our land, he said. Ours. And there's nothing more than that. Let them come and try to take it.

And if they do? I said.

They have the militia. Thirty soldiers, maybe, in Baton Rouge. We could beat them all.

And what about Red Kate and the boy?

We can get them to Randolph's across the line before any trouble starts.

You're really praying on this, I said. And now, damn it, so am I.

Samuel spoke low and his words were almost lost in the roar of wind and water and the drumming of the rain. Pistols out again, powder-smoke—I can't help that I see it in our future.

That night I talked with Red Kate about leaving. She was holding our son over her shoulder, patting his small back to a rhythm she hummed deep in her chest. I never had a home that wasn't burnt down or a whorehouse, she said. I won't let you abandon this one. Her eyes grew bright in the lamplight and she held so tight to our son that he mewled. She continued: If you have to fight, then do it. By God I won't be put out to the wilds and whims again.

The rain had slackened by dark and when it stopped the water stood at the height of the pilings and could be seen sloshing through the knotholes in the floorboards. Waves came over the porch and by morning the damp was all about the house. Crawfish found their way beneath our bed and there was a constant scuttle of creatures seeking shelter in dark nooks and corners. Next day the sun shone clear and bright upon the flooded land, and Reuben and Ferdinand had to wade out to the Cotton-Picker to moor it at the porch.

This water'll stand for a month, Reuben said. There'll be a plague.

I said, You tell me on one hand to stay and the other to run from a fever.

No, he said. There's nowhere. The cities are worse, most likely. If you can get inland to Pinckneyville, stay there with Randolph till the sickness subsides.

We'll see, I said.

And there would be a sickness on the land. In the coming days news was brought by pirogue, word of who was ailing and who'd already given up the ghost. Red Kate and the widow Cobb burnt camphor on the porch and all about the house, boiled everything, went around jabbing red-hot fire-irons into tubs of vinegar, sticking their fingers in to judge its sourness gone—purifying the air; they scattered ground wormwood, burnt pots of tar on the windowsills. The house's smell was a bizarre and constant assault, and I went through those days with an aching head, stench-to-stench, but none of us took ill.

One morning the corpse of a nigger floated by and became caught in the pilings of the store. Ransom and I had to swim out to get him loose so that he wouldn't stay there and spread contagion; and when we came through the swirl to the bedraggled corpse and pulled it free, the thing rolled belly-up and burst. We thrashed through our own vomit back to the porch-steps and hacked while the corpse sailed off into the bayou channel and soon passed out of sight. The women wouldn't have us in the house until we'd spent a night out there on the porch bathing from pots of scalding water they brought. But we remained free of fever and in two weeks the water was low enough that when Samuel and Reuben returned they had only to slosh through it at their knees. They'd talked with Clark in New Orleans, where the fever was rampant and bodies were being burnt in great piles, and he'd told them that the handover would commence in November, less than four months away. So Reuben was once again flush with possibilities.

Who would've thought, he said, that a French despot would bully the Spanish into giving them ownership of the land, keep the Spanish on it, governing it like tenant farmers, and then sell it right off to the States. What a world.

But there were already rumblings that the Pukes would hold the West Florida territory, and that our atheist president would do nothing but sit on his hands and wait for them to give in. Also that General Wilkinson, commander of the American army, was poised to invade and take the land by force should Spain not give her up along with the rest of the Purchase. There were so many rumors in those days I couldn't keep them straight. When the water had entirely receded and the land now appeared balded and riven as a lake-bed, Pintado and the alcaldes would ride by, harassing us with writs and claims; and so we began going about well-armed.

Don't be foolish, said Kneeland one day. Fools come to fools' ends.

And the work of fools was many and varied in that country. For there was the night that Basil Abrams, on a drunk, beat his wife near to death at their place on the outskirts of St. Francisville. He came thundering to our house on his horse, rousing all of us with the beast's stamping and his shouts of consternation. We came outside and saw Abrams leap down from the horse, only to be cracked across the skull with a musket-butt by Ransom O'Neil, who'd taken him for a Puke rider come to ambush us. Abrams lay prone in the yard and Reuben said, God shit, Ransom. He went down to tend the man and we followed.

You might've killed him, said Samuel.

Serves him right, riding up like that, Ransom said, panting and still holding the musket.

At least you didn't shoot him, I said.

O, said Ransom. If it was light and I could've had a mark—

Shut up, all of you, Reuben said, lifting Abrams like a rag and bringing him into the house, where he was laid out across the settee and his wound wiped with rags by the widow and Kate. We all watched him for a while, hearing the horse still tearing circles outside.

Of a sudden Basil Abrams awoke with blood in his eyes and bolted up, saying, I killed her. God help me I think I killed her.

Reuben took him by the collar and demanded to know who.

Abrams' head lolled and the cut across his forehead began to bleed freely so that he had to blink. With my own hands, he said, holding them up; and we saw his knuckles were well-split.

Who? God damn it! shouted Samuel, who'd by then also taken a-hold of the babbling Abrams.

Lily, he said, eyes fixed on the widow and Kate as though they were a double vision of the one he'd struck down. My poor wife, he groaned, then crumpled again, and the brothers let him collapse and turned to me.

He's killed his fucking wife, I said.

Samuel and Reuben's eyes were alight.

Should we ride out and check? said Ransom. To be sure?

Abrams, laid out, moaned and mumbled something about love and women.

No, said Reuben. Basil wandered in here, drunk and wild, and passed out. That's all we know, you follow?

Before Reuben's words had time to sink in, there came the sound of more horses riding up. I was first outside and saw Kneeland and Senator Smith dismounting. Kneeland was hastily dressed, but the parson-politician was in full riding kit, having eagerly accompanied the alcalde on this official errand of territorial justice, to see the puny and sordid workings of the province of which he was a pretend-citizen. It was near dawn and both looked haggard and their horses were frothed. Abrams' beast, wandering loose, was popping its head to the side of Kneeland's; he bent to check its haunch, saying, Yes, that's the man's brand.

Then he's here, said the Senator, excitement in his voice for a minor adventure to tell at table in the capital.

Kneeland shoved away from the horse. Do you have Basil Abrams in your house?

From behind me Reuben answered that we did.

Then, sir, let's have him out!

What's the trouble? I said.

He has assaulted his wife, said Smith. To a vicious extent.

She hovers near death in my parlor even as we speak, said Kneeland. Let's have the wretch!

Reuben pushed me aside and went down the steps to meet them.

Samuel said into my ear, We may just have it out here and now.

The man rode up here drunk, surprised our boy, and was knocked quite bad across the head.

Then he won't be difficult to take, said Kneeland, starting for the steps.

Reuben took him by the arm and hauled him back. This is my house, surveyor, and until the commandant's writ is up, you've got no right to be on my property.

Reuben, said the Senator, be sensible. The woman is beaten to a pulp.

Kneeland whirled loose of Reuben's hand, saying, She came crawling to my doorstep, eyes black, lips smashed, all manner of gore about her. My daughter is fighting to keep her in this world so that she may depose the villain you say you will keep in your house!

The villain is unconscious, said Reuben. And he's said nothing of doing her any injury. And did she tell you that he did it, with her busted lips and blackened eyes?

You, sir, are a cad and friend to worse. To defend such a man—

Reuben, said Smith, you know I won't allow the man to be harmed. We simply don't want him to flee the country before there's justice done.

You've got no power here, said Reuben. Save your spit for Washington. And you, Mister Kneeland, can hie your way back home and make a complaint to Pintado.

Kneeland stamped his boot and tugged at the front of his nightshirt. His voice broke into a high whine when he spoke: I did not, sir, watch my wife suffer and die of fever this very month just to have a man who savages his own wife go unpunished!

Stay calm, Ira, said Smith.

I shall not be calm while a brute like that—

In that instant I stopped him with the only words I'd speak to the alcalde that night, saying, If he awakes and tells what he did, I'll personally lash him for it.

My brothers turned and looked at me cockeyed, shrugging while the two others shook their heads. Both pairs shirked my words and went back to their stand-off.

And I should trust any of you with justice? said Kneeland. Wild savages yourselves: coarse, illiterate—

Reuben took him by the throat and raised Kneeland's feet up off the ground, saying, I can go inside and pick out a volume of Gibbon and break your skull with the spine of it. He cast the surveyor to the ground and Smith quickly stepped between them.

I should not want to add another assault to the night's tally, the Senator said.

You may add a bloody murder if you like and this dog keeps flapping his trap.

Give me a reason, Kneeland said, to bring the militia upon you all.

Smith turned to his friend and patted him on the chest. Ira, this is fruitless. Then, turning back to Reuben, he said, We shall return for him in the morning. And once they were both saddled again: Reuben, you are no wicked man.

The hell he isn't, said Kneeland.

In an instant Samuel leapt from the porch and made for the surveyor with his hands. But his brother caught him up and held him back until they left, with Smith giving his parting parson's words with a jangle of kit and livery: I do pray that you will consider your way.

Reuben was silent but Samuel hollered after them, Consider your fuck-lording way, you bastard!

Back inside, standing over the unconscious Abrams, I said to Reuben, Why didn't we just give him to them?

He's a friend, said Reuben. And there are points to be made.

Points? I said.

They have no right to come here and trouble me, he said. I had to show them.

I waved him off and was going to find a drink of gin when Basil Abrams sat up, the blood upon his face and head now dried into a swath from which his wild eyes peered out.

In the woods, he said, I saw a spider big as a man.

With that his eyes rolled up in his head and he collapsed back to the cushions, and stayed that way until, in the late morning, I hauled him out, tied his hands to the front porch timbers, and thrashed him across the back fifteen times with a whip. I shouted at Abrams for how many times he'd hit his wife, but the man babbled that he couldn't remember. So I made my own account of things and when I'd finished and Abrams, now fully sobered and bearing a hatch of wide cuts across his back, was weeping on his knees, I untied him and said, Last night Sam and Reuben saved you from the rope, but not a man alive can stay God's hand. You go and show the alcaldes these scars and tell them you have paid.

His screams had woke the whole house, and now my brothers and the women were crowding the doorway. And it was that Basil Abrams' answer, breathless with pain and exhaustion, was a strange one.

My friend, said Abrams, stumbling to stay on his feet. All my good and dearest friends—I only hope my Lily's alive.

I stood there in disgust, gathering the whip into a bloody coil, and understood what it meant to prove a point, when the theater of its provation was meaningless and nothing mattered but making others see how fiercely you believed. It reminded me of preaching, of being a man of God. All fault, all sin, the infinite wrongs of the world, could be twisted into proving the Lord's plan. And didn't they?

Later, after he'd ridden off with blood soaking into the back of his shirt, Basil Abrams would go to the house of Kneeland and find his wife alive. It went that she would testify no charges against him, much to the anger of the alcaldes. So Abrams only had to pay a fine for disturbance of the peace, a fact which he reported to us the following week, when he stopped by our house with his wife, to buy for her one of the disused mirrors gathering dust in the store.

I want her to know that she's still beautiful to me, he said.

Lily Abrams sat in their cart. Her bandaged face shifted a bit when he spoke, and the eyes that stared out were pale and sullen. Ransom came with a bone comb he'd brought from the store and handed it to her. She mumbled him thanks.

You should've killed him, said Red Kate to me that evening.

And that was all she said to me until the night, a month later, my boy spoke his first word and she saw the enormous spider crouching by the trees near our house. She dropped the pot she'd been emptying in the yard and came scrambling inside, shakily confirming the existence of the thing. She told me to go outside and look; and I did, with Samuel and Reuben, but found nothing. Back inside, I found her over our son, who was laying in his cradle by the table, and as though to comfort herself for the terrible sight, she'd begun talking to him—a steady stream of words, the names for everything in the house; and he commenced to gurgle but the noises coming from him changed and he looked at her and gabbled, MaMaMaMa. And my wife's eyes filled with tears as the boy sputtered out the word for her over and again.

She plucked him up and I raced for them both and took them close, the boy still jabbering and she now sobbing with delight.

So soon to talk, she said, shaking her head at the miracle. He's brilliant.

And he was, with his wisp of curled towy-red hair and in his swaddling dress, repeating again and again his word for *Mother* and what would become his word for everything else. I held them, and it was at such times very easy to forget the troubles of the world, and to want to keep the land where such wonders came into being.

Smith departed before the end of August, going to take his seat in Washington with a send-off by the planters the same as when he'd arrived. We watched him from the porch, sitting on the top step this time with shotguns in our laps. And the Senator looked back as he boarded, thankful, I believe, to be out of the country that harbored such people as us. I'd come to like the thought of fighting, of standing the bastards off—this feeling being steeled in me as much by my wife's constant admonishments and the brothers' growing boldness as by the insults and glares of the alcaldes, who were at the dock, glancing back at us now and again.

The crowd dispersed when Smith had floated off, and the alcaldes made a file going by our porch. Most went on, but Pintado and Kneeland trickled to a stop at the steps.

I do not like the way you seem to be turning, said Pintado. Go and set yourself on your land to the north, he said. Build yourselves a place there. I would personally guarantee you good workers if you would commence such a project.

No, said Reuben. I believe we like it here.

The corners of both brothers' mouths cracked into smiles, the stocks of their shotguns sounding a low *chock chock* as they nudged each other.

It doesn't matter, said Kneeland, savoring the words in his drawl. Come February you will all be gone, plucked like ticks from a hound's back.

Sharpen up your nails, nabob, I said. We'll be hard to pick. And we may just kick the bitch herself to death before we're through.

The Snares of Government

Reuben left aboard the Cotton-Picker in early November, first for Natchez and Aliza, then New Orleans, bringing with him Samuel, who'd taken melancholy since the night a few weeks before when Ezmina sent him home without satisfaction. Over the course of the succeeding nights she persisted in her denial of his love and barred him from her favors and her place with but the barest explanation.

She said she needs time to rectify her life, Samuel had said to me one morning, returning from another blighted attempt. His eyes were full of sleep and he'd thinned riding so much and eating so little.

I made my own rides those days, with Ransom out to my land on Thompson's Creek, hewing logs and clearing a patch for a cabin. We had four months ahead before our eviction date, and I'd decided to be prepared regardless of what Reuben or anyone said. The ticks might be pried from one spot, but they'd have another place to sink their teeth into. Though the work was slow, in the cool air of late fall it seemed no awful toil. And to raise a house by skeletal frame and lay it with timbers high above the ground was a fine thing when all my life I'd known roofs and homes only by charity.

By the time the brothers departed for New Orleans to pay off debts, we had the foundation laid and the lumber cut to boards and lengths. My son was crawling now, and when I'd return from my work and take him up he'd brush the sawdust from my face and gather it in bunches in his small fists and clap it into clouds, giggling. At such times Red Kate would come by and kiss the patches he'd cleaned from my cheek and smile to us both.

We'll be fine, I'd say, telling her of the house and its future.

As long as both my men are in it, she'd reply.

Christmas neared and the house was quiet, with none of the tumult of the past year, but the three of us, like a small fire in a great lamp, lighting the place with our own good blaze. Ransom, for his part, went up Bayou Gonorrhea for comfort on occasion with the inheritors of the legendary Sara, picking up a bad case of the blue buboes from the home-girls there so that Red Kate had to prepare a makeshift syringe and break a pair of thermometers in the store for their mercury to fill it and for me to inject into a squirming Ransom while she sat by with our son and told to him the words *disease, clap, quicksilver,* and *syringe.* Poor Ransom howled and suffered and claimed for days that there'd been broken glass in the tincture. But he was healed and we were soon back to work at my tract, joined sometimes by Abrams and Arthur Cobb.

We boiled sap for tarring and made our days good as winter came on. And looking out upon the cabin slowly gaining form, I was visited by the memory of the pilgrims and their toil to carve out their camp in the bitter prairie cold. I would tell Kate about it, and she said mine was a poor premonition. Still we brought the beams up and the bones of the cabin rose day by day.

Each week brought belated news from Samuel and Reuben in New Orleans, where the handover of the Louisiana Territory was commencing. In our slow and quiet part of the world, I read over their letters and imagined the city. Reuben noted Samuel's sadness didn't break, even with the whores of The Church, nor with the fine ones of New Orleans. He said they went one night to a circus, put on by the Pukes to commemorate their departure from the city, in which a bull was made to fight a pack of dogs, the surviving dogs fought a black bear, the bear then fought a tiger imported from Bengali, and the tiger, torn and bleeding, fought the strongest bull in the land. Reuben told that the tiger brought the bull down and lay exhausted in the ring, whereupon several men came out with fireworks and strapped them to the creature's back and lit them, to the cheers and laughter of the crowd. The beast roared and ran in circles trailing wailing hissing sparks, cast itself against the embankments of the ring, sending plumes of fiery color into the watchers until Samuel leapt the railing and, with the flaming tiger charging towards him, shot the monster down with his pistol. The beast lay at his feet, still throwing off sparks and whistles, and, so Reuben said, the crowd poured into the ring, lifted Samuel up, and carried him out into the street, where a military band played the anthem of the Spanish Crown and they wouldn't let him down for some hours. Samuel had dropped his pistol in the tumult and once he was on his feet and being sloshed by all the offered cups of wine and rum and whiskey, a child appeared with the pistol wrapped in a cloth and knelt to present it to the man now being hailed in jabbering Puke and French as *el tigre decampo* or *le tigre sauvage*. They wanted to cast the pistol in bronze, but Samuel dissuaded them, taking instead a gift of the tiger's biggest teeth on a thread of silver, which he wore about his neck when they returned to Bayou Sara and rattled often for my son.

Before they returned, however, the brothers were caught up in the gears of government. The French representatives, eager to ply their Spanish tenants, had arrived before the American representatives, and as the brothers sat one day in a coffeehouse Daniel Clark stirred them with the worries of President Jefferson: that the niggers and locals might rise up in rebellion; horrors like those perpetrated by what the president called the cannibals of the terrible republic— St. Domingue—and that the only proper thing was to form a force of

American guards who'd oversee the handover and keep the locals and their chattel in line.

Reuben said he wished I could have been there to see the sight of them as they left the shipyard and went tavern by tavern, gathering up nearly five hundred countrymen to stand and face the royally attired Puke soldiers in what was then known as the Place des Armes and would later be General Jackson's Square. The American guard wore black cloaks and black ribbon upon their hats and tied to the stocks of their muskets. Black so that the French, the Pukes, the niggers, and all the people of the city might know that—while they'd soon be under the red, white, and blue—the men who stood watch were beholden to the black flag of no quarter, no yield.

With the winter-withered bushes of the garden between them, the Americans stayed in their line for two weeks, staring down the Pukes and the smattering of French soldiers accompanying their consul. They ate standing, passed standing, slept for minutes, all on their feet. In that time an impression was made upon the people of New Orleans, so my brothers said; and it must've been that these were madmen, and of furious endurance. Claiborne finally came and greeted Reuben and his men warmly, saying that with such sons here present, the United States were sure to hold the country in good stead. And on the twentieth of December, when the ceremony of the handover was finished and a pole brought up and sunk and a flag raised upon it, even then the American guard stayed watch, on through the revelry and balls that followed in commemoration of the New Year and the new country.

Samuel stayed mostly with the men and Reuben followed after Clark and Claiborne, who in one letter was a fine man of principle and hatred for the Pukes—assuring Reuben that the president did in fact claim West Florida in what he termed an *interesting transaction* to soon be played out—but in the next was a coward and a fool, a stripling whelp for the atheist in Washington. What happened was that a few weeks after the American possession Claiborne confessed that the States' claim to the Floridas was to be one in word alone. Evidently they were content to hold the Orleans and all the rest of the country, but they bowed to Spain for now on her holdings from Feliciana to the coast. Reuben felt hollow of the business, he said, betrayed by the weakness of the inheritors.

What would you have a man in my position do? Reuben asked the newly invested Governor Claiborne after a ball that had set itself apart from the others by the fight which had broken out over which dances—American, French, or Spanish—would take precedence.

Governor Claiborne had seemed exhausted, almost as much as Reuben was those days. He was accompanied by the bloated authority of General Wilkinson, who even then Reuben knew to be a bastard. They were of the same age, so far as Reuben could tell, and both shared Virginia as their birthplace but had been away for so long that it seemed a hazy memory of childhood. When Reuben pressed him with his question, the new governor leaned over his tankard and said, I would have you wait, sir. Wait on the grace of our government.

But it's not my government yet, said Reuben.

It will be, the governor responded.

But when? Reuben demanded.

At that moment, a man ordered a round for all present, so long as they'd drink to the damnation of Thomas Jefferson. The glasses were already in hand, and Reuben said many were raised happily at the words, but many more were sent flying at the toaster and the place exploded into a row. He believed he was struck by a pewter cup in the back of the head, awakening on his knees to see the man who'd made the toast being held down and Claiborne raising his ceremonial saber up, and striking the man across the face with the broad side. General Wilkinson, who was there also, approved the action with a nod of several chins.

Reuben had gained his feet when Samuel and some members of the guard appeared, thinking the fight was still on and intent upon suppressing it. Instead Samuel brought his brother to their hotel, where he lay feverish and wasting for a week, his delirium only stirred by the chambermaids who came to wipe his brow and change the sopping sheets. And what followed in those days he wouldn't put in a letter, but told me when they returned, giving it like one of Christ's visions: the door opening one morning and in lumbering the figure of General Wilkinson, his regalia clattering like a tinker's cart. The general took a chair and sat himself at Reuben's bedside, overlooking him like a bosom friend.

I've heard your troubles, said the general.

And when Reuben cleared his throat to speak, Wilkinson raised a swollen hand and said, No words. It's not a conspiracy if one man talks and the other only listens, eh? Now, there is a natural principle of decay inherent in man and all his works. The Spanish government of West Florida is in such a state, and you would like it if they came to their final corruption, would you not?

The general produced a cigar and lit it. Naturally you would, he said. Who wouldn't? I'm afraid the officers of King Carlos serve to give heart-burnings and stomach-aches to many a man in their territory. But I'll have you know that there are men now in our government who would see West Florida taken this very day. . . . Were you ever in the profession of arms? I suppose you were too young for our war.

My father was at Valley Forge, Reuben said.

Not under Colonel Burr? Wilkinson said.

No, said Reuben. Captain Marshall.

Ah, said the general. I can't say I know the man, but there were many of us in those days. . . . Now, as I was saying, with the proper guarantees of internal support, we could depose the Spaniards easily.

Reuben asked him what he meant by *internal support* and Wilkinson hoisted his sword-belt about his belly, saying, A show of will by the inhabitants of the country. A popular effort which would perhaps drive the Spaniards to rash action near the border. If that were to happen, my job would be made quite easy. With an imminent threat to the border, I would be fully justified in sending in a force of men—and if the outcome of such an event was that we gained the province, then that's the way the biscuit breaks, is it not?

He answered Wilkinson with a foggy-headed nod.

I'm at liberty to give no names as yet, but we are supported by a man in the highest offices of government, and within the season he will come down here with his own force, if conditions are favorable, and our armies shall meet and sweep the Spanish out from here through the Pacific. Again, no need for words. We've formed no junto or cabal. I will only await yours and the actions of your countrymen as a signal.

Reuben, stunned, lay in his bed for a time after the visitation of the general, drifting in and out of sleep but now filled with mounting energy. And it was late in the afternoon that Samuel and Clark appeared, bringing with them Governor Claiborne, who gave Reuben his wishes for a speedy recovery and, after much badgering by Clark, the following assurance:

If there were to be any trouble in West Florida, he said, we would not be disposed to look unfavorably upon it. There could, of course, be no physical support, and I must deny all knowledge and pleasure at any such incident—but know that the wings of the American eagle would take you to her bosom.

With that the governor was off to more pressing duties, leaving Reuben and Samuel now filled with the same sense of urgency. What words my brothers exchanged I don't know, but I imagine them shattering the room with excitement. They would be in New Orleans another week, leaving once the Spanish commander finally quit his post and Reuben was able to walk.

The Spider

I was out most days at the cabin-site, which was becoming a regular homestead. We broke stone from the hillocks overlooking Thompson's Creek and made mortar and a fireplace in a single day, just Ransom O'Neil and me. And it was that we were out one afternoon cutting clapboards for the roof when Ransom let out a scream, and I looked and saw the enormous spider at the tree-line, its dark fur and crouching aspect. Our rifles leaned against a pile of saw-off and I ran for them, only to hear the spider cry out, My God, Angel!

Hearing this creature say my name, I judged it was a demon sent to drag me down to Hell, and I grabbed at my gun and Ransom was soon behind, taking his up, and the spider was now shambling out of the low branches, still talking.

Don't shoot, Angel! It's Johnny! Johnny Crabbe!

I knocked Ransom's barrel aside and he fired into the air, Crabbe falling flat to the ground mid-way between us and the cabin.

What the hell for? said Ransom, trying to grab my gun from me. It's the God-damned monster!

No, I said, wrestling him for the piece, which I finally tugged free. That monster's a friend of mine.

Crabbe raised a claw out from under his matted furs and waved.

Dear sweet Jesus, Mary, and Joseph, Ransom said.

I approached Crabbe and he rushed to me, hugging me in a grip of claw about the legs.

He said, I don't know how long I've been running. O, Lord. Since they came upon us. It was awful.

I shook loose of his claws and squatted down to eye him. Crabbe, I said. You've been out here for more than a year?

Johnny Crabbe's red face had grown pale from lack of sun, from months of skulking in the woods, and I saw now that his fur was a cloak of black cow's skin.

I took it off a dead one a while back, he said. Had to use a rock to cut it. Crabbe shuffled loosely in his skin. I don't believe it fits too well.

Where's the Reverend? I said.

I don't know. I ran off when you said, but I watched it all happen. They didn't take the Reverend, though. I heard the soldiers cuss that.

Whatever joy I might have had at seeing Crabbe again was quickly devoured by the knowledge that the Reverend Morrel still walked the earth.

Are you mad? Ransom hollered.

Come on over, I called back, and see.

Ransom warily approached and Crabbe stuck out his head, saying, See, I'm no monster.

The hell you aren't, said Ransom, stumbling back.

Watch your mouth, I said. I know this man.

You call that a man?

I call him Crabbe and that's good enough, I said. You hungry, Johnny?

Yes, he said, and cold. Cold as shit.

Then let's go home, I said. And we went, Ransom riding up ahead and Crabbe clinging to the saddle of my horse while I led it by the reins. I felt full of the spirit, like what I did was a Christly deed. Crabbe asked me if I still was preaching, and when I told him no he said that sure was sorrowful news.

At the house I left Ransom with Crabbe in the yard and went inside first to prepare my wife for the sight of him.

You've brought the spider home? she said.

He's who everybody thought was a spider, I said.

Red Kate felt for a chair and fell into it. She gaped at me as though I were insane.

I knew him when we were with Morrel. I told you about him.

You told me about plenty of his creatures, but—

He's been hiding in the country like a dog.

Like a spider, she said. Scaring the piss out of women.

He's cold and hungry, I said. And if you see him and aren't struck with pity, then I'll send him away to starve and die.

My wife thought this over and our son came crawling to her chair, pulled himself up by the leg. I rubbed his head and he smiled, jabbering.

Let me put him away, she said.

And so I brought Johnny Crabbe into the house and Red Kate did receive him. She gave him a basin of steaming water with a dollop of soap-fat floating in it and told him to go outside and bathe, which he did. When Crabbe came back inside, scrubbed and without his stinking fur, Kate set him a plate on the floor and had to turn her face for the way he ate, mumbling thanks over mouthfuls. That night he slept before the fire and Red Kate kept my pistol on her pillow. Thereafter he stayed in the storehouse with Ransom, who soon grew used to him—and though he'd deny it and still called him a demon, he was glad for the help and company. He went so far as to rig Crabbe a special saddle with straps out of two that were disused so that he could ride with us out to work on the cabin. Other visitors still yelped when they saw him, or simply wouldn't look, like Arthur Cobb, who'd cup his hand over his eyes to block Crabbe from his vision. For his part, Johnny Crabbe was happy to be fed and housed, given work, and treated somewhat human. And there were times when he'd ask me to preach a little, and I'd oblige him.

* * *

My brothers returned to Bayou Sara the day after the arrival of Reuben's last letter, which I read with some fear that he was dying, though the fear was soon broken by the sight of the Cotton-Picker floating home. Crabbe knew Samuel was onboard and awaited him at the landing, and when Ferdinand saw the crouching figure he refused to get off the boat. So Reuben and Samuel had to bank and tie her, the elder brother keeping a distance even as Crabbe embraced Samuel.

Samuel wore the necklace of tiger's teeth over his shirts, and after greeting Crabbe with a smile and kind words, his features hardened back. Even when my son reached for the teeth and Samuel bent and shook them for him, he seemed stony. My brother forwent eating and instead saddled his horse and rode out to see the widow Cobb. So we sat to dinner without him and Reuben told of what he hadn't mentioned in his letters; the claims of Wilkinson and Claiborne's side-mouth support. I listened, but I didn't believe it would come to that. He said he was worn of drinking spirits, and so it was the rest of us who raised our glasses, toasting what we did not know. Crabbe, from the floor, held his cup high and said, Home's the thing to toast. And we agreed.

I come back from the city of strangeness to this? Reuben said. But my brother wasn't filled up with horror or disgust as others had been with Crabbe. He even filled his cup from the table, passing it down to the slurping thanks of the once-was spider.

Let's go and give him a look at the cabin, said Ransom, proudly.

You've gone through with it? said Reuben.

It's very nearly done, I said.

And damn fine, said Ransom.

I'm whipped to death, said Reuben, but I could use a ride after this meal.

Red Kate smiled and as we left I kissed her on the cheek, leaving a patch of cornmeal there, then put lips to my son's forehead.

The way up the Thompson's Creek road was shadowed that afternoon, and as we went we listened to Reuben talk in more detail of his sickbed intrigues, seeming renewed as he told of what he called our new possibilities. Ransom rode with Crabbe on the makeshift saddle-works, and it was him who first noticed the smell of smoke upon the air.

We were a half mile from my tract and we thought nothing of it, but as we rounded a bend and the trees began to shorten near the path I'd cleared which led through the undergrowth and timber to the house, we saw the cloud rising up above the trees. I don't know what I said but I spurred hard and whipped the life from my horse as I tore ahead, forgoing the path in my madness to see, being cut by limbs and brambles as I rode towards a furious light until finally I burst out into the clearing where our tools and lumber lay piled, wedges embedded still in logs, and saw the cabin on fire. I made circles of the place and I was at the pilgrim camp again, a helpless witness of the great conflagration. The others were soon there and I heard their voices in pitiful narration. When I stopped circling, Reuben came up beside me, putting no hand to my shoulder nor saying a thing. There was a low roll of thunder, moving off into the distance, like a wave receding in the Gulf.

Lightning? said Ransom.

Again the thunder sounded, heading further away from this gathering of fools atop horses wild with fear for being so close to the fire, which now rose with the wind and shot up in a pillar, sucking the breath from my lungs.

Damn the lightning, said Reuben.

I think I saw some earlier, said Ransom.

It's no God-damned lightning did this, I said.

That's right, said Reuben. They mean to have us out of the country.

The roof had collapsed and its boards blew in shriveled husks upon the air. Rills of brighter fire worked between the beams and walls, and all was engulfed. I felt for my Bible at my breast, feeling instead the empty place above my heart as the flames roared louder and the near wall fell, revealing the inside of the cabin where we'd built the fireplace large for cooking and with good walls of river-stone for my wife to sit beside in the cold of mornings and be warm. My face was burning from the imminence of fire, and I was brought to childhood once again. And there was a coal upon my tongue and it was righteous hot.

My face didn't cool even on the ride back to Bayou Sara, which we made in silence save for Crabbe and Ransom asking questions neither I nor Reuben answered. The thunder now was so far distant that I could no longer hear its sound, but felt its trembling in my bones. And when we came ashen into the house, we found Samuel sitting on the floor before the fireplace with his ladle and mold, melting lead and molding shot.

Did you see the fire? I asked him.

Samuel opened the clasps of the mold and a ball clattered to the floor. No, but I saw the smoke when I was passing.

Why in hell didn't you stop? said Reuben.

What is it? said Red Kate, our son pawing at her breast and whining.

Samuel watched the lead bubble in the ladle, poured it into the mold. As he tamped the shot out he said, She says she's going to marry Ira Kneeland. Then he resumed his work. Later he'd tell that he'd seen a man visiting the widow on a few of his rides out there, but he'd had no idea until that day that it was Kneeland, who could not resist the beauty of Ezmina any more than she could resist his money.

This whole place is rotten, said Reuben.

And I looked upon both my brothers, my friends, my wife now bringing our son to suck, life continuing even in the moment which would mark the end of normalcy.

The rot will be carved out, I said. By the wrath of God, it will.

IV

Israel Enraged

May–June 1804

Our Preparations

Samuel's compulsion was catching and others brought their molds and ladles, and we had so many by May, when Commandant Grand Pré's deadline was a month past, that we ran out of ingots and rendered everything else made of lead to smelt; and there was a constant sound of the balls of shot rolling along the floor, and they were found in the cushions of seats, in the corners of rooms, spilling out from cabinets as though they bred there in the dark. Each morning they were poured from boots by the men who'd now gathered with us; Abrams, whose wife offered no complaint over him leaving her to hole up with us, found one in his corn-mush one morning, and Arthur Cobb—who'd come to us after being a month in the debtors' prison in Baton Rouge, cursing the name of Kneeland, who'd sent him there for the duration of his wedding to the widow and their honeymoon—swore, after a day of head-ache, that he had one jammed in his ear; Samuel Kirkland brought his son William along, and Henry Bradford brought his boys, John and Henry Jr., who flung small-caliber balls at each other when they were bored, breaking several of the windows, much to the displeasure of Red Kate, who in turn was visited by the wives of the married men like Bradford and Kirkland, sitting for a while with my Copperhead for a respite; and soon the house took on the air of a family reunion, with men in various states and children and women hustling through, and always the sound of lead rolling or dropping heavily to the floor. Ransom swept the shot up in the yard as Crabbe skittered by trying to get a claw-hold on the ground while borne upon a wave of them; and every cup, sack, cask, and barrel about the place was filled with shot according to its caliber, the containers marked DRAGOON PISTOL, KENTUCKY RIFLE, BESS, BUSS, SHOTGUN, and so on. The pockets of our billiard table overflowed with them, the bright red and white balls forced into a corner by a gray tide of seventy-five-caliber shot. Red Kate tolerated it all, sternly plucking lumps of lead from the mouth of our son when she feared he'd choke; but mostly she let him work his teeth, for she'd had to hide the whiskey she'd used to rub his gums from the others, who were all awaiting the day we'd face the Pukes' men, getting steady drunk.

All of us were weighted down with lead in our coats, in the pockets of overalls, in sacks tied to our belts; and we also bore powder-flasks always about our necks and were bandoliered with arms, adding to the weight. We moved slowly those days, and that shared heaviness seemed to give our party the weight of purpose.

And for the first time since Chit, when Deacon Kemper showed us his collection of armaments, I was in love with firearms. With every new recruit came the weapons we required; and we emptied the racks of billiard cues and filled their places with guns. The house became an armory, and now the problem became one of not having enough men to shoot all the guns; and so we were all carrying three at a time.

We had near a dozen men by the first week of June, mostly wifeless jacks who lived alone in the wilderness and clung to patches of rented property; they were often ones who charged with us at the store, or owed great debts to their landlords and were contemplating soon the cold walls of the debtors' gaol in Baton Rouge. And the house was now so crowded with guns, shot, powder, and all the tools of fighting that there was scarcely room enough for my Copperhead to move and go about her daily chores.

She didn't grumble or weep when I loaded her and our son up in the cart one morning and rode them across the line to the house of Edward Randolph in Pinckneyville. But this was because she was in her head, and had other plans. Reuben's letters were now carried directly to Randolph, and for weeks since the elder brother's return to New Orleans I'd made the ride up there to receive his missives and reports on our support from Claiborne and the general. This day would be no different, but that I carried with me my wife and son, intending to leave them there to avoid the imminent fray. She said not a word on the way, and I should have known. Red Kate had resigned herself to what would be my deeds. She'd spent the past weeks in a houseful of men and boys and suffered with little complaint. Similarly she made the ride up Thompson's Creek, passing the remains of the widow Cobb's house, which Samuel had put to the torch a few days before.

When we got down and the Randolphs came from their porch to greet us, Red Kate went off with Polly, the wife, to have tea, and I thought this was the end of the matter. Meanwhile, Edward Randolph asked after our progress at the house and gave me Reuben's latest letter.

The day's to come, I said. They have to know what we're doing.

217

It's well-known, said Randolph, even up here across the line, that you intend to defend your property, but you must remember that these men are fools. They think all they need is the law to make a man bow.

For my mind, I considered them not fools but sore afraid.

Randolph continued, You know, my friend, you could draw quite a few more men up here. There's plenty who'd rally to your side when the time comes.

When the time comes, I said.

Consider this as counsel from a friend, he said. Rather than one bloody stand-off, why not give them the house now and come up to Pinckneyville, have time to plan. Draft a proclamation perhaps, make your aims clear. People hear gunshots and they know there's a fight, but if they see a declaration of intents as well, they know it's a revolution.

That's what it is, I said—half-believing my agreement. The thought of turning a paltry land dispute into something greater seemed mad; but didn't the Children of Israel fight their wars first for land?

You'd better come to accept it. You're revolutionaries now. Come up to Pinckneyville and we'll hash it all out.

I like the sound of it, I said. But I won't be run off, not by the few measly soldiers they have in the country.

They'll have the militia, he said.

Samuel and Reuben seem to believe that most Americans there won't be a party to it.

I fear they may be wrong, he said.

If they are, I said, then whatever Americans rise against us will be made to suffer.

Randolph, eyes shut, nodded solemnly. I simply don't want this to be finished in a bad way before it's even begun. This is a movement, he said; we can't have a revolution start and end on the same bloody day.

I held up Reuben's letter, saying, Any word on when he'll be back?

Your brother, said Randolph, is staying in New Orleans as far as I know. Most likely he'll miss the first of the action. He trusts you and Sam to start things off.

I'd rather have him here, I said. It's his business.

No, said Randolph. It is all of our business. You're the vanguard of what will drive the Spanish out. Reuben will be there when the time comes.

I considered the elder brother; far from the fight, sitting daily in the coffee-houses, forming and joining the various American societies and clubs, seeing Claiborne when time allowed. And it went that Polly and Red Kate came out the house, and I heard my wife tell her that they did have quite a fine place, but—

Dear, said Polly Randolph, I can't persuade you to stay?

Your pardons, said my wife, looking from one Randolph to the other, you do have quite a house here, but I won't leave my husband. Then she, toting our son, walked past us and went to the cart, climbed up, and took her seat, awaiting me there with a stony look upon her face.

When I was at the cart, looking up at my wife, I said, You will stay here.

Red Kate glared down at me and shook her head, and our son seemed to do the same, nuzzling into her breast.

I won't have you or my son killed, I said.

Red Kate's face twisted and she hissed at me in a whisper: Then why do any of this shit if you aren't willing to risk us? Do you not know me? Do you think I've never seen blood or heard a gun sound out and people screaming? I saw my daddy's hair peeled from his skull while he was still alive and my mother's brains were in my lap. You're my husband and father to my son, and you forget me. You think all I've done was lay on my back or cook meals? I've killed, love. Killed and killed that night until my arms were sore, and that was just for me. Now, what do you think I'd do for my son?

While she spoke our son had begun to grouse, and once she'd finished my wife pulled aside her dress-front, took out her breast, and pressed his face to her. Her pap was dark and somehow it seemed to swirl in anger against me as my son drew from it, taking her fury into him. Most men with sense would have struck her a blow across the face, then drug her to the Randolphs and left, but what she'd said worked in me like a contagion, revealing the selfishness of every unsurrendering fool—that it was somehow a finer thing to put not just what you owned but the lives of all you loved at hazard.

On our return, passing Cobb and Abrams pitching horseshoes in the yard, the Bradford boys pinging each other with shot, I found Samuel and we shut ourselves up in the back and read over Reuben's letter. Elder brother would remain in New Orleans as an emissary of a kind. He'd miss the first of the fight, but, he assured, he'd be there for the final settlement. For now he needed to keep at Claiborne, and with the grace of God and the United Sates, we would be victorious.

I thought as much, I said.

Samuel was bent over a shotgun, cleaning it. He's doing what's right, he said. We need him there.

We need bodies. Not diplomats.

My brother turned from me so that his necklace of fangs dangled down and trickled against the barrel. Worry about yourself. If even half of what Reuben's doing works, you'll be thankful.

I'd be thankful if he was here, I said. But then again, I'm not sure he can back up all his talk.

I waited for Samuel to speak, but he only went on cleaning.

During the days that followed, I gave readings from the Book concerning war, giving sermons at the slightest provocation. Our gathered friends never seemed to tire of my words, nor of our gifts of drink, and they were filled with the spirit. And it was that Senator Smith passed into Feliciana without us knowing, until days later when Ransom and Samuel came tearing towards the house of an afternoon, their commotion causing many to burst outside with weapons loaded and raised. Presently, they said, he was housed at Pintado's plantation, under the guard of five Puke soldiers. That June morning there was a feeling that the time had come, and yips of nervous laughter filled the house amid a flurry of pouring powder and the knapping of flints; the balls of shot were rolling and drummed the ground as they spilled from shaking hands; Red Kate hurried off into the bedroom with the shotgun and hatchet I'd given her, the blade of which bore the impression of a weeping heart, and in her arms our son wore the necklace of tigers' teeth, Samuel's offering of peace; and everywhere there was the sound of hammers nailing shut the windows and bars slipping heavily before the doors.

The First Transaction

We'd been wrong about the Americans, as would so often be the case, and the yard that evening was filled with some twenty men. The only foreigner among them was their leader, the limey Stirling. Samuel raged upon seeing that it wasn't Kneeland who'd been sent to head the militia, and gave a punch to the wall where he leaned to look out one of the barrel-peeps I'd ordered left in the boarded windows.

Bastards, he said. Piss-legged running dogs.

They know not what they do, I said.

Samuel looked to me, deciding whether or not I was joking, and said, The time for quoting scripture's passed.

My Bible had resumed its place at my breast, its pages now rubbed by the pistol-shot I kept there also, and below that the pistol itself, lashed to me with a leather bandolier which also held a small patch knife and a long butcher's blade. In my hands I carried a buss tamped with seventy-four and a few nails I'd pulled from the ruins of my cabin to the north.

Some neighbors, said Arthur Cobb.

Better we know now than later, said Henry Bradford.

Crabbe scuttled to the door and said, Should I go around the back and spook them off their horses? I'll have them running for the river.

No, said Samuel. We go out and meet them.

And I had no time to go back into the bedroom and give a kiss to my wife and son before Samuel unbarred the door and he—followed by Ransom, Cobb, and Abrams—stepped out onto the porch and I followed.

Sirs, said Stirling from his mount with an air of mocking deference. Behind him, his men, our neighbors, held their guns and stared us down. Only a few were on horseback, and these tottered uneasily in their saddles.

Look at all you wretches, said Samuel. Not a Puke among you, yet you do their wicked works.

This, said Stirling, is a simple civic matter. I am authorized by Commandant Grand Pré to order you to leave this house. And—

Go ahead and order us, you English shit, I said.

I am a Scot, Mister Kemper, he said. And if you do not comply with this order, I am authorized to arrest you, along with any that aid and abet your persons in this open violation—

Abrams and Cobb shared a laugh at this.

Let's have the rascals now, said one of the militiamen, to the agreement of the others.

Come and try, boys, I called out.

Stirling straightened on his horse, trying to bring the full weight of his bearing down upon us. He said, I have with me now twenty men, well-armed as you can see, and by nightfall another forty from Baton Rouge will have arrived.

Is the other forty made up of your poisoned niggers? Mister Stirling? said Samuel. I'd say you'll need more than that.

The alcalde jerked at the reins of his horse. Presently the others of our party came out onto the porch, even Crabbe, who lurked in the doorway, as yet unnoticed.

And you, Henry? said Stirling. You side with this rabble and bring your boys?

I do, Mister Stirling, said Henry Bradford. You and your friends have sown seeds of anger in this country. Don't think we haven't seen how you acquire your land. False judgments, bad deeds, signing away a man's claims and selling them off half price to your friends.

And the rest of you? Stirling said.

But before any other of our fellows could answer, the alcalde's eyes went wide and he near tore the bit from his horse's mouth when Johnny Crabbe came around to the front of the porch, a pair of pistols in his claws.

Good God, he said, reeling. I thought—

They do have a monster, said a militiaman.

Saints alive, said another.

That's no monster, I said, but a man. And he's a reminder to all you rotten sons of scabby bitches that there are horrors in this world, and we will visit them upon you if you cross us one more step.

You are worse off than I thought, said Stirling. Keeping a creature best born dead—

Another word, said Samuel, and you'll be looking far worse than him.

The militiamen hoisted their weapons and so the boys on the porch held theirs high as well, and trained. I held the buss at my hip, and catching sight of Stirling's overseer in the crowd, I trained the barrel on him. Slowly the sound of hammers being cocked made the rounds, and amid the clicks I prayed that Red Kate was huddled in a safe place, behind the dismantled bed, the mattress propped against the window by its iron frame. The slip and lock of hammers seemed endless and came in waves until Stirling held up his hand and said, No. I did not come here to be party to a massacre.

Then why'd you bring all the guns? said Ransom O'Neil.

You'll be part of the massacred, said Samuel.

A militiaman piped up, calling, Keep boasting, you indigent—

Quiet! said Stirling. Mister Kemper, I know you have your wife and child in the house and I must say that it's out of Christian charity that I don't order an attack at this very moment.

Eat shit, you George-dog! came my wife's cry from the bedroom, followed by my son's wail.

Stirling looked as though he'd collapse with impotent rage. He wasn't as rotten a man as Kneeland, and the Pukes—always for peace and placation—must have known that he was better to send to try and talk us out. Don't give them your backs, men, he ordered, and he flicked his reins and the militia slowly began to file out sideways from the yard. Their glances to us were like their leader's, with the wish for blood and fire present but thankful also to not have had any.

They took up a position in the high cane near the Thompson's Creek road, as we were told by Ransom, who'd run to the back of the house and peered out after them with a spyglass.

I don't like it, Samuel said. This rat-trap feeling.

We're here for a reason, I said. You and Reuben wanted to make your point, and now I'm the only one who wants to.

We've already made it. But there's twenty Americans with him out there, and more coming. There's no support for us except what's already here.

They chose their side, I said, and wrongly. Let's have it out here and now. We could pluck them off one by one.

But even as I spoke, night, which had been creeping upon the land, began to fall.

They're splitting up, said Ransom, squinting over the glass. Spreading out a bit.

They're setting a trap, I said. There's nowhere else to go. We've felt them out and now we know their taste for fighting.

We didn't shoot either, Samuel said.

I would've, said Arthur Cobb, God Almighty I was ready.

Damn right, said Sam Kirkland.

Then what? said Samuel. Do you all say stay with Angel and have one bloody battle, or break for it and when the time comes take the real prize—the country.

The men were all silent. The quiet was only broken by the two Bradford boys, who said, The small prize isn't what we want, eh? The whole pie's the thing.

Then why in God's name did we stay here to get surrounded? said Kirkland.

If they'd wanted to fight, Samuel said, then we would have obliged them. See, now we know they've got no orders to fire a single shot. If we get out now, we'll make it unmolested. They'll think they've served their purpose, but we'll be riding to Pinckneyville, where more men await to join us.

How in hell can we know that?

Samuel ignored him, saying, Ransom, keep an eye on the horses. Mind they don't try and tamper with them.

They're gone past what I can see, Ransom answered. I believe they've gone on up the road.

We can get around them if we wait till full dark and we split, said Samuel. Then, turning to me: Or would you rather have your one moment on the cross?

That's all it took for Christ, I said. Just one time.

You might learn one day, brother, that you are no Christ.

We stared at each other, and I felt the pistol burning at my belly like an iron.

And what about Kate and the boy? I said.

That is your own damned fault, said Samuel. You should've had her submit when you had the chance.

Like you did with the widow Cobb, I said.

Enough of this, said Samuel. I love you, brother, but you're trying me.

Samuel went from me and called out for the boys to gather up all the guns and shot they could carry and make ready to ride. They commenced to collecting up their arms and scooping handfuls of shot, and I struggled to accept that we'd retreat.

And if they pick us off when we go out to the horses? I said.

Samuel, taking a pair of muskets from the cue rack, said, I'll be the one to go out first. How's that?

So will I, said Ransom.

I left them to their work and went to the bedroom, and, opening the door, I found Red Kate standing there.

I heard it all, she said. Why're you being weak?

Quiet, damn you. Get the boy and whatever you can carry.

We'll go without a shot? she asked.

I told my wife I couldn't fight alone, but she refused to hear. Finally, I filled so much up with anger that I said to her, If I have to bind my son to your breast and your hands together with rope, you're coming with me.

But Red Kate only closed her eyes and said, Why do you bend this way to him?

He's my brother, I said.

And I'm your wife, you fool, fool man.

And the good wife submits to the will of her husband—so says the Lord. You say you've seen blood and spilt it, then you shouldn't be afraid of riding out. When I come back I expect you to be ready.

True to his word, Samuel was the first to go out, bristling with guns and keeping low as he could down the high steps, around the pilings to the horses. When he was atop his and there were no shots, he waved us to follow and one by one the men slipped out the door, keeping an eye to the road and the high cane, from which there issued not a sound. By his order they formed a line of cover for me to take Red Kate, clinging to our son, out to my horse. She cursed me under her breath as I pushed her up, and she rode angrily before me in the saddle as we split ranks, forgoing the road for overgrown and wild places. And there were shouts of sentries as we tore off, but not a shot issued from them. With Samuel riding beside me on our way to the Tunica and then north, I held my wife and son close, feeling his small form jostling rough with every fall of hoof, his mother's heart going so hard as she whipped her head to give one last look to our house that I could feel it in him also.

There was no moon that night, and as we rode I could only imagine the others lost in brush and cane-breaks, trying blindly for the border. But they were soon forgotten when, as we made to cross a carriage road, we came upon a pair of men afoot, posted there as sentries. They must have been asleep, for one jumped quickly up and jabbed at the other with his musket when we appeared, the second rising groggily, then quickly snatching up his own piece.

Hold there! said the first, and I saw then that it was Stirling's overseer; and likewise he took us for who we were.

Samuel was between us and the men, his pistol out and aimed. Shakily they held their own weapons on us.

Hold now, said the second.

We'd come to a stop and I could see from the overseer's face that he was gleeful. I can't believe it's me who gets you bastards, he said.

You see I've got my wife and child here, I said. I wouldn't want her distressed.

I don't give a damn, you scoundrel, said the overseer, leaning around Samuel's horse.

Are you well, love? I said, feigning husbandly tones, into Red Kate's ear.

What's this business? said the overseer.

Christ, I'm fine, came her hissing answer.

Cover the boy's ears, I said. It's chilly out.

Red Kate wrenched around and gave me a look of vicious bewilderment, though her hands did presently move to cup our son's head.

Enough of this nonsense, said the overseer. Down off those horses!

Can you stand a shock, Copperhead?

I'm fine, God damn it, she said.

Good, I said, turning wife and child from me as much I could with one arm; and with the other hand I drew my buss from the saddle and shot the overseer.

In the after-roar my son was wailing and the horse in reel; the second man scrambled off for the roadside woods from which we'd come, tripping on the overseer's splayed-out body, which yet twitched with life. Samuel fired after him, but we wasted no time in pursuit. For an instant I held my bead on nothing but air and my wife thrashed in my grasp and my son's shrieks seemed louder than the shot had been.

My brother growled cusses, trying to right his horse. He spurred across the road and I followed after him, seeing as I rode over the overseer's corpse that his boots no longer kicked and that he was torn in half from arm to neck. I leaned my face into my wife's as we rode through the limbs and she was speaking but by then I couldn't hear in the rush of wind and dark; and I felt her teeth at my jaw and she bit me deep enough to draw blood and take a chunk when I pulled free. I saw her spit, then she huddled down over the boy. The air stung where she'd bitten me and the barrel of the buss was hot against my thigh and in that moment, thrashing through the dark, I found myself filled up with glory, and knew that this was what I'd wanted.

In Pinckneyville

The Randolphs were going madly among the haggard men now scattered in various states of exhaustion in their yard, pouring coffee and offering hunks of cornbread, which mostly lay uneaten on the chests of those now dozing. All of our men were there—a miracle; Crabbe bore a powder-burn at his face, Ransom earned a ball in his back for having turned to shield Crabbe from a scout's shot, and Basil Abrams had a fleck of lead in his arm, which was being picked out by another man. Samuel went along with Randolph as he made his rounds, gleefully asking after everyone's condition. Grunts were given in response, Abrams snarling as the man plucked at him with tweezing tongs heated in the cook-fire, and I was similarly hailed as I brought Red Kate and the boy to Polly, who hustled them inside.

It was the sensible thing, Randolph was saying. Now we can reconnoiter for the grand coup.

The what? asked Arthur Cobb, not bothering to lift his hat from his face.

It's the great move, said Samuel. When we take them once and for all.

Precisely, said Randolph. But there are preparations to be made.

And where's this horde of volunteers you promised? I said, looking about the ramshackle houses of the town, most of which were empty and the rest shuttered.

It's early still, said Randolph. I've organized a party tonight, and I expect the people will attend.

Will there be whiskey? Abrams said.

Certainly, said Randolph. Two hogs are already roasting out back.

Ah, said Ransom, sitting up. That sounds hellish good.

And, my friends, said Randolph, pulling Samuel and me aside. There's the matter of policy. From what I'm hearing you haven't captured the hearts of the Americans of West Florida.

Damn them all, I said. If they don't want saving, I'll take their hearts on a spit.

Randolph frowned. Don't be so quick. The men there, even the ones who marched in militia against you, all have the kernel of independence in them.

Like corn in shit, I said.

Enough, said Samuel.

And I did shut my mouth, seeing then how my brother's face was drawn, his eyes deep in his skull and awfully reddened.

Go on, Ed, my brother said.

Randolph shielded his mouth with a palm as though what he'd tell us was a secret. Independence, he said, is in their hearts. All it needs is to be awakened. And how do we stoke that fire? By declaration of our aims.

A damned pamphlet, I said.

No, said Randolph. A declaration of independence, written up and posted all across the land. Let them read that and not be moved to side with us.

And you'll be the one to write it, I suppose, I said.

Samuel had his arms folded, giving his eyes to the dirt. And when he looked up, my brother said, That's the thing. That's the mothering thing.

You think some paper will make them rise up? I said to him.

I think it worked in seventy-six, he said.

Those were gentlemen talking to gentlemen—

They were talking to a whole uncaring world, said Randolph. And they made this country, and the man who wrote it is the president of the very place he made with a piece of paper.

That's what you want, is it? I said.

I've got no motives other than helping my friends, said Randolph, and to extend the United States into their rightful place as masters of the continent.

And what if we don't want the land to belong to the States? I said. What if we want our own country?

It's inevitable, said Randolph.

And the land will be worth much more if it's American, I said.

Brother, Samuel cautioned me.

No, said Randolph, that is true. Land will have its value added to considerably, once it's fully open to speculation. But tell me, is there something wrong with that? With doing a good thing and gaining by it as well?

That's right, brother, said Samuel. Not a damn thing wrong with that.

And I must say, Randolph continued, that the news from Reuben is also most promising.

I looked to Samuel and he said, Claiborne has agreed that, since we're foreign nationals, we can't be arrested or held by American forces. We won't be hindered or molested.

Then we can do what we want, I said.

Indeed, said Randolph.

Samuel unfolded his arms and put his hands on Randolph's shoulders. Thank you, Ed. For all of this.

Edward Randolph took his thanks; and I considered asking, All of what? A patch of dirt to lie in? A house to take shelter in? The smell of the roasting pigs came to me then on a wind, and the smell of the sweet char and wood-smoke was a hand pulling my mind to the earlier times, when there was nothing more to life than man's original goal, which wasn't gain or the hollow ideals or even to better know God, but to be joined with woman. I left Samuel and Randolph talking excitedly over the prospects of the night and went to see my wife.

She was thrashing at her hair with Polly Randolph's ivory-handled brush; her head leaned almost to her shoulder, which was bare, for she'd unbuttoned her dress, revealing the blood-spoor of freckles there. My son was bundled on the bed, sleeping. When she saw me in the doorway, she stroked harder with the brush and cut her eyes away. Neither of us heard our son awake, nor heard him unfurl his blankets and crawl to where we sat at the foot of the bed, and neither did I feel his small hand fishing in the pocket of my coat; but my wife caught him with her elbow while she was furiously brushing, and we both turned to see him sitting there, staring at us with his mouth puckered and his eyes the color of gun-metal. Red Kate reached with her free hand and had him by the cheeks, and she squeezed until he spit out the ball of lead he'd taken from my pocket. She plucked the shot up and put it in my hand, closing hers over it tightly so that I felt the wetness of my son's mouth, and she drove the ball into my palm, saying, When I met you, you were a street-corner sharp, and now you're robbing for far bigger things. Do it. But do it by your heart. When you have a-hold of the country, don't let go.

She turned loose my hand and our son was laid out across our laps, his head in mine and threatened by the pistol and the sheathed blades of my knives where they were still strung to the bandolier which now seemed so heavy. I took out my small patch knife and scored a cross into the ball she'd taken from his mouth, put it in the pocket with my Bible.

Red Kate stroked our son down his side as he slept. You're a man of God, she said, and if you mean to fight, it's God's fight too.

And it was a strange thing to have my path laid out by the mouth of a woman. But she was right: a Holy Land was laid out before me that would make Preacher-father's pitiful attempts pale. I didn't have a hate for the Pukes the way the brothers did; I'd barely seen any besides Pintado. They were nothing more than what was between me and a country in the governance of Christ. Their lackeys would be driven out at the head of them; and any man who couldn't stand the power of the Word would be cast out also. All of them were Amalekites, Hittites, Amorites, and Philistines, to be overcome on the way to the Promised Land.

Later I would tell this all to Samuel. And I believe that he did hearken after my purpose as well; but it was also that he loved Reuben and, like his brother, was dug deep with the claws of the American eagle and couldn't see beyond the stretch of its wings. He stayed quiet while I told him, that afternoon as the Pinckneyville men and those of the surrounding area came to Randolph's promised party, and sucked at the hollows of his cheeks deep in thought when I'd finished talking of the Holy Land and a government of Christ.

Let's get first to Baton Rouge, he said. Then we can make it what we want.

I didn't press him further—his skin gray as my son's eyes—but let him pass on into the crowd now huddled around the casks of whiskey and beer, encircling the spit where the hogs turned and they sliced off hunks with their knives and ate the steaming meat off the blade. Crabbe tugged loose a foreleg and brought it to Ransom O'Neil, who leaned against the side of the vacant house at the edge of Randolph's lot. The Bradford boys were having a sport of throwing hatchets at a fence-post in a contest officiated by their father. Abrams still grumbled over his wound, but now between gulps of whiskey.

Myself, I went to the nearest cask and took a cup to the spigot, filled it, and found when I turned that Arthur Cobb stood behind me.

You think we can make a run across the line tonight? he said.

I drank my whiskey and asked him why.

The bastard Kneeland, of course. I know Sam'll want to.

Arthur, I said, you aren't whipped after last night?

Not a bit. I want his ass.

Don't you worry. He's on the list.

And there would be a list drawn up that night, by Randolph and Samuel in shifts going back and forth from the party to the house; our enemies were laid out and numbered; and soon the list became but a piece of parchment clutched in the eager hands of my brother and our friend, both of them grown so excited that Samuel, renewed though he still bore the mark of sickness, swept to the ground with one arm all the plates and cups and gnawed, marrow-sucked bones from a table outside for Randolph to spread out the drafts of their declaration. An inkpot was set down, sloshing black and smudging a page, and a lamp to read and write by, as now we gathered around them to view the composition. Samuel held up the pages to the light and the paper looked like thin slips of tanned skin veined with crooked trails of blood. My brother read snippets to the crowd, drawing laughter from our boys with the proclamation that we'd harm none but the Spanish. There were whoops at the words *tyranny* and *despot,* and by the time he was calling West Florida and its people free and independent, the boys joined voices with the Pinckneyville men to cheer, and my voice was among them. The papers of the declaration were brandished and bandied, soaked with the splashes from upraised cups and glasses, until Randolph retreated inside to make more copies, leaving Samuel there to exhort them.

A Pinckneyville man called out to ask who were our enemies, and Samuel said, The Pukes. The dons of Spain who right now have men in stocks in Baton Rouge and sip wine while you squat on land and eat corn-shuck.

But you're citizens of their country, said one.

Before my brother could answer, I spoke: We're citizens of God's country, which knows no borders.

Now Samuel was glaring at me, whispered something about preaching, and our boys were whooping, egging on the others. A grinning Crabbe appeared from out the crowd and handed me a tin pitcher full of beer, crying, Baptize us all!

You'd turn a battlefield into a revival, Samuel said.

I grinned at him as if to say, There is no difference.

Some Pinckneyville men did step back, but others stayed. Ten or twenty more, watching me as I took both handles of the cup and raised it up and spilled the contents of the cup in a foam-mottled golden out-pour over them even as some were pulling the hats from their heads and others' hair was slicked to their skulls. Crabbe shouted, Praise God! And all the people there assembled lifted up their voices in thunderous joy. I flung the cup into the air and jumped down from the bench, Samuel edging away from the crowd, who filled clinking glasses wrecked by overeager fists as the ground grew muddy and both the fine liquor and the swill swirled at our heels, darkening the red clay.

Through the sloshing praising tumult came the clopping of a horse's hooves and the crowd parted for a man to ride through: Abram Horton, planter and business-enemy of Randolph's. He was small and in a fine outfit, staring contemptuously down upon us all.

What is the meaning of this ribald? said Horton.

We're baptized, Mister Horton, called one man.

The following cheers startled the man's horse and he caught a few claps of beer and whiskey to the face, which he spit furiously.

Are you the Kempers? he said, fixed now on Samuel and me.

We are, I said.

Well, said Horton, I will not stand for this sort of . . . rascality in this town. And do you men even know who these fellows are?

Hell yes! the men called out.

You do? said Horton. You know they are murderers, thieves, fugitives? My own friend, Mister Alexander Stirling, was assaulted—

We didn't touch the son of a bitch, said Samuel.

You live here? I said. In Mississippi?

I do, sir, said Horton.

And you're friends to the good Mister Stirling?

Yes indeed. And to his brother-in-law Solomon Alston.

I spread my arms and looked to the men. His dear friend owns twenty thousand acres of land! And that's the man that came to claim my brother's two hundred acres! The same men whose friends burnt my own house to the damned ground!

The men were growling low when Randolph appeared, pushing his way through to Horton.

Abram, he said. What's your business here?

To quell this bloody riot, said Horton.

This bloody riot is a celebration and it's my land it's on. So you'll take yourself back home.

Abram Horton chewed his cheeks. I will not stand—

It'll be damned tough to stand, I said, when you're shot in your fucking knees!

The men roared and had begun pulling Horton from his horse before he beat them back with his crop and tore out from Randolph's yard.

There's an enemy, said the author of our declaration.

Piss on him, said a Pinckneyville man.

That's right, friend, said Samuel.

But what's going on now? said Randolph, suddenly taking stock of our sopping persons.

The true religion, I said. Isn't that right, boys?

Samuel shook his head, bent to whisper in my ear as Randolph asked what Horton had meant by murder, but both were drowned out by the voices of the drunken men.

Whether my brother wanted it or not, we were all saved; muddy and soaked and stinking of every kind of spirit the territory held, and some it couldn't, which burst out in gouts of vomit from the mouths of the gutly penitent, who were only encouraged by their fellows to down more. The row went on for hours, into the night, with more and more converts coming forward. By dawn, when the revels finally died and most were slinking off to sleep, their heads throbbing with goodness, we had nearly thirty pledged. Some were puny and bad-off, but others were grown men and fierce. All they'd needed was a cause, and we were happy to oblige. God, there was such beauty in it then, as the whole thing came to be in riotous inception; and we were proud fathers stomping our feet happily in afterbirth.

The First Incursions

The patrols were thick about the border and Bayou Sara was garrisoned with Stirling's militia, only there were still no Puke soldiers present in the force; our opposition was wholly American.

They're like the drowning man who fights you even as you try to pull him from the water, said Samuel after hearing the reports from our riders, who now made forays into the country not only to post the copies of our declaration, which were quickly torn down, but more and more to impress the arms of the inhabitants into our service, whether willingly or not. Guns have no qualms, so said my brother. And I came to enjoy the looks on the faces of men, working out in their fields, harrying their niggers in the bright June sun, when we'd approach and level our barrels at them, order them to their houses accompanied

237

by Crabbe, who'd emerge with claws full of muskets, rifles, shotguns, sabers from old wars, and all other manner of death-dealers, so that soon the once-vacant house on Randolph's plot was filled not only with us but the smells of oil and steel and lead; and my wife, when she wasn't scolding our son for his habit of sucking on shot-balls, was bent to sweep up the drifts of powder-grain which collected like dust in the floorboard cracks.

So we made ready for the assault on the capital, and because we rode in such small groups there was little order to the enterprise; but this allowed us to break the militia's pickets, which were more haphazard even than our rides, and go into the country even in broad daylight.

I admit we did much of it drunk. Randolph had a love for revels and we kept the spirits flowing on after the baptismal night, much to the frustration of his wife and the solemn tolerance of mine, who at first delighted with each gun we brought to add to our armory but soon was as eager for the true attack as any of our riders.

You've done enough jackdawing, she said to me one day. It's time to use the bloody things as something more than a place for you and all your boys to hang your hats and coats.

Samuel had already tried and failed at burning down the house of Ira Kneeland. He'd laid his torch at the back, so he said, to flush them out so that he could have a shot at the surveyor before the eyes of his new wife, then sit back and watch the mansion devoured by flames. But I believe he bungled it out of hold-over love for the Ezmina Cobb. My brother said he'd seen her through the window as he laid the torch, dressed in mistress's attire and holding a tiny glass of liquor in her hand, chatting with another woman of her new-found station. Arthur Cobb had come along, wanting his own chance for Kneeland's scalp, and when the flames refused to take purchase, Arthur said they ought to just storm the house, and Samuel was about to agree when some of Kneeland's slaves, who'd seen the flames, came upon them and with wild cries began to beat the fire out with blankets while others ran to alert the master. And my brother amid the swarming Negroes saw Ezmina at the window, looking down at the flames and then to those who'd set the fire. Arthur Cobb raised his musket to kill the woman he'd lurched after in his heart from the time she'd married his brother, but Samuel struck him across the face and the shot hit a nigger in the leg. My brother dragged Arthur Cobb to their horses and they rode home, where Arthur sulked for a few days, picking at the scabbed slash that the butt of Samuel's pistol had left on his head. When he was fully cup-shot, he'd admit his love for Ezmina and try to get Samuel to join in his lamentations over the wicked woman.

Should've let me shoot the bitch, he said.

But Samuel wouldn't hear it, and for a good while he avoided the house of Kneeland. His grayness grew worse despite our rides and he took more to the whiskey. Myself, I was deep in the barrel on the day Ransom O'Neil came leaping from his horse to tell us that Senator Smith was lodging at the house of John Mills in Bayou Sara. So I saddled and with Ransom went to kill the Senator. Reuben had ordered in his most recent letter that we weren't to harm Smith, so that he could have him broken in the American courts, which Claiborne assured him would find in our favor. When I'd read that, I'd thought again on the madness of the man who'd rather see his enemy in penury than in the ground. So it went that I wouldn't tell Samuel of my designs when I rode out that day, for he was hard bit to obey his brother, who remained in New Orleans for the bloody duration of our revolution. I cursed Reuben just enough that I wouldn't have Samuel's hands about my neck. He still held his brother high, despite what I saw as cowardly dealings and plotting. I didn't care for the orders of our absent leader, and so I loaded my pistol with the shot I'd taken from my son's mouth and etched with a cross; had to ram hard to tamp it in, for the caliber was too big.

*   *   *

That decrepit founder Mills stood before his house with a shotgun, and he cocked with rickety fingers the twin hammers as we approached. Smith was on the porch in a rocker, peering at us from the shade.

No further, lads, said Mills.

Damn, old man, you're prescient, I said.

What's that? Ransom asked me.

It means to know when you're about to die, I said, loud enough for Mills to hear.

That's what you've come to do, then? said Mills.

Your brother, came Smith's voice from the porch, has been writing rather foul letters to the commandant and Mister Stirling.

They'll get more than that soon, I said.

It's doing nothing to help his cause, said Smith.

We're here under the orders and protection of Governor William Claiborne of the Orleans Territory. Shoot us, old man, and you'll have the damn Army of the United States coming across the river from Pointe Coupee.

Liar, said Smith.

Let them come, Mills said, lifting his shotgun. If they're sided with trifling hooligans like yourselves, then they won't be much trouble.

I ignored the old man, had my pistol out and was raising it to put the bead on the Senator's heart when the first shot burnt past my head and we turned to see a company of militia riding for us. When I looked back Smith had disappeared inside and Mills was on the ground, covering his head. Ransom fired his rifle into the pack and I did the same with my pistol, but saw none fall. They came on through their own smoke and the air buzzed with their shots. I spurred, calling for Ransom to follow. I heard the next shot from closer and my horse was screaming and his eyes were rolled up to fevered whites. It was all

I could do to keep him from going down, which he did a half mile on, and come to find that Mills had given him a load of buckshot to the haunch and blown the beast's ass away. I had to leave my saddle and climb up with Ransom, the firings of the militia now but hollow pops in the distance. We splintered the bridge at the crossing of the Bayou Sara and rode east to Thompson's Creek, where, in the yard of the abandoned house of the widow Cobb, Samuel was crouched over his flint and a pile of pine-needles which he'd bound to a stick and lit. The bedroom window was broken and my brother strode to it with the fire in his hand and pitched the torch onto the bed where he'd spent so many nights with her. We didn't stay to watch it burn.

That same day, Basil Abrams and the Bradfords, who'd ridden in to Feliciana to see after their wives, came upon a small guard of Puke soldiers marching along with an ox-cart up the road from Baton Rouge. Basil fired on them and the Puke soldiers fled, leaving behind their cart, and the boys discovered, after lifting the tarp, that it bore a pair of small cannons that fired balls the size of billiards. They took the cart and the Bradford sons drove it back to Pinckneyville, hollering happily as they approached the yard, which soon became the scene for an even wilder romp than was usual. In their drunkenness, the boys loaded the cannons and gave me and Samuel a two-gun salute. But in their drunkenness they'd aimed the cannons too low and the shots tore great sections from the roof of our house and killed a neighbor's pig when they finally landed on the other side of the village. The people of Pinckneyville who hadn't joined us thought the war had come to their dribbling little town and poured out of their clap-board houses in fear, only to find the party in full swing.

When the cannon-balls had torn the corner off the roof of the house, Red Kate didn't even bother to come out. I had to go in to see that she was safe, and found her with our son laid over her knee, whipping him with a switch for his crime of sucking lead.

241

The boy didn't cry out even when she finished and turned him loose. He stayed silent, and I thought then that it was because he'd inherited my strength for taking pain; and I was proud, though I'd begun to notice that his words hadn't grown since he'd said his first one back in Bayou Sara months before. In fact, they seemed to shrivel in him, and he often as not was quiet, and if he did speak, as when the pair of cannons were rolled into the house for storage that night and he caught sight of them and grew excited, it was only Ma, ma, ma, gesturing with his thin arms, his gray eyes alight as they could be. My wife worried over him more than I did; she was there in the days when he'd go from smiling to fits which lasted hours, or when he'd dull and contemplate nothing for a time; and always secreting his balls of shot until she grew so tired of slapping them from his mouth that she ordered all the guns but one, my pistol, taken from the house and stored in a shed out back.

Before the end of June Reuben sent us printed copies of the declaration hidden in barrels of flour; and we commenced to make a snow of them across Feliciana and eastward into St. Helena and St. Ferdinand, and even south into Baton Rouge, where with Samuel I rode through in the dark of night and nailed the declaration to the flag-post in the square and to the columns of the house of the commandant. I'd never seen the town before, and didn't see it proper then we were in and out so quick. I saw my first Puke soldier there as well. He had his pants around his ankles, squatting to shit in a dusty courtyard. He stared at us in disbelief, our arms full of papers, and we were laughing too hard to shoot him. And I imagined that soldier and the other residents and straggling troops awaking in the morning to the fluttering declarations now adorning every house, and the papers' sound being like the noise of a hawk's wings when it swoops down upon its prey.

V

The Lord Shall Roar

July–August 1804

Wanted Men

Dead or alive, come July. The month rolled in with the news of Grand Pré's latest proclamation, which was for the heads of Samuel, me, and even Reuben, who they thought rode with us, and Arthur Cobb tossed in for good measure. The rest were to be pardoned should they turn themselves in to the authorities. So we celebrated by riding down and getting two of us wounded and six taken prisoner.

We'd gone with the idea to strike down along the east bank of Bayou Sara, take Stirling's plantation, which was being used as a post for the militia, then go on to St. Francisville and in one bunch of fifteen move south to the bend of the Mississippi towards Baton Rouge, while the other fifteen came at the city from the east. When the capital was taken, we'd go out among the countryside and rectify the ones like Kneeland. But we were fool enough to misjudge the craftiness of Stirling and Pintado, who laid in wait for us above the indigo man's plantation with two company of militia.

Pintado's men were tucked in a blind turn in the road, and we were riding so wild and loose that our number was far strung out ahead of Samuel and me. We heard the firing and screaming when the first few rounded the bend, and so we kicked hard and rode into it without thinking.

Henry Bradford was already on the ground, being dragged off into the bushes, and Pintado was waving a saber, hollering in Spanish to men who couldn't understand him. Then smoke was everywhere and I fired into it blindly with my pistol, hearing others of ours screaming and more shots from where we'd come, and now Stirling's men had swung into the road to trap us. I was struck with musket-butts and Samuel was roaring through the smoke at hands and barrels, one of which was jammed in his face, but he took it and shoved it away as the militiaman pulled the trigger. I spurred forward, trampling some, and rode from out the smoke on down the road and turned my horse, seeing Samuel coming also, followed by Ransom, Crabbe, and Arthur Cobb.

We'll go back and charge, I said, and was drawing the buss from my saddle when Samuel put his hand out to stop me. He was shot through the right shoulder and another had grazed his forehead. His rifle was gone, and there still came the clatter and screaming from the fray ahead.

From the left-hand side and out the woods came a group of the Pinckneyville men and the Bradford boys.

It's worse, said one.

And so we hied further down the road, until the sounds of battle died down; and I saw then the wild look in the eyes of the Bradfords, and that their father was gone. Samuel was asking all who was taken or killed and the answers varied. His face had gone full gray now and I wondered briefly if he wasn't shot worse.

How many are missing? he said.

Let's go hit them now, I said.

Wait, said Samuel, leaning low upon his horse.

Wait? said one Bradford.

They got our pa, said the other.

Fuck that old nit, said a Bradford. I want my pa back!

We can't, said Samuel. We got to move.

He kicked into his horse and headed away from us and the dying skirmish. And so it went that we followed and my brother formed his plan on the fly. We think we're in retreat, he shouted to me when I rode up and was pacing him. But really, said my brother, we're on our way towards win.

Pintado'll take them to Baton Rouge, he called out so that all could hear. We're between him and his house, so we burn the God-damned thing.

But what about Pa? a Bradford cried.

They took ours, Samuel said. We'll make them pay.

At a tenant-house on the outskirts of Pintado's tract, we kicked in the door and took the lamps for their oil and broke the legs from the table where the family sat at dinner, watching us in terror, and we made torches of them and rode across the fields of cotton to where Pintado's slaves were slowly filing out onto the road to their houses. Some shrieked and ran but others kept walking with their hands hanging at their sides or just looked at us. Many we ran off the road and I believe Arthur Cobb caught one across the back of the head with his torch. Sparks flew and we jumped the fence and rode down Pintado's garden and were in the yard, circling the place and seeing where we'd lay the blaze. Samuel, Ransom, Crabbe, and Cobb took the big house, and I rode to the cotton-house with the Pinckneyville men and the Bradfords. There we set our torches to the piles of white and the gin, and everywhere went niggers screaming about fire.

Samuel and the others were beating back a horde of them when we returned to the big house. Cobb threw his torch through a downstairs window but some house-slaves inside had already put the blaze out. My brother tossed his onto the roof and it took in a corner. The cotton-house was engulfed and even still the niggers were fighting to work the water-pump and draw buckets from the well.

Damn it! I screamed to them. Come on and be free! Let the bastard's house burn!

But the niggers were now slinging buckets of water at the roof, and every time you knocked one down another took his place and pitched a stream.

O for Christ's sake, cried my brother.

I rode through the slaves, knocking at them with my buss. In the name of God, don't any of you want to be free?

This is shit, Sam, said Arthur Cobb.

Won't be shit long before that fire takes, said Ransom O'Neil.

But it didn't. And it became evident in the chaos that we'd either stay there and wait for one of the niggers, who'd surely gone for help, to return with the militia, or we'd cut out, abandon the ride for Baton Rouge, and regroup across the border. Before we left, I saw Pintado's black-clad wife and daughters streaming out the front of the house like a line of crows, jabbering in Spanish. So we beat back across the fields and took to the north and the woods, hacking our way through the wilderness so as to avoid any further strikes against us. The Bradfords cussed and pouted all the way back. And I couldn't blame them for it, but did grow tired of their voices. Samuel now rode up ahead, silent, never giving any hint that his arm must have been throbbing or that he was even touched with pain. Polly Randolph doctored him that night

as the others who'd escaped rode into Pinckneyville and gave us the
butcher's bill: six captured and carted off to the capital.

There would be no more charges, no more fires. Take prisoners—a few
alcaldes—and bring them to Baton Rouge, where we would drag the
commandant from his house and use him as the chip to secure the surrender of the fort. In truth the plan was mine—less bluster and boldness, more secret and swift. We chose our quarry and in the following
days our men made night ventures into the country, and judged finally
when Pintado and Stirling would be at their homes and unprotected.

It was Ransom and Arthur Cobb who brought the news, and
along with them were ten men of the West Florida country, youngsters no older than O'Neil. I was shocked at the sight and bore some
thoughts of outraged fathers. Samuel, for his part, greeted them with
cries of joy.

Arthur Cobb dismounted and stood with his hands on his hips as
his recruits got down and introduced themselves.

These boys, he said, taking one around the shoulder, all they had
to do was hear what evil the Pukes are commencing in Baton Rouge
tomorrow night, and they came right along.

That's right, said one. We won't stand for it.

And which evil is that, Arthur? Samuel asked.

Well, the execution of the forty prisoners, of course! Cobb said,
betraying his slyness with a smile to Samuel.

Of course, said Samuel. Their outrages won't go unpunished—will
they, boys?

The boys were howling hell no and how they'd save those poor
wretches down in Baton Rouge from torture and the rope.

See, said Samuel to the wild-eyed entrancement of the recruits,
it's not just them the Pukes mean to hang, but forty more men in the
districts are set to be captured and killed.

One of the Bradfords was beside me and I had to take his arm and pull him aside to tell him it was a lie.

Then nobody's to be hung? he said.

It's just a way to drum up business, I said.

But the rest isn't lies, is it? About taking the country and getting our pa back?

No, son, I said. The rest is God's Own Truth.

Though he was only four or five years younger than me, Bradford seemed a stripling and I an old heaper of lies. But I knew even then that lies are the mortar in the foundations of revolution. You have enough iniquity and right to raise the structure up, but you need something more so that it holds fast against the winds of human frailty. I left Bradford, telling him that he could tell his brother that there'd be no executions of anyone else. He called me *sir* and said he'd justify my confidence.

Meanwhile, Red Kate tended to our son; and when he'd exhausted his word and his arms grew tired from their endless flapping and pointing, trying to form speech out of air, she would put him to bed and fix a chair before the door, then go to the Randolphs' house, where she and Polly had begun a project of sewing. I'd see her make the walk between the houses from where I sat at the open fire in the yard among the other men, drawing lines and arrows with sticks in the dirt and using pine cones and bent mule shoes as marks for towns and plantations. I'd look up from our little war in the dirt and see my wife, and also the face of my son pressed to the window of our bedroom, lit by the lamp which she left burning for him, and which one night he put to the wall and, spilling oil, set fire to the room where he was kept, so that Ransom, who first saw the smoke, had to break the window and dive into the clouds of black and emerge with the boy, alive and staring vacantly, and put him in my arms before he went back with Crabbe and others to beat the fire down. Red Kate had come from the Randolphs' house to us, and as I held my son it was that I thought she'd snatch him up and press him to her breast, but when she reached out for the boy her fingers took him by the face and she squeezed a handful of lead balls from his mouth.

I felt like dropping him, but his weight was like no weight at all, and I bundled my son tighter and whispered to him prayers for his mind to be cleared of the demons which fogged it. And my Copperhead did snatch him up then and stormed back to the Randolphs' house, where she tied him to her rocking chair and resumed stitching with Polly.

Samuel came to me and we stood sharing a bottle of whiskey in the yard, amidst the excitement of the fire dying down and the men laughing about the wildness of children.

It's a punishment for not serving well enough, I said. God shows His displeasure this way.

We'll be doing right by Him soon, said Samuel.

I hope, I said.

We'll make it so, my brother said. Reuben says that the garrison from Pointe Coupee is awaiting the news of our strike at Baton Rouge. When they get it, we'll have the American army crossing the river.

I listened to him, but heard Reuben's voice behind his own, that deep need to please the brother whose absence plagued him as a judgment not unlike the Lord's upon my son.

I'd lately given up on Reuben's letters and the intrigues of government, and took whatever news they contained third-hand from Samuel. The boys had resumed their places by the fire and I saw their boots stamp out the marks and scratches of the battle plans I'd made. Later in the night, I went to find my wife and tried to lay with her in the smoke-stinking bedroom, but she rolled over, facing the wall where our son had put his fire and where the burn had left a wide black swath in the shape of a cowled man, bundled herself in the soot-streaked sheets, and said to the figure burnt into the wall that there'd be no love until we'd won and she was back in her good house in Bayou Sara. I left her and the smell of smoke, the black shape she'd given her words, and went out into the house where our son was laying on a pillow, tethered by the ankle to one of the small cannons. I undid his leash and slept that night with him in my arms. And it seemed a dream that in the early morning there was a voice in my ear, a small rasp telling me over a mouthful of shot the details of our coming victory. But when I opened my eyes I found my son curled into the crook of my arm and all he gave off was breaths smelling faintly of lead. I fell asleep again and Red Kate woke us both with a kiss a-piece, and her wrath seemed somewhat cooled. I spent the day cleaning guns and readying the horses for the ride, which, with the news that Pintado had retired to his house and Kneeland to his also and the militia was strung out in patrols, was to commence that evening.

I saw nothing of my wife or son and was back to the dirt with my twigs and exhorting the boys, who now were knapping their flints and boxing them, some taking turns slapping each other across faces which burst forth with streams of whiskey, others jumping through the fire in the yard, whooping. A Pinckneyville man had out a mandolin and was playing The King of the Cannibal Islands, but no one could keep up the tune. Randolph came to see the preparations, and he was chided for not joining in the ride. I didn't join the gibing for I knew even then that the authors of declarations and constitutions rarely took up arms, preferring victories in papers. And Samuel was there giving an oration on the coming enterprise, invoking the name of his Reuben like a talisman to men who'd mostly never met him. It was then, when we were at the pitch of fury and ready to saddle and strike, that the women came from Randolph's house and the boys parted for them. They carried between them an unfurled flag, which had been the object of their stitching. It was of three blue and white stripes and in the left-hand corner a field of red set with a pair of gold stars, one for me and one for Samuel, and beneath the stars were stitched the words *Thy Will Be Done*.

Samuel turned to me. Why's there no star for Reuben?

Red Kate, smiling her freckles into a bunch and looking square into my eyes, also carried our son half-hidden by the banner. I went and gave a stroke to where I thought his head would be.

Let him stitch his own, I said, when he shows up.

My brother said no more as Crabbe appeared with a broomstick and the flag was lashed to it; lots were cast for who would bear it, and finally Ransom won the honor and as we all mounted in the dying light, he planted one end of the stick in his stirrup and I gave a prayer for victory, and the Bradfords gave one for their father, and Arthur Cobb gave one for the damnation of the Pukes, and Randolph gave one for freedom, and my wife mouthed love while our son gave the only word he knew, and Samuel, biting back on anger, finished them all, giving the order to ride as the moon shot up above the trees and the air was riven with the noise of our departure.

The Way to Glory

We stopped at the road before Stirling's plantation and I followed on foot behind one of the new Pinckneyville men, who went to the door and told the slave who answered that he had a friend dying down the way and he'd been told there was a man here who could write a will. I struggled not to laugh, crouched below the porch-steps, when Stirling appeared and took the matter as grave and hurried down in his night-clothes after the man.

You'd have signed the will over to yourself, I said, rising as he came to the last step, bringing the butt of my gun across Stirling's face.

The alcalde toppled and fell to the ground. But I'd given him no credit for strength and he was soon afoot again and grappling with me.

He had me by the throat and was cussing in his brogue until I reared back and put my forehead into his teeth. His nose had burst and he sat now with his hands fingering the split. I towed Stirling by the scruff to where the others waited with rope and bound his hands and set him up on the saddle behind the man who'd told him about his dying friend.

You bastard fools, said Stirling before he was hushed by a jab to the ribs and the laughter of the men as we proceeded on our way.

When we'd crossed the line, earlier in the day, the new recruits had drawn out hunting horns and blown a signal for others to appear, which they soon did. We were forty and expecting more from the St. Helena squatters who said they'd meet us at Buller's Plains, below the houses of the men we were to take.

This time we had enough torches and Pintado's house was consumed and so too his cotton-gin; and when we had him, rope about his neck, held by Samuel on that tether out in the yard, the fire spread even to the surrounding fields.

The dog owes me fifty dollars, said Basil Abrams, who'd gone with us into the house to drag Pintado out, and taken for his payment a pair of fine pistols emblazoned with the seal of the Spanish king.

Pintado's words slipped into Puke when he saw his wife and daughters running out from the conflagration.

Your world's falling, said Samuel with a jerk of the rope. And you'll bear witness to it. If your commandant in Baton Rouge is kind, he'll let us trade you for the prisoners. If he isn't, he'll watch you die.

Pintado jabbered in hateful Spanish and shouted to his women, who were by then heading for the slaves' quarters, which were unburnt, their black dresses fluttering against the air, bright with fire. His face was black with soot from crawling through his house, trying to save his maps and instruments. It had been me who pulled him from his office, braved the flames, drug him out the burning house and into the yard, where Samuel awaited him with the rope.

Now my brother and I were again exhorting the niggers to come with us and to take their shovels and trowels and forks as weapons. But they only ran from us as though we were devils. I was up on my horse again and Samuel whipped the rope tight about his wrist, gave a look to Stirling and then Pintado, and said, You don't ride. You run.

On we went, Crabbe fighting against the banner which blew over Ransom's shoulder, more red-faced than usual and filled with glee.

You think you'll gain from this madness? called Stirling. Nothing but a bunch of bloody brigands.

The boys hurrahed and fired off shots.

What in hell's a brigand? asked one.

Nothing but a common robber, spit Stirling.

Big talk from a man who sits back while eighty men are about to get hung, called another.

Who's hung? said Stirling.

At that, Samuel raised up his voice and said, Then let's show him what brigands can do, right, boys?

Amen, I hollered.

Pintado ran, struggling for breath against the rope, and now and then his slack would get too much and he'd trip over it and fall to the ground. This went on until it became clear we had to horse him, hauling him up still bound and sitting him behind one of the Bradfords.

Many of the boys now rode with silver coffee-urns the size of children in their laps, china-ware dishes that tottered, fell, and shattered in the road, and even some captured slave women and children, who by midnight were pitched off for their weight and tumbled down into the road, where the lucky ones hit their feet but many were ridden down. So we left behind us a wake of busted bodies and finery on our way to Baton Rouge.

There were no St. Helena squatters to be found at Buller's Plains. We were forty men and twenty miles from the capital, spelling our horses and waiting for reinforcements.

My brother cursed their cowardice.

We don't need the weak, I said. The Lord provides according. This just shows His faith in us.

Dawn came as we rounded the bluffs along the Mississippi River heading for the fort on the western side of the town, where we'd planned to split, with one bunch hitting the barricades while the other went east to take the commandant in his house. But the Lord saw fit to spread his indignation upon us that night, and we rode straight into a picket of Puke soldiers, who rose up from behind a hasty battlement of cotton bales and sugar sacks and fired.

I can't say how many fell, but the flash of their muskets was like Christ snapped his fingers and said, Now prove yourselves to me.

And so Samuel shouted for a volley and we let our irons bark and the Pukes fell back from their picket, scrambling through the piked palisades for the fort. The one I'd shot with my buss was near halved, and I trod my horse through him as we came to the pikes and the earthworks, and a rain of shots came down from overhead. I saw a Pinckneyville man fall and we beat back to the safety of some scrub oak near the river.

The sun was fully risen now and the river flooded gold behind us. Samuel shook with rage and barked plans and orders to the white-faced men.

You thought they wouldn't find out? said Stirling. You fools, you rode through like a pack of Indians! How couldn't they know?

Let's draw them out, I said. Send a prisoner to talk over the exchange.

They're probably hanging them all right now, said a West Florida boy.

No one is to be hanged, Pintado said, too quickly for one of us to shut him up. Turn yourselves in! We know you've been deceived by these *bribónes*!

I swung my empty buss and struck the Puke over the head and he fell to the ground, but now Stirling had taken up his call and was yelling to whoever listened that there would be amnesty for any West Floridian who'd quit the present madness.

It's not a damned madness, I said. It's how nations are made.

Stirling heaved a breath and said, You are the sorriest bunch of idiots afoot in the land. And led by even bigger fools to attack the blasted fort, undermanned and outgunned, and for what? The promise of the Kempers?

Somebody hit that bastard! Samuel shouted, unable to stand another word; and Arthur Cobb did, putting Stirling in the dirt with Pintado.

A volley sounded from the walls of the fort and tore a hunk from the scrub oak, where now the faces of the men betrayed their growing doubts.

You turn your backs on us and you turn them against God, I said. And my voice rang weak, belching old coal-dust, and the alcalde's words became my father's in my head.

But if they aren't hanging anybody—

And there's no troops from Pointe Coupee—

They'll come when we take the son of a bitching fort! Samuel howled. We've already sent the messenger! He had his pistol drawn and was waving it about the doubt-wracked faces of the men.

I said to the doubters, You'd rather listen to the Pukes' dogs here than to men you know?

Listen to him, said Ransom. We're here to take the thing one way or another.

Damn straight, said Basil Abrams.

And as for you, said Samuel to Stirling. You're going to the fort and you're putting our proposition to Grand Pré—release the prisoners and we'll turn the rest over. Go and tell him.

The indigo man was cut loose and driven to his feet and off towards the battlements, where he had to step lightly over the slain Puke soldiers, and among them I saw the body of Arthur Cobb, dangling from his stirrups, his love at an end. I pointed him out to Samuel, who had no time for pity.

We'll see what the old Puke says, said my brother.

Meanwhile we poured powder and reloaded, prepared ourselves for a reckoning. I loaded Deacon Kemper's old dueling pistol and set it in my lap while I made sure the rifle strapped to the saddle was ready; and its weight was like the weight of my son, pitiful and hopeless.

Stirling returned and said the commandant refused to negotiate with pirates whose only object was plunder and riot.

Then you tell him to get ready to watch you die, said Samuel.

And His Honor the Commandant wishes me to tell you that he will execute a prisoner for every man you shoot. All others, besides the Kempers, may turn themselves in and depart in safety. I've let the commandant know that you were misled, gentlemen. Consider your conduct well. Stirling smiled with busted lips as Samuel doubled over in rage.

Myself, I was quiet, thoughts of my wife and child upon me—not that I missed them or wished to live on for them, but that I wanted to die and be rid of them—wicked thoughts as the day wore on, the sun glaring bright upon us and the boys beginning to bitch for water while the Mississippi made its enormous pull against the land, ongoing and unstoppable.

I say we ride around and go into the town, I said. Draw the bastards out.

The Americans from Pointe Coupee should be coming any minute, said Samuel, sounding miles away.

The Bradfords tossed down their guns and rode for the fort without a word, followed soon by the other West Floridians, leaving us with Abrams, Ransom, Crabbe, and the paltry ten Pinckneyville men, who soon quit us, to the spitting shouts of Samuel and me.

Cowards! Samuel called after them. Fools!

But Stirling also was shouting to the fort, that there were men departing home and not to shoot.

O, that's just damned honorable, Samuel said to him.

Stirling said nothing and went to where Pintado was standing, just apart from us, at the foot of the scrub. They talked amongst themselves for a moment.

Just as honorable as shit, I said.

Pintado shook the rope about his neck and said, That is the difference between us, Mister Kemper.

By noon we were in a daze, and it seemed we'd live out our years in that copse of scrub oak beneath the looming fort. The day was windless and I saw in Ransom's hands our banner drooping and wilted. Stirling said something in Puke to Pintado, and they, in a slow strange dance, went to the foot of the scrub oaks and lowered themselves flat to the ground. Samuel laughed as he watched them, before the daze of heat and sunlight was broken and the banner ripped to shreds by gunfire from the riverside. We had no time to talk, to plan, but rode against the firing and it harried us as we tried to circle our attackers, who were so shrouded in a cloud of powder-smoke that we couldn't sight them. So we fired wildly into the cloud, whirled our horses, and rode at where we thought they were, only to end up slopping in the river, having to haul back up a hillside now strafed with shot; we turned to ride northwards up the river, fools, outcasts, and failures, and I was at the back of them and saw Crabbe crumple and fall from Ransom's back. Then Ransom, feeling the weight of his friend gone, threw down our shredded banner and went for him. I pulled up and fired my last shot into the oncoming militia, seeing Ransom O'Neil jump down from his horse and crouch on the ground beside Crabbe, who was alive enough to put a claw to his shoulder and be half-hoisted before both were finally brought down by the next volley. A fire lit in my ribs and I knew I was hit. Hearing up ahead Samuel and Abrams screaming for me to come on, I hunched to my burning rib and spurred on after them, leaving behind Ransom and Crabbe and my hopes for fulfilling God's Will, all equally dead.

We followed the Mississippi fifteen miles until it bent with Thompson's Creek, thinking the patrols would be heavy near Bayou Sara and Feliciana. We met no resistance, and even this was galling, as though we were so insignificant and foolish that the world no longer paid us any mind. Hunger-bitten, we were swallowed in the giant cane and the sun was so merciless that it shone even there and further up in the woodlands and the northward limestone seeps. When we slowed to give the horses rest, Samuel said we were not finished.

God's overthrown us, I said, and set darkness in our paths.

Lot of good your damned preaching did, said my brother.

And what did your damned brother do for us?

It's not over, said Samuel.

After that we didn't speak, save for Basil Abrams mumbling about his wife. And there was nothing which spoke of being finished like the land we passed through on our way to the line: a miles-long stretch of sugarcane fields which had been burnt for fallowing. The furrows still smoked and we rode through the ashes of our failures; and it could have been made no clearer in that black and shriveled land that the love of the Lord was gone from us, that we meant nothing to His plans. I didn't have the strength to beg Him, didn't have the spit to ask Him for a sign. I bore His mighty hatred and resolved to give it back to Him in kind. And if Satan himself had rose up from the ashy land and asked me to join him in his fight, I might've thrown in right there with him, I was so sorrowful tired of God's love, if this was what it was. But there came no Devil and there came no answer from on high, just a sullen breeze of wind-blown ashes drawn up to the burning August sky. Samuel was at the head as we neared the end of the burnt country, and he didn't see that I took his father's pistol from my bandolier and dropped it to the dust. I'd tell him that I lost it in the fray.

VI

Dregs and Wretched Remainders

Pinckneyville, Fall–Winter 1804

A Cure for a Felon

News came shuffling into Pinckneyville for weeks and fell on ears too dead to care. At least my own were; still ringing with the gunfire that sent us in retreat, and the shameful sound of it was deafening. And it was better to be deaf those days, when what came from the mouths of all I knew were either the whispers of new conspiracies or the wild yowls of my son which served to punctuate his frequent silences. There was indeed an amnesty, and all our captured followers were released on bond; the Pukes were kind in their pardons, as though to mock us further, and the country subsided back to peace. Arthur Cobb, so we heard, was alive, but Ransom O'Neil and Johnny Crabbe went unmentioned, as though they had never existed. Perhaps it was that the good people of West Florida couldn't suffer to think that such a horrible thing as Crabbe had shared the world with them, and worse that it had a friend who'd died by its side. So they were erased from all memory but our desolate recollections in that rotten Mississippi town, and even these grew fewer and fewer as the time passed after our raid.

Samuel and Randolph kept abreast of developments and egged each other on. Randolph had no reason not to; he'd never heard a shot fired. Samuel, though, should have been worn of such ideas, but he took each snip of news, whether from the mouth of a traveler, Reuben's letters, or the territorial newspapers, like they meant something other than shit. He railed and stormed over them nightly. It was said that the governor of West Florida himself shipped over from Pensacola with a column of troops, bypassing New Orleans and landing in St. Ferdinand. From there and with a full brass band at the head, a pair of large cannon at the tail, and himself borne upon a gilded litter hefted by a dozen West Indies Negroes of ferocious character, the governor marched his column all the way to Baton Rouge, where Grand Pré received him with three weeks of fireworks and balls. The great cannon were filled nightly with champagne and on the corner of each street there was a woman singing with a detachment of the band.

I wonder if the bastards are having a bear-bait, said Samuel.

And as much as I tried not to hear, I did, aching with the piss-rotten knowledge of the revels held to celebrate our failure.

The night we'd arrived back from Baton Rouge, Red Kate dug the ball from my ribs and patched my wound with what she'd heard was the cure for felony: a poultice of onions applied three times a day for seven days straight, and held in place by porter's plaster. Once Polly Randolph was visiting and overheard my wife remarking on the progress of both my wound and my soul.

After listening a while, Polly said, But, dear-heart, a felon is a canker on the finger.

Red Kate gave her a look like she was a perfect fool and said, My uncle wasn't hanged in Georgia because he was a canker on a man's pinkie. I know what *felon* means and this, so I hear, is the cure for the condition.

At that, Polly went away and my Copperhead finished applying her second poultice of the day, saying, I kept my family from the fever and flux in that flood. And that woman tells me I don't know cures?

Her hands were so often mixing plaster that they were white and cracked to the elbows. I didn't care what was true and half-hoped that her stinking wraps would cure me of my hunger for misdeeds. But truly the job had been well enough done in Baton Rouge—at least for a time, until the devil-worms reawakened. For now, I wanted only the touch of those dry, bleached fingers; and it did draw me from my desolation some to find that she still loved me. All her talk of winning was of the same piece as mine and Samuel's, Reuben's and Randolph's; in the face of defeat there was nothing to do but endure.

And Reuben was enduring quite well in the comforts of New Orleans, scratching out his correspondence to us and claiming he'd come to Mississippi soon. In fact, he'd gone many times to visit his Aliza in Natchez, where travelers who'd passed through the West Florida country during our rides had put out wild stories to the papers—nearly all of them wrong or garbled, and most calling Reuben the one who'd led our boys to Baton Rouge. I learned, sitting in the Randolphs' house while Samuel read the clippings, the way history is truly made—through the eyes of gossips and fools. And when, in late August, Randolph was erupting with the story that the vice-president of the country had shot the treasury secretary in a duel, I snorted and waited for the corrections of the rumor. None came, and the shootist's name struck me from the memory of one of Reuben's old letters: Aaron Burr. I was glad upon the news to know that there was still someone with steel in the world, that a man could kill his enemy outright and upstanding, unlike the way we'd so pitifully protracted our rebellion and revenge.

Claiborne stayed true to his word, and when the new governor of the Mississippi Territory sent a district judge from Fort Adams to Pinckneyville, all the old man did was question us and spend a night drinking in Randolph's house.

Judge Rodney was portly and of good temper, though tending to fury a bit. With his first snifter of brandy he let us know that we were still beloved of the United States, and by his fourth he was deep into thundering denouncements of the Pukes.

The bastard dons have placed a tariff on American goods in Mobile Bay and Baton Rouge, but do we tax their goods in New Orleans? No, sir! An avaricious people to be sure.

No doubt, Samuel said.

And your fellows down in West Florida, said the judge, they're feeling the sting now, I assure you. The dons have deigned not to allow any new American settlers into the country.

He went on and I listened, caring little for what amounted to another in the endless recountings of the Pukes' injustices. But Randolph and Samuel were rapt.

The judge said, They're selling off all their land to their alcaldes and planters so that when the takeover comes there'll be none for American interests to own. It's a devious business. They know their downfall's coming and they mean to make it hurt when our diplomacy wins out.

We've been failed by diplomacy, said Samuel.

Judge Rodney righted himself in his seat. Now, my good man, you were failed in your own designs.

It would seem so, said Randolph.

And I would urge you, the judge continued, as a representative of the American government, to not protract your plans any further. I should think you've had a taste enough of it.

We have indeed, said Samuel.

The judge seemed contented with the lie and left us, saying how we'd done a service to our country. And the moment Judge Rodney packed off, my brother fell again to planning with Randolph. They unfurled maps and drew up laborious lists of all the men who'd wronged us and the ones considered traitors; and there were so many names inked in those pages that I believe many were of their own invention and lived only in ink and parchment for them to hate and plot against.

Those nights I returned to my house on Randolph's lot—which Reuben in his kindness had leased for us as permanent, along with a house further in town for Samuel and the ghostly Basil Abrams, who stayed drunk and out of sight most days, unless to be found face-down in the street—and Red Kate would hold our son down while I read to him verses of the Bible which might drive out the demon from his mind and put an end to his affliction. But God had turned his eye from me and the boy grew more and more enraged until one night when my wife was weeping as she clutched his thin arms in their struggle, I felt the Word on my tongue like a gob of rotten meat and I snapped my Bible shut and flung it to a corner of the room, where it would remain almost a year in the roach-dance darkness, gathering dust and twists of rat shit to its pages. Thereafter I'd try and be the doting father. I took my son on walks and rides into the countryside, never going south or near the line, but into northward groves of grape and honeysuckle, where his sullenness was all the more terrible set against the last glow of life before the winter.

On such a day, in October, we strayed into the outskirts of Abram Horton's plantation, where there was a fine stream of water full of creatures for the boy to watch, and the man himself came riding up while we sat beside the stream and hollered, I do not believe this! Get on out of here!

Easy there, I said, toeing the cool water from the bank.

Horton bellowed, You and your whelp quit my property this instant!

I was broken, a numb fool sitting barefoot by the lilies watching my malformed child slap at frogs, but not near enough to take words from a planter before my son. And so, seeing that Horton held a fowling gun across his lap, I sat there and let him ride nearer and soon his polished boots were at my head and I looked up to see his jowled and powdered face looking down on me with scorn.

Do you understand me, Kemper? The law here may tolerate your character, but I shall—

Before Abram Horton could finish I rose up, snatching the shotgun from his hands and him from his saddle. He fell to the reeds and was sloshing on his hands and knees when I gave him the first kick to the face. He horse cantered off a ways and I circled him, stepping down into the gentle flow of the stream, and cracked him again, wishing I had on my boots. He was gurgling curses and trying to stand when I felt the weight of the shotgun in my hands, and I brought it up so that the barrel was between his gaping eyes. The water at my ankles grew warm as I cocked the hammers back, and I felt good and whole for the first time in months, soaked up his begs and pleadings, which were as much a balm to my soul as any onion poultice.

And I should have killed Abram Horton, for later he'd prove his planter's enmity, but I broke the shotgun and emptied its load into the water, cast the thing off to the stream. Then I took him by the throat and held his head under the water till I was sure he'd tasted mud.

Listen to me, Mister Horton, I said once I'd released him to gasp for air. You and every other son of a bitch in this pisshole town needs to understand that I am not beholden to any fucksaken planters, and I will kill any man who speaks out of turn to me. You follow? So consider your God-damned mouth when you pass near me. And tell your little clutch of masters to do the same.

Horton's lip was a-quiver, and I was so damned pleased with myself, so full of the spirit, that all I did was bend to spit in his face, then turn and gather my son, who smiled dully as I brought him to where my horse was tethered. On the way I reared back a hand and slapped Horton's wandering mare across its haunch, sending the beast darting off into the woods. Laughing now, I set my son in the saddle and mounted behind him. As we rode past the sopping, red-faced Horton, I said to my son, See, that's what a sinful man looks like.

Ma, said the boy, pointing at the glaring planter.

That's right, son, I said, a sinful, stupid man who knows better now than to piss about with us.

Colonel Kemper

We set to work converting Samuel's house into a tavern before Christmas. We had no money to speak of, but bought the lumber and later liquor on credit from Randolph, who considered in his fool's way that the eventual profits would finance our next revolution and that having customers would offer a steady stream of fresh ears to hear the railings against the Pukes. And there was always such talk, even as we hewed boards to make the counter and polished railings of brass for travelers to rest their heels upon, took stock of spittoons and ashbins, enlarged the fireplace and built, in the yard behind the house, a ramshackle still which, when it cooked, seemed constantly near explosion and produced such a mean cane liquor that the drinkers called it the Blight-Cock. I went about the work for the sake of something to do, hewed and planed until I was whipped each day and shuffled back to my house so that I could avoid the nightly prattle of future rebellions, now spilled over from Randolph's parlor to the newly christened Kemper Bros. Tavern, where chancing men gathered from all-about— deserters from the army and even Indians from the Creek nation to the east ambled through to have their taste. Randolph wore his throat out from talk within a month, but my brother seemed bolstered by the business somehow, as though the guzzlers, who only listened to his voice when they weren't fighting or singing, were the shades of our departed army.

It was about that time that they began to call me Colonel Kemper. The first man who did was but a drunken traveler staying the night at the tavern who'd heard wild stories of our fight; and I thought he meant it for a joke and so dragged him out into the road and beat him till my fingers were like loose sacks of bone. But stories of our revolution had grown so wide-spread, and were so warped, that you'd have thought we'd won; and more and more who passed through called me Colonel until there was no stopping its proliferation and it spread like a fever; and the men of the town said the word when I passed them, tipped their hats and offered makeshift salutes; soon Samuel, who was always glad to shirk glory and praise onto someone else, introduced me as such to newcomers and guests. He called me the leader of our uprising and corrected those who asked if I was Reuben. Accounts of our wasted war were so often called for by the drinkers that my brother did beg me to make appearances, and to wear something besides my working clothes when I did. Those times were only a few moments of me stepping in to hails and hurrahs for my great effort against the Pukes. And it was like a ghastly joke played on the minds of men: to think that what we'd done and failed at so miserably was something great.

When winter grew bitter, Samuel was laid out with bouts of his recurring sickness, which a New Orleans doctor had given every name from ague to feverous impetigo. More than once he called me to his bedside—a pallet in a back room of the tavern—and had me hold his sweating hands and pledge that I would carry on the fight. I didn't have the meanness to ask him what fight he meant, the only one present being his and Randolph's paper war, their endless correspondences, and the tavern battles fought between tankards of liquor.

The ship, he said one night. A black ship just bristling with guns . . .

I was kneeling beside him, his hands cold in mine. He was deep in fever and rambling on a trip to the Bahamas, a British commission, and the warship we'd take up the river to rain down retribution on the Pukes.

We'll reduce them, said my brother. Hammer them to fucking ashes.

I told him that, yes, we damn sure would; sat with him through visitations of both our fathers, which, shuddering and wracked, he'd describe to me. And I saw them also, a pair of old gangling ghosts who he'd shout were chasing him around the room, breathing fire, though my brother was on his back and bundled in sheets so that he could only kick his feet to run from them. It was only in his sickness that I saw guilt ever take him, addressing Ransom and Crabbe with tears in his eyes. His fever finally broke with the news that Reuben would be coming to Pinckneyville in late January on his way up to Natchez, where he'd winter with Aliza. When Randolph told him, Samuel's face cleared of grayness and he sat up in his pallet like Lazarus from his tomb, more-so for the fact that his color remained that of a fresh corpse before it yellows and blackens.

I lived in a world of gentle madness and in the face of it all I worked. My pistol was in the ashen ground and my Bible untouched in its hidden corner of the house. Red Kate swept around it, cleaned all about it as though it were a piece of the furniture. Shameful, but I had no godliness in my heart and only wanted things to do with my hands. I helped my wife put in seed for spring, laid on a porch to the house, when Samuel was down toted casks filled from that rattling roarer of a still, and made my brief shows as Colonel Kemper. And when Reuben did arrive, fattened by New Orleans and surveying our holdings with a sorrowful look, I gave him a haggard hello, like to a man passing by on the road, and would have been content except that Samuel brought me to Randolph's house, where we sat with coffee and cut it with Blight-Cock. He was alone, having sold Ferdinand to pay a debt.

You're famous, Colonel, said Reuben.

I shook my head; no words would come.

You gave it hell, he said, meaning our rebellion. I don't know if you understand the way you've inflamed the country.

Which one? I said, thumbing the bib of my overalls.

Reuben cut his eyes. The United States resound with your accomplishments.

What God-damned accomplishments? I said.

Reuben didn't hear me. He was looking to Samuel, squinting at his face. Lord, brother, you're looking poorly.

Samuel, soaking in his brother's false pride, said, It's a fever keeps coming back to me. But I've seen some of the write-ups.

Even in Philadelphia, coughed Randolph. As far as New England even—

They haven't captured the spirit of the thing just yet, said Reuben. Though I've tried—

I hear they say it was you, I said, who led us.

That's been common, said Reuben. And I've suffered for the mistake.

You've suffered? I said, reeling. He was as impressive a figure as ever, but his paunch now strained at his waistcoat and the sight of it galled me.

By association, said Reuben. Claiborne's about exhausted himself over you two. He won't have any more of me. Damns the ground I stand on. But Governor West of Mississippi still maintains you won't be hassled.

We don't need Claiborne, Samuel said.

Not with Colonel Burr, said Randolph.

And with the invocation of the great man's name there came a hush over our talk, the three of them leaned in close and began whispering over the Mexican Association of New Orleans, which Reuben had evidently founded, and their discussion carried on to the opening of the tavern, where sodden Abrams was given the task of tending bar and the Blight flowed freer than ever while they huddled at a table and strew their dreams about.

When the three of them had dribbled off towards the tavern, I'd peeled off to my house. Red Kate had the boy gently lashed to a chair and was feeding him a supper of eggs a local had bartered off for drink. The house stank of sulfur. My wife greeted me with a bunching of blood-spray freckles and jabbed the wooden spoon into our son's mouth.

They smell rotten, I said, going to sit beside her at the table.

You can't smell, said Red Kate.

And it was such a thing as Preacher-father would say back when my tongue was ruined. I hated his words in her mouth and I caught whiffs of my own damnation in the brimstone air as the boy spewed out the scrags of egg across the table. My Copperhead caught him lightly across the cheek with the spoon and the next time she came with it he chewed, watching me. I sat at the table and saw Aaron Burr eating steak and baked pears in syrup and with the future of the world at his fingertips among the crystal service and polished silver. In my mind he was a cross-breed of my father and Morrel, only wiser, more determined. There would be not a stitch of white upon him, and the great man would shine like black glass.

I said to my wife, I believe I'll go and have a drink.

Reuben's back, she said, clacking together her front teeth to show the boy to chew.

It's only a drink, I said.

Red Kate mimed chewing at the boy, who gave me a look and then spit out his food and mimed right back at her until she cracked him again with the spoon. His cheek was red and now my son took sullen, as he would, and looked to the far reaches of the room without ever fixing on a spot. She jabbed him more mouthfuls but they only gathered on his tongue, spilling out onto the table, whereupon Red Kate flung down her spoon and kicked her chair away, going off to the bedroom and leaving him in his chair, mournfully casting his gray eyes on nothing.

It's fine not to eat, I said, getting up and undoing his bonds. Those eggs weren't right besides.

I took my son and brought him to her. When I sat him on the bed he scrambled off and went to hide in the underpinnings. I could feel him at my feet as I sat beside my curled-up Kate. She'd months before taken me back to the bed, in fact had tried the very night we returned from Baton Rouge, though I was then too busted weary for the charity of her love. Lately it was a comfort to me, but in our rolls together I felt the way her bones had begun to strain her skin, and it was also that she no longer grabbed at me and had no true hunger for it. I had now what the Book said was best: the wife who submits. And I hated it for the clawing thought that when I went at her she took me on like a customer.

She rolled over and snatched at my hand and put it to her breast, never giving me her eye. The boy was scrabbling beneath the bed and she sighed at the sound of it.

I do love him, she said. But I wonder what the sin was that made him.

There's no sin, I said. He's young still.

She didn't hear me. You're going to the tavern?

For a bit, I said.

Well, said my wife, letting go my hand. Do thank Reuben for the house.

Colonel! Basil Abrams hollered when I came into the tavern. The drinkers raised their glasses and I gave them all nods as I went to the table where my brothers and Randolph huddled. I sat with them and Abrams brought my drink. They were all wild-eyed with talk and plans, Samuel hiding his weakness behind slaps of the table, and Reuben taking me by the shoulder often and shaking me. And I was glad to be drawn into their false world, where we were statesmen and generals and colonels; it was a better place than what was real. I drank deep of the Blight and listened.

So it came about in their talk that our patch of West Florida was now but a minor concern in a continental enterprise. The name of Burr was bandied, for even now, Reuben said, he was preparing to come down the Mississippi with the first frost-break, collecting himself an army on the way.

Jefferson's taking a soft hand with him, said Reuben. He'll be untethered in his aims.

Is this from General Wilkinson? said Randolph.

From Clark, said Reuben. Wilkinson is on the side. As I aim to be until they make themselves clear. Mister Gutierrez believes we can raise a force in Mexico, if given the time and money.

You're dealing with Pukes now? I said.

Gutierrez is no Puke, brother, Rueben said. He's a Mexican and born to his country same as us. And he wants the same thing we, Colonel Burr, the president, and all other good men want—to drive Europe from the hemisphere.

This is no hasty ride-and-shoot, said Samuel. It'll take time.

Maybe years, said Randolph.

We'll see, Reuben said. I'm not so deep in it that I can't extract myself if things begin to look dire. All we need is time. Hell, I've even got my case with Smith in the dockets of the American court in New Orleans in the summer.

Well done, said Randolph. You'll break him there.

For now, said Reuben, we wait for them to play out their hands and see if we'll throw in behind them. I want to be sure that it's an American enterprise.

I say either way we do, said Samuel. If the president's with them—

Reuben frowned over his cup. The atheist is doing them even worse than he did West Florida. His support isn't even tacit. That's the hazard of it.

Then it's up to Wilkinson to throw the army in, said Randolph.

If the fat man can be persuaded to act, then we've got something.

He didn't help us at Baton Rouge, I said, breaking the dream for an instant.

Good sometimes comes out of folly, Reuben said. Your incursion means more than you know. By this spring I'll be back in New Orleans, with Sam, if you'll come—I think the town may do you good—and Burr shouldn't be far behind. We'll know more then.

Randolph said, Justice, though slow, is sure, and vengeance overtakes the swiftest villains.

Yes, indeed, said Reuben.

And Samuel stretched his hollow cheeks into a smile, saying to me, See, brother. I told you we weren't finished.

I laughed at it then, but my brother would be proven right. And there was the part of me, the colonel and the devil-worms that went a-churning as the talk wore on, that did love the prospect of another chance, and that wickedness plowed over the bones of friends and the lives of my wife and son for a view of glory. What a bastard truth it was, that our war, started in such a measly corner of the country, would never be through so long as there were lands that hateful others held and there were men like us who, by the Grace of God, would try and take them.

Book Four

IN THE WILDERNESS

I

Israel Renewed

Summer 1805

The Great Man

They have compared us in the papers, you know, said Aaron Burr, smiling.

We sat at my table, sundown darkening the panes, candelabra brought from Randolph's house making shadows of us all, and I was nailed to the floor by the man opposite me. When I'd tried to bring the colonel to Randolph's, because it was far finer than my own, he insisted that we stay at mine. He'd been too long, he said, at the fetes and balls of New Orleans and would most appreciate a spell of normal life. Randolph was in Mobile on matters of business, and I was some afraid that I'd be receiving the colonel alone until he called for the ladies of the place to come and join us, saying that there was no conversation that couldn't use the voice of women. My wife went to go and fetch Mrs. Randolph, who couldn't resist changing from her day-clothes into a gown and bringing her china and candle sticks to dress up our mean table. When she appeared, Polly Randolph curtsied with her finery bundled in her hands. Red Kate, for her part, didn't change out of her work skirts or curtsy to the colonel. I don't believe she knew how; nor did this seem to trouble him.

Are you sure it wasn't to one of my brothers? I said.

The colonel flicked his fine hands, which bore no jewels other than the wedding ring of his departed wife, and said, I've met them. I'm sure you know that. But the eastern papers have garbled you into a Trinity of sorts—three brothers in one person, as it were. And from what your brothers said to me in New Orleans, you are the one who acts.

That's a kind thing, I said.

Truth, I hope. What do you say, ladies? Don't be silent, now.

Polly Randolph shuddered at being addressed but Red Kate didn't blink. He's the one, she said.

Yes, said Burr. It's not hard to tell. There are men who plan and men who act.

You seem to do both, I said.

I try, he said. My trip has been only a fact-finding venture; though I do like what I've found. This is a spirited country.

Colonel Burr had come into Pinckneyville that afternoon on horseback, hailed like Christ Himself; if there were palm fronds in the country the people would have scattered them on his approach, but the townsfolk could only take what was at hand and so plucked petals from the magnolias and flung them before him as he trotted through the town. For a time outside the house the planters went disgruntled, wishing for an audience and cussing that the great man would rather sit with such a low character as me. They departed before nightfall for their mansions on their fine horses, and I was poisoned with pride at their grumbling and the jingling of their liveries as they rode off.

There were slips of white still stuck to Burr's boots and mashed in the button-folds and lapels of his coat. He didn't brush them off, but let them stay there, fragrant and bright and marking his months of success in garnering support throughout the South and West. His voice was a strange thing, slipping often into mirroring my accent, but always with the jagged diction of a northerner.

Polly Randolph mustered enough to ask Burr where he would go now.

To Nashville, madam, where I stay with Colonel Jackson in his new home.

Colonel Jackson? she said.

A fine man. Prompt, frank, and ardent. Not unlike your brother Reuben.

And so I was caught up among all the colonels of the world. In his letters from New Orleans, Reuben claimed that he and Samuel were called that these days as well. For now I sat with the great man, who, when I offered him spirits, refused them and tippled only at a little wine and tea with our supper of catfish cooked in milk from the few head of cows I'd lately bought.

I do like your brothers, said Burr. They say your father was a man of God. And that you are as well.

That's true, I said. But I've quit it.

So was my father. And his father before him. The colonel leaned back in his chair and narrowed his eyes so that they were all blackness. They trained me for it, he said. But I was not meant for that life.

The Lord's a harsh master.

Indeed, said Burr. And so are nations. How do you stand on democracy, Colonel Kemper?

I don't know enough about it to say.

Burr laughed, flashing his teeth. Ah, that's the truth. Most of our countrymen will grow old and die without knowing it. . . . I hadn't enough time with your brothers to find what sort of government you planned for West Florida, had you taken it. May I ask you?

They wanted it to become American, I said. But I wanted to make something else.

Your own country, said Burr, breathless.

That's right, I said. In the image I thought at the time was the Lord's, and according to His will. I don't know if democracy much figured into it. Either way it was a failure.

Don't flog yourself on it, man. Do you know what the same papers that compared us say about me? Burr is finished. Democracy can now do without him: therefore let him be suppressed.

A vicious slander, said Polly Randolph.

No, madam, said Burr, it is true. At least up to the point of suppression. Like the existence of God, might I say, if the existence of democracy is not made apparent after years of toil in its name, does it not cease to exist? Or perhaps never has existed?

I listened. Times past I would have struck a man who said such things a blow, but I had no love for the Lord at that time. I saw that night he had his own reasons to turn his back on the God who'd so forsaken him. We were alike in that way—and in that our Gods would one day roar back upon us both.

I served the nation well, he continued. I loved her as bloodedly as any man can. But she is ruled by men who conspire and pass over the best in favor of those who would cow and bow. I loved the United States as you love God, Colonel Kemper. But if God is revealed to be nothing but whims and nations to be nothing but land—then what are we left with?

Nothing, I said.

No, Colonel. We are left with ourselves. Men, women, and the land they live on, far from the houses of power. It is the same in Mexico. I have heard it from your brother's Association. Young Mister Gutierrez tells of how the people suffer there under the decaying yoke of Spain. We liberate Mexico and cut the head from the Spanish dragon in the new world. The rest will wither and die. Then, Colonel, the western territories will have a choice as to their governance. And who will they side with, do you think? The eastern states and the business interests or a union of their own, like-minded people?

But aren't you an eastern man, Colonel Burr? said Red Kate.

Burr's eyes lit. Yes, my dear. But I am also my own man. And if democracy can do without me, then perhaps I can do without democracy. As can you.

I said, I've tried my hand at nation-making—

There is much to do. Much work and preparation. I do not intend to go into this enterprise without the most careful considerations. What I require of you is small. I will bring down fighters from Tennessee and Kentucky next spring, and coupled with the armies of the downtrodden in Mexico, we will have a magnificent deportment. Wilkinson will strike from the north, at the Sabine River in Natchitoches, and we will split our forces, shipping some to Vera Cruz and the rest overland through Orleans. There will be more than enough men. What I need from you and your brothers is friendship and information.

Why didn't they give it to you already?

Well, said Burr. Therein lies some trouble. Your brother Reuben smarted a bit when I told him he'd been recommended to me by Senator John Smith of Ohio. And I see in your face that you are equally surprised. You may be further surprised to find that while Senator Smith was your enemy in the late unpleasantness, he could not help but see your spirit, even if you did not succeed.

I wouldn't like to be attached to Wilkinson again.

The general has his uses, he said. I know his limitations just as well. That is why I intend to have enough men and supplies to abrogate the need to rely solely on him. If he comes through on his talk, which I give you is as likely as not, it will be a fortuitous event, but not a necessary one.

And despite my misgivings, I was growing more and more enraptured with the man and his designs, how he saw none of our failures, how he treated me as though I were great and had done great things. And even now I don't believe his way was sinister, but that he saw the best in every man, and wished to raise all around him to the heights of what he called *destiny*.

The man who sees his destiny, said Burr, can put aside the enmity he holds for another to further his own purpose.

I thought on this, judged it true, and said, What about the president? He can't stand by and watch the country split.

Burr looked to the ceiling as though Jefferson sat there on high, presiding over him still. He said, Old Tom knows my designs to a point. The severance of the Union is inevitable. But I believe the East will be the one who makes the move. They'll suffer no equality with frontiersmen. Think of it. When we have all that country, we offer land to the eastern mechanics and tradesmen and they will pour across the border for the chance at a better station.

But the president, I said.

My friend Tom owes me more than he can ever repay. He knows that. I have given him a presidency and removed his foremost enemy from the world. And now I will offer him an empire of the Americas. What man can deny that debt?

I'd say no man could.

Right, said Burr. He leaned across the table now and took me by the hand. And what man can deny destiny?

The word *destiny* broke over my head where there had been only providence and the Will of God. And so the Lord's path was usurped by the way of man. When Burr said it, the sound was like the wind I'd heard blowing through the blighted plains of Chit, carrying the embers of the pilgrims' camp, the hissing stillness of the fort at Baton Rouge, the sound of a hand so often beaten down now doubling into a fist.

In early morning the colonel set out for Natchez, unheralded and alone, and traveled on his way from our house through town on a road still strewn with flowers; but the night's rain had drummed so that the twists of petal were now ground with dirt and horseshit.

He'd given me instructions for the next year, to write him in cipher care of Colonel Jackson, and later of Senator Smith in Cincinnati. I watched the great man pull himself a-horse, thanking us again and giving a bow and sweep of his hat to the women.

What a pity, said Polly Randolph. It was so pretty yesterday.

The colonel turned in his saddle. The earth makes trash of all man's pomps, he said, setting off at a gallop down the mucked path and sending up clods of soiled petals in his wake.

Some hours after Aaron Burr passed out of view and we'd gone back inside our house, there came the sound of a rolling thunderous wave from the south, and I hurried out onto the porch with Red Kate following to the doom-crack screeching of thousands of crows in great clouds swiftly moving across the sky. Burr's rear-guard, they swept in peals of black beneath the clouds and swirled northwards, never lighting on house or limb, but moving after him. And I wondered when they'd overtake him on the road, and if when he saw them the great man wouldn't smile, dark eyes alight, and consider them brothers.

Before the Fall

I notched the ears of my calved-up cattle in July, and kept the tavern going in the absence of my brothers, who, so their letters said, were feeling out the situation with Burr. Reuben was cautious, but would keep up his own ciphered correspondence with the great man. They stayed in New Orleans despite the wrath of yellow fever then in season, Samuel already bedridden most days and there being no sickness that could stop the elder brother. In fact, Reuben said, he was sorry I couldn't see the city this time of year, in the plague-quiet when most Frenchmen and Spanish had retreated to the temperate outskirts and the place left to the hands of the hearty. The plans moved a-pace: Daniel Clark was shipped out to Vera Cruz with a cargo seemingly innocuous, but the flour sacks were filled with gunpowder and the hogs-heads of sugar contained pistols and short-swords. There he'd meet with Gutierrez's confidants and dispatch his wares, looking also to the defenses of the port and the determination of the people to revolt.

A gift came from the brothers in early August: a uniform of sort made for me by a German tailor of the town—of black fabric and with gold embellishments about the high collar and the wrists of the coat and down the leg, denoting a rank in our imagined army. Both, so they said, had similar outfits they wore to meetings of the Mexican Association. Red Kate laughed at how loose it hung about me when I put the uniform on, and she spent a few hours tailoring until she was pleased with the figure I cut.

What a handsome father you've got, she said to the boy with her needles in her teeth as she cinched cuffs of the pants to where they'd fit tight under the lip of my boots.

Ma, he answered, scurrying about her.

And when my wife had finished I regarded myself in the window: a colonel of illusion, and not unpreacherly in all that black. My Copperhead stepped behind me and took my hair like that of a horse and gave it a yank to turn my head and kiss her. The misery of days past was forgotten in our house, and all the war-talk now seemed like great play and fantasy.

How'd you like to be a duchess of Mexico? I said at supper.

Red Kate blushed over a plate of steaming potatoes. It won't be called that though, will it? she said.

No, I said, laughing. Colonel Burr'll find a better name.

Burrland? she said, grinning.

We laughed together and even the boy in his table-bonds managed a giggle; and though it sounded like a mock and not a normal child's joy, we were glad to hear it and unlashed him and each took him by the hand and swung him, dancing, about the room. And it went that at the end of that happy night, when I lay exhausted with my wife in our bed, she said she'd been without the blood since July. Far too soon to tell whether a child had taken in her, but, she said, she knew.

A letter from Samuel detailed the planned gathering of guns and men and the resurgence of his health. He was wearied of New Orleans and sickness, of bed-sores, and, when he was well, of being called to meet with the Association or to preside over bear-baitings. He said he'd be glad to see me and talk over what he called our happy expedition. And so we were all caught up in the dream.

I read the brothers' boasts and news with my wife set up in bed beside me, in the calm of the passage of our son's spells. Lately he'd quieted more, his fits of screaming grown internal so that in his moments of misfortune the boy would collapse to the floor and silently writhe. We suffered his convulsions far better than the screaming, for now it was only to jab a spoon-handle in his mouth and wait until he'd shaken out, at which times Red Kate would bundle him and sing hymns I heard for the first time with the ears of an apostate. My Bible in its corner continued to be a house for vermin. I had no urge to touch it, and by August had forgotten where it lay. And her half-remembered verses were nothing more than any other lambkin lullaby, fit only for the ears of children and the lips of mothers unknowing in their kindness. I'd built him a bed with sidebars where he could thrash in the night and not fall to the floor, and we set it up at the foot of our own and I slept so deeply that my Copperhead would have to shake me awake even after sunup. In the last days of August it was still too early to judge whether she'd taken child again; but in her way she knew and I'd wake her of a morning, feeling her belly for the lump yet to come.

I suppose he'll be born in time for the next war, said Red Kate on such a dawn.

This one will be better, I said.

The baby or the war? she said.

And the choice she gave me meant more than what she innocently said and made grave all our jokes. Or maybe I give Red Kate no credit for offering me then what she'd ultimately later ask. As it stands, I wove a finger through her hair and felt the fat at her mound and wished it to swell as I wished the Mississippi's waters to rise and carry down Colonel Burr and his army.

Both, I said.

II

There Shall Be Desolation

September 1805

Bonds and Yokes

I thought at first Basil Abrams was drunk and needed something for the tavern, for it was his voice at the door, calling for someone to answer. I fought for sleep, hearing Reuben, arrived two days before, go to the door and answer him. Past midnight and the moon beat our bedroom panes and I edged closer to my wife's warmth and saw with eyes half-shut that my son was standing up in his bed and he was trembling. That was when I heard the horses and the door crash open and my brother holler murder; and they came upon me before I could get out my bed. Black faces and figures, they took my arms and legs and I raged against them; Red Kate had a knife held out and was slashing at them, but one struck her and she fell to the floor; I fought, toppling my boy's bed so that I heard him wailing as they dragged me out. I bit at their hands and tasted boot-blacking, spit it, howling and hearing a man say, If the bitch says another word, kill her.

They flung me from the porch into the yard, where I saw Reuben on his back with a pair of men kicking in his face with their boot-heels before the clubs began to rain on me and I struggled to keep my knees, spitting teeth, until one caught me across my nape and I fell to the dirt. I was rolled over and held down, seeing now the faces of the men who were upon us. They all were black, but only some were true—niggers with cudgels milled with painted bounty-men and their masters. The boot-black was smeared now from the faces of the whites and in streaks and moonlight I knew them. The hirelings I didn't recognize, but I saw Kneeland and Horton drawing knives before my brother's face even as they called out orders to their slaves and hires. Kneeland was the first to make his cut and I cried out louder than Reuben when he pulled the blade across my brother's cheek. Some of the bounty-men were on Randolph's porch and they'd drug him and his wife out and were tearing through the place. Hearing me, Horton hurried over and called for his niggers to hold me fast and when he bent low with his knife I cast my head at him but he pulled back, laughing.

You won't catch me that way twice, you little son of a bitch, he said, and flicked his knife to my face.

My eye was filled with blood and the blade screamed against my brow-bone when more bounty-men on horses rode into the yard, one with a rope round his arm dragging Samuel at the other end. The rider stopped and my brother lay there and didn't move. Horton put his boot into my stomach and stood. His niggers were mumbling yessirs and driving their cudgels to my ribs. A bounty-man came and tossed the niggers rope and Horton said to lift me up and tie me. And when they had me on my feet I saw Reuben being lashed with rope about his hands and neck and Samuel still unmoving. I tore a hand loose and grabbed at the slaves' eyes and at their throats but my hands were weak and the hemp came twisting about me and I was facing Kneeland and Horton, who stood together, watching.

Let me see my wife, I said, sputtering blood.

At that moment there came Red Kate's voice shrieking from the house and she was at the door, clawing and crying out in rage. One of the bounty-men knocked her back with his shotgun and slammed the door shut.

You're coming to Baton Rouge, said Kneeland. You won't see your whore again.

I was screaming that I'd kill them all when the sassafras root was pulled over my mouth; and I gagged on rage and tried to force the root from between my teeth. Blood and spit gathered in my throat and came burning out my nose as the rope was cinched about my hands and the bounty-man gave it a jerk and I stumbled forward, past Reuben, whose face was slashed and busted unrecognizable, his eyes wandering balefully to Samuel, now being pulled upright by Horton's niggers only to crumple again and again to the ground.

You like to make people run, said Kneeland, now a-horse along with Horton. So we'll see how you like it. Hup!

The horses reeled and we were dragged towards the southward road, and in those first steps I wondered was this justice that I'd called down. Reuben blew gouts of blood from his nose as the pace quickened, and we passed on the road Basil Abrams, who we had once saved from this very man, sitting high atop a fine horse and holding a bottle. The men all gave him tips of their hats and Abrams wouldn't meet my eyes. Samuel hitched in his run and now and again shouted through his gag. And it was worse to dwell on his pain than my own, and in his wounds I saw the first fights of our youth and our brotherhood in its infancy and I wept, eaten up with fear for my wife and son. The niggers ran beside us, and one came jogging by me, cudgel pumping in his hand, and he skirted towards Reuben and struck him across the back. Reuben fell and was dragged so far in the road I thought they'd let him die that way, before Horton saw and called his bounty-man to stop.

Damn it, Minor! he said. Wait until we're there!

The bounty-man, Minor Butler, slowed to a stop and we were on a ways before he trotted back, grinning, Reuben slouched and trailing with his head down. And the wrath of the Lord washed over me, for this was truly His hatred of us made manifest. And even Christ Our Savior in his agony did break. He screamed to His father, asking why he'd been forsaken. So I did on our run, harried by that horde of blacks and bastards and knowing that the end of my world had come. And when I could howl no more for breath I chewed the bonds at my mouth, left some teeth in it before the end. The riders were whooping and I saw that Samuel would fall again and I jogged over to my brother and gave him my shoulder to lean on as we ran. And it was that my kindness was jeered by the bounty-men, by Horton, by Kneeland most of all, and even by the niggers who trotted alongside, singing, Bad men! Big bad men! Ain't but shit now, bad men!

It was near dawn when we crossed the line into West Florida, and not a dozen yards from the demarcation stood Alexander Stirling, holding a lamp at the head of a few more men. Our train stopped and I couldn't help but fall to the ground along with my brothers, and we lay there half-piled like whipped dogs, gasping and heaving while Horton and Kneeland spoke to their fellow.

You're late, said Stirling. It's almost sunrise.

Kneeland said, I only wish that I could see them all at the mines in Cuba.

Speaking of which, said Horton. I must get my boys back to the house. Too much excitement, you know. Wouldn't want them too riled to work.

Minor Butler dropped Reuben's rope and began herding the niggers together for their journey back. And I put my elbow to Reuben, trying to rouse him, but my brother wouldn't move. Once Kneeland and Horton had gone, the bounty-men got down and lashed all our ropes together, which Stirling took up, hauling it taut. I ground my teeth into the sassafras root and tried to help my brothers stand.

By the Waters of Babylon

Water poured over the pirogue's lip where we were set with a tarp thrown over us between Stirling and a bounty-man called Barker, who held the barrel of Stirling's shotgun to the back of my head. The other hirelings manned three more boats and we floated down the bayou heading for its mouth at the Mississippi, where we'd turn and go to Baton Rouge. I sucked at the muddy water some and heard one of my brothers do the same. Sweltering under the tarp, I gave chew to the root once more and felt it break, but my hands were still tied and I held the root in my mouth, hearing the paddles dip and slap as we passed into the low roar of the confluence and were drawn into the current of the father of waters, which had borne us down here years before when we were searching boys, and which now seemed would carry us to damnation.

The pirogue spun wild in the swell and the bounty-men hollered to one another and Stirling and his man battled with their paddles, giving us kicks with every stroke. Our boat rocked and leaned and was caught now and again in rushes that spun us round until they'd beat the water enough to right the thing. Samuel lay beside me, and I don't know if he slept, but I could feel his breath against my face there in the dark beneath the tarp; and my life wound out before me as the river; I felt it rushing under my cheek and its taste was our blood that had gathered sloshing at the bottom of the boat and churned with muddy water and the spice root now pulped from all my grinding. I sucked what was left of the sassafras like the coals of old, knowing this too was punishment.

I gave out over and again, waking when the sun had gained the sky and beat down on our tarp. The men in the other boats were chattering, having games of dice and singing until Stirling called for them to quiet.

Edge to the east bank, Stirling ordered.

What's that? called a man from another boat.

Away from the American side, damn it!

I took from Stirling's fear and the way they went hard to the paddles that we were nearing Pointe Coupee, where we'd pass at the outskirts of the American fort. By then I'd nursed my root of all taste and I spit it out and whispered to Samuel if he was awake. My brother groaned. The sunlight shone through the tarp, showing his and Reuben's busted faces, their eyes swollen near-shut. Stirling's boot came down hard upon Reuben as they thrashed the water. Barker's heel was at my side, but he'd put his shotgun down to paddle.

Who goes? came a shout from the western bank.

The bounty-men were cussing up ahead and our boat tottered for the fury of Stirling and Barker's paddling. The sentry called out again. And so I pressed my palms to the belly of the boat, caught one last sight of my brothers gaping in their bonds, and flung myself up from under Barker's boot, sent him toppling backwards as I tore my way from the tarp into the clean air, spitting sassafras root at him and seizing the shotgun, and its weight was glorious as the shouts of fear now from Stirling behind me.

It was a few soldiers on the American bank who stood washing pots in the river and I swung the shotgun on Barker, crying out, It's the Kempers they're taking to the mines! Come get us, God damn it we're American!

Barker was upon me and I fell back atop my struggling brothers and had the barrel of the shotgun jammed into his stomach, but when I pulled the trigger there was only misfire. The soldiers were calling to their fellows and I heard their boats take to the water and their oars slapping fast. The river swole and roiled while I fought, and Samuel was up now, beating at Stirling with his bound hands. I buried what teeth I had left in Barker's arm, at the elbow, and I bit and he was beating me with his oar when I heard the first shot fired.

The soldiers were calling halt and I brought the shotgun hard between Barker's legs, hearing Stirling's lamentations as both wrecked brothers piled atop him; and I had my foot raised to stomp Barker's manhood when we overturned.

As in the days of Preacher-father, the Mississippi embraced me and drew me down into its whirl, and with Reuben and Samuel lashed along we spun in the murk, fighting each other, kicking whoever was closest, battling to drown rather than swimming together to live. The rope caught round my throat and as my brothers thrashed and yanked I spun and came facing the surface of the river, which seemed miles away, and the sunlight was gleaming upon it and upon the oars that broke it and the blue-cuffed hands of men reaching down while darkness gathered at the corners of my eyes. I was between them now, my brothers, and the rope coiled about me in all its length, so tight around my neck that when my jaws pried open on their own to take a lungful of water none could pass my throat. The rope went slack, our fight lessened, and we were sinking into the dark reaches of the river, and there was in me, on that downward glide, a coward's want to die for the thought of the world I'd have to survive in: wife dead or worse and holding our unborn's fate, idiot child I loved as much as hated. And it would have been better that way, for all three brothers, the two blooded and me the false third, to be sucked out of the world in that instant and rendered sopping to the gates of Hell, where the endless heat would dry us to the bone the instant we stepped inside; it would have been a blessing to the world for us to die, but there came at that moment our final baptism as the poles and oars and bale-hooks of the soldiers jabbed into the water and snatched our rope; and I saw Reuben grab for one pole and draw himself to it and we were suddenly rising towards the surface, cupped by the hand of God and the soldiers now in the water kicking us lightwards.

We were strewn like flotsam on the bank at the foot of the American fort where the soldiers had brought us, and some were sawing the gags from my brothers' mouths and pushing the water from their bellies and others now made to sever our wildly tangled bonds. I rolled my head and saw that Reuben and Samuel were breathing and up the bank an officer was shouting questions at Stirling and Barker, who sat cross-legged with their heads hung. Later, when we were being doctored, they'd tell that the rest of the bounty-men had escaped to the Spanish bank. I was the last to be cut loose, and when the soldier came with his knife I lifted my hands for him, and while he went to work, saying that we were some lucky fellows, I looked again to my brothers—Samuel on his side now, eyes shut, retching water and blood.

Brother, I said, can you see?

Samuel hacked himself empty and his corpse-color was worse than ever. He raised his head from the ground and searched my voice with squints. Not a bitching bit, he said.

And what awful broken dregs we were of those boys who'd blacked each other's eyes back on the plains of Chit.

Reuben groaned and I saw the wounds in his face which one day would become horrible scars; and I sat there dumbfounded when he rose up and gained his feet to the surprise of the attending soldiers, and hobbled up the bank towards Stirling and Barker, who rose and made to run, but were restrained by the men as Reuben came lumbering on.

He couldn't see either, but he wobbled before them and one man said, Why not let him get in a lick, Cap? Reuben swung at the air, and I was on my feet and would've joined him before an officer stepped in and put a stop to it.

Christ Almighty, said the officer. Get them to the doctor and let's have this thing sorted!

Stirling and Barker were hollering that we were criminals and fugitives from justice when they carried us off for the fort. It took four men to load Reuben onto a plank, but Samuel and I needed only a pair a-piece to haul us; and I remember them saying how my brother was strangely light for such a big one. I was begging them to send riders to Fort Adams in Mississippi and to Pinckneyville, babbling the names of Horton, Butler, Kneeland, and Basil Abrams. I know I sounded like a madman, for when they set me and Samuel in cots in the garrison hospital, where Reuben was laid out stripped on his plank and the doctor was bent over his face with compresses, I looked at the sick men now leaning out of their beds, eyeing us with wonder, and when one said, Damnation, fellows, where's the war? I laughed and wept so long and hard it hurt the nubs of my teeth.

Fort Adams and the First Justice

Judge Rodney sat behind a table piled with papers, a skull dug up from an Indian mound serving as weight to one teetering stack, scrivener at his side taking down the particulars of a case that was now, in the mind of the worthless Mississippi court, finished.

I am sorry, gentlemen, said the judge, but neither Mister Stirling nor Mister Barker are citizens. And as they committed no crime above the line—

Bull-shit, said Reuben. They were in conspiracy with men who did commit crimes above the line.

And Mister Horton has been apprehended and bonded, said Judge Rodney. You gave us no other names.

Give me an hour with Barker and I'll have them, I said.

That's probably true, said the judge. But the fact stands that we're in a wild country, my friends. We've got no felony laws on the books for simple assault—if we did you'd have damn near every man in the territory clogging my courts. Kidnapping, no—the only people who kidnap are Indians and they'd be killed outright. No need for a felony law there.

Samuel said, They stole from Edward Randolph's store, sacked his damned house!

I understand that, and they've been charged and bonded back to their own country. A thousand-dollar bond is no mean thing.

It is when you've got twenty thousand acres and a hundred fifty niggers! said Reuben.

And what about Horton's niggers? I said. They were in it just as much as any white.

There's no way to charge a Negroe with a crime he's been led into by white men, and especially not when their master has fled so there's no one to speak for the property. Could I level charges against the horse a highwayman rode? No. Could I charge the ox that tramples a child? No, you make the master pay. And for the time being I can do nothing with draught animals, bipedal or not.

You could shoot it like a mad dog, said Samuel.

Judge Rodney sat forward, elbows threatening tobacco-stained territorial writs and missives. The sockets of the ancient Indian skull were cocked sidelong at him in shared confidence. I guarantee you, said the judge, that even if Mr. Horton doesn't return and forfeits his bond, you'll have him or his heirs in the civil court for damages.

We did as you said! Samuel whacked the table, jigging the skull from its perch. We made no more moves against West Florida, no more plans—

Let me say once more that it is early yet in the process, the judge said. It's not a blasted fortnight since this dismal incident took place.

I chewed my cheek with the nub-shards of my teeth and let my brothers roar.

What about Barker and Stirling? I said.

What about them? said the judge.

How long will you hold them?

Not much longer, I'm afraid. When their bonds are posted they will be escorted to the line.

And when can we go? said Samuel.

Immediately, Judge Rodney said. On honor that you will not raise trouble in the Spanish country. A collection has been made from the town, and you have three horses outfitted for your ride home.

Fine, said Reuben. But I will hold you to what you said about the civil case. The stitching in his face turned any look into a snarl and the flesh under his right eye bunched and puckered as we made our bonds of paltry honor and left the judge's chambers.

We stepped out into the courtyard of the fort on feet busted from our run, and there, not two paces from the door, stood Edward Randolph, blanching, so I thought, at the look of us: our beards grown patchy and scraggly, as none of us could shave, for the blade would open our wounds; Samuel's head bound in bandage and held in place with plaster, the corpse-color briefly abated. Reuben worst off, not from Kneeland's knife but from the skin split by cudgel blows.

When I took a-hold of him, asking of Red Kate and my boy, Randolph was apologizing for his lateness, turning his face to not look upon mine.

They're well, he said, well as can be expected. Polly's been with her since that night.

She's pregnant, I said.

I—Polly's with her, Randolph said, and would say nothing further though I shook him and in my fit caught him across the face, screaming for him to speak. And my face then was mauled worse by rage and sorrow than it could ever be by any blow, my cuts opened, stung with tears as Samuel dragged me back and held to me. Go on, he said. Go to them. We'll handle the pair here.

Randolph, picking himself up, said, I am sorry, Angel.

I tottered in my brother's grip, clung to him.

Come on, said Reuben, who remained stony, hiding with his hand the blighted eye from the sun. We'll walk you to the stables, brother. I need to see the man there about some whips.

The Fires of Home

I made Pinckneyville with Randolph in a night and a day, riding straight and crossing Bayou Sara the second evening with a fog heavy on the land. The soldiers at Fort Adams had taken to us—Reuben had made sure of that—and their outrage at what we'd suffered, plied with beer and whiskey we brought for them from the outlying town didn't dampen their desire to be helpful. And in the stable the day I left, when Reuben asked the livery-man for two good whips, he'd been happily obliged. Later, my brothers would tell me how Stirling had been spirited across the line by an officer while we were still in Judge Rodney's chambers, but also how Barker was given a guard more fitting his station—four corporals, who my brothers drank with that night after I was gone. The detail was to escort Barker to the line in the morning, arriving there sometime in late evening and bivouacking with the patrols now swarming the border-lands. The soldiers, they said, were amenable to their plans; and so my brothers left the following morning under the eye of Judge Rodney, were presented with pistols for their safety by the commander of the garrison, and, with their whips packed away under their saddles, took the southeast road for Pinckneyville but cut west some miles down and crossed over Tunica Bayou and awaited there, a few yards above the line, the arrival of their new-found friends, who came, singing Yankee Doodle, with nightfall.

When Barker was brought down from the wagon and saw my brothers, he tried to run, but the soldiers held him, and with few parting words they made their exchange and set off north, leaving Barker bound at the hands and legs with rope between my brothers. The way Samuel told it, Reuben held the lamp low on their walk across the line and they happened to see in the light the piss-stain growing at Barker's pants.

A few yards over, where the trees resumed, they moved into the woods and tied off the end of Barker's rope to the low limb of an oak.

They told me Barker only jabbered questions and that they made him understand within the first half-dozen cracks of the whip. He screamed so loud they thought the whole damned country would hear. So Samuel took Barker's shirt and made a knot of it and bound his mouth, and the brothers took their turns.

Samuel said that when he undid the gag from Barker's mouth, it was so soaked with sweat and tears and bile coughed up in his agony that it wrung out in a great stream while the man told what he knew. When Barker had finished Reuben told him to say it all again—slower this time. They'd been organized by Horton's overseer Minor Butler, some from Woodville and Pinckneyville in Mississippi, others from West Florida, St. Helena mostly. Stirling and Kneeland oversaw the West Floridians, who were mostly squatters they'd promised to pay in deeds and titles to the lands they lived on. Their names were repeated in a litany, the names of their wives, their work, a jabbered collection of names misplaced, switched from town to town and country to country, blended equal and alike in pain-wracked recognition, and even as he gave his last sob-stuttered recollections of the men and circumstances that had led him to this sorry fate, Reuben was finishing the job of digging his grave.

By that time I was home, on my knees on the porch, holding my wife and my son while she wept and when I could open my eyes for my own weeping, I saw he stared at me same as if I'd never left. His dead glances didn't hurt me; that there was life behind those eyes, whatever kind, was all that mattered. I tried to lift them up, my wife and child, and carry them inside, but the ghosts of the cudgels were at my head and ribs and arms again and I faltered. Red Kate wrapped my arm over her shoulder and helped me stand when she shouldn't have been on her feet herself.

Our second child had been born a puddle at the bottom of a basin-pot not five nights before, which I imagined, once I heard, that Polly Randolph spirited away to empty in some secret place, a better place than the trough at the far edge of the property.

Back to bed, dear, she said, tipping me into a chair which I soon flung aside, making quick apologies to Polly and following the thin figure of my wife to our bedroom, hearing from behind our son yawping and being taken up in the arms of Mrs. Randolph. I shut the door and thought as I did that I'd put a brace on it and cut a good length of stout wood for a bar, cage the windows with iron, fix pikes in the yard as what guarded sorrowing Emily, and how I hadn't saved her or Kate.

A believer in the healing powers of the dark, Polly Randolph had snuffed every wick in our bedroom, and Red Kate slept beside me while the darkness was emboldened and surrounded us. I lay there, fearing it, careful not to grip my wife too tightly round her middle. Truly I can't say she was sleeping, for she was turned away from me, and if I took my face from the hair at her neck when my breath grew too hot, raising my head like a swimmer for air, she'd inch closer into me.

I wanted light, and so I left the bed and went searching for matches and, finding them, lit the lamps. Red Kate sat up and as the wicks burnt off their top-oil, I went to her. A horseshoe of yellowing bruise wore her right eye and her jaw was swollen on the left-hand side. I knelt at her bedside and the lamps sent black twists of smoke to join the dark. I took her hand and made myself a wretched thing, begging her for forgiveness like a sinner at the foot of Judgment until she said for me to shut up.

These were all they did, she said, touching her face.

Thank God, I said, and my thanks felt immediately loathsome. I told her that I'd kill them all. I'll bring you their fucking ears, I said.

Not tonight, said my wife with more steel than any man. Stay with me tonight.

But I was shook and I told her, jabbering, what Reuben and Samuel would do; I told it to her thinking that this first vengeance would soothe her heart, and I was too foolish to know that such things never do and revenge is a sorry balm for the wronged. I don't believe I ever understood that. I hate to think it's true, but whether I knew or not I saw it in my wife's eyes that night and I denied it in my heart.

Polly came and put the boy, pink and still warm from the hot water rag-down she'd given him, to bed with us. I took him and suddenly realized I was still in my clothes, my soldier's boots hiked over woolen pants, the pistol still tucked at my belt. I set my son between me and his mother. Polly leaned against the doorframe, lingered for a moment, and before she shut the door, in the light from the outer rooms I saw a place in the frame where a cudgel had struck and the wood was dinted and hairs of splinter shone.

My wife had awakened and taken the boy from where I'd put him and as the light shortened I saw she had him curled in front of her. I heard her pat the spot behind her and I returned there, aware now of the pistol pressing to my side, trying to edge it away from her back. But when I did she rolled partway and stayed my hand, saying, Keep it there.

301

God damn you, stay, said Red Kate.

I'd been tossing in our bed for a while and she'd cussed me when I sat up. There was no chance for sleep, my mind wrought with the fear that Abrams and the bounty-men might have run too far to be caught, that I was in bed while Horton and all the rest were getting further and further away. The awful idea gripped me in a claw of bones. Horton's slaves slept peaceful, not ten miles from here; Kneeland and Stirling were dozing in their fine houses in a country that stood only because I was too foolish to take it. No sleep, but I stayed with my wife that night and was tormented, by Red Kate's comfort and the way she seemed resigned, by the thought of retribution slipping through my fingers.

When they returned the following afternoon, Samuel sat with me on the porch at my house. His pallor was poor and we talked over the details again. I learned the names and whereabouts like scripture, like the endless lists of begetting. We'd find them all. Samuel stretched in his chair and put his hands on his knees. We were looking out on the yard where we'd been beaten and bound, and the marks of our struggle were in the ground amid the hoofprints and weeds.

Do you recall how many you've killed? asked my brother.

Not enough, I said, that's how many.

We sat together until we were too tired to talk. And passing sleeping Reuben on my way inside, hearing Samuel lay himself on his mattress brought over from the tavern, I wandered to the far corner of the room, to the wood-grate by the fireplace. There, as in a dream, I reached my hand behind the grate and felt in the cobwebbed reaches for my Bible. Slip of dusty leather at my fingertips, I seized upon it, shook the twists of vermin shit and insect husks from the testaments, and gathered the good book to me again; that night it joined me in my sleep, slipped in my belt alongside the pistol; and this was how it would be: boots, weapon, wife, child, Word—never, I believed, to be taken again.

III

The Covenant Renewed

Fall 1805

Woe to the Traitor

We rode in circles about Basil Abrams' hovel and talked loudly of burning him out, so that he'd hear. The fool had left a trail of ill tales, smashed bottles, and pawned possessions from Woodville eastward to Pattersonville on the Amite River, which was where we found him, in the first days of October, living on the outskirts of town in a hut of pine limbs.

Come on out and take yours, Basil, I said.

Reuben should have killed you for what you did to your wife, said Samuel.

Abrams was retching; the thatch-work of pine-straw trembled with his gagging. When he was empty, he called back, I know it! He should've! But I won't go out, you hear!

His cries were so pitiful they shamed me for a bit. Well, I said to Samuel, it's our own fault for not doing it.

It is! Abrams cried. It's you bastards' fault! You tricked me into all of it!

We kept you on, you son of a bitch! Samuel said.

I didn't have nothing! Lost my house, lost my wife—

Because you beat hell out of her, I said.

Because of you Kempers!

Samuel's clay-daubed features were twisted in anger. We'd figured right that Abrams would be easiest to catch, and so we felt fine going after him while Reuben was in Natchez. A letter had arrived in Pinckneyville the week before, saying that Aliza had been stabbed. The deed was done by a new whore. They'd had strong words between them, and one morning the girl had put a knife into Aliza's side as she went upstairs. The letter said the lady was recovering nicely, but the stabber went unmentioned; most likely she was weighted down with stones at the bottom of the river.

I hope the bitch is alive, Reuben said, hitching to the saddle not ten minutes after he'd read the letter. I mean the one who stabbed my Liza. He stroked his beard and said he wished he could shave. These damned cuts. I'll make a poor bedside companion.

Reuben's eyes were full of tears as he swung and left for the northward road. At least now he could compare scars with his wife. So it was the two of us brothers again, at least for a time. And the ride in search of Abrams had been long and sorry; following his drunkard's trail was like pursuing a tuck-tailed dog for days and days just to give it a kick in the ribs. It almost made what we'd do seem hollow.

I say *almost* because it wouldn't. If we'd have found Basil Abrams in a cave of lepers eating his own foot, it would have still felt good and righteous to kill him. In his sordid weeks of travel since that night in September, Abrams had gained a scrap of legend, and the people of

Pattersonville whispered of the whiskey-pickled creature in the woods; their children sang songs about him and pelted him with clods when he ventured into town. When they asked our names, we said we were the Roy brothers, which was the name we used in our ciphered letters to Burr and his men.

We'd brought no torches or oil, so there wouldn't be a burning, and though we were far enough away from any ear to rattle off as many shots as we wanted, neither of us fired. Instead we made our circles and shouted to the squalling Abrams.

God, he cried, be done with it!

Then come out, I said.

O, for Christ's sake, Samuel said, rearing his horse and riding off to the edge of the clearing. There he straightened the beast to face Basil's hovel and, jabbing his heels deep to horseflesh, charged.

Abrams made it partway out before his hut was trampled to splinters, and the horse's hoofs were stuck with sappy limbs and blood as my brother reared his mount again and again to drive Basil Abrams' spine through his ribs and into the dirt. Basil screamed at first but soon the sounds he made were of gory air being forced from his crushed bellows. Now my brother rode over his flattened form again, wiped the sweat from his brow, and asked me if I wanted a turn.

Well, I said, cantering and gripping twists of rein, why not.

My wife hadn't cried or said a word when we'd left three days before. Red Kate wore her own bandolier, strapped with knives and a pair of pistols, when she'd walked me to the door. She said she wouldn't take them off till I returned. I thought of her as I made my last few gallops over Abrams, the man who'd bought a mirror for the wife he'd beaten, and there was Ransom O'Neil sheepishly handing a comb to the bandaged woman. Ransom was dead and my wife had suffered greatly, all because of me. And now death was my gift, my mirror and ivory comb, proffered to a woman who'd endured so much for my sake. There was nothing to do for Ransom but live on, protract the dream. I struck hard with my heels for the last trample and trod, wondering was there a difference between me and the one we left amid the splintered limbs and pine-straw to rot. No point in concealing him, a scrape-trough of red flesh pocked through with bone; he'd have no mourners. The children in this lonesome town would find something new to sing about.

The Lord's Passover

The Lord made His will known in the ease of our passage into the country, across the line here overgrown and wild and into the district of St. Helena, the parts of West Florida where there were no planters, no Puke patrols to hinder us.

At the first squatter's house, a cabin guarded by a herd of skinny pigs, we said we were surveyor Kneeland's men, here to inspect their tracts for claims and future titles. We'd had our hands ready to draw pistols if the owner of the place was one of our bounty-men, but he was an old man eking out a living in the backcountry alone. His name I don't remember, but when Samuel asked him the names of the other squatters nearby, he gave them and I had to fight back a smile at hearing that five of the hirelings were among them. We walked with the man and gave survey to what he considered his property; I even jotted notes, mapped the country with a pencil, the way I'd seen Kneeland and Pintado do when they eyed land. I had him show me on my drawing where the houses of the other squatters were, their distances and particulars. We left him in the afternoon with assurances that his claim would soon be recognized, his toils not in vain.

I remember that he blessed us, called us good men as we rode away with our map.

The houses of the bounty-men were scattered among the other squatters' plots, in a dead line down the western bank of the Amite.

That night we made a fire and looked over the map, figuring how and where we'd make our strikes. We slept in shifts so as not to be surprised, but nothing came and we set out before dawn. We'd ride to the southernmost house and wait until evening and make our way up from there, so that if things went poorly we'd be heading north and back to the line anyway. It was twenty miles back to Mississippi; our work could be done in a night.

Crouching in cane, on a hillock overlooking his squat, we watched Nehemiah Hunter jab his dusty rows with a hoe-blade and go about the other chores of his day, bending to dig out potatoes, which he left in piles for his scraggly children to pare of their roots and bring to the house. Afternoon he went inside to dinner, and returned to the field as the sun began to set. His name was among the ones we'd learned by rote, though I didn't recognize his face.

But he knew our faces, for when I came upon him, riding down from the hillock and with my pistol out, he dropped his hoe and gave a yelp. Samuel had ridden up ahead to keep him from the house, and when he saw this, Nehemiah Hunter tripped on a pile of dirt and potatoes, then rolled onto his back with his palms up as I closed on him.

He was saying, No, no, no, when I shot him through the chest.

And there came a woman's shriek from up ahead, where Samuel was. I rode past the corpse of Hunter towards my brother, who whirled as a shot sounded from the cabin. He wasn't hit, and so we kicked off and passed Hunter's wife where she knelt among the squealing pigs, trying to pour powder and shot into the barrel of a musket, wind whipping the black grain from her shaking hands. The sun was low and the shadows long upon the earth. The wife was crying, spilling powder and ball; she looked up at us, red-faced, and revealed her toothless mouth in a scream of fury, casting down the powder-horn and all the implements of firing, screeching that, damn us, she didn't know how to load it.

Nightfall and five miles north, we kicked down the door of George and John Barton. They lived on their own, so the old man had said, and were whiskey-makers. We didn't know which was which, but both sat before a fire with their bare feet propped on the knees of a squaw who was rubbing their toes. The Bartons tried to stand and I swear the squaw gave a little smile as we shouldered our shotguns and fired each to each. I'd shot the nearest and he lay on the ground with his neck mostly gone, while the other had received Samuel's shot to the belly and was hunched over the hole in himself, mumbling. He took no notice of us as we turned over his brother's body and checked to see that his wound was good. He didn't even pick his chin up when I bent to look and saw through his gut to the ladder-back of the chair he sat in, seeing also that the squaw had been caught in the scatter. She lay at our feet and the bare feet of the Bartons, still breathing, a smile on her face. I said a prayer for her. She'd been heating water in a kettle, I supposed to wash their feet, and there was an empty basin set beside the fire, which I kicked away as the kettle began to whine and we crouched among the dead and dying to reload our pieces.

Samuel huffed a breath and said, Shit.

It was my shot that did her, I said.

Damn, said my brother.

Job was a good man and God took his children, I said. We can't help who's huddled up with shits like these if they get in the way.

Samuel nodded. The squaw's eyes rolled up in her skull as though to catch my glance. I'd never killed a woman, and even if it was by accident it didn't make a damn—killing felt the same, like the last twitching moments of love, when you can't keep your seed from spilling; you have no control and are the glorious instrument of the Lord's Will. Samuel couldn't know this; it wasn't in his nature. He sorrowed over the squaw and for a long time would pray daily for her soul and his own. Myself, I was content to slaughter the world. Until the Lord put a stop to me, until I felt His hand on my shoulder and heard His voice in my ear, saying, Enough, I'd go without guilt, which seemed like nothing more than weak and brittle snakeskin to be sloughed from the hearts of the righteous.

Next was Roger Washburn, who surrendered himself like a fool without a fight. He'd heard our horses, evidently, and came outside armed, but threw his rifle to the ground and pled mercy for his family if we'd take him. He'd cast the rifle beside a fire-pit, upon which cooked a pot of pitch, perhaps for tarring his house in the morning against the draughts of winter. It was midnight and he was dressed in his nightshirt same as I'd been when we were taken; he seemed about my age, worse worn by life. Scattered about the fire-pit and steaming pot were trowels, spades, and ladles. Washburn was on his knees, hands clasped, saying, It was just for money, sirs. The Bartons were the ones who thought it up—they said Kneeland would grant us our titles to the land, said we'd all get our plots and more for free.

We were down off our horses and candles shone in the window-hole of the house; before the netting that was tacked where glass would be a woman and a pair of young boys peered out.

I said, We've got no time for this.

But Washburn's words caught Samuel, his story of being led down a wicked path by wicked men.

Barker didn't say that Kneeland had promised them land, Samuel said.

What difference does it make?

For a poor man, said Washburn, it makes a matter.

The pitch was roiling in the pot and I was tired of this talk. I looked again to the window, where the woman and her sons were pressing their fingers to the netting. I shouted for them to get away from the God-damned window before I filled it with shot, and the woman hustled her children off.

Spare them, Washburn said. You got me.

We will, Samuel said.

Another hissing spit from the pot struck me under my eye. Do you like to paint yourself black? I said.

Washburn turned from Samuel to me. It's what the others said to do.

Did you think playing nigger would help you? I said. Do you think that hides you from God?

It's what we were told, said Washburn.

Just because the Lord turns His eye and favor from the black man doesn't mean He can't see him, I said. So I say again—do you like to be made black?

I don't follow, sir, said Washburn, turning to Samuel for maybe more sense.

My brother looked to me; I'd taken up a ladle and presently dipped it to the pitch and drew it full. The man's face was dumb and unknowing and I was reminded of the words of Judge Rodney about punishing beasts of burden. I held the brimming ladle for a moment, then slung the pitch into Washburn's face.

His screams drew his wife and children from their house, but Samuel kept them back; and I was shouting over Washburn's wailing, How's being black? How is it, now?

Washburn batted his hands at his tarred face, rolling and thrashing so much that I had to stand on his legs to hold him still enough to shoot. In the after-roar of the shotgun I heard his family crying. Samuel had started for his horse and I followed after him, giving a kick to the tripod leg and toppling the pitch-pot over. I had to scamper fast to escape the flow of black that spilled out onto the ground and swallowed the dead man.

When I'd caught up to my brother and was saddling, I reached and took him by the coat and said, Don't, by God, go weak on me.

You don't tell me that, he said, then gave his horse a thrash and rode on ahead.

Our last was called Will Everett, who lived but a few miles from the man we'd first met. And it was a strange thing to ride to his house in the silence of the pre-dawn hours, when we knew that behind us was miles of screaming and death. We didn't kick his door in but shouted alarm and for help in the yard until the man came out. He was shouldering a musket and he trailed it between the two of us, asking what the trouble was.

You're William Everett, I said.

That's right, he said, jabbing the mouth of his musket at me. And who the hell are you?

Samuel gave our answer with his shotgun. I saw the flash of blue out the corner of my eye and Everett flying backwards like a doll flung aside by a child. Another house full of screams, another flick of the reins to our tired horses; and as we made for the road, closing on one another, Samuel popped me in the leg with the butt of his gun, saying, There's not a weak bone in me, brother. Know this.

I smiled as he charged on ahead and I felt more whole in that moment, more blessed by God, more full of the spirit than I ever had. Even now I can't curse myself for what we did that bloody night; that's the way of vengeance. So it went that we crossed the line just after sunrise, going a few miles in to find a place to spell our horses for a while. My brother's anger at me had cooled and morning broke to find us knelt in prayer, and I read from my Bible the story of the sword of Gideon.

IV

The Coded World

Winter 1805

Visitations of the Law

It's a bloody outrage, said Justice Baker.

There's more bad men about lately, I said.

Deserters from the army, Samuel offered. Gamesmen from Kentucky. They're all wild, and as long as the Spanish government's so weak, I'd expect it to continue.

Head tilted gravely above his cup of Blight, Justice Baker said, At least from what I hear it wasn't blacks. We can all take heart in that.

Late December and outside the frost was being battered from the trees by hailstones as we sat with the justice, who'd braved the weather that day to come down from his court-seat in Woodville and inform us we were rich. Moreover it seemed he was there to test us over the night in St. Helena. Justice Baker had ears and was no fool; like the rest of the lower Mississippi, he'd heard tell of the Passover night and his conversation wound back to it. He was shrewd, and as I sat with Samuel at our corner tavern table, listening to Baker bemoan the lawlessness of the lower country and the hail pelt the world in rattling drifts, I was happy in the knowledge that since that night we'd done more of God's good work, and the justice would never know nor could he wield any law against us.

Speaking of Negroes, Samuel said. Would it be possible to take part of the payment in Mister Horton's slaves?

I don't believe that would be a prudent measure, given the circumstances.

And if you were a money-loving man, the circumstances were fine indeed. The settlement with Horton's estate, made in the absence of the man himself, was just over twenty thousand dollars, to be divided principally amongst the three of us brothers, with a provision to pay Randolph for damages and hurts incurred. And I judged it sorry that neither Edward nor Reuben were there with us to hear our wealth proclaimed—elder brother still in Natchez while his wife's wounds knitted, and Edward Randolph down the road in bed with the sickness that would carry him over before Christmas.

At first I thought it was Samuel's fever catched and spreading, but Randolph bore no corpse-color; suffering aches, chills, and yellow flux, his illness was entirely earthly, and so after a week's worth of torment our friend would be put into the half-frozen earth, interred with a miniature of our revolutionary flag which Polly used to dab her tears while I read the service. I told her, when the last shovelful was patted down, that she could take heart in the judgment we'd gained, meaning both Justice Baker's and another, the knowledge of which her husband had taken to his grave, whispered to him the day before he died: that Abram Horton was dead by my hand.

We went for him on the Sunday before the justice graced us, having heard the night before one of the tavern-goers say that he'd seen Abram Horton's son, a boy no more than twelve, riding from their plantation every few days with a bundle of supplies. The man knew what his words did and he told his story loudly, the way I found that countrymen did bark when they wanted trouble stirred amongst others than themselves. He went on to tell that the boy was riding south and east to the Bayou Sara, Sundays and Wednesdays, he said, regular as clockwork.

So we waited until the appointed day, when at an out-wash of the bayou, the boy appeared, tethered his horse, and dragged a pirogue from the bushes, then loaded himself and his bundle in and shoved off into the swamp. We kept low until he returned, when it was nearing sundown. Horton had a better son than he deserved, who'd ride the roads alone knowing we were about. But from what I've seen sons often do exceed their fathers and this one I wouldn't make suffer for the sins of his. We let him pass. And so the good son returned from his errand in the swamp, pulled himself atop his horse, sat there for a moment puny-looking, then hied for home, supper, mother. It hurt me some to think of it; but then I'd had neither home nor mother, my meager suppers wasted on a tortured tongue.

We paddled quiet as we could, thumping cypress knees and edging past the moon-struck eyes of alligators, hearing the slosh and coil of snakes slipping from the low limbs to the water. Samuel rode at the fore, and we craned and peered for any light ahead on our slow progress. In the belly of the boat rode our shotguns, tamped and ready. The light grew, wriggling shadows between the trees as we neared a small island where two men sat talking before a campfire. By their voices it was Horton and his man, Minor Butler. There was a good stand of cypress between us, and so Samuel pulled the paddle from the water, set it in the boat, and we floated there, listening. We were no more than fifteen feet from the island, a patch of soft-suck mud where nothing grew but a scattering of bright green moss. I took up my shotgun, wondering why in God's name was this man such a fool as to not have gone below the line. Pride, I figured. But what pride was there in skulking through the swampland? I couldn't grasp it. All I knew was there he sat: Abram Horton, spooning beans from a pot and chatting with his overseer; they were covered up in furred blankets for the cold, which grew worse in the damp. Brothers to the deep, we'd act together and without words, all in murderous motion. Samuel had his shotgun up and aimed, covering Minor Butler; and I raised and leveled mine, balancing the barrel on a branch, thinking, We are all made to pay in kind for our foolishness and pride.

Abram Horton was telling a story of his youth: a night in a bawdy house in Virginia. From the sound of the overseer's laughter, he'd heard it more than once. Butler was turned more towards Samuel, who had a good shot at his front, while Horton had his back to me. It didn't matter—the shot I'd tamped in my piece was of a brutal gauge; it wouldn't spread far, but put a knothole through to his chest if my aim was right.

I fired first, followed closely by Samuel; and in the briefest noise and flash both men dropped. We held to the trees, for the force of our shots had the pirogue near to swamping; we negotiated the trunks of them and banked upon the island, where the two now lay dead. Butler had taken his in the chest and was splayed wide with his arms outthrown; Horton was face-down, the evidence of my shot staring up at me from the fist-sized hole in his back.

What followed was the hours of struggle through the swampland, after we'd loaded the corpses in the pirogue and shoved off for the deeper reaches. Over and again I swore I felt Abram Horton stirring at my feet. I'd give a jerk and prod him with the barrel, but he was only ballast; and my brother's mind was also on ghostly things as we inched our way through low brambles and tangling vines, until what passed for land in the bayou rose up beneath our boat and the paddle struck in muck. Samuel debarked first, stepping knee-deep into the slough, and held out the lamp, revealing an expanse of sallow pock-marked mud which wriggled when he moved. Looking out, I realized it was the color of my brother's face when he'd neglect his clay and powders; and he peered into it as though contemplating himself in a window.

He said, God, this would be the place you'd find Sara herself wandering.

The ancient, deathless killing-whore now skulked through my mind—her toothless mouth, the seat of her womanhood still filled with the contagion that had damned her, moving like a water-bug, picking bony limbs up high and swift to go circling us atop the mud, which presently accepted me in suck and chill up to my hips. We tried to move forward, hauling the boat behind us, but made little way.

Shit, I said, let's put the bastards here. No one's braving this.

We hustled and grumbled as though we served some master other than ourselves. Perhaps we complained against the Lord, as we laid hands on the bodies of those we'd slain, hauled them atop the jiggling mud and in the light of the sinking lamp pressed against them until they were deep enough in to step up on like ramps and drive down with our boots. Abram Horton's eyes had been open, his mouth agape; and as I'd shoved him down his head had bobbed through the parting mud, nodding to me—the only kind of deference I'd ever have from such as him.

In the following days my lungs filled up with bile and my throat was burning, but Red Kate made me honeyed drinks and though my throat still felt clawed it was like the good rasp a full day of preaching had given me in the past. It let you know you'd done your work.

The storm went on and worse cold came down upon the country, freezing drops first into sleet and then the hail which kept up its rattle-pat falling throughout Justice Baker's visit.

The justice reared up in his chair, giving rise as though he sat at the bench before a pair of misbegotten boys. Listen now, he said, and listen well. I'm not so loose in my doings as Judge Rodney. We are trying to make something out of this country, more than just scrappers and a few scant plantations, and I won't have it ruined by acts which engender reprisal either here or from below the line. When war comes, it comes. But for now I want peace and control. Now, I'll let this matter lie, but I want to have a handle on your doings. When your hands are idle, it seems, they end up covered in blood. So I intend to make sure you aren't idle.

There's no blood on us, said Samuel.

Be that as it may, said the justice, you are twenty thousand dollars in my debt, and moreover you owe me for turning an eye to your acts.

Here it is, I said.

Is this ingratitude?

Before I could answer him, Samuel cut me off, saying, What would you have us do to show that we were grateful?

For Christ's sake, Sam, you'll cow to another of these—

Enough, said my brother.

The justice looked to each of us, studying, measuring, as though he could see the seams wearing out of our brotherhood. I understand, he said, that in your time in West Florida you had your own trouble with squatters and timber-thieves?

I kept shut my mouth, for anger and disgust, as Justice Baker told what he required: his land outside of Woodville was being preyed upon, and he needed men to clear it of what he called *ruffians*. Like most of the horsed and booted, he was awaiting the arrival of what he thought were better settlers, people from the East with money and designs on homesteads who'd eagerly sign papers, pay rents, subject themselves to liens and forfeitures, incur debts, and allow their landlords and creditors to make for them paper nooses out of mortgages and titles, shackles out of law. I listened to him talk of his acres awaiting the axe, how his holdings would provide for his descendents with the coming flood of immigrants if they could only be preserved from poachers, and I wanted to spit. They had, he said, despoiled fine quarters and some had gone so far as to harass his carts of cotton on their way to New Orleans. The justice hadn't enough constables or militia, and he wanted to keep the matter private so as not to stir up further indignation; he grew more excited, saying how he eagerly awaited the new blood coming into the country, once the Spanish matter was settled—The coming tide of sober, industrious folk would serve to wash away the trash.

They are illiterate and rude, he said. Of low morals and unworthy of public confidence or private esteem; they will never take a foothold because they are disunited, and knowing each other, distrust each other in kind.

He went on like that, the justice did, blind as all his kind are to the trajectories of trash—the trash who came on prison-ships windswept across the Atlantic to the new world, where they were indentured or set loose in the wilds of Georgia and South Carolina, and there carved out a life for their children and grandchildren to abandon for the promise of the southern motherland Virginia, where though they went among those who for a century had sent tobacco leaves to English queens and kings, they were still trash; and it was our fathers who quit the cavaliers' commonwealth and set out for the western territories, going willingly into newer wilds whereas their begetters went in chains for stealing fish from an Edinburgh monger's cart; and they brought with them into the wilderness the sons they'd sired, our generation. And though the names of ones like Baker and Smith bore the marks of menial origins, that past was forgotten, or worse, remembered but kept locked away in a strongbox, buried underneath their ever-rising wealth. Already Samuel was nodding in agreement, and I, damn me, was too weak to tell him no.

Yes, gentlemen, the justice said, this will be a fine new country in the coming years.

Now we were rich and had something to protect, something owed. I wondered if I could put it in a letter to Colonel Burr, ask him how it was to be beloved of the low man and the high alike, but I couldn't figure how to put it rightly into cipher. If in our letters men were flour-sacks, then should I ask him how it was to bear the cheers of the coarse Kentucky flour but eat only bread made of the finer grain? In his last letter the colonel had flattered me, said how pleased he was at the sound of our stores and how he so looked forward to doing business with a merchant of my quality.

And in our lives outside the letters, we worked within the indexes of code. Land meant more than dirt and trees, cotton more than bloom of bole. The books of the Bible had to be deciphered for their meanings, and we were the characters in one of Christ's red-lettered parables; lead shot was candy in my son's mouth and for my wife the knives and pistols in her bandoliers were jewels. And all was like the visions of a fevered man, wherein the bedside lamp becomes a block of ice, a loved one's hand seems a smelting ladle pouring drops of lead upon the sweating brow instead of cool water from a rag, sheets and blankets turn to jangling chains with every thrash and roll of the afflicted.

I thought of Edward Randolph, wracked in bed, dreaming of Daniel Clark's ship in the port of Vera Cruz, its hull packed with munitions but its manifest reading CLOTH, COTTON, TAR, and NAILS, and Clark himself there in name as a merchant of goods but in fact a salesman of revolution. And, in his delirium, would the cipher be reversed—guns splinter into nails, powder bleaches into flour, as all our codes and falsehoods are made clear when the accounts are parsed in Heaven?

I couldn't have put any of this to Randolph if I'd wanted. That night, after the justice left for a room at a house in town, we went to see our friend and found he was too bad off for words. I could hear his teeth grinding from the doorway when Polly led us in. His eyes were squeezed shut and he wouldn't know that we were there. Regardless, Samuel knelt beside him and talked to Edward Randolph of the declaration he'd written, how one day it would be famous from here to Mexico. I stood a ways back, at the foot of the bed with Polly. I told her of the money judgment and she took my arm. She said we'd been such good friends to her husband, that even with the trouble we'd been good. And, watching Randolph thrash and writhe while my brother tried to give him peace, the awful knowledge dawned on me that I'd lived beside this man for two years, preserved by his kindness, and that I didn't know him. His wife squeezed my arm as he stained his sheets with yellow bile; then she let me go and went to clean him, drawing rags from a sloshing basin as Samuel tried to hold her. I didn't know the man at all. In two days he'd be dead.

The Season of Giving

We waited until Christmas passed to do Justice Baker's work. Since the hailstorm there'd been no rain and the squatters' camps were dry and ready for the torch. As for killing, there was none. Instead we fired in the air and over grizzled heads to frighten and speed the stubborn on their departures. Most of our time was spent hollering and blustering them out. Skinny and gray, wearing too-old hides, most of them complied; and these we helped as much we could. Game was scarce and their few crops had failed.

We're starving, said one withered woman, hefting holey blankets to their wagon.

Then you'd better find somewhere else to starve, I said.

Her husband spit at me and I rode back and watched Samuel give them his ration of dried venison for their journey, speak some words of comfort.

The ones who refused had their houses set aflame and we left them naked to the elements. Thankfully, they'd cut enough trees so that the fire wouldn't spread.

I was hardened against their plight. I'd killed enough to know that it was mercy of a kind—they were poorly off wherever they were. The justifications of a hired hand, hired man; I was become like the ones I'd put to death in St. Helena. And so trash is set against trash. It took two weeks to clear them all out, and I sat coldly presiding over the enterprise with the same empty feeling as would visit me in later years when I chased runaways for sport or, still later, stood by tallying my gains at the slaver's block. On the justice's errands, I came to know that killing was better. I did it well. Never could plan, never could lead, but I could lay waste to a man and know I was right with the Lord. It was my only talent outside the Word.

So I drove the people from their homes with the memory of my own fireside close upon me, where on Christmas Eve we'd opened the crate of gifts sent down from Aliza and Reuben in Natchez. For my boy there was a rocking-horse, upon which somehow he managed to sit still. From her old mistress my wife received a dress in the latest fashion and a parcel of candied orange slices accompanied by a note in the lady's hand which said she remembered these were her favorite. I sat before the fire as the gifts were opened, my son straddling his wooden horse, and asked Red Kate if this was true. She said of course it was, plucking a bright slice glinting with sugar to her lips, chewing gratefully. And I worried that perhaps I didn't know her either—like Randolph, whose gift was a gilded desk set. The sight of it drove Polly weeping from the room, followed closely by my brother. She'd only taken part of the wrapping off before she'd seen the note and dropped the present clanging to the floor.

Samuel stayed with her in the back for a time, and so we went about balling up paper, stuffing-straw and twine, and pitched it all into the fire. I knelt with my wife and we watched it all consumed atop the embers. She smiled, red as ever in the firelight. Our son was at my side, holding fast in his still ride, and so I put my hand to the haunch of his mount, pushed down, and made it rock. He screamed so loud that Samuel and Polly came running from the back to see what was wrong.

At the last house there lived a pair of brothers near our age. We put the case to them with pistol out, and at first they both agreed. The elder, full-bearded, went to gathering their tools and horses while the younger stepped within their house, only to come suddenly out, brushing aside the blanket tacked for a door with a musket so old I couldn't judge its make, strange locks and mechanisms hissing sparks. Before I could fire it exploded in his hands; and the man ran shrieking into the woods, waving arms that ended fingerless in the air.

The shock of it drew nervous laughter from the wicked depths of me. I couldn't stop it and doubled on my horse, fighting against the bleating black cackles until there were tears in my eyes and Samuel was screaming for me to stop, God damn it, stop. And the laughter was my father's, like the time in Richmond when we saw a drunkard tottering from a tavern and fall onto the iron head of a hitching-post, killing him outright. Preacher-father, laughing, stepped down from the crate where he'd been giving his sermon to a sparse, jeering crowd, took me by the back of the neck, and brought me to see the dent in the dead man's skull. He held him up by the hair and said, loud enough for all to hear, See, son. The sinner gets his due, one way or another. I'd fought the laughter down to bitter hacks when Samuel took the bearded man to search the woods. I was choking on stillborn anger, the hatred for that voice, by the time Samuel and the man returned, having found no trace of his brother.

V

That Cursed Name

Spring 1806

The City and Her Associations

April in New Orleans and the slates and tiles of the roofs dripped rain-wash upon my false-colonel's uniform as I strode the city for the first time, brought along by Reuben because Samuel was down with another of his fevers. There was work to be done, transactions to be made, creditors to sate, and meetings to make.

Now that we're afloat again, Reuben said.

And we may have been bobbing upon Horton's money, but the bowl of the city was rapidly filling from the downpour, which had been constant since we'd debarked that morning. Reuben hulked ahead of me, his shoulders draped with a great-coat oiled against the rain, pointing out spots of incident or importance in the city, which was still small in those days, but teeming. The American merchants we met along the way gave him tips of their wilted brims and occasional salutes, sending droplets flying from their soaked gloves. Storm or no, on our way to the meeting of the Mexican Association at the house of Judge Workman, he'd take me to the Place des Armes and show me where they'd stood, his American guard, in their bloodless victory. Men hollered from King's Coffee-House at the sight of him, unmistakable in his size, but Reuben waved them off and said we'd see them later. From the open doors of little shops there issued the clucked haggling of Frenchmen; others stood beneath awning tarps struggling to eat sweets which crumbled to mush in their hands. And it was such a world I'd stepped into, with none of the honesty of Natchez, where all, at least below the hill, were united, if only in brawling. New Orleans seemed a clutch of islands populated by various tribes of outcasts, who only dealt with one another when there was no other choice.

You can tell the Spanish, he said, by the way they look at me.

And it was true at least in that the Pukes went hushed at his approach. There were many still scuttling about the town, long-time residents along with holdovers of the late government, whose uniforms signified as much authority as mine. They were gathered in the darkened porticoes, waiting out the rain, as we cut around the old church tolling mass and the smell of popery wafting out its doors borne by airs of Latin. We passed one clutch of them close by, fresh from their morning meeting with the Whore of Rome, their language jagging shrilly off the stone-work faster than seemed possible. It had been a while since I'd heard Spanish, and it sounded as it always would, like an endless disagreement. They cut their eyes and went quiet as we skirted them and came into the square, the drooping sodden stars-and-stripes suddenly in view, as if to tell me, And who are your enemies? Who have you killed but Americans? You fool, these others are a mask. You fight yourself.

I edged beside Reuben and let myself be buffeted by wind and rain. The flag, too heavy with water to unfurl, slapped soggy at its pole. In the far corner of the square, facing opposite the church, stood a scaffold for hangings.

Grinning and with a quick nod back to the Pukes, Reuben said, If they only knew, eh?

What's that? I said.

If they only knew it was you.

By the third course my belly had grown to the lip of the table. I watched the others for what to do with the thing which sat upon the plate before me, a soft-shell crab fried and swimming in cream. Following suit, I pried off one by one the spidery legs and ate them along with sips of sauternes. Slaves set saucers of butter before us and tied napkins round the necks of the more eager eaters. One black, seeing that I'd flecked cream across the front of my uniform, tried several times to bib me, same as the others. I had to grab him by the frills of his shirt and say that I'd crack his woolly head if he approached me again, to the laughter of our end of the table.

Reuben, myself, and Daniel Clark—tanned from the Mexican sun and his transits of the Gulf—sat opposite Judge Workman, who reigned at the far head behind a bucket ringed with shrimp and filled with steaming ice. A judge in the superior court of Orleans, he was delicate-seeming, not portly like the other judges I'd encountered. Workman styled himself foremost as a man of letters, his apartments crammed with books, most prominently copies of his own slim volume, a play called Liberty in Louisiana. Upon entering, those of us who'd never shared the judge's table were impressed with copies. Those who knew had brought their dog-eared own, producing them at the door like talismans to the delight of the host. Reuben nudged me early on, pointing out those who sat at Workman's left and right.

That's Lewis Kerr, he said, pointing to a tall man with powdered hair and spectacles. He's president of the Bank. Last I heard he was suing for divorce from his wife. She had one of their nigger girls tied to the bedpost and whipped her to death. By the look of him the matter may have been settled at last.

Was the black girl his mistress? I said.

A man who sat beside Reuben and had been listening leaned round and said to me, Are you sure you've never been to New Orleans, Colonel Kemper?

Seems so, said Reuben. You understand the city already. And to the right there is Gutierrez.

The Mexican was young, offset by the older men. He wore a uniform of blue and gold, thick black side-whiskers tufting at the high collar as though they grew down his neck. From what I saw he didn't speak, only watched the others with bright eyes peering out from matted hair. He had the appearance of a wolf in disguise, hair bristling out the worn seams in his man-costume.

Throughout the evening, as the crabs gave way to broiled fish and then to spring lamb and sweetbreads, Workman was encouraged by knowing guests to recite particular passages of his play. It was a comedy on a greedy Spanish don faced by a pair of buffoonish Scots-Irish grifters. I watched Daniel Clark redden each time Workman affected a brogue. After a time, the host noticed as well, standing a bit to address our end of the table, glass of wine held high as if in toast.

O, my dear Mister Clark, called Workman. I do hope you aren't taking offense? I'd hate to upset our first congressman.

None at all, sir, said Clark, raising his voice to be heard above the laughter of the guests. I only suppose you selected Irishmen for the quality of their language. I only wonder when you'll give us your next play.

Workman winced at this, let his attention be drawn away, and I leaned to Clark to ask him if it was true, was he a congressman?

Absolutely, he said. This mick takes his seat in the fall. Clark took up my copy of the play from where I'd crammed it among the china, shook the crumbs from the cover, and began to thumb through its pages.

See, said Clark, leaning in and pointing to a page, it's better to be humble in such instances.

His finger tapped for me to read a line in the frontispiece, which humbly stated that it was considered by the best critics a work unexcelled in the realm of literature.

Impressive, is it not, for a play that only stood for a night, Clark said, slapping shut the book and returning it to me. Reuben heard this and grunted. He was facing up-table, trying no doubt to catch a snippet of business amid the performance and guffaws.

Workman stood again, glass in hand, and proposed a toast to our new congressman. Clark bowed as we returned it.

Now, said our host, is a happy day, to have support in congress for our enterprise.

The guests murmured for a moment, then went hushed.

I speak freely not because of wine—though that's been quite fine, eh, gentlemen?—but because I know the sentiments of all you gathered here. Whether you've attended formal meetings of the Association or not, you have been spoken to by members and your character deemed hospitable to our designs. Is this not the case?

Hear, Hear! came the voices of the guests. The more flamboyant tossed about huzzahs. I kept quiet and so did Reuben, whose hands were flat upon the tablecloth, fingers drumming.

Excellent, said Workman. Now the project moves apace. I have lately received from Colonel Burr a letter detailing our new fortune. At this moment he stays in the house of Senator John Smith of Cincinnati, whose shipping concern has been awarded the contract to ship arms to all the American forts along the Mississippi. These shipments will be, shall we say, diverted on occasion. So you see, gentlemen, we shall not want for shot or powder!

More cheers, huzzahs, clinking of glassware. Reuben's jaw was jumping as he listened and his hands were bunched in fists.

Workman continued, And it has come to my attention that Senator Smith and our dear Colonel Burr have entered into a compact to build a canal around the falls of Louisville. A grand undertaking, which in time will provide us with profits and speed the access of settlers and volunteers to our country.

The blood was gone from Reuben's knuckles, and I thought I could hear, above the clinking glasses, the sound of his teeth grinding.

Daniel Clark stood. But, sir, such a *grand* undertaking will no doubt take time to yield. And what shall we do for financing in the mean?

A smile spread across Judge Workman's face and he put a hand to the shoulder of Lewis Kerr. Why, he said, we'll just rob the Bank, won't we!

The men only began to laugh when Workman and Kerr signaled it with their own. I thought Reuben might overturn the table.

Mirth aside, said Workman, I shouldn't be concerned over financing, Mister Clark.

And what of the governor? said Clark. Does he still stand with us?

Workman frowned, glancing to his glass, now empty. He returned his eyes to the guests and said, Governor Claiborne is a mauled bitch. He shrinks at whatever master's hand is raised.

The table squealed with Reuben's rising, fists bunched and pressing to the linen. Gentlemen, he said. I know that I'm a ways on the outside of this project, but would you grudge me a question?

Mister Kemper, said Judge Workman, by all means. Let's hear it, so we might make clear to all who have similar misgivings.

Reuben looked for a moment at the judge, then swept his eyes over the guests and started. You've read me right, sir, to say I've got misgivings. Don't fear, though, I won't go running my mouth. I know for a fact that Mister Claiborne damns the very ground I stand on. But he has been forthright in his dislike of me, while a man like John Smith— by God he's in the pocket of the dons and the worst back-dealer and smiling liar in the country. And while I'm at it I might add General Wilkinson to the measure as a pocket-man. He sold my brothers out on their first try at a similar business. With such a great enterprise at hand, how can we put our trust in these men?

The guests went murmuring until Workman stood and spoke. Well put, he said. But, Mister Kemper, the thing about pocket-men is that they can always be plied to the side whose pockets are deeper. I wager to say that the Spaniards' are growing rapidly thin, with little chance for them to fill again, while our own have the prospect of being so loaded down with cash that these men will have to fight to keep their heads above it. They see that, and so cast their lot in with us. And you must also not forget that with us they have the prospect for glory—isn't that right, my friends! And glory, I trust you agree, Mister Kemper, is no mean prize.

Glory, said Reuben, working the scars in his face. And is this glory to be the separation of the western states or the acquisition of West Florida and Mexico? I'm hearing too many different stories and designs for my liking. From the sound of it tonight, we mean to take New Orleans.

Workman plainly was fighting down anger. In the meantime I sat there, hidden behind Reuben, damning that everything had to come back to Smith. That he couldn't put it away for this.

I'll say this, Reuben continued, because I would have no part in any action disloyal to the United States. I will happily help enrich her borders, or set up a more friendly country on them. But I will not put asunder what God Himself has joined.

And there, behind this inexplicably voiced supposed loyalty, there was a hint of Baptist boyhood. It worked upon the guests, his preaching, and if some didn't share in his misgivings, they had begun to. Myself, I knew it for a lie.

Workman brought his full might and judicial tone to what he said next: Mister Kemper brings up valid points. And we must all recognize that out of all of us, barring Mister Gutierrez, he and his brothers have suffered the most because of the Spanish dominion.

Reuben winced and worked his scars again as my own were being gawked at.

Hear! Hear! said the guests.

And Mister Kemper's misgivings, said Workman, are indeed justified and welcome. For they give me the opportunity to state once and for all that we will foment no disunion. Our enterprise is not to separate the states, but to add to their bounty, to do, as our president has expressed many times, the work of driving monarchy and European influence from the continent.

Yes! cried Gutierrez, raising his glass so that the wine flipped from out the lip and doused a nearby candelabra. The guests were clapping. Reuben still stood, buffeted by their applause for Workman's words.

We few, said the judge, we happy few; we band of brothers must hold steadfast to our lofty goal!

Clark nudged me, whispering, At least he has enough sense to quote a better playwright.

However, Workman said, we cannot in our high-mindedness dispense with the more immediate needs of supplying an army.

Then it's true, said Reuben.

If, Mister Kemper, we are to enact this project—

Cry havoc, and let slip the dogs of war? Reuben interrupted.

Workman, ignoring him, pressed on. If we are to set out for Vera Cruz, Mobile, and Pensacola, we need ships in port. We have that in New Orleans. And if we are to get our army to these ships, we cannot simply march them to the wharf without notice, nor even gather them in the city itself if the authority here is hostile towards us. No, sir, if the Isle of Orleans is taken, it will not be in our possession long, but be returned when hostilities have ceased and we are victorious.

You won't hold it long, said Reuben, with every damn American fort turned against you.

We won't have to hold anything, said Workman. We know the number of our national forces nearby, and now, thanks to Senator Smith, we have control of their provision. Furthermore, as we will take Baton Rouge first, I believe the government of the United States will see the worth of our project. As we offer everything but ask nothing, the government can sit back and apologize to the Spaniards for our actions while we do the work the army should be doing. And might I add, Mister Kemper, that you have been made a party to our project despite your failures in a similar effort and because of the recommendation of the same John Smith to whom you seem so opposed.

Reuben stayed standing after Workman had sat. He wouldn't be alive to recommend if I'd had my way.

Bull-shit, I said.

The guests about who heard all started at my words, and Reuben, still facing the judge, could only give me a glaring corner of his eye.

I am sorry to hear that, Mister Kemper, Workman said. But if we cannot count on your support, then can we at least trust in your confidence?

By my honor, said Reuben, easing himself back into his chair, where he burned beside me with such anger as to melt the iced cream which followed. Sweet wine and thin glasses of liquor were given us by the slaves, and Workman, his good humor returned, announced that he had a treat in store for us all. His pen had been busy of late, so he said, and he'd gathered up a troupe of rather interesting players to give us the first act of his new play. And so we were led into the large sitting room, where were arranged at the front various sofas and plush chairs for us to sit in while we watched the show.

When all were seated, an Indian girl, naked save for a string of shells and the hair of her mound braided with glass beads, stepped out from the back of the house and began to declaim her half-memorized lines of dialogue, tripping over what was meant to be simple, savage speech. Satire upon satire. Reuben and I sat at the back of the others, the anger in his face as clear as the shivering of the naked girl. She was cold, her paps puckered and risen. Her beads and shells tinkled piti-fully together as she lamented being made a sacrifice to the great spirit. When four of Workman's Negroes, painted a terrible red and decked in the garb of braves, came in bearing the sacrificial totems, Reuben stood and made for the door.

Before I could follow after him, Clark caught me by the arm, say-ing, You should've said your piece.

You can let them know. I'm for it.

Do you think you can talk some sense into Reuben?

Workman watched us while he coached his players in whispers, waving for the Indian girl's arms to be held above her head.

Does he really make a damn? I said.

Clark said, That much depends on you.

He let me go and I slipped out as the girl was being tied to the stake.

And that's what you want, is it, killer? To throw in with Smith?

It was past mid-night and we were on Bourbon, the lone streetlamp dangling in the distance near the Carondelet Canal. Reuben was in such a rush to be out of Workman's that he'd pulled his coat only partway on; it flapped heavily as he swung his arms about and raged. He said Smith like it was the worst of cusses, fit only to be spit from his mouth at one of the many trash-heaps we passed which spilled from out the alleyways in drifts sweetly stinking in their rot.

I said, All I'm saying is we don't let what's past come in the way of us being a part of something that will work.

Past? he said. Past? It may be past to you and Sam but I live with that bastard's usury and treachery each day. I just got my fucking suit against him put in the American courts, for God's sake! You don't think that's why he's recommended me to them? No, he wants me placated so I don't beat him with the law.

And whose court will it be in? I said. You think Workman will speed your case right through, eh? Tie up one of Burr's financiers?

Reuben doubled over in his anger. God damn it, I am trapped. This twisted world and that cursed name. I'll never be rid of it.

The few people out that night scuttled from our warring path like roaches to the walls of the houses, disappearing into the dark as though they feared the light of the distant, bobbing lamp. We came to a corner, not a block from the canal, and we were full of meanness.

I won't be God-damned part of it, he said.

Who gives a shit? I said. Smith will always be there, whether it's him or another bastard in government. They're all the same. Why not throw in when they're onto something good?

You prove yourself wrong, he said. They are all the same, and that's the thing! Your precious Colonel Burr? He's worst of all.

He's a great man, I said.

Toasted in the same breath as Smith and Wilkinson. They're rotten great men.

It's your people doing the toasting, I said. Your Association.

It's not mine anymore, said Reuben. Tonight I've parted interests.

Well, I said, I'm not as weak as you.

Reuben stopped beside a shuttered coffee-stall and glared at me, swung one fist and buckled the paneling. The latch fell from the shutters and clattered to the ground. A voice called out from above for us to clear out.

Ask my ass! Reuben called back. And you, you think you want to be a part of this grand glory, eh?

If I can have a clear shot at dogs like Kneeland and—

Reuben blocked the way ahead. Seems to me you take your shots by ambush anyway, and you can do that anytime.

What are you saying?

I'm saying that you are a bone-picker and a sneak-man. Reuben squared to me and stepped close. You hide and skulk and don't have the stomach or the skill to make a fight square.

Fuck you, I said. Where was your noble ass when we were in Baton Rouge?

And you couldn't win that one because you're too damned stupid! All you can do is murder by surprise.

You telling me that, foreskin-cutter? You plan to whip a confession out of me?

For Christ's sake, he said. The foreskins were a show. None of it was real, nothing in the jar but pigs' knuckle skin. It started as a joke we liked to tell each other while we courted, but everyone was fool enough to believe it, that's all. . . . See, I am not like you. I'm no fiend for slaughter.

Right, I said, you're just a liar. And a coward.

Reuben had me by the shoulders and I took him by the coat and in our struggle we toppled the coffee-stall, hit the pavers so that the breath was knocked from me by his weight. I was growling and swinging at his face, knuckles glancing the wounds I wished to split anew. His monstrous weight was upon me and his hands smothered my face, squeezing my head as though to crush it like a coon-box. It was like when we'd gone into the river, bound together but fighting each against the other; and likewise as the blood hammered in my ears and even Reuben's cusses were drowned out by his fingers digging at my skull I felt Samuel was there, twisting away on his own end of the rope. I felt the plates beneath my hair unhinging and my jaw set open as I tried to give him a knee to the bollocks but failed; and from out the dimming corner of my eye, rounding onto Bourbon, there came a light.

I brought my knee up again but to no use and the light grew brighter, turning onto the street, and at once a great bright haze but also a collection of many pinpoints which only became one when I was squinting with the pain as Reuben let loose his grip and turned to see the light engulfing us. Slowly, knee to foot, he stood, and from the wreckage of the coffee-stall I sat up and saw the light was candles, held in the hands of a procession of Negroes. I lipped the blood from beneath my nose and lay my throbbing head against the busted boards, tried to stand but couldn't. Only Reuben had his feet, facing now the flame-point river and the dark faces it lit—too dark to be free, and in cast-off black suits with their collars pulled high for the chill and drizzle, hiding ragged work-day clothes, their candles fighting against them. And only when the bearers passed, shouldering the coffin, did my half-mashed mind come to understand it was a funeral.

The Negroes were utterly silent, not the ever-singing dance-abouts the world would have them be. A fine, solemn function; and I thought, watching the last of their train go by, that this was a good way to go to ground. Reuben didn't move, nor did I—we were fixed like a monument to the white man's bafflement, and the funeral-goers took no notice of us. At the end were children holding pine knots and nubs of wax-melt molded into candles their own size. Even these were silent. I drew out my pistol and aimed it at his back, leveling the gun in my blasted sight while he contemplated the tail of the procession. When darkness returned and Reuben stood round, I cocked the hammer.

Well, little brother, is this the end you wish to make?

You tried to kill me, I said.

That may be the difference between us. I try and you do.

And don't *little brother* me.

I haven't treated you as a brother? he said. If not, then shoot.

Reuben would have been a hard target to miss; he ate up all my vision as the shouts and calls that a killing was commencing began to issue from about the street. Of course we hadn't been alone. From out the trash-heaps and the rain-barrels and the bottom-floor brothels people peeked out or gave voice, the bored encouraged and the frightened alarmed.

Christ, he said, enough. But Reuben's voice bottled up in his throat and he stopped, bending to retch out the courses of Workman's fine meal. Spit strung from his lip to the ground and I was laughing as he shuddered out the last of it.

I put my pistol away and Reuben stayed bent, contemplating the cat-pile he'd left on the ground. I would have had to walk around it, there was so much, but he took it in one stride. And his voice, continuing, was fat with breaths straining not to bring up more.

All this shit, he said. That's what it's worth. Burr and Workman and Smith.

The Pukes? I said.

Reuben grunted a laugh, then staggered off to vomit again. The second time he was finished, I went on, saying, I'm still for it. I want to win.

Wiping his mouth, Reuben said, And I want it too, but not with these men. I was wrong to fall in with their like.

It's all the same, like you said. If sinners can be used for a holy purpose, then why not?

I'm not all that sure it's all that holy, but you would know, he said. But then again it seems the Lord only comes up when you need Him.

Isn't that His way? I said. He comes to me only when I'm in need.

I meant to justify, he said, whatever fool or rotten design you're after. That makes me think it's less the Lord's will and more yours.

They're one and the same, I said. I'm but a vessel.

Christ, said Reuben, choking back another bout. I guess he's picked worse.

If their plans show promise come the fall, I said, I'll join in with them.

I swear to God I'll stop it, he said.

How's that? I said.

Spread the word, he said. I'll go all the way to Washington if I have to.

If you're so sure it'll fail, then why bother?

That's the thing, he said. I'm afraid for it to work. Then instead of the Pukes we'll have an empire of Smiths and Workmans.

We've already got that, I said.

Stop, by God, trying to convince me.

You were so hot for vengeance, I said. But now you've softened.

Reuben arched his fingers so the knuckles popped. No, he said. And I'm not giving up on our retribution. That'll come in time. But I don't want me, or you, or Sam caught up in this disaster.

So it's gone from being foolish to a disaster, has it?

You more than most should know how one can lead to the other.

Sam's for it, I said. It'll be hard work for you to change his mind.

I brought him into it, he said, and I can bring him out.

All he's ever wanted was to do right by you. It's why he came down here in the first place. Back in Chit all he could talk about was you.

Reuben heaved his shoulders as though the weight of his brother's admiration rested there. And what about you? Why'd you come down?

What did I say about the Will of the Lord? I heard it and I followed.

Reuben rubbed at where the scars began, or ended, at the hair of his temples.

And what if Jefferson himself supports the enterprise? I said.

Then I'll know where I stand, said Reuben. We'll know.

And even as he went from clerk to clerk over the next few days, paying off his bondsmen so that we could leave the city, he tried to ply me to his side. I had stoppered my rage and began to think coolly. Whatever his aims were, I wouldn't have to smash them; all I'd need to do was work the loose threads at the seams. Let him holler and spout; I would be quiet and calm and watchful. If Reuben did go crow at the capital then Burr would know before he left Mississippi. I'd make sure of that. I began to think of how to put it into cipher, slipped into the coded world again.

VI

Many Returns

May 1806

The Safety of Home

Pinckneyville was late awake the night of our return, high spirits for a Tuesday in early May. From upcountry there had come a group of strangers, ten or so, who brought with them brindled fighting dogs and coops of roosters to pit against the local talent. When they arrived in town that morning Samuel was well enough to rent them the lot behind the tavern—where they dug a great pit to hold their exhibitions of animal violence—and to sell them scrap timber which they quickly threw together into tiered benches filled by afternoon with townsfolk screaming out their bets. There was also a brisk business in Blight, so Samuel said, the strangers having agreed not to sell their own drink. In exchange, Samuel had given them a pittance price to set up their camp a mile or so down the road, on Randolph's patch of land where years before the Reverend Morrel had struck his last revival. They said they didn't want to sleep in town, and if things went well there'd be more festivities to come and they would need the room.

When I left, said Samuel, pairs of men had broken off and were boxing even while the dogs fought.

And they say *we* ruined the character of the town, I laughed. We were at Randolph's table—I still considered it his though he lay months-dead and Samuel had taken up residence in his as-yet-unspoken dealings with the widow—the three of us brothers, Polly beside Samuel, and my Copperhead close to me, holding my hand under the table. We'd put the boy to bed soon after I arrived. I supposed he was glad to see me, though he didn't return my kiss and I had to lift his limp arms to hug them round my neck when I picked him up. Red Kate squeezed my hand and sidled closer, the handle of her leftmost pistol knocking against mine, the wooden thunk of our armed matrimony just as reassuring as the sound of dishware being set upon the table or bed-linen being beaten for fleas.

Reuben grunted, stretching the crick which had developed in his neck on our journey up, made worse by what Justice Baker had said to him when we'd stopped in Woodville the day before. We left the Cotton-Picker in New Orleans and traveled overland for just this reason—his preparatory go at raising the alarm over the designs of the Association. At first the justice feigned surprise, said he'd heard similar rumors, made half-hearted promise that he'd look into the matter. But when Reuben kept on pressing him for what actions he would take, saying that he himself intended on going to Washington, Justice Baker stiffened and said that he did not recommend such a course. Growing flustered, Reuben demanded to know why, and the justice looked at me, then back to Reuben, and replied, Didn't your brothers tell you? We'll have a fine new country here before long.

This sent Reuben into a rage, and he stormed out of the justice's chambers, leaving me to exchange a nod with the man, to let him know that I too was a believer. The look upon Justice Baker's face, the strained arch of eyebrow and the tilting head, before I hustled out after my cussing brother, said, You'll have to stop him. Even ranters and ravers are given credence on occasion in the houses of power.

And I wished the justice had tried a little harder to keep up his original lie, for all his honesty did was steel Reuben's resolve, buckle it with anger—his great motivator. What I saw behind that look did trouble me all our way home, the knowledge of it galling even at the table with the sound of cock-call and barking and shouting men coming from outside.

You should see their dogs, Samuel said. Their eyes are different colors. One blue, one green. They look like demons.

Where are they from? I said.

All over, Samuel said. That Kentucky kind. Tennesseans. I didn't ask much. They're just traveling hucksters.

The way we used to be, I said.

Before I liberated your asses, said Reuben, who was spreading and rolling his shoulders in his frustration. And it seemed to work on Samuel a bit, for he gave his head bow and cast at his brother a grateful smile.

Samuel said, I don't think they've got a head man. From what I can tell it's democratic.

We'll need to be sure they're not stealing niggers or horses, I said.

They seem to be content, he said.

We were quieted by still louder barking, then a piteous squeal that lasted far too long and was terminated by cheers.

No one ever is, Reuben said. Right or wrong, every man is always stretching for what lies just beyond his reach. Isn't that right, brother?

Reuben meant me, though he stayed facing Samuel and the yawning widow Randolph, barely cutting his eyes in my direction.

I'll have to plug my ears with wax to sleep a wink with all this racket, Polly said.

Samuel leaned close to her, saying, You'll sleep fine.

Red Kate's hand pumped mine and I knew she had things to tell me, to add some flesh and blood to what I already knew. I wasn't eager for it, knowing that I'd have to hear the same things from Samuel when we were alone. Truth be told, I didn't care much for my brother's need to have the widows of his late friends, but I wanted the hearth and kitchen talk of women more than I could stand to hear Reuben go into the Burr business again, which he proceeded to do, speechifying for Samuel's benefit. So when my wife turned to me, blinking slowly so that her nose, flat like those of the boxers now pummeling on each other down the way, wrinkled and arched its freckles into a bunch, I rose with her and we left.

Outside the barks and shouts were louder, and we didn't stop to see any more than the light of the bonfires and the long shadows cast upon the roofs of the buildings from the party. There was no need; our lives were blood-sport. There was only the question now of who held the bets and what fruit our wagers would bear. We rubbed guns on the porch, kissing soft and kind for the first in a long time, until from within our son began to cry, adding his own wail to the sounds of animal pain and fury. Red Kate pulled away and went to fishing in her dress-bib for the key, saying not to him but softly and to herself, All right, child, I'm coming.

We found him with his head jammed between the bars of his crib, which had been replaced and fitted stronger since the night of our kidnapping. He was facing the ground, wailing, eyes upturned and visible through his dangling tuft of white hair, his mouth open terribly wide. I was frozen by his noise, stood there, unable to offer him comfort, while my wife went to the kitchen and scooped two fingers of clotted grease from the pan. His wailing grew louder as she had him pull his neck out straight like a man awaiting execution, and she daubed the cold grease about his ears, slicked the hair there and down the sides of his neck. I overcame myself, my weakness, and went to him, took my boy by the shoulders and as his screams reached an awful pitch I tugged and he came loose. I lifted him out and held him, shrieking as though he were still trapped while I kicked the bars of the crib to pieces. Red Kate stood back and let me go, and once the wood lay in splinters on the floor, I turned his head from where it had been buried in my shoulder and had him look. See, I said, no more bars.

And I held my boy while his mother swept up the broken wood, shook splinters from his bedding. She went to pitch the pieces in the fireplace, and when she returned we sat with him for a time while he sobbed and jabbered in his way at us, going from my breast to hers and back, soaking them with his tears until his anger and bewilderment were spent and he fell to sleep in her arms, fluttering snot from his nose which she wiped with the ends of her dress, revealing her thighs, bare and beautiful. But I didn't want them and found myself just as bewildered, just as trapped, as my son.

What can he see? said Red Kate. What can his world be like?

God knows, I said, and thought, It must be a torture. Horrors of the everyday.

She held his head and rocked deeper. Maybe it's better that he can't tell it—that he has no words.

That's too cruel to think, I said. If he's afflicted it's no blessing.

Her harsh whisper: You'd know cruelty, wouldn't you? And I didn't say it was a blessing.

She swept him deeper in her rocking and I didn't have the strength or rile in me to press back. I was cursed with words: God's, Preacher-father's, Samuel's, Reuben's, Burr's, my own—all preying endlessly upon my mind and soul. But as it would so often be, none of them

343

were for these two, wife and child, who needed me; my words were then as they are now, far-flung and useless to the present.

Reuben wants to go to Washington, I said.

So? said Red Kate. It isn't far.

I was dumbfounded for a moment before I realized she thought I'd meant Washington, Mississippi. Not the territory, love, the capital of the country.

O my Jesus, she said. For what?

He's turned against the plan, I said. He's angry that Burr is in with Senator Smith and has quit the Association. Now he means to go and warn the damned president.

God, men's minds are fickle. And you'll fall in behind him?

No.

Then you're enemies, she said.

A dog was baying now, victorious. Men hollered for their takes. My Copperhead shifted her dozing burden and searched me in the darkness. It won't do him any good to go all that way, will it?

No, I said. The man's president of the country. If he doesn't know already then it's too late.

This is all a dream, she said. We're little people, not so caught up in this as you and he'd like to think.

If the plan does fall through, because of Reuben or not, I'm caught up enough to be arrested.

But if the judges are all for it like you say—

There'll always be more judges.

Then go with him. Stave his head in or shoot him on some dusty road in Tennessee.

I had my chance already, I said.

New Orleans was eventful, then.

We've got an understanding of sorts.

He doesn't understand a thing, she said. Not even his own self.

Christ, you've done some thinking, haven't you?

Ah, said my wife, now he's full-out. She rose with the boy in her arms, went and laid him in his bed. She came back to the bed and took off her shoes, carefully cupping each with her free hand lest the heels hit the floor and raise a sound. As I would, I left my boots on. In the meantime, the baying was at an end, the shouts of men had died down, and now what could be heard was the dwindling, excited chatter as the spectators returned to their homes, got a-horse to jangling livery and hoofbeats to hurry back and perhaps avoid the displeasure of their wives or to trudge drunk to houses in town.

At least they're done, said Red Kate, laid out straight as a plank across the foot of the bed.

The way they sound, I said, I can't help but think of when we used to rob such men. And as I spoke, I saw myself stepping out with Samuel from behind a corner, pistols out, and looking on the awe-struck faces of those we'd have empty their pockets and beg for their lives.

I've got no fond remembrances of those times, she said.

I pulled myself further into bed so that my boots no longer touched the ground. And in the way which earthly things, facts and realities, often came to me, I recalled how young she'd been when we'd first met—fourteen. In the last year Red Kate had passed the age of her majority. Reaching for her I felt the straps of her armaments, knife-handle or the stock of a pistol, and she didn't move. My wife was stiff and prone as a corpse in its coffin.

The homeward-heading voices were now gone, the night's wildness at an end and the men returned to wanting safety—shuttered windows and the bar behind the door. We stayed awake even as the strangers, it seemed, had loaded up their animals and driven their carts out of town, rending the silence with the squealing of their cartwheels as they turned just past our house for the east-west road and their camp.

345

Sounds like West Florida, she said. The whining wheels.

This gave me pause, and I prayed on what she said until the sound of ungreased axles carried off into the distance and was gone, as we were from that place and time.

I'd only go with Reuben, I said, because I don't think Samuel can make the trip.

He's strong enough, she sniffed. I'll tell you that.

Polly? I said.

This morning, when those men came knocking, was the first time in a week he's left her bed. And I don't mean he's been laid up there sick.

I know what you meant, I said.

I can't be the judge of anybody, said Red Kate, but so close to her husband's death. I've resigned myself to you dying so many times I've lost count. And I know I'd be no wilting lily if you did. I'd go on, but I'd damn sure take no other man. I've had enough of them.

And her words hugged to me close and good as my weapons, though I couldn't judge them true. They were the bedroom promises often made between man and woman; they carry little weight in the light of day. And why should they? Talk of the future blows away at morning like the ghosts of the past which hang about our periphery. I expected nothing of her but to live and to endure me. I could ask no more. I sat up in bed and took Red Kate by the arm and brought her close to me.

Kick the dirt from your boots, she said, easing to the pillows.

Knocking my heels together over the floor, I heard the boy stir at the noise, and more—there was the sound of horses whinnying out back.

The stable, said my wife.

I went from the bed, looking to the black windows for any light or movement in the front of the house as the horses grew louder, feeling in the dark for the handles of my arms.

Get him under the bed, I said.

And at that moment came a shout I recognized as Samuel's, and a gunshot. I had one pistol out and like a fool burst onto the porch, where issued a volley of fire as the door splintered. I fell to the ground, slapping myself with my free hand for any wounds, hearing from Randolph's porch my brothers calling out to me.

I answered with a whoop that came out strange, and Reuben was jabbering that it was ambush and murder, trying to raise an alarm in the town, which was so oddly quiet that I could hear the men rushing through our yard, taking better places to pick us off while their fellows in the barn drew out our horses. Inch by inch I stuck my head out to look at Randolph's porch, where both brothers crouched in the doorway, lit by lamps and candles from within. Samuel held a shotgun out, barrel wavering; Reuben had both his pistols up.

I ducked back in and another shot sounded and a ball struck the frame where my head had been. Again the brothers called out, but this time I didn't answer and the men moved closer, rustling through the weeds. I leaned against the inside wall, and there I slowly stood and waited. Boots upon the boards and evil whispers, approaching. Samuel's shotgun sounded and the men on my porch dropped, but were unharmed. They croaked to one another their condition and the one furthest to the right returned fire.

Deafened by the after-roar and the blood pounding in my skull, I drew out my second pistol as Reuben tried his shot and failed, cussing loudly. And it was a pistol which first entered through my doorway, jabbing in, followed by a scraggy thin arm and a wild bearded face which was lit by the hang-fire of my sparking, hissing flint in the instant before the powder took and sent my shot through the side of his head. The man dropped and I slipped in his gore on my way to throw open the door, which was slick with him also, and, eyes burning in the powder-smoke and the back-blow of the dead man's blood and brains, I stepped out and shot his fellow in the back as he scuttled down the steps, threw my pistols down and drew my third and last. The second man was still alive; he'd fallen in the space between the steps so that he was caught by them at the waist, dangling there like the target at a gentlemen's shoot. I saw that his hands were empty, feebly reaching for the smoking hole in his back, and so I resigned to let him wail and bleed out rather than waste another shot. Above his screams I shouted and was answered by my wife and both my brothers.

Hell yes! Samuel shouted. Hell yes, Angel!

And now came the calls of the other men, who were still out back at the stable. They taunted us some country cusses, said for us to come on down. I slipped back inside my house, went to take my shotgun from my kit, hearing Samuel say, There's two of you down already, boys! You want more?

Piss on you Kempers! shouted one.

Come and take your dues! called another.

The back-shot man was still shrieking, his arm-flailing now more floppish when I came outside again. I waved to my brothers that I'd go round the left-hand side of my house, for I judged the space between mine and Randolph's to be the killing-range of their poorly laid trap. In fact, the foolishness of their ambush did remind me of ourselves, the way we would've done it with Ransom and the boys. Only I'd say we would've had some cover fire in the high grass near the river, so that I wouldn't have been able to step round the porch-trapped man and descend from my house, passing by the window where my wife leaned half out with her guns, nodding sharply to me as I went around the side and made my way along the wall, trampling her truck-patch, shotgun parting the spring corn's shoots. To my right the rest of town was quiet—not a voice, not a man without his house at all the screams and gunfire. Now hoofbeats sounded; they were mounting. Stumbling through a tangle of squash, I resolved I might burn Pinckneyville to the ground, test the citizens' indifference that way. I thumbed to be sure that the hammers of both barrels were cocked.

I was coming out the garden when the dark moved up ahead, enormous and stomping towards me. I crouched and fired lucky, saw the rider in the flame-plume of one barrel which tore away his shoulder. He fell and I fell atop him, for the horse, which I'd later find was mine, clipped me in the face with his back shoe on his way through the plants. I picked myself up, finding my right cheek was stoved. I thought my eyeball might droop loose, but still there was no stopping me. I squinted it shut, to hold my eye in, and threw my back to the wall of the house. I peered round and fought to see. A lantern within showed the open doorway of the stable and the men, another three remaining, all on horseback, riding about between the stalls, arguing confusedly in their high-mountain accents. In the mean, Samuel and Reuben had done the same as me—gone round the outside of Randolph's and drawn beads.

This don't end with us, Kempers! hollered one from the stable.

I was gasping too hard for breath to answer, but there came Reuben's voice, calling back, Well, if any of you make it out alive you can tell your Spanish masters that they'd better send something more than a bunch of Kaintuck pig-fuckers!

Piss on the Spanish, the man said. You're marked worse than that!

That so? Samuel said, mocking. Then who is it?

A good man, who you wronged, answered the man.

You bastards must be drunk, said Reuben.

The Kentuckians yipped and hollered. Whoever's men, they were clownish. Still and all there were three of them, and they were mounted. The lid above my busted cheek did tremble to keep my eye skull-bound; and I wondered were they mad enough to charge.

And they were. The lantern-light disappeared for a moment before it was made clear that they'd tossed it to the hay, which took fire as they rode howling out from the smoke. It was only fifty yards or so to cover before they were between the houses, but in that space we laid a volley down that put two to the ground. I threw aside my shotgun and lurched out, pistol in hand, breaking into a run, every step jogging my loose eye and bones until I met my brothers in the middle, saw the escaped rider turning to the front of my house. And it was that when he passed out of sight there came a pair of gunshots. Running again, brothers close behind, past the one trapped between the steps, now dead and drooping, and into the yard to find a horse turning circles, unmanned, and its rider twisted on the ground at the edge of the yard.

Be damned, said Reuben, who was turned towards the house.

And when I looked to where he did, I found Red Kate standing at the top of the porch, both her pistols smoking. I took her in my eye, and she was a fury, holding tight to her weapons and bringing them close to her chest as she started down the steps. Her leather enwrapments creaked, as did the boards, and when she passed the trapped man she kicked him in the back of the head and came on down to meet us.

We were huffing breaths, my brothers giving wild glances between us all, grinning at the strangeness of this woman, who, coming close, appeared so small, but burnt there in the dark like a lit match. I'd put my free hand to the stoved side of my face; and my wife parted the brothers, took me by the wrist and brought it away. I'd had it there for I could no longer hold the squint, and so as she shook her head and looked upon me, my eye gave way and dangled out upon the wreckage of my cheek.

O Jesus, love, she said, reaching out to cup it back as I winced and spit for pain.

But even as I spoke my good eye darkened, and I saw through a narrowing pinprick tunnel in the blackness my brothers reaching for me. Overtook by blindness that would last for days and in an instant all my weight was gone and I was light as ash. I didn't even feel their hands upon me, hauling me up the steps to where I'd lay out on the porch for the night and early morning, raving bewildered when my wife brought out our boy, saying, How in Christ could he ever sleep? And she set him beside me on the porch, kissed both our foreheads, and returned to her hasty preparations, for we would leave as soon as possible. Feeling for my son, I hurt him when I pulled him close. He moaned his word, then settled; and we, in our way, oversaw the sorry night's-end progress, left the horses to rot, gifts for the buzzards and the townsfolk, who had shaken off their indifference enough to venture near the slaughter-ground, though there couldn't have been much for them to see—scuff-marks in the dirt, the holes pocked in our doors; above all, the smoldering ruin of our stable. Samuel and Reuben bartered with them for a wagon and the beasts to pull it even as the men gave pitiful croaks about legal repercussions and their worries for the safety of the town.

By then my boy, wrapped in a blanket and swaddled close, had joined in, imitated them in gibbered harangue. The men of the town resumed their grumbling; their voices were of awe and wonder, as I imagined they would be for generations, at having had people such as us within their midst. We'd hear later that, not an hour after we left, Pinckneyville was visited by a storm of awful power. The whirlwind formed at the river and slashed against the land, drawing up the newly buried killed and the bloat-bellied horses, along with many houses and goods of the living, and several themselves were caught in the pillar of wind, beaten to death by their doors and stoves and porch-beams. And, so we'd hear, when the raging column had passed and the people, mostly naked, came out from their hiding places, they found our houses and tavern to be the only things untouched by the storm.

Book Five

THESE ARE THE WORDS

I

O Jerusalem

Natchez, Summer 1806

Bring Forth the Blind

I was brought to Natchez as into the womb, a place of darkness where I floated amid the dulled noises of the world, jarred and bobbing in the shuttered, bolted madness of Aliza's household—now reduced by that lady's fears to herself and the necessary slaves—as in the waters of my first home, which was rotten. This I considered in my time of darkness, while being shuttled about The Church by the hands of the sighted—that I was grown in a house of pestilence, my mother diseased of body and my father sick with the Lord. From the rot sprung and to the rot returned.

Come on now, the Negroe Barbary would say whenever she'd heard enough of my mumbled ravings. I won't have another crazy person here. I can't hack more of that. She was chief among Aliza's servants and had seen, since the stabbing, her mistress grow stranger, running off all of her whores and shutting up, window-by-window and lock-by-lock, the house once full of laughter and sweet voices until it became the close and fetid vault we entered to the sound of bolts unshot, chains unlatched, bars lifted.

It had been Aliza's voice, thin and rasping, which answered Reuben at the door. She'd seen us from her spyglass, which she manned now constantly. And if her voice didn't tell the tale, it was the jangling of her safe-guards—more than I recalled—being undone to let us in; and when Reuben told her of our troubles, it just confirmed her suspicions of the world, that it was peopled with deceivers who sought only to destroy us, invaders and assassins massing at the gate. She talked of danger and betrayal while her slaves brought our wagon to the carriage house in back and unloaded our things. Reuben, I could feel, tried to hold on to his wife, but she'd allow him only brief grasps as she sliced on through our company, giving bony embrace to each and all: to Red Kate, who she kissed and called Katie; to the boy, who she asked how he liked his horse, and was answered only by his single word.

He doesn't talk much, Red Kate said.

O? said Aliza. Well, you're still young, aren't you, dear?

And on the mistress went, gasping at my wound, then to the shuddering widow Randolph, her affection strained, as bizarre as the blade of a guillotine fettered with flowers.

When Reuben spoke I groaned, and my son groaned with me. He'd continued, since the night of the attack, to be a mocker. At Fort Adams, where we were hailed and toasted and given a guard of soldiers to ride on with us to Natchez, he'd taken up his bowl of corn-mush and begun to pat it on his right eye, so that he'd have something like my plaster patch—or so I heard by Red Kate's shouting as she jerked him up.

It was Barbary who was called to bring me and the boy upstairs, to Red Kate's old room. She talked to me all along our way, saying how she'd seen me give the wedding sermon, and how it was a pretty thing. She toted the boy in the crook of one withered arm and led me with the other, slipping it out when we reached the bedroom door. Then, holding me there with a fingertip, she said, When I brush the mistress hair it falls out in hunks.

She sick? I said.

Worse, said Barbary. She's lost.

Presently the boy let off a moan and the slave brought us both into the room where I had lain first with my wife in that time when all things were possible, but now the spices and perfumes were faded on the air after being shut up for a month or more, and the sheets, when the Negroe turned them down, gave off the smell of mold and were cold and furry to my touch.

I wouldn't have told you she was lost if you weren't the preacher, she said.

As you see, there's not much I can do.

Because you blind, she said.

I eased onto the bed, dust swarming at my nostrils. The boy was curling into the pillows; perhaps the memory of his mother's scent, mixed in somehow with the grime and disuse, but more likely the leavings of more recent tenants—the brow-sweat of the one who'd plotted Aliza's death and those who'd knocked the notion into her.

Barbary said, Let's have all that nonsense off before you lay your head.

What she meant was my cures. My condition had become the chief feature of our stops along the way; every farmer towing carts of manure-caked produce, every wizened crone, every rich man with his retinue of slaves, all proffered cures for blindness—some of which even Red Kate had never heard of. I was uncaring, and by-the-by they'd

357

been applied—chickweed and bay leaf in compress, vials of water draped about my neck, a knotted crown of possums' tails—applied and endured only to be drawn from me piecemeal by Barbary, clucking derision as she held the warm bulb of the lamp close that she might better see.

I suppose you know a cure too, I said.

Miss Kate knows cures. Used to doctor all the girls.

She only did the plaster, I said.

I cried when you took her, Barbary said. I knew, right then, all the good was gone and things would be sorry from then on out.

I didn't know you were there.

Course you didn't. You weren't supposed to. Barbary went about the room, found the wash-basin and tray, clattering the empty china. She said, Nigger's a ghost. Can't be seen unless something else's gone wrong. . . . I'll bring back the basin.

When she'd gone, I reached round the underside of the bed for the pot and, lifting it, found that the thing was filled, its holdings hardened but heavy. I threw the pot down and put my head to the pillow, which didn't smell at all like killer's sweat but the sopping feathers of scalded fowl before the pluck, and I pulled my son close to me; and when Barbary returned, she took the pot up with a cuss, saying, Damn, devil, shit. I cleaned this out before I closed the room. I know it.

I snorted as Barbary went to the door. There came the slave's voice again: Lost, lost her way.

And I thought, Dear God, who among us hasn't?

I'd never spoken so much with a black, but it went that in the gathering of dark days to weeks old Barbary became my eyes and company. I could hardly stand the others: not Reuben in his talk of Smith and Washington, nor Samuel always either in dog-trot at his brother's heels or cooling the fears of the widow Randolph. Their daily lives were mysteries to me, for I was untethered from the sun's rise and fall and slept during the day and was awake most nights. Barbary, it seemed, never slept. She said she was too old for it.

Red Kate wandered through the trappings of her former life, asking where things were as though she didn't know. She had, in her kindness, brought my letters from Colonel Burr. I would teach her the peculiars of our cipher—happy nights of code and symbol, when I'd stand behind my wife and hold her hand, which itself held the pen, and move it for her so that she would learn to make the proper marks herself. So she became complicit in the enterprise, another agent of what would later be misknown as a grand and far-reaching conspiracy of empire. Lovingly she'd read me Burr's old letters, or take down notes for the messages I planned soon to send. We worked against my brothers even as we shared a roof, all of us paired-off in that mad land-bound ark. And Red Kate did seem to find joy in our nib-scratch sessions and whispered talk of map-lines and the movements of men into foreign countries. She was with me above all else, in the way that pairing-off makes conspirators of man and woman in the union of their hopes. And ours were the coming army of Colonel Burr and the war meant to unify the continent by rending it at the seams of its invisible borders. Moreover she'd taken on my growing hatred for my brothers—chiefly Reuben, who never really was, and Samuel for his doggish acquiescence—and would be glad to see them fail in their designs and be rid of the pair.

Red Kate twitched happily with plans, and sometimes, in our symbol-scribble sessions, she would grow hasty in her words.

We have the money, she said. Letters of credit good in all the country. We can quit this house at any time and set ourselves up far, far away.

Where can I go like this? I said.

Do I have to take that little Bible from your pocket and read you about all the great blind prophets?

All cases of charity. Only fit to be healed by greater prophets. And I don't see many of that kind about.

You may yet see, she said. Not the right eye—it's shriveled as a ground-fallen grape. But the left I think may just be clouded by sympathy for its fellow.

That's a resource hard to come by these days, I said.

O? said my wife. Pitying, are we? Then let me show you some sympathy, love.

We'd have to turn the boy out.

Red Kate coughed, quick and sharp. Well, then let's get on together with the writing.

Right, I said. And we stay because the colonel will be passing through Natchez on his way down with the army. We'll be here to hail his entrance, having done right by him.

The first order of the letter was to warn the great man of Reuben's intentions, that he would soon be heading north to give the president a personal forewarning and, as I'd gathered overhearing snatches of his drunken late night talk with Samuel, that he'd take up gladly a federal commission and drum a force in Pinckneyville to repel Burr's invaders, naturally in exchange for a monetary settlement with Senator Smith.

When I heard this I was being led from the kitchen by Barbary, in earshot of my brothers where they sat in the receiving hall, but we must have been out of sight, for they gave no pause in their conversing. And Barbary knew my mind well enough to tarry for a moment at some task, so that I might catch their gist.

But who's there to follow us and fight? Samuel said. We aren't exactly popular in the place.

As far as the atheist knows, said Reuben, we're heroes to the whole country.

But so, it seems, is Burr.

It won't matter, Reuben said. He'll be caught and had before we're back in Mississippi if all goes well and we're heeded. And when I tell him that Smith, one of his own Republican senators . . .

Scheme upon scheme. Barbary drew me on and I was thinking, as Reuben's words were drummed out by my footfalls, that at least they knew that no one would follow them. They'd be alone in their efforts, or so I thought. None of us would know, until later, that General Wilkinson was setting out plans to wreak all the havoc he could within his pudgy reach.

So Red Kate would put down my words in cipher, laying out my brothers' plot. But when I came to telling that I thought they'd get no volunteers, my speech trailed and I said, But neither can I. No one will follow me, nor could I lead them if I wished.

I sunk into the bed, jostling my son, who'd been crouched there giving off streams of murmuring as I talked. I saw my usefulness withering. My hand couldn't even be trusted to write the letter; my lines would start out straight, but by mid-page, as my wife described, the sentences would snap off at their ends, dangle in the blank to be over-written by their fellows, and be rendered indecipherable.

The boy's imitations of me had lately worsened; when I refused to bathe or sleep, he'd do the same; he'd taken to my way of walking, combating chair-legs and overturning lamps and side-tables. When he could escape his mother, I'd find him underfoot; and I dared not speak unless to hear my voice echoed in his small and singular speech.

Damn it, said my wife one night. He's taking after all the worst of you.

So I would sit awake and listen to the town—which suffered no small-hours but sprang to roaring life in the late night—the constant commotion of the old streets where with Samuel I'd nicked and laid in wait and searched out the history of the brother who'd now led us back split and set against each other. I heard the shouts and laughter

---

and the weapon-seller's cart making blade-and-iron music on his way to the next brawl.

Mornings, when the revels became silence for the briefest time and soon turned to workman's grumbles, I would go to sit with Barbary in the kitchen, where the other slaves mulled reverently about her while she oversaw their work. There, sipping coffee and gnawing twists of bacon, I listened to her history over the clang of pots and the occasional scream of the kettle. She'd come late in life by the name of Barbary; before that she'd been Rona, Sally, Lucretia, Ruth, Sara, and the lastmost was her name when she'd been taken—for she was of the continent true and not American-born—from her country, which I cannot recall. Her current name, the one she supposed would be her last and if the graves of slaves bore names would be etched upon her tombstone, was given by the mistress Aliza: Barbary, for her nose was long and hooked, her skin light.

She considered this name second best and fitting; her father had been an Arab man-merchant in the port town of her origin, and she the product of his meddling with his wares during a time of storms when no ships would pass his stony castle. The storm, she said, lasted for six years, and so she'd been allowed to grow into a kind of mind before the day at last came when the ships returned.

By sunrise I'd be fighting sleep as the others were awaking, lurching downstairs one-by-one. I'd try and wait until they were all seated in the dining room to have Barbary slip me out from the kitchen, but on one such morning the old slave was occupied and I took off on my own. Miscounting the footsteps and the groan of chairs, I was met at the foot of the stairs by Samuel.

He had to halt me with his hand. Brother, he said, why don't you stop with this and join the living for a day.

You're still here? I said. The hour's growing late—you may miss the president.

The congress is in session until September, he said.

Now you know the government, eh?

We've been studying the papers.

A lot of good it'll do you, I said, and started up again.

His hand returned. You know we won't go until you can see.

Well, shit, I said, at least there's somebody with hope. Then I stepped aside and continued on, my busted cheek and socket, which in those weeks had begun to knit beneath the plasters, drumming hurt.

That day Red Kate would go with Barbary to market. Polly Randolph caught wind of it and, eager to escape The Church and take the sun, begged to accompany them. So I heard later from my wife, Polly stood firm.

I would rather be knifed in a back alley than be prisoner in this house, said Polly Randolph. I will go this time and in the future, or by God Samuel Kemper I'll go further than the market!

And so it was decided that both Reuben and Samuel would accompany them. Red Kate told me, giggling, how the brothers squinted at the sun and were easy to slip once they'd all passed into the teeming stalls. She lost them among the vendors and, finding a runner-boy from the docks, drew from the bib of her dress my letter to Colonel Burr and pressed a piece of silver on him to have it delivered to the mail-packets.

She took the boy, who was skinny and no more than twelve, by the arm, and before she let him go, said, And if this letter doesn't reach its destination, I'll have your wee balls for baubles. You hear?

The letter would pass first, of course, through the supposed Patrick Fitzroy of Nashville, who we hoped had an idea of the colonel's whereabouts. I knew it would be bold luck for the letter to ever find the great man's hands, but I was glad when Red Kate woke me in the afternoon to say she'd had it off, sent out all my dreams of destiny and retribution and the Grace of the Lord, now hers as well, held within a few scraps of paper glyphed with strange markings and language unintelligible to but few, a tiny, tiny thing fluttering into a vast and wild country, borne upon more than hope, with all the chance of a single whispered prayer rising up to meet the face of God.

Faces and Features

As if to mock my blindness, the talk about the house turned to appearances.

My freckles, said Red Kate one day, are fading. And in July at that, with the sun bright as can be. Pretty soon I'll be as milky as a German girl.

And on another, Barbary pronouncing: Your brother, Mister Sam, he's turned full green.

That's just his way, I said to her. It means nothing.

He looks a dead man.

He is dead, I said. I killed him. Two years past, yet he haunts me still.

There's some sense, she said. But that's how it goes with dead folk, I suppose.

No, I said, thinking better. He doesn't haunt me, I carry his corpse upon my back.

And if my wife was turning white and Samuel was greening, it was not for lack of sun. Red Kate's trips to market had increased, and she brought back with her more than fixings for our meals: news that Mother Lowde was still alive, and wished desperately to see her boys. Samuel would ask me to go with him on his visits, but I saw no point—saw nothing, as it were. When he'd return, he'd tried to tell me what she'd said, but, feigning tiredness, I'd go up to bed, where I'd have Red Kate make notes for the next of our letters, which now bore the address of a tavern in Door-Knock Alley, the owner of which she paid a tidy sum to be recipient of the return letters with no questions asked. She'd thought at first to ask Mother Lowde, but I cured her of the notion, saying how the old whore couldn't help but give away our secret to Samuel, who called on her more and more, even bringing along the widow Randolph, herself having taken on something of a Natchez twist, her words grown sharper and cussful, her dresses bawdy and low.

I'll be a fuck-stuck goat! Polly cried one morning, upon finding a Negroe's hair in her tea.

While I awaited Colonel Burr's response, Reuben was received in the hill-top town; and I imagined him being hesitantly toasted by the nabobs, eyeing him as an oddity, the brutal boatman and backwoods brawler, but yet—I could hear them whisper—so mannered and accustomed. Not the kind of man you'd wish to cross; for hadn't he, time and again, slaked his need for vengeance upon the Spaniards and their country? Reuben wouldn't have been a one to disappoint them with the truth. Sure he seethed and ranted and let spill his anger, though not against Colonel Burr, who he despondently reported was a great favorite of the gentry there. He would reserve his bile for the Pukes, and little did the planters know that all his rage and what they surely saw as steel resolve sprung not from righteous patriotism but from a shift of papers—the contracts of a speculator and the accounts of backwater stores. And while they sputtered over their claret at their strange and hailed visitor, the planters and gentlefolk were also thrumming with the news that the Pukes, from their Mexican outposts, had crossed the Sabine River with an army of two thousand, and were billeting at few miles from Natchitoches. War, as always, was imminent.

What was fresh news to the hill-top planters had been bandied and sung up and down the docks a week before, so when Reuben spoke of it, I was already smirking with the knowledge. The Pukes were giving an excuse, a reason for the enterprise to be outright draped in the

American banner. It was only for Wilkinson to come down from St. Louis with barges packed with soldiers like cord-wood, march to the violated border, and ignite the glorious conflagration.

And when I grinned with foreknowing, my right cheek bunched at the lip of my new eye-patch. Bought for me by Red Kate when it became clear that my bones had healed, the patch was black velvet strung upon a leather thong and emblazoned with a cross in thread-of-gold. The color she had to tell me, but the cross I could feel for myself, whenever fingers went to searching, as they often did, to ease the itching of my skin, freed from the plaster and revealed to my touch as puckered and riven with lines as the sorry plots of Chit. My wife spoke admiringly of the needlework as she went about untying the snakeskin from the tail of my hair, letting it fall so that she could brush the knots out. With the fine patch had come a return to appearances; I was shaved, and bathed with scents and oils unearthed from the abandoned cabinets of rooms long vacated by their whores. My uniform was put to a hard wash, my boots drawn off and filled with wadded paper dusted with salts to draw the stench. Similarly, my son suffered a new cleanliness; often I would hold him and feel his small hands working at his skin, then rubbing his fingers together close to his face, unnerved that there was no dirt to bead between them. From the same seamstress who'd made my patch, a child-sized colonel's uniform, in replica of mine, was ordered for the boy. He wore it proudly about the house, which sounded with his tiny martial stomping. But before this could all come to pass, I would be stripped, forced to part with my lanyard of pistols and knives; but I still kept them close, before me on the bed while my clothes were boiled and pummeled and my boots packed and polished by wincing slaves, my stockings cast out into the trash-heaps to be bedding for river-rats.

They say they never smelt a thing like it, said Barbary when she came in to bring me coffee. Those boots would stun a horse. Don't know how Miss Kate could stand you.

She perseveres, I said.

I had to gather my weapons close, hoard them, for the boy, naked as well, would climb a-bed and try to play. I had to call for grease to pry his finger from the barrel of a gun, where it'd squirmed in search of lead to suck. He cried out with his word while we worked him free, and when his mother had gone I let him suck his finger, take what he craved, even as I worried the embroidered cross before my eye. It was fine work, but unlike me to celebrate embellishments. No, my filigreed patch was more to the taste of a man like the Reverend Morrel.

See, it wasn't Burr alone who occupied my mind those days; there was always the specter of the Reverend, perhaps in congress with the surviving alcaldes, Kneeland and Stirling. But they were only shades— he was the one behind it. More than from the Kaintucks' words, I knew it in my bones, felt it written on my soul. Of course, it couldn't be proven; the word about town held nothing of his name but the tales of bygone days. Thinking he'd regain my trust, Samuel had, on his most recent visit, put the question of the Reverend to Mother Lowde, who said that all she'd heard was that he'd escaped the soldiers and the hangman's rope, but hadn't been heard of since.

This once I would quit my lie and listen to Samuel's words. Lowde believed him to be dead, for word of such a man was unlikely to not be spread.

She still adores him, he said. Gave me a hot minute of hell when I told the way we parted from him. . . . And she adores you too. Misses you greatly.

She knows more than she lets on, I said, wondering darkly whether Mother Lowde was tough as I remembered, how long it would take to beat the knowledge out of her. The old whore had been so kind to me in my boyhood, not so long ago, and I did shudder some thinking of the man that I'd become. No helping it—blood and bone-crack cruelty were the music of the devil-worms turning in my gut. I saw myself,

367

once the country was taken and remade in the image of Burr, as a kind of magistrate, ruling the unrighteous in whatever province the great man saw fit to seat me; blindness wouldn't matter, I'd be justice itself, and wherever I put down my boot the wicked would be crushed.

Forget the Reverend, brother. He's a dream.

And what about Ira Kneeland? I said. Have you forgotten him? Forgot the ropes at our necks? I know you've got yourself another widow, Sam, but—

I'd spoken just as heels clacked upon the boards in approach and fell to thuds hushed by carpet. What stopped me was the voice of Polly Randolph, breathless, saying naught but Fuck before she made off. Samuel had raised partway from his chair with a squeak of pegs, and with the clap of her slamming door he fell back.

You've turned to a mean little bastard, he said.

And you've become a lap-dog to a man who'd rather shame a paper enemy than have his own country.

In bewildered voice he said, My God, would that you knew that I still loved you as a brother. Even as you spit at me, not even a friend.

You're dancing, I said. Answer—would you go, right now, with me and finish Kneeland? Fulfill God's will and vengeance?

Haven't I killed enough with you to prove it? Shall we count the skulls? And for Christ's sake what stupidity is this. Go with you? I couldn't help you on a horse in good conscience. Much less ride with you on a killing. You'd shoot me in the back. But maybe you'd do that anyway. Don't think that I don't know you're up there scribbling to Burr.

It's nut-cutting time, I said. You've made your choice and I've made mine.

Samuel growled: For a month I've held Reuben back from going, said how it'd be wrong to leave you here alone and blind—

So you wouldn't, I said.

No, damn you, I wouldn't.

And you've told Reuben that you think I'm warning Burr?

I've said nothing. But I'm sure he suspects.

As always, I said, you give your brother more credit than he deserves.

Roaring off went Samuel, to beat on his bedroom door and shout for the widow to let him in. I sat alone, hearing another door burst forth, to Aliza's chambers, and Reuben's voice booming for this damned foolishness to stop.

The Blood and the Light

I'd not put more than a few weeks' worth of creases in my fresh uniform when Colonel Burr's response arrived, delivered by a rider to the Door-Knock tavern, and fetched by Red Kate on a Tuesday's marketing.

Giddily she woke me, pressed the letter to my hands, and I drew out my knife from the lanyard and slit papers open, tried for a moment to feel the imprint of the words before I handed the letter back to her. My wife was by then so versed in the coded world that she could read it without the help of a cipher. So she read and read again, we both rocking in bed like excited children, our own child silently doing the same.

Burr spoke of my great worth, my unparalleled assistance. My place in the enterprise, he assured me, was elevated and secure despite what he called the misfortunes of my condition. You will, he wrote, attain the greatness inspired in you by the God of your fathers. I made Red Kate several times repeat that line. How couldn't young men wish to follow him? He saw the greatness in you, and his only desire was to bring it to full flower. In his letter and the ones that followed, the colonel spoke of thronging acolytes, of hearts leaping from the

369

breasts of would-be soldiers. He was apprised of the Spanish crossing of the Sabine, and judged Wilkinson would soon have his troops in Natchitoches, if they weren't there already. Himself, he was presently at Philadelphia; he planned to leave in early August, gathering along the way the men and makings of the glorious event. Spread the word judiciously, he said, be prudent in who you choose to tell and what you say, and plan for my return.

All the household, free or not, was asleep; early morning, the false watchmen of the under-hill town barked lies about the time for sport. On the hill-top criers were in pay of the city government and called the hours proper, but by the river it was left up to whatever drunks caught the chronomic urge, so that at two in the morning you might hear a man fighting his own laughter to yowl, Nine o'clock and suck prick! The effect was to unseat you from your sense of forward-marching time, to make you think that the night was constantly in lurch either backwards or ahead and you were trapped in the limbo. So if you were watchless, clockless, or blind, you learned other ways to track the dark hours. My son might've been awake, doing as I did, but Red Kate had taken to lashing him to the bed, and he'd likely struggled himself to sleep. It was only me and Barbary, our usual vigil kept in the kitchen, my boots up by the stove and her tending pots atop, grinding cloves between her knuckles, dropping in bay leaves, her hands smacking slimily after cutting okra.

There's things I do remember by and by, she said. Things I don't forget.

And among them was the Reverend. Before Samuel had gone questing of Mother Lowde, I'd asked the people Morrel most preyed upon—the blacks. All the slaves of The Church remembered him, a decked-out man in black, and most had heard his legend: freedom, the months flush with cash, and then the final sale. They shook their heads for the fate of country niggers, who would've benefited greatly for their city knowledge. Only Barbary knew his dreams of stirring revolution among slaves.

She'd said, He told me it. Came down about one in the morning, stinking of the girl he'd laid with, sat right there in the chair you're in, and told me how it'd be. A woman like you, Barbary, he said, you could be a queen. White and black alike would curtsy to you. No more mistress or master, everybody free. And who'd be king? I asked him. He said he would, naturally.

Barbary gave no truck to the Reverend's claims. Said the mention of kings and queens made her mistrustful. That talk's for dazzling simple brains, she said. And when I asked if she'd heard whether he was still alive, or moving about Natchez, her answer was that I should go uptown to the auction and find the weepingest nigger on the block. Ask him, and you'll know.

Something put a stop to the crier's pranking; it sounded like a bottle—a pop of glass and a crumple to the ground. Barbary snorted. Jeers followed, turning into calls to buy the hero rounds. One swift move, a snuck blow dealt from behind, and the hours were righted. The world could move on, knowing now the night would end.

Bitter mood returning like the tide, that evening I'd been awoken with word from the docks that General Wilkinson and his army were still in St. Louis, and the fat man had seen fit to keep the Louisiana troops in garrison, unable to march without his orders. And so it seemed the Pukes had matched his inactivity, staying encamped fifteen miles from Natchitoches. A test, a provocation untaken. If they were paying Wilkinson, he was giving them their every penny's worth, his weight in reales. Burr knew his treasons, as did most men of substance in the country, but it was thought at last we'd found a situation that called for Wilkinson to act; after all, what difference was Spanish silver whether received in a hogs-head at the dock in St. Louis or by the sword in San Antonio? Surely more to be had that way, but all mis-judged the quality of the general's laziness, and that he was smarter than us all—understanding that power didn't care that you betrayed a country, so long as you didn't do the same to the administration.

I'd yet to receive Burr's next letter, but could guess its contents: Wilkinson does not matter. If he chooses to cover his expansive ass and thus reveal himself to be a pensioner of a foreign country, then so be it. His action against the Spanish would be a happy eventuality, my boy, so carry on and look ahead. And remember that the path to greatness is littered with ones such as him; their bones are buried and they are forgotten, while the men who stride over them on their way are remembered forever.

In bed that day my dreams were terrible, and whenever my son would try to nuzzle close, I'd put out my hand to keep him away. I thrashed, felt his blood on my face, saw his gape-mouthed expression as the slit opened in his throat. In some dreams he spoke words beyond that which he'd know in life. I woke once, wiping my brow. Was it blood or was it sweat? I tasted salt and was drawn back into my torments, this time deeper.

When next I awoke, it was to pain in my left eye and swirls of fire burning in the blackness of my vision, eaten away. I was squinting, so hard that I had to pry my eyelid open with my fingers, quickly shut it back for the fire and hurt. I reached about the bed, found my son, felt for his throat, which was still there. The light like an arrow out of Heaven, shot through my left eye. I couldn't open it but for the barest crack, the blazing arrow stabbing deeper, its tip churning the blackness of my brains. I knocked the boy aside, the room filling with light as on the night of his birth, me stumbling out of bed to draw the curtains, sinking to the floor and seeing, dimly seeing in what was the last light of afternoon, the bobbing blur of my son. And when, soon after, Red

Kate came into the room, she shrieked with joy so loud that the whole house thought me murdered, instead of risen, which I was.

Unwinding the Knot

They were packing, the brothers; coming in and out from the carriage house where quartered the two new horses they'd bought in the time since I'd regained my sight. Shapes and bounds hardened their lines, realizing again their forms. I tripped and stumbled worse than when I'd been full-blind—my senses having grown acute to the feel of space and darkness, I was untrusting of the blurred world which slowly came into being over the course of a week in which August broke and Reuben and Samuel readied for their journey. It was the night before they'd leave, and I sat with the women while the brothers worked, careful where I turned my head, for a glance of lamp or candle would burn spots into my vision like the dullard gets from staring at the sun.

Virginia, Reuben said, for the first since you were—what?—twelve? Longer, said Samuel.

On this trip they were carrying tied parcels of clothes fit for their reception by the president, who was evidently an appreciator of frontier fashion: buckskin suits cut in the latest style, hats fringed in coonfur. Reuben had heard of the president's tastes, and he intended to meet the mark, blend in among the walls draped with head-dresses and Indian costumes, the stuffed specimens of our American wildlife, to seem at home propping his boots up on Jefferson's footstool, which legend held to be a mammoth's skull. Once Red Kate had seen the clothes, she said to me, Why don't they just wear their best day-suits? Now they'll look like pioneer buffoons. While she shook her head I'd laughed, saying, Let them look like fools.

Now my wife sat beside me on a couch, facing Aliza and Polly Randolph in their separate chairs, the mistress's throne-like and enormous, its occupant the sharp and angled thing of my memory. I wondered how often Barbary darned and patched the seat for the slip of elbow-blade or wrong turn of razored hip. Polly, for her part, was plumping, powdered flesh a-strive at her Natchez dresses. She eyed Samuel on his to-and-fro, the nibble of her painted lip betraying her poor nerves at the prospect of him leaving. She did it so often that red soon showed on the tips of her front teeth, as though she'd been sucking blood.

According to Red Kate you could tell they were worrisome because they'd both dressed and made themselves up so fine. The pair had made work for the slave-girls, piled hair held carefully by pins and charms, Polly's borrowed from the mistress, perhaps thinking that what one brother sought so would the other. She was more right than she knew. Supposedly it was all for their farewell dinner, many courses and champagne dusted off from Aliza's cellar, which had ended but a few minutes before, the brothers springing immediately from their settings of half-eaten cakes and going to their final preparations.

Another hurried passage bearing necessaries, chatter of roads and routes. And would the horses hold it all?

They're like boys, said Polly. So excited.

Off on an adventure, said Aliza, smiling until the brothers were gone, then allowing her face to glint into a scowl.

But, so Red Kate had said, it wasn't for the dinner that they'd dressed. Now that Polly Randolph followed her fashion like a courtier, Aliza would've imparted this wisdom: dress finest before they go, give them guilt not for coming but for having left. My wife had asked if I remembered how she'd always be in a fine dress, different from the one she'd worn before, whenever I'd leave The Church. Make you dally in the barroom, give me time to change and make up, then come downstairs resplendent to lay the parting memory upon you, just as

Miss Aliza had taught her. That memory could drag a man back from half-way across the country. I'd said that she never played such tricks on me, but stayed in bed until I'd go. Hearing this, my wife had turned from her mirror, where, refusing slaves, she did her own hair and powdering, and considered it true. I guess I never gamed you, she'd said. Knew I didn't have to.

Presently came Barbary with a tray of brandies, doling them out to us in silence and departing without thanks. That night had seen my first supper taken with the white people of the house since we'd arrived. I'd returned to sleeping nights, and Barbary no longer gave me words, but treated me as any other master. Once, forgetting I could see, she'd tried to take my arm to lead me upstairs. I'd snatched it away, and on her face there was the briefest look of hurt before she turned stony and went on about her work. She hadn't lied about her features—the Arabic hook to her nose and the light, papery skin—but by week's end she'd blended in appearance with the rest of the slaves, not to be looked upon directly in the face, just hands that brought and bodies that should move quicker, damn it, we're waiting.

A rifle and shotgun, scabbards to be lashed to their saddles. Reuben would be the long shot and Samuel the scatter.

Aliza, from between her teeth, said, It brings home the nature of their trip, does it not?

Polly Randolph, a-shudder, answered, I worry less over him leaving than being here unprotected—not that we are, she said, nodding to me. But the things he may encounter on the road—

I said, Samuel and me came a greater distance, and with but two pistols and a rusty rifle between us. Young boys. And Reuben, God knows he's traveled.

I stopped talking when the brothers came through again, and when they left I was accused by their women's faces. So much for comfort. Finished, they came into the parlor and towed chairs to sit

375

beside wife and widow. Samuel was indeed coloring worse, his skin splotched with black like smears of ash or gunpowder. At first, when my vision returned, he was but a greenish blur. He'd spoken little to me that week, once it'd become clear that I could see and that they would leave as soon as was reasonable. Reuben had said nothing but to clap me on the back and claim how glad he was my sight had returned. I'd thought, I bet you are, you bastard. Now you can go without guilt.

A toast was made, our brandies drained. The standing order to keep all windows shut and nailed at their frames had allowed a mighty heat to settle in The Church, which remained even into the night. Broad and strong, Red Kate sat solidly beside me, the sweat upon her giving her a look like she'd been working in her truck-patch, while Aliza and Polly had begun to crumple; as it goes with weaker women, their backs were humped and sucking in their hollow breasts. Aliza called out for more brandy, her voice cracking to a shriek. Reuben put out a hand that covered both her knees, perhaps not without guilt of a kind, I considered.

How young were you, asked Polly of her man, when you and Angel made the trip down?

Twenty, Samuel said. Twenty-two? He was but a whelp. Fourteen, was it?

I never knew my age, I said. And anyway we didn't come directly down. We went east, to Cincinnati, because he wanted to find Reuben. Then south for the same reason. We got waylaid from the search. It was almost a year.

And I was the one who found you, said Reuben.

I never knew that it was just you two for so long, said Polly Randolph.

It was, said Samuel, elbows on his knees and staring at the floor.

I looked at my brother, seeing now that he was thinking ahead, of the long road and a journey which would take months, encompass half a country and their final dissolution: the unwinding of the last two cords from our knot. Mine was already gone, a fallen twist withering in the dust at Pinckneyville—if it'd ever been rightly bound at all. Samuel felt his face; his powder had worn thin. I wondered if the president, in his fascination with the odd, might forgo their discussions and wish to examine his skin.

II

A Man of Business

Fall 1806

We Cannot Fail

Tavern gabble and chinking cups, the hacks of smoke-choked throats soothed by beer and liquor, above it all I hollered. I was preaching Burr. At first I wouldn't use the great man's name, but instead spoke loud of frontier destiny, eastern treachery, flags planted by the shores of other seas. But in the first week of September word was flapping about the country on the wings of a territorial rag, The Western World, which had printed some of the more egregious rumors and stated outright that Colonel Burr stood at the head of a treacherous imperial enterprise. So my work was simplified.

From the dock-side houses where the men stank of Mississippi water to the barrooms at the edge of the under-hill town where manure musk and plant-shrift reigned, I preached. The boatmen knew some of the enterprise and would invoke the colonel's name or even that of Kemper, demanding to know where were the other, giant brothers. On a mission of importance, I'd say, the knowledge of that mission's purpose burning in my throat like the remnants of my childhood coals. I promised the men of the river open commerce and an end to shipping tariffs. The farmers, fresh from being cheated at the markets, solemnly fumed and worried their corn-silk fobs. Sun-burnt and raw-knuckled, they regarded me, and I would make their eyes go wistful and watery with assurances of things to come: a country for the tiller and plowman, power taken from the merchant and his eastern master. This dream-nation I invented, caring nothing that I lied, so long as I was preaching; make the enterprise all things to all men just as any preacher knows to say to a cocker that Heaven is a great run and pit full of fine fighting birds, and to a drunk that it's the draught that never ends. I gave instructions purposefully vague as those for Armageddon; I could've been telling them to await the trumpets and hundred-headed beasts as I railed and bought their drinks.

I said, When the call comes, we have a man in Ohio ready to lead his force, a man in Kentucky, a man in Tennessee, a man in Orleans. Brothers, be ready, for if the whole of the South and West will answer—so should you.

From one wag: And what kind of men are these?

Men of prominent station, I'd say. Men who can command the loyalty of troops.

Another calling out: And who'll be the man in Mississippi? You?

At such words I'd raise my glass and give a tilt of my head, squaring the gold cross of my eye-patch to the unbeliever's face. A nod, a bow of confidence; false, of course, for I commanded no force nor held any civic station. But I knew that I could, with time and the Word, stir war in the hearts of rough men. It was a glorious return to younger days, striding out of taverns to battle in the streets and silence with fists the doubters and unbelievers I couldn't quiet with words; the tedious unlashing of my lanyard of weapons, the other drinkers following after, choosing sides and laying bets. After a while my backing grew great, my odds small. One man knocked me to the ground with his first punch, but I rose up and drew my Bible from my coat and struck him down with its spine. Some desired true satisfaction, and so the weapon-seller would be called for and the matter soon settled, whether in the street or rowing to river islands or riding miles out of town to stand on some hillock and dispatch a man whose name I'd forget by morning. By early September I'd fought four such duels.

Red Kate tsking briefly at a slash in my arm or a powder-burned cheek: I knew I'd be glad when your fire returned, she said. Pretty soon Colonel Burr won't need an army. Just bloody you.

And that fire had arisen from the latest of Burr's letters, received not a day after the brothers' departure. Gone were the pronouncements, in their place facts and figures. The detachments from the territories, what he called a host of choice spirits, numbering some four thousand—notwithstanding what my efforts would yield—would convene at the mouth of the Cumberland River on the first of December, arrive in Natchez between the fifth and fifteenth of December, and from there meet with Wilkinson, if he were not engaged already with the Spanish in Texas, and decide which first to seize: New Orleans or Baton Rouge. It ended with the proclamation:

We cannot fail.

Even in cipher the words stood out, condemning you to action. And I knew which city I'd advise. I could see the Pukes' heads on pikes, the houses of Feliciana in ruins. Samuel may have forgotten the rope, but I never would. My fire was so fierce that I considered taking a week to ride down by myself and murder Kneeland and the rest, but I thought better of it; when the time came so would my vengeance. And how much greater would it be to extinguish them as they watched their world go up in flames.

I kept to matters within my reach—my tavern-preaching, stirring the people to glory. I kept no rolls of names, for what use was it to list the multitude? I'd tell them to be as a great voice and, when the call came, holler back. Afternoons I'd have an early supper with Red Kate and the boy, clean and oil my pistols, unload and reload them, making sure my flints were knapped. Polly Randolph hung about Aliza's crimping and would only take meals with her. She pretended strength but, as Red Kate would say, you could see her sometimes strangling the air with her hands, or plucking and picking her fingers as though leafing the pages of letters yet to come. Sundown would find me at the door with my wife, kissing her goodbye like a tradesman off to work, undoing the bolts and locks and bars, then slipping out. On the way down the street, more than once I looked back at Aliza's spire and saw that lady in the window watching, sunlight glinting off the lens of her spyglass.

Red Kate told her I was on a wild tear, drinking and brawling and God knew what else. She laughed it to her former mistress, playing the part of the shrugging wife aghast at her husband's revels. Aliza posted slaves, like a guard, at the front door peep to be sure it was only me asking entrance in the early hours. The lady was no fool—Reuben had told her, no doubt long before, that I stood opposed to him; Samuel would've said the same to his widow. But, so it seemed, it was better to keep me close and watchable. Seeing Aliza in her window, hawking me, I'd smile and wave before I headed on.

He'd better watch himself, she said one night to my wife. At this rate he'll have his other eye put out. And then where will you be?

Knowing we weren't long for The Church, I made arrangements to let rooms in a hotel on the hill-top, where, if the mistress turned us out, we might look down upon her and the widow as they flitted about in lonesome madness. And Red Kate didn't tremble at these plans; she was ready for her own place in the world.

We've been strung to others for too long, she said. It's time we struck out for ourselves. But strung we were, bound now to the fate of a man a thousand miles away, the last of my leaders, teachers, fathers, and the one I'd know the least. Perhaps that was why it was so easy to believe in him, in the plans of the great man and my place in them.

I was of furious energy, going from place to place, giving up the Word, even unto the hill-top town, where, after arranging for the rooms to be kept open for the near future, I took on an agent, named Stephen White, to help increase my wealth and standing, bolster me in the business of the upper town. I brought my money to the territorial bank, my writs and liens against Horton's estate. And it was for White to wield them in the markets. Through him I came to know the workings of the auction-block, the yield of slaves and the futures of cotton and sugar. He was older than me, but appeared somehow younger in his flower-patterned waistcoats, his hair cropped, his face smooth and scarless. He was late of Tennessee, and in his short time in the territories had advanced himself considerable, being in his other work an assistant to the surveyor general of the Mississippi Territory, a bitter old Quaker named Isaac Briggs. Introductions were forthcoming, and by such ways I'd slip into the houses of government. The nabobs, though, wanted little to do with me; they'd had enough of the novelty of back-woodsmen, so it seemed. And I didn't cut the same gallant figure as Reuben, tending more to harshness and what was said to be a devilish appearance.

They don't mind so much the duels, said Stephen White one day on our way from his office to the market. But it's that you fight them against low men.

I considered this, and Stephen, thumbing snuff before he breached the crowd, said, Better wait back, sir. Even the niggers, it seems, are afraid of you. You unnerve them, patch and scars and all, if you'll pardon me saying. Go have a drink and let me tend to our success.

So it went; and leaving Stephen counting coinage in the evenings, I would repair to the taverns on the down-hill side, less now to preach than to be hailed by the converted. And in my energy I neglected not my other duty, the search for the second of my teachers, the Reverend Morrel. When Samuel and Reuben returned I might have the Reverend's head in a hat-box, show them, in this way if nothing else, that I knew better. Burr's troops would be marching through the streets and while my brothers slumped dumbfounded at the sight of them, I would take out Morrel's head and perhaps the tongue of Ira Kneeland, and bring the knowledge full upon them: I am the one.

So, I said, where is he?

Mother Lowde gave a look of puzzlement; she'd made me wait half the night, while she tended bar and went about serving her patrons, until the morning, when, smiling, she brewed her beer-mash and coffee just as she had done when Samuel and me used to sit with her and read her verses, when we were boys.

You know who I mean. Just tell me where.

Lowde, shaking her head, poured me a cup and I took it. She said, Why'd you do the Reverend that way? Not that treachery hasn't treated you well, looking fat-pursed and press-suited, minus the eyes and the gouges in your pretty face.

That's not what I asked, Mother.

Lowde went on: If you'd been sweeter, you might've earned a living by them looks alone. They used to say it, all the girls. Some chaps too. She laughed. If it weren't for your disposition and that voice, who knows?

She'd talked that way all through the night, blithely twisting away whenever I tried to press her, shouting to her patrons that I was a pretty prodigal returned, how she'd cut the eyeholes in my robber's mask. How I might've picked one of their pockets, and did they recall being nicked by a boy five or so years back? They mostly grumbled that they'd been robbed too many times to tell. One man played along, feigning the memory and bellowing rummy indignation to Lowde's delight, until I screwed my eye at him, parting my coat for to show how many times over I could kill him. Now there were no patrons, her tenants shuffled up to the attic room once mine, and I was growing angry at the way she talked as though to ghosts in the wall.

He sent men to kill me, I said. And Sam, and Reuben, and my God-damned wife and child.

O, yes, she said. Sam did tell me you had a boy. And who does he take after?

No one, I said. He's not right. And that's not the point, besides. So enough with the fuck-about, now tell me.

Mother Lowde sipped her coffee, batting the steam with her lashes. Fine enough, she said. And why should the Reverend wait five long years to revenge himself on you?

So he is alive, I said.

As you or I, said Lowde. But that blow your Reuben struck him, those army men, it finished him. He's long since retired to shrivel and sulk. Not doing harm to anyone anymore. Not even horses or niggers.

There was a harelip, I said.

Mother Lowde drained her cup and flung it aside, pewter clanging on the boards, the only bell to be heard of a morning in the under-hill. And maybe the Reverend was drunk one night and telling about how you two boys deserted him so meanly, and maybe one man heard and told another, and the story floated thus. So after a while some rough bastards with an eye on reward hear the tale and set out to claim a prize from a man what couldn't pay in the first place. Or maybe you've made so many enemies, my dear, that you can't keep them straight, and are going for an old man who only ever treated you with kindness. Like it's a diversion, a game like your little duels I hear about.

You hear that, eh? I said.

There's so many stories about, she said. And have been since you left.

Like when you told us about Reuben cutting foreskins, which was a lie.

All I do is hear and tell. Give me a story that's not got lies in its stitches. Even from your blasted little book.

So you're telling me it's because of a fucking story?

I'm telling you shit, son. For all I know they might've been some men you cheated for a horse, or whose houses you burned in West Florida. These old ears just listen, and the old brain between them knots things together best it can. Lowde was weeping now. I just try to make answers that fit. The Reverend had no part of it. He wouldn't know your face if you walked up to him. Christ knows, neither do I.

And where could I show him my face?

Fucking hell, you are a stupid thing. He's not in town, is he? But I know him, so he's close—sad, scrounging in the dark with freaks for company.

The Devil's Pisspot, I said.

Bleary-eyed and pained, she smiled her nubbin teeth at me. There, she said from between them. For that gem of intelligence did you have to come and torment me?

I'm settling accounts, I said, before everything changes. I want to start anew.

Get out with your accounts, she said. Take them to the street with the other shit.

And as I rose to go, Mother Lowde was saying, It's what I deserve for being a ma to you. God how things do change.

385

I held open the door, surveying in the bare dawn the piles of dung, then turned back to her. They'll change even more before I'm through with it, I said; as though I had my hands round the whole world's neck, forcing downwards and telling it to swallow its coal or so help me God—

Hail Columbia issued in a growl from a smat of patriotic throats, which by the look of their owners, grunting and wobbling on the wharf-boats where the general's barge was lashed, had been the very gullets that had filled with puke the ruts and hoof-clots I'd walked over on my way to the riverside. The barge was decked and draped with the country's colors; red spilled in torrents down the balustrades, the goods, the pilot's perch, the tiller, and carelessly trailed in the water, staining the white stripes between; stars in their fields, as stars go, were everywhere, overlapping one another so that you couldn't be right sure how many states the nation had. Because we numbered them with stars, the possibilities were likewise infinite. So down towards the monstrosity through the chattering others at the landing, an easy crowd to part, and at its center, stepping down to a lamentable call of Three Cheers for the General! was Wilkinson.

I'd never seen the man, but from his size straining at his regalia, I knew him. Doffing his plumed hat to the crowd, the general glanced back towards his barge, wherefrom there came a bed-stand litter shouldered by well-dressed Negroes, its posts all draped over with netting-cloth, and beneath that, a figure.

Christ, said a man beside me, who's dead?

At that, the figure sat up and hacked a clot of blood into the netting. And as the litter approached, I could see that there were many such expurgations, dried and spattered on the netting.

Jesus, the consumption, said the man beside me, backing off.

General Wilkinson, urging the litter up, turned at the disease's name and regarded the place where the speaker had stood with piggy fury. Orderlies were fast approaching, and now swarmed about him. I saw his mouth say, Arrest that man; a doughy finger jabbed from brocaded cuff, indicating a spot beside my face. But the orderlies only craned their necks to see through the crowd, and by then the general was waving the litter on ahead. Within it was his wife; stricken with the bloody-lung and not long for the world, she'd been brought down from St. Louis by her husband, to be housed at a nabob's mansion for the final term of her infirmity. Wilkinson would make her the excuse for his delays, and for coming first to Natchez rather than heading straight for the Sabine and his confrontation with the Pukes. He'd dragged the poor thing across the country for an alibi, saying that he waited for the last of the summer heat to break so she could better tolerate the arduous journey.

When the litter had passed, all that remained was Wilkinson and his aides, followed by a pair of drummers rattling a march. The general seemed bewildered, cast about for a moment as the tappers approached and might've let them crash into his bulk if not for the hands of his aides, who led him onwards. I looked to the barge. He'd brought no army; the garrison remained at St. Louis. The foul memory of West Florida, of his promises to Reuben, was upon me. But perhaps they marched overland; there was no way that Wilkinson, chief of the armies, could let himself appear incompetent—no way, so I thought, to parlay losing into gain. As it happened, I didn't know General Wilkinson, nor his capacities.

But I aimed to, and so scampered along the crowd, which soon grew sparse on the general's way through the under-hill town. He'd not stay here, dear God, but would have carts and carriages hired by the time his party reached Gorman's Hill, and from there would ride up to the finer side, leaving behind the river-stench, the hoots and calls of a populace unsure of who had arrived.

A king, said an old woman who I dusted and sent tumbling as I hurried after the general. I caught him at the corner of Front and the bend of Door-Knock Alley; an ox-team was blocking his path with their slow progress, separating him from his blood-bedewed wife, who was on towards her own destination.

I tried to sound urgent: General, sir, an important message!—General Wilkinson, please, I must speak to you!

Disregard from the general, staring at the plodding oxen laying pats as they went, his face tucked, tripling his chin at the collar. There were others shouting to him, whatever came to mind. I imagined Colonel Burr, when he'd made his visit the year before, stopping with each one and talking knowingly to them—a voice of great understanding—until they forgot what it was they'd meant to say and remembered only him.

The general would make no such efforts. I shouted again and shouldered through the last of the crowd, who were keeping a respectful yard of distance, and came to his cordon of aides. I said, My name is Kemper and I'm a friend of—

Recognition wrinkled high on his hairline as an aide's hand shot out and tried to push me back. The ox-team was at its tail-end.

I'm no mess-boy, I said, batting the hand away, which was followed by a voice of eastern indignance, saying something about seeing me in irons.

The general kept looking ahead, to where his wife had been, but also back at me, testing the wine-besotted tracts of his memory for my face, tapping at his mechanism as though at a toe prickling with gout. And while he did so, I thought for the first in years of Brother Zach, and the way the Reverend Morrel would look upon a slave as though he'd known him all his life.

Yes, yes, said Wilkinson, feigning recognition. Of course, sir. Approach.

Seeing the general close now—his jeweled fingers, the polished brass-work of his buttons and medals—I considered that the Reverend would've liked this man's style, maybe chided him for gluttony while admiring his baubles and pomps, all the while scheming how to slip the rings from his fingers. And getting near enough to smell the perfume on him, I said softly, I'm a friend of Colonel Burr's, and I must speak to you.

Wilkinson said, Ah, I see. He put out a hand and I let mine be sunk into it. The oxen were gone; only the steam rising from their leavings remained. His head jerked for the open path and without looking at me the general said, I'm billeted at Concordia Plantation. Do you know it? Come by and we'll talk, given time.

He patted me on the shoulder and hurried off, calling for his men to follow. I stood there, thinking that I should've damn-well asked him why he wasn't at the Sabine, but knowing also that my life was now of behind-doors dealings, not the way I'd grown up—shouting the world's troubles and hacking them out on the street-corner for all ears. The aide who'd tried to hold me back—a spotty man, tall, with a pinched face—was last to go; he said to me, I'll boot your ass before you meet the door. Then he clicked his heels and started off.

I called after him: I've chewed the fucking livers of better men than your footman self!

The aide didn't turn, nor did the general, who was too far ahead and moving too quickly to hear.

Aliza's eye screwed out the peep, and I crouched and matched it with my own. When it was gone and the lady was about her unlocking, I could hear her hiss and mumble behind the snapping movements of metal and the rattling of chains.

Stephen White, I'd decided, could acquit himself without me that day, so I'd headed for The Church, and rather than going to the carriage house, saddling my horse, and riding to the hill, I went to the door, thinking: I unnerve the trade, I unsettle the moneyed interests; best to wait till evening and pay him a visit while he's tallying the take. But soon I'll quit this house and its shard of a mistress, now opening the door and stepping back to let me in.

So, I said, you saw who came this morning?

Aliza, stiffening, said, Took the general by the hand, did you? Old friends?

Reuben's the one that's met him, I said. Not me.

Don't you dare speak his name, she said, slamming shut the door and hustling to her locks. I know your designs. I've been keeping a close watch.

Lord, I know it.

Hunched and scraping with her nails at the locks and latches, she flashed her eyes at me and I went on: It's not as if I'm setting traps for them on the road or paying Indians to ambush them.

Aliza straightened herself into her natural blade-posture. Her hair stood up in golden shivs, paling in what light had managed to sneak through the curtains. I thought of my own, our similarities in blondness and harshness of appearance, and how, if anyone was watching—and surely slave-eyes did accept this scene—we might've been mistaken for brother and sister arguing an estate.

I don't doubt you would, she said.

I mean neither of them harm, Aliza. They're still my brothers.

Aliza let a hand creep to her right side, just below her rib—the one I'd preached the wedding day sermon over in this same parlor, in the days of light. It was where, I supposed, she had been stabbed. And in times of worry, which for her were constant, it was her tic to set a trembling hand to that place. Soothing phantom pains reawakened by her earthly woes.

But they aren't, she said. They aren't any brothers to you. Not by blood. Not by anything more than years, and even that you've thrown away.

I considered how easy it would be to reach out in the darkened parlor, take up Aliza like a biddy hen, and wring her neck. I imagined the deed accomplished, her dropping to the rugs with a sound of breaking glass; and would she lay there like the shotgunned squaw? Open-eyed and glaring? I saw myself stepping away from her crumpled form, finding that her throat-bones had cut my hands.

I hope, I said, that they don't think as you do.

They put no thought to it, she said. Today was Reuben's first letter. They were in Nashville last week, and now they're going east. The next will be from Washington. You see, they've put you behind them. You're only here on their good graces to your wife and child—both of which I gave you, if you remember. That two dollar biter, Kate, and the brat you had by her.

Well, you can absolve yourself of graces. We'll be out soon enough.

Aliza grew pinched, but made a show of puffing out her tiny breast, saying, Good. I'll see to it that—

You'll see to nothing, I said. You'll see just what you can from your spyglass.

Down the room the stairs creaked; at the last step, her hand upon the railing, stood Polly Randolph. Her hair half-undone and flapping, face unpainted and pale, she'd come down looking for Barbary to help her finish.

I turned back to Aliza, who, still looking to the widow Randolph, gave her a nod to stay.

Are you that afraid of me, Aliza? I said.

Her hand was at her side again; her eyes cut a vicious jag to take me in. I've known things, she said, that would make you blow away like a cloud of fucking dust, little preacher. But I do feel the blade twisting in me day-by-day. Not just in me, but in Reuben and in Samuel. And yours is the hand that holds it.

My pair of broad blades, sequestered amongst the pistols, weighed heavy at my chest. One swing and her head would be on the floor. But I walked away, and passing Polly on the stairs, she standing there bewildered and agape, I said to her that I was glad to hear her man was safe. Then on and up, to roust Red Kate and make ready. Our few belongings were trundled onto the porch by slaves, my Copperhead striding downstairs past the wisps of the two women, carrying in her arms, like some exotic creature which glared and bobbed its head, our son, who yelped and covered his eyes when he was first brought out-side. I left them there, went and paid a runner to go and hire a carriage, beside which I would ride, aching with freedom, on our way to the hill-top town—there to take my seat briefly at the table, the better to kick off its legs.

Devilments and Conjures

Chandeliers glowed above Condordia's ballroom, where companies of guests were twirling and others lined the punch-bowls and the tables set with oysters, and still others, arguing, slung wine through air sifted with wig-powder and cigar smoke—all of them feigning lordly indif-ference to General Wilkinson, in whose name the fete was held by the governor of the Mississippi Territory, Cowles Mead.

Damned, sir, if you didn't move fast, said Stephen White. Three weeks of business and you're up on the hill. Two nights on the hill and you're in the governor's mansion.

My agent grinned at me; he'd been the one to secure my entrance to the fete, usher me past the scowling slaves at the front door, through people casting eyes at my get-up, and into the party itself, where he pointed out the risible and the serious, distinguished cotton-man from governor. The general stood off to a corner, more decked with braids, brass, and jewels than when I'd seen him the other morning, receiving what comers made it past his guard of sublieutenants and aides.

The next step, I'd wager, is Washington, White laughed.

I was thinking more Baton Rouge, I said.

How's that? asked Stephen White, who then went on to try and explain his joke.

I let him, thinking: You just worry on the money, Stephen, and I shall put it to use.

The real money, as Stephen called it, would be forthcoming; we'd only have to wait. These weeks had been shouldering out the planters' men sent to auction, or cornering off small but sizable fractions of Kentucky flour shipped downriver, undercutting cask-by-cask the respectable buyers until we could set the market price, send a gang of boys down to the docks and disrupt the other shipments. When he told me of this, I could see Captain Finch snorting and cussing, waving his blade as his barge was boarded by swarms of filthy youngsters, overturning the goods and upsetting his trade.

In the first week we'd hit upon the notion of buying up indigo niggers and renting them to the government as workers hacking out the new northward road. Proper planters wouldn't rent their hands out for the federal project, not with harvests soon to come and the money of no great return. It was my idea to go for the indigo slaves, their cost little more than nothing—promises to their masters to secure discounts for their next batch of fresh bodies—and with some tinctures and the small cost of cast-off clothes to replace their own rags dyed that horrible blue, they appeared no worse than overworked cane-cutters. When several died, a few days in, Stephen laid blame on the poor conditions—tentless in the autumn cold!—and the government men were too stiff with federal money to care, so they simply ordered more until we had to impress the granddads and cripples from sugar-growers' grinding houses.

The afternoon before the ball, I'd drafted out a letter to Abram Horton's widow, conceding her the remainder of the judgment owed me in exchange for ten of her field-slaves—saving her, I added, a substantial sum, by my agent's reckoning, and advising her that there was no need to bring Justice Baker in on an act of kindness. In two weeks I would receive her letter, feminine scribble flourishing with gratefulness; she would agree to make no mention to the justice, and was glad to put the matter at an end—for her husband's wrong-headed actions had cost her so much already. Consider them, she wrote, on their way and ready for my uses.

She must've had some inkling as to what those uses were, or at least the slaves did, for when they arrived in Natchez near the end of October—after Wilkinson had departed for his stand-off with the Pukes, and Colonel Burr stood in a Kentucky courtroom against the accusation of treason—they were much afraid, clucking and shivering in the cart which had borne them up from Pinckneyville. I would stand there, Stephen and the indigo man's agent beside me, and look closely upon the black faces for a hint or feature of those that attacked me in my house. But it was that they all appeared alike, undistinguished by grace or sin. By then I was far-gone on my progress of becoming a gentleman of the South, gazing pitiless upon dark faces wracked with fear. I would ask no questions, prod them not for knowledge of deeds now a year past and into which they'd been led by their former master, dumbly obedient; I would no more have asked a horse why it stepped on my boot. Justice Baker's words stole into my mind, but were gnawed back by my own: But neither would I miss the chance to take the offending beast out back and bludgeon it to death behind the barn. The indigo agent, taking stock of them and slipping the bill of sale into his coat of striking blue, would smilingly say, These ones here may last two seasons, by God!

Women fluttered by in loose, silken dresses—not of the stiff, bedizened, and brightly colored kind favored by the ladies under the hill, but pale, fragile, and thin. They wore their gowns like funeral shrouds, their hair braided and battened down close to their skulls by Roman garlands; and I wondered how Red Kate would've burnt among them, a vanguard of the barbarians somehow slipped among the marbles and white columns to unsettle ghostly ladies delicately fingering the foam from their punch and flicking it to the floor.

My wife was in our rooms at the hotel. She wouldn't trust a slave to watch the boy, though I'd offered to pick a worthy one up. Trust comes with time, she said, and I'm not giving my child to the watch of some nigger-woman I've known but for an afternoon. She'd said this while swallowed in a flowery chair, watching the boy as he played with his new lead soldiers, which I'd bought him to ease his discomfort with moving, to see that he overturned none of the delicates and gilt-edged finery scattered about our new home, situated nicely on the uppermost floor of a grand house on the square, a few minutes' walk to the offices of Stephen White and the ride out of town to the mansions and plantations not long enough for the smell of horse-sweat to set on your clothes. When she wasn't looking, the boy would snatch up a dragoon or two and suck upon their heads.

There we are, said Stephen White, pointing to an older man who was limping towards the general's retinue. My sometime employer, Master Isaac Briggs. Let's see how he acquits himself.

I could thank him for his help on the road contract, I said.

That you could, White said. But he'll smart at the mention of slaves, the Quaker snit. He owns none himself, for it's a sin, you see—but damned if he won't use them to clear road.

So we headed across the dance-floor, catching hems and throwing dancers out of step, until we came to where Wilkinson and his men stood, having parted to receive the surveyor general. Stephen stepped aside to let me make the breach. A flash of recognition on Wilkinson's red face when I approached, but it appeared this Briggs had engaged him in an argument, and he acknowledged me only with his glass, which was near empty. The old man held in his hand a rolled copy of the Mississippi Messenger, no doubt filled with bile over Colonel Burr's movements, nor sparing the general any ire for his unwillingness to engage the Pukes. By the bristling of his aides, it seemed the man had accused him outright of treason.

But General Wilkinson was smiling, buoyant-seeming. He drained the last of his glass and said, Strange, isn't it, friend Briggs, that I, a Spanish officer, am now on my way to fight my employers should they not retire to their borders?

Stephen White took Briggs by the arm and led him off like a doddering uncle. I could hear the *thees* and *thous* trailing off as I shook the general's hand.

The younger Kemper, then, he said, though not the lesser, I'd wager. I was talking to your brother in New Orleans while you were the one thrashing about against my supposed employers in West Florida.

You're among the first to get it right, I said. You and Colonel Burr.

I am always right by the facts. Facts are my weapons beyond shot and steel. The fact being, Mr. Kemper, that I took ten thousand from the Spaniards, though they owed me upwards of forty.

He'd whispered this last bit, leaning in to give it, wafting Madeira my way.

Perhaps, I said, you may call in the measure owed you once we're in Mexico.

I can't deny that I myself see the prospect of such a happy accident occurring—should the Spanish overstep.

Haven't they already? I said.

They are on thin ground, he said. A wrong move and the surface crumbles and they will be consumed.

I hope to see it.

The aides had closed us off in a cordon, to let the general speak of matters best unheard by other guests. He waved his empty glass to one and the fellow scurried off to fill it. Meanwhile the general withdrew from his coat-pocket a silver flask, turned it up, chins bobbing as he drained it.

I leave in the morning, he said, to meet General Cushing in Natchitoches.

Then it's coming, I said, eagerness in my voice. They'll have to try and face you.

Perhaps, said Wilkinson. Or they may retire back to their own borders.

But you can't allow that, I said.

Wilkinson tapped at his flask, the silver ringing hollow. I can't?

If the Spanish retreat, we have no grounds for West Florida.

The general shook his head. West Florida is a pittance. You must understand that.

That's not what Colonel Burr thinks. He'll be most upset to hear you're wavering.

Ah, and you presume to know what that man thinks? The general now took on a fatherly air, saying, Mister Kemper, you know nothing of Aaron Burr. And, it seems, you know even less of how little you or West Florida matter in the scheme of things. Burr you'll never learn, but you can learn your place.

I know he'll have your ass before it's through.

We were locked in a stare when the aide returned with the wine, brushing past me to place it in the general's paw, lean in, and whisper in his ear. Finished with his message, the aide withdrew and the general downed the glassful. Smacking and with a look of distaste my way, he said, Keep well, Mister Kemper. I'm afraid we must part. I've just been told that I must go and watch my wife give up the ghost. . . . Remember my advice.

I made to stop him, but he pitched his glass aside and, surrounded by his guard, strode out onto the dance-floor and in martial shout announced his departure, which was met by only perfunctory cheers and salutes.

His wife wouldn't die, not that night, but it was, I judged, a fair way to make an exit. Stephen White found me and was telling how Governor Mead had been calling Wilkinson a blackguard up and down the hall, but I was shuttered to his chatter, thinking instead of the rotten admonition offered in the general's words: know your place; it's other hands that move the pieces—you just polish the board.

Fine enough, I thought. Let him fail or try his hand at power and he'll soon see who holds the western states and their people in his sway. For Burr a crown, for the general a gibbet. Should the fat man flinch, I'd be the one to set up the cry.

But there it was again, his voice and the voice of all fathers, saying, Boy, know your place.

The Errand-Boy

Sam Swartwout chewed a chicken leg, working a beard of grease as he talked.

Two thousand miles in two months of travel, he said, all to miss the general again. Pick up and go, Sam, that's all there is to it. But, by God, Colonel Burr will be in New Orleans and the war at terminus before I find the fat man.

We were in a tavern off the square, him picking clean the bones and me with an untouched glass of whiskey, observing this creature not much younger than myself, who'd appeared that afternoon in the fore-room of my hotel, sole-worn shoe crossed at his knee, packets and bags scattered round about him on the floor, the slaves eyeing him warily from their posts. I saw him there as I entered from my day at the markets. When he stood and said he'd been looking for me, I might've drawn my pistol and shot him, but he skittered immediately into telling of his service to Colonel Burr, how he'd been sent to give a special message from the great man to General Wilkinson. He'd been given my name as one of his contacts, should his journey take him to Natchez. And it had, by the long route. First up to St. Louis, so he said, but the general had quit the place; then on down the river, hearing he'd been headed first for Natchez to put up his consumptive wife. No luck here, and so he found himself with the prospect of still another journey, toting letters growing older by the day. And if any man doubted his story, the smell of the road upon him told the truth. It stood out even among the piss-tang of the horseflesh dealers and quarter-race men seated about us.

If he'd sent the letter by post, I said, it would've been there months ago.

Swartwout looked at me as though I were mad. Too delicate, he said, to be trusted with some clod-hopper on a horse, wedged in his sack with the love-letters and condolences.

Damned if that's not how I've gotten all mine from Burr, I said.

That's between you and him, said Swartwout. But I'll have you know the colonel keeps up many correspondences. Too many letters from too many different places for one man to read. So he puts his trust often in associates. . . . Who is it you address your letters to?

I sign them as Thomas Roy, and they go to John Fitzsimmons of Nashville.

I hate to break it to you, friend, but those letters you've been getting back are probably not from the colonel himself—though, hearten up, they are in his spirit and from a trusted friend.

There was nothing I could say. Know your place.

All I know, said Swartwout, is that I'm bound to hand-deliver the message and it's of great importance. The colonel did assure me of that.

He was a New Yorker, his talk a harsh ramble, as though the thoughts were heading too fast on their way and intersected strangely. And he was a young man, face fresh despite the road-grime smeared across his cheeks, no lines for it to gather in, no scars like mine to hold it. Aloud he wondered how many years these months of travel had put on him, holding up a wishbone, offering.

I didn't take the bone, instead thinking, Did the dust of those same roads try my brothers' joints? Did Samuel gather it in handfuls to hide his putrefying face? No, I judged, they'd be out of the West by now; in the capital, plying the president's fears.

And so, I'd later come to find, they were: Jefferson cloistered in his office among the curiosities when in walked two more. He was unimpressed by their size, for he himself was a tall man, but he was piqued by their appearance, which even among the hides and head-dresses and strange brass tools stood out. For a week they'd been waiting in Washington, wheedling and lying and trying to worm their way into an audience with the atheist, who coolly received them, bade them sit upon chairs made of fossilized wood. Reuben had claimed, to the president's men, that he was there to discuss the prospect of contracting out the building of a new road from Pinck-neyville north through Tennessee, as the one that stands now, Mister President, I assure you, is lousy with brambles and sinks, places for highwaymen and runaways to skulk. The way Samuel recalled, Jefferson watched while Reuben made his proposition, but he didn't listen. He'd heard such cant before; he was inoculated. What he did was keenly look, taking measurements for the taxidermist, taxidermy being a skill he may have possessed, so plentiful, it seemed, were his interests; among which was not the construction of a new road, for one was presently commissioned and being dug from Natchez up, so the atheist said—my road, little did the brothers know, paved with the bones of indigo slaves.

Swartwout held the wishbone out again, fat upon it shining in the lamplight. Come on now, he said. For fortune's sake.

This time I took the bone, squeezing for a grip; and with a wide smile and a roar of glee Sam Swartwout yanked his end, coming away with the wish still whole in his hand. He puzzled over it and shook his head at me. Too slick, I said, tiring of his silliness. He laid the bone aside.

The atheist needed no deftness, no supreme turn of phrase to maneuver Reuben into revealing his true purpose; he blundered into it directly; having built himself too small an entrance with his talk of road contracts, now he knocked the door-jamb loose with his shoulders—blacking Burr's designs, holding up Senator Smith as foremost among the conspirators, implicating Wilkinson and the businessmen of New Orleans. Jefferson let him unspool: Do go on, no need to say their names again, Mister Kemper. He was quite capable of remembering even the paltriest of details. And these two were among the insignificances.

The president made no mention of our rebellion, but Reuben would invoke it like we'd served at Yorktown: we did right by our country, trying to add to her borders. Then of course there was the attack upon us not long thereafter, which he recalled to Jefferson also: our patriotism in the face of foreign attack. I read, said Reuben, that even some members of congress were for raising an army in reprisal. What came of that? The atheist tried his best to stay out of the affairs of legislature. Our glorious separation, he called it.

Now Reuben was back on Burr and meanwhile Samuel had been sitting in his chair of wooden stone, growing iresome in his quiet. It had been a long trip: sorry roads and houses, buggy tavern beds, the heat withering away and in the highlands the leaves gone orange. A season he couldn't recall, for down our way everything just died, got straight to the business of winter. He felt his own color changing like the leaves, only not so prettily.

December's still the goal? I asked. He'll be here then?

Last I heard, said Swartwout. The Ohio rich have outfitted us with enough boats and meal and pork to feed five hundred for eight weeks. He should be in Tennessee now, and there's another man in that place who'll give us even more.

I said, I thought the colonel convened the armies at the falls of the Ohio in November.

He will. He'll have to travel back up through Kentucky. Rotten place, but not as bad as the Ohio country. He's just in Tennessee to iron out the details. The man's put in almost as many miles as me!

More to come, I hope.

Jefferson seemed displeased that their meeting had lasted long enough for a slave to come in with coffee. By then Reuben was bulling on to his purpose. Let it be known that none of the Kempers are involved in this scheme, and that they have, once again, done right by their country, this time in the face of a cabal who'd have it split West from East. They were, he said, so willing to do her right that he requested a commission to raise troops to defend Pinckneyville. We could easily fall back upon New Orleans, reinforce her when she's under siege. They'd take a commission on grants of land or the dispensation of some debts from the treasury, which he'd heard had been done in the past. So it's come to that, has it, said the president. Samuel had been watching him, wondering why was the man so unsurprised. His vice-president out to split the Union and march on Mexico, his senators and generals in support—how could he be so cool? Unless, of course, he knew.

I said, Do you know if he's dead-set on New Orleans?

Of course, said Swartwout. Absolutely. We need it for the navy. The port. The banks, for financing. Mister Kerr has promised silver from the vaults enough to recruit, feed, and arm seven thousand men. And more, it's a point of leverage. Our men down there haven't softened, have they?

Not from what I know, I said. They were strong for it when we last met.

No letters?

It's been tough to keep in touch.

If anybody knows that, it's Sam Swartwout. He rolled his neck for cricks and stretched wide for his aches.

The same aches trying Samuel's joints, Reuben's words, in outpour, heaping weight upon the hurt: that for expenses paid they'd harry Burr all the way down to New Orleans, keeping yourself, Mister President, informed of his whereabouts and movements. Jefferson, as he'd done with all of Reuben's offers, took it in—agreeing to nothing, giving nothing away. He'd already sent a pair of confidential agents west, two weeks before, and these men would be at Burr's heels, seeing that he went before a grand jury in Kentucky. At the end of October, he would send another, in official capacity and with the blessings of his cabinet, to oversee the proceedings of the court.

So it was an era of errand-boys. All the great men of the time delighted in their Christ-like position of sending others out on missions—Jefferson his Lewis and Clark, then his spies after Burr, who had his Swartwout and what-all else tramping the roads; even Wilkinson had dispatched someone, a man called Pike, into the far reaches of the southwest, to scout out the mountains and dry red-baked lands he assumed to conquer. All of them traveling, through trial and deprivation, for the ill-defined sake of America.

Samuel never told me whether he numbered himself among those missionaries of the United States, with so many miles to go and naught to do but sit there sipping bitter coffee, but only that Reuben—having talked himself to the end of his abilities—grew frustrated by the atheist's lack of alarm, and so invoked the newspapers. Surely, Mister President, your papers here have the same stories as ours do in the West; the plan and its allies are all laid bare. The atheist angled: I do not trust the newspapers, he said. I rely on facts, by which pamphleteers and newsmen are not governed. Then, sir, said Reuben, take what we've said here as fact. From experience and worthy of your concern and that of the entire nation. Jefferson looked grave. Of course, he said. Reuben, rising from his seat, asked: And what of the commissions? At least let us serve. Meanwhile, in Samuel's hand the china cup had grown cold. His brother's words, the damned *us,* he saw falling at Jefferson's feet like the multitude of birds about the office, briefly on the wing but quickly downed, their fate to be stuffed and mounted for the president's pleasure, so that he might know the varieties of wildlife.

Tell me again, said Swartwout—what would be the quickest way for me to reach the general?

If he's still in Natchitoches, you'll take the Red River up. Two days, nothing more.

Thank God, he said. If I didn't have to rush Wilkinson's response back to the colonel, I might return here and settle in for the wait, which should be brief.

You should be on your guard with Wilkinson, I said. The man didn't act as though he had much love for the enterprise.

The colonel's told me how to deal with him. And, besides, anything's better than the cutthroats here. First I was told you were in that lower section; spent a day floundering down there. Christ, the people. The fishmonger who held your letters wouldn't tell me, didn't even know your name—you must've paid him well. Another sent me to this monstrous brothel—what they said was a brothel, though I've never heard of one where the whores jam a pistol at you from out the letter box. You must've spent a bawdy night there, sir, for the whore says to me, His bastard ass is up the hill. Go and find him there and spit in his eye.

Aliza, I thought. Or it may have been Polly Randolph, the mistress whispering the words in her ear. When I first brought Red Kate into our rooms at the hotel, I'd made a joke of promising her that we'd get our own spyglass, watch the pair of them fret and wither. She hadn't laughed with me, but the boy did mock a chuckle. Instead, she went from room to room, touching the furniture, the rugs, the wall-paper, asking me how much a dent this put in our money. We're fine, I said; there's more to come. And anyway I want you in a good place for when the general comes and I march with him, I don't know for how long.

Rubbing the tassel-fringe of a cushion between her fingers, she looked up at me. I forget what lies ahead, she said. Spyglass or no, I can't make fun. When you go I'll be just like them.

And among the curiosities, as darkness fell on Washington and their audience neared its end, the brothers listened to the president's response: By your own admission, you have served your country admirably already. I should hope not to put you to further trouble, you who have at great expense and hardship brought me this intelligence. Reuben's scars were twisting, blood fattening his veins; he said, It is no trouble, sir. We only ask your favor. The atheist waved his favor away with a flip of his long thin fingers. I am in no position to give out commissions, contracts, or dispensaries, he said. I thank you for your fidelity, and ask only that you return home and maintain you considerable vigilance over the matters of your country. By then Reuben was standing, his bulk in full fury threatening the glass cases of preserved eggs, the tubes and bells of glass blown by the same lips which now dismissed him. When Samuel rose and led him out, he was shouting only names: Remember these, the betrayers. But as Samuel hauled his brother off, the name he shouted over and again was that of Senator Smith. Reuben cried it in the hall—Smith of Ohio—as though it were that man alone from whom all troubles sprung.

Swartwout fiddled with the carcass of his meal. The people down there, in that rat-trap, talked a great deal of your duels. Four in a week?

I believe so, I said.

Not unlike our Colonel Burr, he said.

I thought he only had the one.

Well, hell. Swartwout flushed. One's all you need when you use it to take out a man like Hamilton, with one shot dispatch the greatest cause of evil in the country!

I considered this, evils and their multiplicity. Did this boy, who I wished to reach across the table and take by the lapels, know their number? The world would be an easy place if evilness were reconciled to but a single man. Instead, I thought, it holds in the soul of each and every one, twisted and tormenting until it is let loose.

From the White House to the muddy road which led into the town—a few buildings set among open fields filled with the stumps of trees—Samuel brought his brother, who still raged. By God he'd follow Burr himself, raise alarm in every town he came to. Sling so much bile in Cincinnati they'd hang him right there. He'd have him sunk in the river. Samuel let him go, knowing who his brother meant. He was tired, and going back to their tavern-room through the bare-bones capital, where there weren't enough citizens for even pigs or dogs to roam the streets, he saw that it was all a waste.

I finished my whiskey, left coin for the meal, and rose to go, bidding Sam Swartwout good luck on his mission.

Ah, ah, he said, holding out a finger for me to wait. Grinning, he found the wishbone, took it in both hands, and broke it.

All Hallows' Eve

When the runner came to fetch me to the offices of Stephen White, Red Kate, feeling the pull of her Irish ancestry, was doing the boy up so as to ward off any ghosts or demons straying about on the night before All Saints'. He let off short moans and wobbled on his feet, so I thought from discomfort at the costuming; a paper mask folded into the shape of a skull hid the face which had grown gray these past few days, but it didn't hide his eyes, gazing dully from within.

She'd seen me scoffing and said, It's your people, Scots, too who do it. But then again you're of the kind of Scots that burned and hung folks for celebrating Hallowtide.

The day had seen Horton's slaves trundled off to the indigo plantation, the month of October borne witness to the sorrier prospect of Wilkinson's dallying at the border. At his arrival the Spanish had receded west of the Sabine River, broke, and rolled back like a bank of fog. Wilkinson advanced his forces to the east bank, and the Pukes remained, sending him missives, making a show, their commander no doubt leavening his letters to Wilkinson with so much silver-dust that the general was placated by the prospect of his rewards should he not act. This I heard, or read, and filled the gaps with my own speculations. Wilkinson would ignite nothing, but still he had called up damn near all the troops from New Orleans and the river forts to join him at the border. And if the initial aim of the enterprise was the capture of that city, the general had done right by us indeed.

But, as it went, there were things I wouldn't hear or come to fully know until much later.

Swartwout had at last reached his destination and, beaming I'm sure, pressed upon the general the letter which he'd use to destroy the entire enterprise. In it—at least in the version Wilkinson sent out to the president, de-ciphered and in his own malignant hand, and by early November given print in all the country's papers—Colonel Burr revealed New Orleans as the object of his grand designs; not the culmination, but the jewel in the crown. He claimed the assistance of a pair of British warships, which would come up the mouth of the Mississippi and guarantee the port. He claimed the American navy too stood at the ready to spring to his call. He claimed enough to put stars in the eyes of any man. And though he'd never mentioned the British to me, I know much of the letter was true, for the language, full of pomp and promise, matched the colonel's, or at least the men who wrote in his name. Burr's great mistake, so I'd find, was not so much in spelling out Wilkinson's involvement, nor in giving him all the details of the plan, but in committing the sin of reducing Wilkinson to his lieutenant—Second to Burr only, the letter said. He should've known that such men are not accustomed to being subordinates; they smart at the thought and it riles their blood. But Burr was used to young men eager to be seconds, men like me or Sam Swartwout—who Wilkinson kept on at his camp for some weeks, wining him and prying him for information, until at last the general would turn him loose and in the hang-fire send the alarm and the de-ciphered letter to the president.

In ending his letter, Burr had written: The Gods invite us to glory and fortune. And that night, when it should have been elsewhere—on the prospects of the plan, on the hitching and groaning of my son—my mind was on fortune, on wealth and gain.

The runner was waiting at the door for his coin, my wife now folding herself a witch's face out of yellow paper. On the floor beside her the boy sank down and sat cross-legged, sulking; he'd tugged the mask from his face. She'd bought a shrift of all-colors, the sheets played out across the writing desk, waiting to be made specters.

While we're blaspheming, I said, make one for me. From that red there.

Red as the Devil's ass, said my wife, smiling. It'll have to be for the likes of you.

I falsed a laugh, and at that moment my son rocked back and forth a few times, tugged again at his mask, and vomited into his lap.

My wife had him before I could, hauling the child into her arms so that the vomit spilled from where it had pooled between his legs and dribbled down to his ankles as she hurried off with him to the bedroom and the pot.

From the doorway the runner spoke: Sir, I can go tell Mister White—

I held up a hand, listening to my wife cuss the food in this fucking place while the boy wretched. She returned, shaking her head.

The third time this week, she said. They cook this dainty mess and he can't hold it.

You didn't tell me, I said.

You're usually not in so early, and I didn't see to trouble you. Red Kate held up her hand as if I'd see the truth there, saying, There isn't any fever. It's just his stomach. Knew I shouldn't have let him eat those cakes. If we had my propers I'd make him something to calm it.

Call up a nigger and have them get what you need, I said.

I tried that already, she said. They brought back all the wrong things.

The boy had stopped retching, his gags sputtered dry. We listened to him heaving breaths.

There, she said, he's done of it.

God damn it, you'll tell me when he's sick.

Then I'll make you a damned list of what he needs, she said. Hurry and you'll get it on your way to meet with Mister White.

On a sheet of her colored paper she scratched out the necessaries, gave it to me, and whipped round and off to the bedroom. I paid the runner and headed downstairs and into the square, where mercifully no Irish were about, jabbering their demonologies—all sequestered, as they were, in the under-hill town. From between the cracks in the buildings you could see it down there, red and smoky. They'd be yipping wild tonight.

Dusk settled as I made the stalls of the tincture-seller, assembling her cure in little parcels. And as the bundle grew, my anger bled away. He'd been sick his whole life, the boy, and tonight was nothing different. Red Kate would care for him, and though she was stern with the boy when I was about, I knew also that she coddled him the instant I was out the door. She'd be cooing softly songs while he sang along with his single word, his name for her.

I thought I could hear them, the voices of my wife and child, even in Stephen White's office, holding unlit the cigar he'd given me, seated in a cold leather chair before the window overlooking the street. I told him my son was ill and to get to the point, which he did.

Land, said Stephen White. Buy up land.

Christ, Stephen, I don't want a plantation.

Let me finish, he said. I've come into some knowledge, formed a plan that will make us both rich beyond our dreams.

Then speak it, man.

A bill, in this past session, has moved through congress—a bill to put a ban on the importation of slaves. The Virginians believe we're devaluing their commodities, which they so like to ship down here for us to do the hard work of selling. They say they'll put an end to it within the year.

Then why wouldn't I just put my stake in slaves? Their value will only grow because of this.

That's one way, said Stephen White. His lips curled into a smile as he bent and adjusted the bell of the lamp upon his desk so that he could light his cigar from it. The other way—and I speak this in true confidence—is to bring more in. I don't mean to put you or myself in the position of—

Growing tired of his wheedling, I stopped him, saying, Stephen, I've made my way in darker alleys than you'll ever know. Tell me the plan.

Do you know the Attakapas country? It's in the southwest of the Orleans Territory, runs along the Atchafalaya River and down to the coast, terminating in a place called Berwick's Bay. I've been looking over maps since I heard the first rumblings. Even called up copies of the land grants thereabouts from the offices in New Orleans, at my own expense.

You must be convinced, I said.

I am. Buy land at the mouth of the river, in Berwick's, but also on the coast itself. The Isle Dernière, it's called. The Last Island. It stretches some fifteen miles, and would offer ships from the Caribbean a place to anchor and unload their cargo; then those souls would be transported by pirogue up to Berwick, given papers, and off they go to New Orleans and sale.

And who'll bring the slaves?

If you give me your confidence, and some expenditure, I will go to New Orleans within the month, hit the sailors' hostels, talk to Bahama-men, talk to the Barbary pirates for all I care, and I swear to you we'll not be short of eager parties.

Any squatters on the land? I said.

Fishermen work Last Island; Berwick's is empty, since the bay draws so little water. I tell you, Mister Kemper, if we accomplish the feat but once, you'll have your money doubled. If we can continue judiciously to bring the niggers in, our coffers will spill over.

It's a long wait, I said, until the bill's a law and put into action. And besides, think of all the men to be paid—whatever pirates bring the niggers, these fishermen and the others about will all ask coin for their silence.

No different, said White, from what we pay whenever we bring slaves to market. Pay for the pens to hold them, pay the guards to keep them, pay doctors and cooks to fatten them, pay the fucking fiddler to play so they can dance in the yard. I've done the figures, sir, and with the increase in their worth with the coming law, we stand to make fair profits. And as for any of the rougher aspects such trade may require—no offense, but I don't see any wharf-rats and sailors backing you down.

Stephen, I said, are you so ready to become a criminal?

White sat back and tried to look determined among his piled papers, ink, and gum. I saw the maps now, rolled and piled on the desk. He said, I'm here to make my place in the world. If we don't do it, others will. And in a way it seems more honest. If we're selling souls, then it's better to do it sneaking—cover of darkness, as it were—than with creditors and eastern investment bankers on our backs, handbills and advertisements.

He paused, and I let the idea take root in my mind. I'd been in the slaving business not more than a month; but it would come to pass that it encompassed the rest of my life, and brought me the fortune no war or revolution ever could—though God knows I tried, taking on blood, fire, and the ride the way most men of business went on holidays. And did I foresee it then—all the days I'd spend smelling the piss and shit of the pens, how many dancing black bodies I would witness beating with bare feet the dirt floors of exercise yards, the endless voices of the auctioneers, the stream of agents I'd assume to help me in my awful work?

No, my sight those days was poor and the Lord was far from my heart. I still carried the little Bible at my breast, but not even in the way most men carry flasks, drinking occasionally to fortify themselves. Instead I wore it like a tumor, too close to a vital organ to be removed, but nonetheless despised. And it was that the Lord saw this, saw my wicked heart, and though He would allow me earthly rewards—for White's plan would later prove a glorious success—He visited His wrath upon me in His way.

Haven't you heard? I said. Orleans may not long be American. The law won't apply with a new government.

The Burr matter? said White. Anything that's spread so much in the papers can't be true, or at least not as serious as they say.

That so?

I know where you stand, sir, but may I say that it's precarious. Why not take my proposition as a bit of insurance. And besides, there'll still be a market for slaves, duty-free and no-questions-asked. If we spread west to Mexico, think of how many niggers they'll need.

I sat my cigar, still unlit, down upon the front of White's desk. Insurance or not, I did like the plan. None of Reuben's mercantile nonsense, but bodies and beating hearts and hands to work. The country needed bodies more than cloth or tools. And what it called for, I'd provide—and let it provide for me a fortune in kind.

All right, I said. Draft up the money you need and go to New Orleans.

Stephen White rose from his chair, reached across his sea of papers to shake my hand. You'll not regret this, he said. Not a damned bit.

I'd been there not a quarter of an hour, but what transpired in that time would seal the fate of the following fifty years. The blighted trace of my overlong life, its music the sound of coin clinking in a purse, the same as ball-shot in a bag, the noise of souls swiftly stolen by Death's footman and stuffed away into his woolen sack.

Dark had overwhelmed the few streetlamps of the town, and I made my way as in those blinded days, reaching out to touch the unfamiliar, cradling in one hand the parcel of makings to soothe my son, and with the other feeling in the cracks of plaster walls and lines of brick-work the demons to which this night belonged. They brushed by me, Satan's messengers, whispered in my ear, You will be a rich, rich man. So I stumbled on, mistaking the odd clop of horses here and

413

there to be their cloven hooves, until I came into the square and saw the hotel, which was well-lit.

Coming on, I could see through the bright windows that the floor-rooms were full of people, the doorway open and crammed. Their faces turned to me, awaiting. Nervous chatter as I made the door, and from out the crowd came the owner. He tried to take my hand.

My God, sir, I am sorry. A doctor was called, but—

I was past him, shoving guests aside who'd come down from their rooms to witness. I remember their hands, reaching out, trying to touch me. I remember one of the chamber-niggers leaning by the stairs, weeping. Upstairs, still clinging to my parcels, and into the rooms, where there stood among crumpled masks of colored paper the belated doctor, who I passed without a word, and to the bedroom, where a single lamp burnt low, revealing Red Kate curled upon the bed, stroking the pale hair of our dead son beside her.

Their faces both were bloody, hers in smears and his in a great wash from his mouth down his chest. His eyes were closed, but hers turned on me as her mouth began to part and widen into a black and tortured gape, screaming though she didn't make a sound.

Rites and Offerings

Where was he christened? said the cemetery clerk.

Nowhere, I said.

Baptized?

By this hand.

On what authority?

The Lord's.

In the offices of the cemetery clerk, I sat with my fists as stone. My throat was poor of words, my eye reckoned nothing but the bare outline of this fool man, who read me territorial statutes as to why my child could not be buried in the city cemetery. He was a large man, seeming more a farmer than a grave-tender. But there came the thought: Does he not plant and till the earth?

So you have no papers, he said.

None.

Not for your marriage, nor the birth.

Write Justice Baker of Wilkinson County. He'll guarantee whatever you need.

That would take time, sir. And I need the documentation.

How much will it take?

The papers—

No, I said, how much money? Give me a fucking figure.

Sir, said the clerk, I am a public official, and the penalty for bribery, even in such a delicate matter—

God damn you, I just want to put my son in a proper place. With a good stone.

I understand and you have my sympathies. . . . Have you tried the churches?

I'll die and go to Hell before the flesh of my flesh gets put in a papist yard or the damned field of the Church of England.

You may find them more receptive to your . . . offer, he said. And it would be better than what I can give you.

Which is?

There is a corner of our holding, for the—pardon—indigent, the unregistered.

The potter's field?

We do not call it that. There's a prince of France buried there. It's not so mean a company. And you could put your stone as you wish.

A monument among the paupers and niggers dead of dropsy, eh?

The clerk said that I must understand his position; he'd been eyeing, since I'd entered, my pistols, worn according to the law uncovered and outright in plain view. I squared him in the cross of my patch. I can kill you; put your brains through the back of your skull so that you'd be only a mess of teeth and blood-meal. Or the gut-shot, an hour of writhing on the floor of your office with the fires of Hell-pain burning in your belly, your friends calling in a doctor, who messes his arms to the elbows toiling in your innards, but too late.

The doctor had said it was poisoning, hemorrhage resulting. He'd called me from the bedside and my silent-screaming wife, then gone about the rooms in search of the cause. And after a few minutes he crouched at one of the couches and reached beneath it, withdrawing with a knowing sigh one of the boy's lead soldiers, sucked of paint, which the doctor said was no doubt a glaze of sugar-of-lead; the soldier stood upright with his musket, black and terrible and ready.

They should ban the use of it, he said. I've seen it from cookware, utensils.

Staring at the black soldier, I said: He liked the taste. When he was little he'd steal lead shot to suck.

I should think the poor little soul would have suffered an earlier fate if that were the case.

He was troubled, I said. He never spoke my name.

The true evil is the glaze. The lead for shot is less insidious, slow-working. Where did you buy the toy?

A vendor in the street, I said, trying to remember voice or face, but finding nothing.

Where? asked the doctor.

Under the hill, I said.

Bastards, he said. You cannot trust them down there a whit.

I left the clerk unharmed, his mumbled apologies and bureaucratic sympathies, and returned to the hotel, where the body of my son was laid out on a stand in the sitting room, shrouded in fine cloth so that only his face showed. Red Kate had done the business of cleaning and powdering his corpse, and now she sat in a chair nearby, keeping the vigil over the work of her hands, her womb. She said nothing when I told her of the clerk, nothing when I cursed the potter's field. She wouldn't speak until after I'd gone downstairs, called for one of the slaves to bring up my horse, saddled, came again into our rooms and began to wrap tight the shroud about my boy, cinching knots at his limbs so that they wouldn't be jolted loose on the ride.

It was then she said, Why?

And in that question lay the measure of her grief. To fill the breach of the silence that followed—so that it might not be filled by all the awful answers—I said that I would go and find a place of worth, a good place to put him in the ground. I lifted up my son and held him shoulder-wise.

She rose as though on strings and said, I'm coming; and stepping near she reached out with hands hard and clammy from where they'd held her eyes, and she pried him from my arms, made a bower of hers, and, folding him into a tuck, carried him down after me.

The day had been the coldest yet, windless and barren, clouds overwhelming the sky, everything impenetrable gray. The slaves of the hotel had my horse out front, hitched and ready, and when they saw Red Kate behind me with her bundle they ran inside and brought back a small step-ladder so that she could, in some comfort, mount. They also brought a blanket for her shoulders and scrambled up the ladder to fling it over her, while she, unmindful, looked away. I rose, careful not to upset her or the burden which would ride between us on our way through the town, stiffened fingers jabbing at my back, bony shoulder giving nudges, as though asking where it was that we were headed.

And I didn't know myself. We rode through the square and to the north side of town, past the pens, the auction-ground, past the office of Stephen White, where that gentleman was bent to his maps, shoring up the plans for his trip, which would commence so soon that he wouldn't know of my loss until he'd returned from New Orleans bearing the good news of finding partners for our venture. And I wondered were Aliza and the widow Randolph at their spyglass now, watching. Had they witnessed the events of the night, and now the sorry progress of the day?

Further up and out of town we climbed higher, and along the road went tenant-farmers, drivers from the plantations which appeared every few miles, distant from the road and white as bone. Still I didn't know, and Red Kate didn't ask. We went on faith or madness both, rounding the hillocks and through places once covered with trees, now reduced to stumps cut down for timber, the country chewed down by the white columns, which did appear like teeth in the faces of the mansions, now more and more infrequent as the trace led us further out from the habitations of men.

At one point, many miles out and nearing end of day, I let the horse go off the road; he wandered and ate the brittle dying grass. The land thereabouts was unfenced, not yet put to cultivation. I only steered him when we came into some trees, and told my wife to watch her face, but she held it high and let herself be cut by the limbs. One pried the patch from my face and I felt the chill deep in my socket, had to let go the reins to tie it back.

And it was that we came into a clearing, broad and free of tree or undergrowth, where stood a pair of hills twenty feet or more high, whose flattened sides showed the work of human hands. These were the mounds of the Indians long scattered and despoiled by those French explorers who'd ventured first up the river a hundred years before, the same lot who might've marooned the whore Sara back in West Florida. The grass upon the mounds was green, still living, unlike what we'd left behind; and as we approached the horse strayed and ate of it, while I looked about in awe at this glowing clutch of life, fed for millennia from the flesh of chiefs and braves.

I hadn't brought a shovel, but once we both were down, I went to digging in my bags and found a small hatchet. I judged which mound was tallest and went to it, found a place near its crest and began hacking at the earth with the hatchet-blade. Through the dirt flung upwards by my work, I could see Red Kate standing with her bundle at the foot of the mound, straight as the surrounding trees and moving just as little. I wanted to holler for her to set him down, but thought better of it, swallowed dirt instead of speaking. Let her hold him while she could; soon enough he'd be in the ground. Let her bear the weight of our small and warped creation for what time remained before he'd be put away.

My blade struck something hard, and I swept away the dirt to find a spearhead of shining black stone, like glass. I pitched it aside and kept on, hitting now and again veins and pockets of ancient knives, arrowheads, and axes—all of stone. I lifted up my head and rested for a moment, thinking: This is a pagan place. Just as bad as a Catholic yard. But there were those who said the Indians were the lost tribes of Israel, forgotten by God and exiled to America. And this was their temple, long-forgotten, of no use to their inheritors. I could go like Abraham and cut lengths of wood and make him as a burnt offering. But the Lord had already taken him, and there was nothing more to give but flesh already rotting. No, he'd go into the ground with the other lost. Those who the Lord saw fit to vanish from the earth. My boy had been born just as Louisiana was born into America, and now I'd put him in the earth among the people who were there before America was a thought, among the ancient means of war, old as man himself.

It was dark before I'd finished, the hole dug into the mound-side like a bier, the piled dirt aside and waiting to cover him over. There was no pain in my arms, nor was I tired. I waved for Red Kate to come, which she did, trudging up the mound, clutching him close. On her ascent the moon broke the clouds and we were cast in a terrible cold light. And I thought I'd have to take him from her, but my wife fell to her knees before the hole and gently rolled him in. I stood by, Preacher-father's voice clawing in my mind: Be sure you bury it deep.

She peeled aside the shroud from our son's face, took me by the pants-leg and pulled me down to look along with her. Some dirt had already spilled onto him, smudged at his mouth and showing in the strands of his hair. Red Kate choked and put the shroud back again.

I'll be the one to do it, she said.

And so my wife reached out for the piled dirt and by handfuls she would cover him over, batting me away whenever I made to help. You dug the hole to put him in, she said. Now it'll be me.

III

All Fall Away

Winter 1806–1807

The Devil's Pisspot

The Reverend Morrel's hands were bare, his rings pawned off one-by-one to supply himself and his following of Blessed, with whom he crouched and scrounged in the great sink to the east of town.

My God, he said, how you have changed.

Having done so for some years, they'd built up shacks of twigs with roofs thatched with pine-straw, lodges of the damned; he sent the Blessed into the countryside and town in search of bits of cloth to stop the breaches, so their huts looked like the nests of thieving birds. And these Blessed had been the first things I'd seen when I'd ridden down into the pit that morning in late November: worse off than what he'd had before, not harelips or legless or four-legged or crabs

421

or girls big in the cliver, but idiots skulking and humpbacked, with enormous heads overgrown with matted hair and far-set watery eyes which regarded me with fear on my approach to their camp, scurrying downwards to warn the others. And was this what my boy would've become? No, they had not even his single word; rather they moaned and yelped, clapped their hands as they ran in circles of the largest hut, four or five of them, until I came into the clear and the Reverend Morrel stumbled out his door of twigs and briars. A few moments of awe upon his face before he recognized me and went to hushing his Blessed, calling them *children*.

It was all so pitiful as to make me wonder why I'd come at all. Mother Lowde had been right, so Samuel and Reuben, and in truth I'd known it all along. But it was also that my soul cried out for something to do besides mourn. November, slow as torture, had progressed; by mid-month I'd read not only of Burr's first hearings before the Kentucky jury on charges of plotting war against Mexico, but also that Wilkinson had signed a treaty with the Pukes and now the land between the Hondo and the Sabine, the decided borders between the respective countries, would be termed a *neutral ground*. The Pukes had found a price to their liking. One war done, another to begin—at least in the mind of the general, for he continued sending messages of alarm throughout the territory, and before he quit Natchitoches he dispatched his troops to reinforce New Orleans. He'd tried to be secret about it, but governors do talk and the march of twelve hundred men overland did tend to draw attention. And as it went, instead of New Orleans being conquered by Burr, it was Wilkinson who, in his way, would take the prize. But not before he returned to Natchez, where he was not hailed and his call for Mississippi troops to be sent in defense of New Orleans was refused by Governor Mead. So the general dispatched personal messengers to the president, and took up his dying wife again on her litter, hauling her to the boat for New Orleans.

Heading to the markets, I saw the litter pass, the grim procession, the fluttering of blood-spattered cloth, the shadowy figure within, delicately coughing. I went on to my work, and at the pens a cotton-man was talking of Mead's measure, how he considered Wilkinson to be as equal a conspirator as Burr. Designs and plans grew indistinct and muddled in the eyes of onlookers, of which, I hated to admit, I was a member—a follower at best, and all that remained was out of my hands. The tavern talk was now confusion: not Mexico but New Orleans, they said. But wasn't Burr on trial? No, no, Wilkinson's move was a feint. But couldn't New Orleans be still another? Convince the Spanish that Burr seeks to dissolve the Union, but all the while he's aiming for Mexico? The drinkers on the hill-top talked this way, privy to knowledge quite different, I imagined, from the people under the hill. And I hoped that if the horsed and booted spoke of failure— another month, they jeered, and he'll be in a cell—then the others, whose news came from river mud and knuckle-busted lips, would speak of success.

And I should've felt at home among the idiots and the failed fouled remnant of the once-great man who presently sat beside me on a log, stirring at the fire with a stick, a pelt of thick fur worn at his shoulders, a wolf's hide. His clothes, once a fine suit, were now frayed and patched; his high riding-boots, which he propped on the stones before the fire to warm, had been recobbled with hack-wood heels and what looked to be buckskin sole.

Five years? Morrel said.

That's right.

And now the prodigal's returned, but to the wrong father. He looked about him, waved his hands to encompass the surroundings, the many scattered holes where he'd buried the fruits of his robberies, now long disinterred, saying, And what do you think of it?

I thought you were dead, I said.

Did you? No reason why you shouldn't, I suppose. Those militia, they tried to crucify me. They tried to hang me from a tree and cut open my bowels. They tried to paint me with tar. But the cross broke before they could nail me down, the limb snapped from off the tree, the tar turned to stone in its kettle. I escaped.

So did Crabbe, I said. Do you remember him?

I remember everything, he said. I've got nothing else but to remember.

But he died later, in fighting.

Your war of rebellion—I know it well. Morrel coughed into his hand, struggled to regain his breath. A handbill, one of your proclamations, blew in on a northward wind and came sailing down from the treetops. Landed right over there. I read it, saw your name. In such ways the Lord has kept me apprised. . . . I'd have it still, but I'm afraid we used it for kindling that winter.

You've been here that long?

I tried my hand in Mobile, he said, in New Orleans. But, son, I came to know that when God tells you that you've failed in His eyes, that you're through and bereft of His love, then you quit from your present path and try to regain. And so I removed myself, like the prophets of old, to the wilderness. I've made friends by and by; they're drawn to me, it seems.

I meant for none of it.

Vanity, he said—to think that you're the cause. Son, you didn't know me for a year, and you think that you're reason for my ruination? And who says I'm ruined anyhow. My black children haven't forsaken me—they pass this way when they escape and I give them shelter. And I have my Blessed. So I'm loved, taken care of.

In the summer, I said, some men rode on my house. Some of them were harelipped. I thought you'd sent them.

The foolish man searches for earthly reasons, causes; he shouts to his fellows for blame; but the wise man knows it's all because of God and simply bows his head. . . . I thought you'd have come further than this. You should've been the greatest preacher in the land. But I suppose there's still time.

I've long given it up.

And yet you look for causes in the world of men, even when your answer comes easy from your own lips. Forsake the gift He's given you, and you shall be forsaken of Him. I knew it that night when you followed after those Kempers like a dog, tail-tucked and willing. You looked earthward when your eyes should've been to Heaven. . . . God, how you sounded when you preached. I was wicked then, enraptured of money and earthly things, but you—when I heard you preach, the Lord's voice was in my ear, and do you know what He said? He said, Morrel, this boy is sent like a Christ. To save the land. To prepare it for the great return. And I knew then that you'd be with me only briefly— though not that you'd shut away the Gospel from your heart. When will Our Savior come down from Heaven if the men who'd speed his return all fall away?

That's not my job, I said.

And what is?

I've been making speculations at the flesh-markets.

I know that path. The lure of our great commodity: the Negroe. The only way a man without standing can make his way in this world. Morrel snatched a fist at his temple, trapping a thought. And no doubt you're waiting for another revolution, he said.

I gave a bitter smile.

You have it in your heart, as did I. I waited all my life for my black children to rise up behind me and tear down their masters' houses. They haven't yet, and still I wait. Vanity; the true revolution is the return of Our Lord and Savior.

Then why aren't you out among the people? Why aren't you preparing the way?

425

I was given my chance. I turned from the path.

That's my answer to you, I said.

You're too damned young to say it. Maybe if you step back on the path, then the Lord will quit trying you.

What do you know about that?

I know that I didn't, he said. And I've been made to suffer for my vanity. And I know you suffer, too. I remember how in your sermons you'd talk about the drowned girl, back in the plains, how you'd put a baby in her that died. And now you've drowned another—that's what brings you here.

I've drowned nobody, I said. I had a son. He died last month.

Morrel sucked his cheeks to emptier hollows, stared into the fire, nodding. I see souls rising up in shafts of light, he said. I look up at nights, like this one, and I see them shoot skywards from the city. I hear their voices in low chorus. They go to Judgment. I heard your boy's voice, singing as he rose, his light a thin scribble, but up and up it went. I heard it and I knew.

You heard shit, I said. You're telling nothing.

Well, he said, that's not why you came here anyway. Not to hear me talk.

At the far edge of the fire a pair of the Blessed were fighting, groaning and bleating at each other and venturing slaps that smacked dully on each other's heads. Morrel turned and admonished them, like a gentle father, knowing and without anger: Be silent. Hush. You are the Blessed and most beloved of God, so be at peace.

At the sound of his voice the pair of them stopped and sank to the ground, looking about bewildered, having forgotten what it was they'd been fighting for. And while the Reverend Morrel was turned, I drew out one of my pistols and leveled it at him. And he must've heard me working at my bandolier, for when he turned back to me he said not a word, just shut his eyes. His fingers, dented where his rings

426

had been, went scratching out of habit at his chest for where the fine jeweled cross had hung in better days. He knew why I'd come: to strike at something, no matter how useless, how hollow, it was. And even if I denied it then in my wicked heart, the Reverend Morrel knew that I could not resist being the Lord's mechanism, and would do His Will.

I stood and came round behind him, thumbing back the hammer. I shot his head into the fire, where it seethed and hissed for a moment as the flames turned black. The pair of Blessed were crying out, their faces looking upwards as though they too could see the light he'd spoken of. Morrel's body fell towards me and I stepped back, giving room for his soul to rise.

Nativity

Christmas nearing, a constant insult: the white sugar-dusted cakes baked into the shapes of swaddled baby Christs, a mockery piled in the shop-windows beside short-bread Marys and Josephs, attendant kings and beasts.

The Natchez people went about their days shaking heads at the confusion of the papers and the government as to who the enemy was and from whence he was coming. Like the days of the Purchase, I heard one saying, when everybody was fearing the French, the Spanish, the Federals, the British! Next they'll say Burr's in league with Bonaparte. Or Wilkinson's sent a letter guaranteeing him the port. All three a gaggle of little emperors!

Mead's refusal of troops had lent the populace a hearty contempt for Wilkinson and the tyranny he presently exercised in New Orleans. In under a month he'd imprisoned most of the Association, sent them to a ship anchored in the river, where they were clapped in irons. Judge Workman, who'd granted them a writ of habeas corpus, was sent to join their shackled company along with Lewis Kerr, the banker. Daniel

Clark only escaped a similar fate by virtue of his being in Washington at the time, in his first session of congress, the bitter winter having no doubt bled the flushed health of the Mexican sun from his face. Similarly I considered the imprisoned: a fine troupe of actors, in the chill of the hold performing a spot-composed play by Workman, while Kerr counted their biscuits and pretended they were silver.

Earliest among the arrested was Sam Swartwout. In the first week of December, before the scope of Wilkinson's awful power was full-known, he'd passed once more through Natchez with a man named John Adair—evidently the leader of the Kentucky faction—on their way, so they said, to New Orleans, where they intended to convince the general to negotiate a handover of the city to Colonel Burr. They'd stayed at my hotel for a night, prattling hopes at dinner, Swartwout counting his miles. The man, Adair, told how Burr had beaten the charges in Kentucky, and was presently assembling the force at the mouth of the Cumberland.

It's coming close, he said. The time is nigh.

Wilkinson will have none of it, I said. He's made his choice.

We'll see how our offer suits him, said Swartwout. He's an agreeable man, and he's done the work of taking the city for us.

He's been screaming alarm about Burr all over the territory, I said.

Screaming to cover your ass is one thing, said Swartwout. Let's see how he acts when we've made him the new offer.

Later I would hear that, in his first week of occupation, General Wilkinson had sent a letter to the viceroy of Mexico: a bill, for thirty thousand dollars, for services rendered in defending the lands of His Catholic Majesty. I'm sure that he was paid. As for Swartwout, he'd have many miles yet to cover once Wilkinson had his hotel in New Orleans secured by two hundred soldiers, and he, along with Adair, was dragged off for the prison-ships and on to Washington to stand trial for treason.

THE BLOOD OF HEAVEN

We must try, Swartwout had said as I was leaving, wishing luck but knowing there'd be none, going to my hotel where Red Kate had shut up the bedroom, never to be used again. We slept on a mattress in the sitting room; and as the month progressed, in those nights, while my wife mumbled in her sleep, pulling pillows to her chest, and I numbered the ever-growing tally of arrests, I could hear above it all Reuben's voice, low, boastful, and assured, saying he was right.

Much of the word out of New Orleans I heard from Stephen White, lately returned. Mid-December he'd arrived back in Natchez, happily bearing the weight of our enterprise high upon his shoulders. As it goes with New Orleans, his time there had been a whirl: from the soggy and bitten sailors' rooms to the whorehouse cloisters of their captains, from the card-tables of the slave pen guards, who kept their watches in towers above the massive brick-and-iron gaols which held the slaves awaiting market, to the French hotels of those who owned the pens. On his first day he'd witnessed a newspaper editor being dragged out from his offices by a cordon of guards, and on his last day General Wilkinson's speech to the Chamber of Commerce. White sat among the men of business, now surely feeling invested among them with the success of his dealings, and listened to the general rail and shout, stomp his spurs and clatter his scabbard to the lectern, saying, Eight thousand men! Eight thousand of the worst, bloodiest, most barbarous horde since the Vandals sacked Rome are presently forming in secret along the banks of the Ohio, hurrying to meet their leader in Kentucky—a man no close second to Catalan or Caesar—liberate him from the law, and pour downward to our fair Orleans!

The man seated beside White turned to whisper in his ear: And how in hell do you keep eight thousand men a secret?

The general went on, declaiming on the stage, where seated at his right hand was Governor Claiborne, now, as the city merchants told White, cowed by Wilkinson into utter impotence. That same speech saw Wilkinson announce that the city was officially under martial law. A little late to give it a name, said one man of business.

But the details of the city and her preparations for the imagined army were only snippets thrown about White's talk, which was mostly of our new business. It's so strange, he said, how you meet people of interest. So it went that Stephen White had been sitting one evening with the guards at a slave pen on Carondelet, playing cards and sharing his flask while outside the niggers were made to dance, when a Frenchman came, a blacksmith who made a measure of his living repairing the iron bars of the gaols. He was there to replace some grating, but the guards held him up, saying, Pierre, Mister White here is always talking after shipping, getting into trade. Does your brother still run ships? The Frenchman smiled and said, Mais yes. What kind of cargo are you wanting? Stephen had tried to be in confidence. A touchy sort, he'd said. Ah, said the Frenchman, and invited him to come round to his shop in the morning, where he told White horror-tales of his escape from St. Domingue—his wife flayed alive before his eyes and despoiled—until his brother, Jean, arrived from the docks.

The younger Lafitte, related Stephen, seems flightier. I believe the elder brother, Pierre, is the brains of the operation. But Jean is the captain, knows the waters well. And he's not afraid to take on a Spanish ship on its way to Pensacola. Despises them, so you'll have that in common. He's had a hell of a time finding what to do with the niggers he picks up as it is. Pierre says to throw them overboard. But Jean has been selling a few here and there, though he says he mostly leaves them on the boat, as they make troublesome cargo.

But he agreed to do the shipping, I said.

Yes, yes, said White. But I'm afraid it will be catch-as-catch-can for the most part. We laid out a plan for a trial engagement in early May, so we can catch the tail-end of the selling season. He'll test the waters on the islands, see how many he can get at a chance. So you'll have to be in Berwick's by then. See how we do without the full force of the law upon our backs.

And the fencer is another Frenchman?

Lamarque, he said. Owns two pens. He offered to secure us papers in advance, but I'll do that job myself.

Good, I said. We're cutting our percentages as it is.

Only at first. Monsieur Lamarque has agreed to a sliding scale. After the first year of sales, we begin to take a majority of the profits. Minus upkeep, et cetera.

Too many Frenchmen, I said. Couldn't there have been an American for you?

Americans, said White, cleave a bit too closely to the law for our purposes.

It's a long time until the prices should rise.

Only half a season, he said. From September to December of next year. And by then we'll be masters of the trade. We'll be like magicians, moving them unseen wherever we wish.

All this on my mind as the anniversary of the Savior's birth dawned, but there was no use in talking of it to Red Kate, lost lately to sorrow and rage, giving damning glances whenever I spoke of the prospect of our future fortune as Christmas Day shone through the windows.

And how do you think you'll find the time for Colonel Burr's war, she said, with all this business?

I was parting the curtains to look outside, see the people milling, congratulating each other on the day. Good tidings. Comfort and joy. I told her it would come by and by.

Christ, said my wife. All the stinking guns and shot and bloody men on our doorstep—only to end up a nigger-dealer.

Is there something wrong with that? I said. With making a way in the world? It's paid so far for all this. Or would you rather a shack in the woods? Or the cabin in Pinckneyville?

There's nothing wrong with it, she said, rasping now, her face contorted into a kind of smile. But I have paid, and you have paid—for all of this. Not nigger-flesh, Angel, but by our own.

There stood my wife, who I'd bought from a brothel at the age of fourteen, myself not much older. Who'd endured childbirth and war and kidnapping and intrigue, my blindness and our child's death. And it would've been less terrible to look on her then if she had aged. But she hadn't, not so that it showed. Outwardly she looked a girl, a rough-country one with her spatter of freckles, broad face, boxer's nose, but a girl nonetheless. Inwards, though, she was a nest of dry and winter-bitten briars, her hopes impaled upon brittle tines.

It doesn't matter, she said. Not a bit. Go on and make a fortune. Build me a mansion in a swamp. Build it out of bones. We used to joke, remember, about me being a queen in the new country? So now I'll be queen of the dead.

In the street below the citizens were nibbling their sweets; wiseman, camel, mother, father, child—all devoured.

Rejoined, Renewed

And so it was, as the old year came to an end and the new took hold like a skeleton fist, that the dead, or those who might as well have been, were rising. It was the start of the second week of January, Sunday, the Lord's Day, and I was standing in the Natchez square with Samuel when a rider came to the government house, crying out that Aaron Burr was landed in Vicksburg with his army.

I looked to my brother and said, You came just in time.

That morning one of the hotel slaves had come knocking at our door, saying we had visitors awaiting in the lobby. I followed him down. And in the morning bustle of footmen and Negroes bearing trays of breakfast were Samuel and the widow Randolph, standing beside a pair of trunks. His color had turned to a deeper green, purpling at the edges of his features. He hadn't had time to apply his powder since he'd returned, not a day before. He'd come alone to Natchez, having left Reuben in Washington some two months past, left his brother to pursue the vendetta alone. Because of this, Aliza had thrown the widow and him out. Before they'd been able to get their things out of The Church, the mistress had taken up a crop and began thrashing them both, screaming. I could see the tattered places in the widow's dresses where the crop had struck her bare, pale arms. Samuel was holding one at the elbow, gently, as though to steady her.

Without thinking, I embraced him.

Brother, he said, letting me go, we have much to discuss.

Samuel made to send Polly Randolph up to our rooms along with the trunks. I stopped him, told him to get his own, and that it was best, Polly, to leave my wife alone. He smarted for a moment, then I said, My son is dead.

The widow Randolph began to cry. She looked away from me, was bumped by a slave carrying an urn of coffee, yelped, the madness of her time shut in with Aliza having overtaken what little sense she'd had before. I could've struck her. I wanted no tears. Then I saw Samuel too was weeping. I left them there, went to the valet and arranged for a room. While I waited at the desk, my brother came behind me. The tears which ran along his corpse-colored features had the look of pus.

Wipe your damned face, I said.

Into the street and chilling wind we went, him leaving Polly to attend to their rooms. He told me of the president, of Reuben's foolish obsession; he said he'd been a fool to follow him all that long way. With some satisfaction I said he would've done no more good here. And these words brought him back to the matter of my dead son.

I'm sorry, he said. God, I am so sorry.

We walked the square, past the government house, turning at the English Church, making the same tread over and again.

He said, in the tones of our boyhood, of a Chit funeral: The Lord does not cast off forever. But though He causes grief, yet He will have compassion according to His mercies. For He does not willingly afflict the children of men.

O, put it away, I said. I've heard enough of scripture babble to last a lifetime. I'm through with it.

Samuel stopped. I thought it might help, he said. I've been thinking on the Bible lately. Had time to on the way back.

And did he want me to proffer him some verse, a balm to soothe his conscience for leaving his mad brother to rail in the streets of the capital? Or were there some other sins?

There is no balm, I said.

Samuel looked to me, a dull giant peering down for meaning. God Himself would've had no better visage reproduced, as He is, in the images of men. He bent over me, his necklace of tiger's teeth spilling out from his coat, reached out a hand and tapped the Bible at my breast, where he knew it would be.

There, he said, you must still believe a little.

I'd felt his finger-tap through the pages of the book, thudding at my heart. I did still wear it, but now not even like a tumor. I said to my brother: Belief's nothing. I wear it like you do your tiger's teeth. In remembrance of something I've killed.

Samuel shuddered, and we walked on. As we rounded the same landmarks, he talked of his journey, of Reuben and how he'd forsaken him—though rightly, he said. For he couldn't bear another day of him, of his plans for Senator Smith. Before the end, Reuben had been trying to find a way to address the congress, was drafting out speeches. Samuel said his brother hadn't even looked up from his desk when he'd left.

He was going on about it all as we turned the corner at the government house and came upon a gathering crowd, above which sat a rider bellowing about Burr, Vicksburg, an army. I felt as in those moments when you're riding through a storm in open country and all around you lightning is touching down in electric slashes, and the hair stands upon your neck and arms and your throat grows clenched, awaiting the strike which will be surely aimed for you. Speed the horse and hurry on.

I listened, hollered over the crowd for the rider to say again. All he knew were those few words. He was the third in a chain of messengers who'd ridden, in twenty-mile stretches, the distance between the towns. By the time it'd gotten to him, the rider before was so whipped as to only give the pertinent details. Fine, I thought. I need no more. I wheeled to Samuel, grinning.

Your faith's been rewarded, said my brother.

Damn faith, I said. This is something more. And you're for it now, aren't you?

Samuel's shoulders dropped to bear upon them another brother's hopes. If this is how it goes, he said, I'm with you.

I took his arm and shook him. More and more came to the crowd and the rider's words were now repeated in yammering chorus. I pulled Samuel through and we made the steps of the government house, came to doors where stood four guards of the Mississippi militia. I told one I needed to see Mister Stephen White, under-secretary to the surveyor general.

Nobody in, said the guard. No admittance till further notice. The governor's in meeting with his staff.

And even this had joy singing in me as we went back down the steps. The crowd had taken sides, one hollering for the honor of the Union, the other for a gabbled mixture of freedom, land, and Burr. When we walked through them they were about to come to blows;

gentlemen throwing down their hats, assaulting the air with their canes, beggars and menials egging them on, switching allegiances as they saw fit.

So, said Samuel as we hurried back to the hotel, will you ride up now and meet him?

No, no, I said. Why kill a horse to go eighty miles when he's coming down the river soon enough? We'll meet him at the docks, or ride down and catch him at his next stop.

I guess we will, he said.

Across the street, before the government house, the crowd was in minor riot. We watched the gentlemen fly at one another, shouting oaths and tearing cravats. The militiamen stayed at their posts, four of them to maybe a hundred in the street. They'd marked the odds and so would let the scene play out.

Finally, I said. The time's at hand.

We were not long in the hotel. Red Kate, unable to stomach my happiness, had sent us off. She still hadn't seen Polly, and when, in the doorway of our room, she caught sight of Samuel, I thought she'd come scrambling towards us and tear him apart with her hands. I could see them working into claws at her sides.

By evening we'd been sitting in the tavern off the square for some hours, watching the crowds buffet and break at the doorway, men shouldering in to continue their riot in a more peaceable place, where at least there was beer. Toasts to the Union, toasts to its death.

I was nearing drunk, going over the details of supplies, what we'd need for the campaign sure to commence. First things first, I said. You'll need a horse and kit. How many guns do you have?

A few, said my brother. But won't we be supplied from Burr's store? That's all I heard on my way down was how much money he'd been given by the rich men in Ohio and the ones in Tennessee.

Poor Reuben, I said. He couldn't see that it was good.

He didn't care about Burr. So long as Smith was broken.

I believe we'll tolerate a Smith or two to have our own country and the crushing of the Pukes at last. I must try and convince the colonel of that. First Baton Rouge, then on to Wilkinson's thousand in New Orleans. Christ, the man's been such a shit down there they'll treat us as liberators.

Clark was drafting a pamphlet against him when I left Washington.

Good man, I said. Wait till he hears what the bloated bastard's been up to now. He'll have to write a book. In memoriam.

A pair of drinkers were bellowing about tyrants, smashing chamber pots for emphasis against the bar when Stephen White came in. Spotting us, he came on, having to hold a hand over his face to avoid shards of china-ware. He sat and I introduced him to my brother, White taking his hand briefly, looking gray-faced all about.

So, my friend, what's the news from the government? I said.

Stephen fell into the chair and leaned his head back. Mead had us locked away all damn day, ever since he got the letter from Burr. So the governor, it seems, will be sticking it to Wilkinson. He'll be the one to accept the surrender, tomorrow.

What surrender? I said.

Burr's, of course, said White. He landed in Vicksburg yesterday afternoon and it seems someone gave him a newspaper that said how Wilkinson was in New Orleans and would have him hang. Evidently he thought better of it all when his neck was on the line. His letter to Governor Mead came early in the morning—he'll surrender only to Mississippi authorities, and on the condition that he will not be extradited to Orleans.

I couldn't speak. Samuel put a hand to my shoulder and we had to duck, for another pot came sailing overhead, smashing against the wall behind us, its contents streaming down the paper. The gentlemen were roaring now; I wanted to join them, to howl.

The Spilling of the Books

Ice crackled in the air, glinting in what little sun deigned to shine upon that day; the governor's militia, collars pulled to their eyelids, hats tucked low, went slipping and stumbling upon the boats of Colonel Burr's surrendered army. Samuel and I wore scarves tied about our faces, looking like the banditti we had once been. Stephen White had secured us Mead's allowances to accompany him and some fifty militia to the spot where Burr would make his end. It was an outlet of a bayou, frozen over, its arteries blocked with muddy drifts of snow, which had fallen in great force all through the night, beginning while I'd been sitting in the tavern listening to Stephen White try and convince Samuel of how fruitful our slaving venture would be.

Looking out from the hill-top where we'd been told to stay while the governor and his men approached the boats, I wondered how could this land bear any fruit. None that wasn't wicked. Rotten on the vine. Burr and his party had floated down almost to Natchez, landing in this place where he could have his shame with the fewest witnesses.

Can you see him? Samuel said.

Down at the riverside eight or nine boats were banked and piled haphazardly with casks and barrels and crates, and among the goods huddled clutches of men whose breath rose in clouds, indifferent to those who now boarded and began to upturn casks, pry with bars at the mouths of crates. They'd outpaced the governor, who'd gotten down from his horse and was now mired in a muddy bar. A man from off the boats strode through the slough and helped him free. This was Colonel Burr.

Damn this, I said, spurred my horse and rode downhill, Samuel following. We stopped before the mud, wet snow tumbling down from the branches of the trees as we tied our horses off. We made the muddy plain, seeing now that the governor and Burr had moved away from the bank to higher ground. Mead wore a gray great-coat, soaked about the shoulders with melt, while Burr was in his black and stood against the snow like the lone tree in a field to have been struck by lightning.

At the boats there were maybe a hundred men, not counting the militia; we trod the boards and ignored the cusses of the Mississippians, taking stock of this beleaguered army. They were young men, younger than me, and in their faces, blue from cold, I saw my foolishness reflected—my vanity, as Morrel would have it. Samuel gave one a light for his pipe.

My father will be pleased, said the boy. Now I'll go home with my tail between my legs.

Where do you come from? I said.

Nashville, he said. He told me not to go, but the colonel has his way—makes you believe, you know? O, the old man will be feeling his oats when I come crawling back, I'll tell you.

Then don't, I said, and strode on. The militiamen were sifting their hands through open casks of sugar, licking their fingers.

That's poor advice, said Samuel.

Why? I said. We never did go back.

It was different for us, he said. These here have prospects. Did you hear his voice? It's an army of school-boys.

Samuel picked his boots up high to step over a passel of them warming their hands around the belly of a small lamp. The next boat was full of long crates, of the kind which might hold rifles and muskets. Some militiamen were now at them, prying with hammers and bars they'd brought from home when they'd been hastily called up in the night.

I don't see why, brother, said Samuel. Why you'd want to come and see this.

I didn't answer, couldn't term it then in all the frozen sorrow, that I would not be such an apostle who would miss the crucifixion. The snow had begun to fall again and the militiamen let out a cheer as the first crate was opened, then cussed bewildered when they overturned it and found that what it held was books.

Volumes spilled out onto the planks, kicked at by the men in their anger. Another crate, the same result—thuds of leather spines, books sliding down and slipping to the water, bobbing off into the ice-bit flow. It was this sight that struck me most of all. He'd come with boys and books, dear God, and this was what I'd been waiting for. And more crates were pried and more and more books spilled, joined their fellows on the decking, their pages swelling and bloating from the wetness of the falling snow. The militiamen were laughing now, drawing up volumes and holding them like muskets in their hands, aiming at each other and the boys who sat nearby on the bank cross-legged and sullenly reviewing the performance; they sniped them out and made sounds of shooting with their mouths. The boys shook with every shot, but it might've only been the cold.

Dear Christ, said Samuel. This was it?

I turned and started back the way we came. And I would've gone straight to the horses and ridden back to Natchez if I hadn't come, at the bridge of the last boat, face-to-face with Colonel Burr. He was the same man I'd seen at my table in Pinckneyville. Brows pushed back from the wide, searching black eyes, he showed no wear or sorrow, unlike his followers, but rather than the petals of magnolias which had been caught all up in his clothes, now his person was gathering snow like any edifice, this one erected as a monument to failure. Frost rimmed the brim of his hat and he made no move to dust it away, but let it fall. He greeted me without any recognition, but as another function of the great machine his plans had engineered, and which was now grinding him apart between its gears.

Colonel, I said. It's Colonel Kemper. Your friend in Natchez.

Burr blinked; he'd been staring off, perhaps letting his vision go to haze so that he might spare his eyes this scene. I'm sorry, he said, but at present you escape me. Everything escapes me now. He shook himself, fixed his eyes on me. Of course, that doesn't mean that you are not my friend.

You stayed at my house in Pinckneyville, I said. I have your letters—

Curse letters, Burr said softly. I'm undone by letters.

I'd forgotten how small the colonel was; how his size was like mine.

My respects, sir, said Samuel. We met once in New Orleans.

Burr nodded thanks, and giving gaze to the boats, this creature who I'd thought for so long to be a great man, to whom I'd attached myself like a tick to a dog's neck, thinking I was also great, spoke these words in parting: Forgive my memory. I'm sure you are a good friend. It's only that I have so many . . .

Aaron Burr then brushed past us and went on, boat to boat, kneeling and giving words to his young men, who, when he came to them, would smile solemnly and listen, as though they still believed.

IV

The Last Island

Spring 1807

Settling Accounts; a Parting Gift

Pinckneyville had been rebuilt since the storm of our departure, but still the citizens watched us with unease from their porches and windows as we took what things remained from the house. Reuben was among them, and stood in observance off with some of the town fathers. If any of them were papists, they'd have made the sign of the cross. Instead wives brought them out punch and glasses of lemon-water to ease their nervous talk; it was mid-April and the heat was beginning to return, the crops blighted by the winter being renewed. Hope broke the soil in green leaflets, the world went on.

Red Kate hefted a stack of pots and handed them to me, saying, I wouldn't have come if I'd known there'd be so little. I don't remember us having so few things.

I put the pots in the cart, between the legs of the bed, broken down but loaded with hopes that she'd sleep in this one—the one where our son had been conceived and born, where I hoped to do the same again. Fallow hopes, and hopes they would remain. But at the time I had some faith, not in God but in my own works. So I climbed into the cart and tested the riggings that held the bed and mattress fast. I'd agreed to come for reasons more than gathering up our meager possessions. There had been, to use Reuben's words, accounts that needed settling—only my accounts weren't made of paper and ink, not yet at least, but were of flesh and blood, and I paid them out with pistol and knife. His words upon me: All you know is the sneak and ambush. Killing out of shadows.

Sun burning in a clear sky above the flat land of Pinckneyville, above its flat people who chattered and tsked and cupped their hands above their eyes, checking the horizon for the makings of another storm, now that we were back. All of this in preparation for the move to Berwick's Bay—take our things down to the barge which awaited us at the river, from where we'd float onwards to New Orleans, cut across to the bay. Stephen White was on his way with the forged papers, enough for twenty, taking some time off from his practice and the affairs of the surveyor to assist me in this first exchange. Talking excitedly on the eve before I left Natchez, he said, It'll be good to do it ourselves, before we find some men to hire who we can trust. Good to get our boots wet a little, eh? Get our hands dirty.

His hands were paltry feelers and spreaders of foolscap; the only blemishes they knew were ink on uncalloused knuckles trapped and under well-groomed fingernails. If he only knew what hands could do.

443

I leaned at the kick-boards of the cart, eyeing Reuben now and again. He'd bought Randolph's plots outright from the widow and Samuel, sought to solidify his place in town with a tavern and a new store, renew his barging on the river. He bore ill will for no one, so he said. In the last week he'd heard the news that John Smith of Ohio was now the first senator of these United States to be indicted for a crime. He crowed the fact proudly since he'd come back to Natchez in February, in time to see Burr brought to trial under Judge Rodney in Mississippi, and there he'd spent a few weeks with Aliza before shutting her back in her cage and heading down. In that time he'd worked over the sale of the land by letter with Polly and Samuel, who'd employed Stephen White in finding them a piece of worthwhile townage in the village of Alexandria, in the Orleans Territory. White said it had room to grow, and would be prosperous of cotton, a fine place for a tavern and hotel.

You want to sling liquor, work a stinking bar? I said.

Samuel, putting pen to deed-papers, said, It's better than the alternative, brother.

By this he meant my slaving venture. Samuel wouldn't be persuaded to join in it, despite my or White's persuasions. He wanted to be upcountry and on his own. He said if it wasn't for Polly he wouldn't have even come this close to West Florida. Last Island and what we aimed to do there weren't to his liking, said it reminded him of Morrel. I smiled when he said that, smiled as I watched him now as sweating, he tossed a chair into his cart. Let him wear an apron and tap casks—I wished him well. I'd even given him a parting gift for the mantelpiece, now squirreled away amongst his goods, hiding in some corner of his cart: the ears of Ira Kneeland, floating in a small jar of pickling wine.

Reuben thought he'd won, the fool. You lied about cutting men, lied about a jar of foreskins for the love of your wife. I am no liar.

I'd made this gift to my brother that morning. I was just returning when he came outside at the sound of my horse. We'd been in Pinckneyville a single night, and in that time I'd made my mind up to settle that outstanding bill. Lying alone in the bed while Red Kate slept out in the open room upon the floor, there came a voice—not God's but mine, saying, You've got nothing. You have failed and what you believed in is a failure. This is your last time near the country you so sought to take. Soon you'll be down at the swirling Gulf, a slaving man. But now, you can ride out one last time. Leave them all in fear. And if you should die, what matter? She'll be this way if you are dead, she'll be this way if you're alive. Once more for blood and screams and retribution. One more ride before you're rich and just like them.

So I went, stepping over my wife where she lay upon the rug in the hall, out into the early night, the moon not even risen. She hadn't said a word, but I knew she'd been watching, resigned.

Twenty miles of the old southward road, where we'd been made to run that awful night, where I'd wept and bled and jogged along gagging with my brothers towards Kneeland's promised torments. I beat the horse down, charged it fast. I wanted not to look upon the places of our suffering. Past the invisible line of demarcation between the countries and into the open land of the plantations. If any had been looking, they'd have seen me coming—lone rider, black and terrible of purpose. And if I'd been still in the habit of belief, it would've seemed divine providence that Ira Kneeland would be riding northwards with a friend on that same road, to what purpose I can't say. I never gave him a chance to speak it.

At first I only saw a pair of men a-horse, trotting slowly, oncoming. I slowed and edged to the far side of the road, hoping for them not to catch my face. But as they came I heard one speaking, talking loud perhaps to frighten off the night and this traveler he didn't know. It was the voice that had called my wife a whore, told me I would never see her again. I could not forget it. The knowledge broke upon me, his face blazing to my eye, in the instant we passed each other on the road.

I wheeled and shot his fellow in the back before they'd gone ten yards up the road. The man fell, shrieking, and Kneeland, in his confusion, trod upon him with his horse. He gave a dig of spur to ride away, but I had my second pistol out and it plucked him from his mount as though I held a rope and yanked him down. The beast tore away and I rode over the trampled man to where Ira Kneeland lay splayed out, blood pouring from his shoulder and gathering in the ruts.

I got down, and when I bent my face above his, showing him my cross and scars, Kneeland understood and let out a long wail. I didn't cover his mouth, though the next plantation was only half a mile up; I let him scream himself out, allowed myself to bask in it like in the heat of all those fires I'd been made to sit so near. Son, you're sure to be damned, so sit here close to the flames and by the end of a lifetime you'll be ready for Hell. Preacher-father didn't know I'd make Hells of my own; whether cutting flesh or bursting it with shot or selling it off in markets, I would be the one who dealt the pain, others the ones who'd endure it. I fell upon the man and held him down, drawing the knife from my bandolier. My knees were on his chest and he was choking now, wild eyes upturned to encompass the blade which would soon pluck them out. And with the stars and moon roaring in their brightest glory overhead, I said to him, I just wish it could be duller.

As it went, I'd have to cover his mouth.

Cart half-full, the loading drawing to a close, I raised the hand that bore Kneeland's toothmarks, where he'd dug and bit in his struggle as I took first his eyes and then his ears, and waved to Reuben. He tipped his glass to me—an act of consolation, so he thought. In a few months he'd have even more to beam about: Smith would be expelled from his country, forced to retire to West Florida, where he lived out his days as a preacher of sorts, with no church or congregation, but wandering the roads and giving sermons on the traps and snares which strayed the path of righteous men.

Reuben thought he'd won, but he was wrong.

Into the house, where I walked the empty rooms with my wife, dust rising from the boards and making her eyes to water. She moved among the shapes in the floor left by the furniture, checking for if anything was left behind, forgotten, slipping in the wet spot on the floor, the handful of string beans from her truck-patch years before, which I'd pulled from their jar to make room for Kneeland's ears.

She shook her foot, mashed the beans into the floor, and kept on searching, her toes catching now and again a ball of lead shot, which would go turning, nothing there to stop its progress, revolutions never-ending, sounding heavy beyond its size, rolling on.

All right, she said. There's nothing left.

She spoke as though reading from a bill, the ledgering of our lives parceled out and blotted. But my Copperhead had misread the lines, for there remained those which she would write by her own hand. She had endured so much and would in awful continuance endure our first months at Berwick's, as I brought my loads of slaves through the bayous and the bay to be penned, tidied, watered, fed. She carried on, a miserable coda to our love. One day she started digging for a truck-patch, and I made her stop. We won't need that anymore, I said, pressing coin in her hand. Go and buy whatever you need.

The product spoke in French or Spanish when they did at all. Generally they were silent; and any man who says the Negroe sings always songs of sorrow is a fool. Sorrow is silence, and they kept it like holy orders as they were, in our secret passages of swampland and then of paper, print, and auction-block, passed into the world of trade.

Tell them, I would say to my Frenchmen hands, that if they speak of this ever I will find them and kill them. And the hand repeated it to unblinking blacks. I quickly learned there was no use in threatening. They were already dead.

And so my own language changed to one of heads and ligature, of breeding stock and field-strength. Red Kate spoke less and less, nor did she take pity on the product; no more than did myself or White. I had her a seamstress's dummy made, carved to her shape from cypress, and sent it to New Orleans, wherefrom weekly would arrive the fine new clothes which she dutifully wore. With the first two rounds of sales, the occupation of some months, I began to build our home. White procured the marble at a fine price, the lumber, the workmen who'd thrown up the grand houses of sugar planters all along the river at whose terminus we lived. And it was to be like the finest planter's palace, the white-columned halls we'd passed on the day we buried our son.

The place was only scaffolding on the day Red Kate abandoned her forbearance. Many times I'd tried to bring her from the cottage where we stayed to the shores of the bay and witness the progress of the house, but up till then she had refused.

I returned from settling the nerves of a customer, a day and night of haggle and soothe, to find my wife sitting on our porch, taking coffee and the sight of me. Lately to embrace her had been a hollow thing, but that day it seemed she shook off her indifference and as I mounted the steps she stood and held out her arms, almost smiling.

Wife, mother to the stillborn dreams of her husband, to children's ghosts, she pressed close, and there were no weapons between us. Gone were her knives and pistols; she had nothing more to protect. In the evening warmth her hair had sweated to her skull, and it was wet against my cheek as once had been drowned Emily's.

Is this all that you wanted? she said.

And I couldn't tell what she meant, or I refused to try. What I wanted in this life was as unreal as the nation to which I'd served unwitting husbandry, as false as the borders and divisions of America, which exist only in the way of spirits, angels, and signs from God. What was there to want? There were only things to take, whether I desired them or not. Red Kate raised her head and kissed me, never shutting her eyes, which trapped in their reflection the darkening sky, as though she sought some sign in mine. Not finding it, she let me go.

She said she'd like to see the house now, and I happily obliged. She wouldn't take the carriage, and so we rode down to the bay each on our own horse. The townsfolk hailed us, their nods and sack-cloth curtsies given no recognition by Red Kate. High and stiff in her new riding habit, she gave all the appearance of a lady of property. Only her features would betray her origins, the trials I'd put her through; and these too, I foolishly imagined, would soften in time.

We came to our inlet of the bay, where on slaving dawns I'd land with the cargo brought up from Isle Dernière. The boats rested at the shore on keel-rutted mud shining golden with the falling sun. She looked on them, to their hollows, gave her reins a flick, the chain-work of her stirrups rattling as she rode on ahead. And as I had the language of the slaving trade, so I had mastered irons. Chains, locks, slip-bars, bits; there was nothing I couldn't bind. The difficulty was in the undoing.

The workmen sat about their tents, the day at an end. Some waved as we got down, hitching off to the nearest pile of lumber. She seemed so eager then, standing before the skeletal beginnings of my great gift to her, boots half-sunk in the yard of mud and sawdust, gazing up at the column beams. They had been hewn from the broadest-trunked trees which could be hauled out of the swamp; some twenty feet high, they dwarfed her.

Too big, she said, still staring upwards.

I came to the column and leaned against it, proudly. I wanted it to be grand, I said, for you.

It'll be lonely here, just us two.

I gave her a smile. We can fill it.

Red Kate shook her head, stepping back, saying, I've got no more in me. I can't. Her heel caught in a pile of tools. Looking down, she stopped, and said, I won't.

I shut my eyes at these words, opened them to the sound of metal, grating, and saw Red Kate with the axe in her hand. She came for me, axe upraised, her face a death-mask empty of expression. And was this how I appeared to my father before I laid him low?

I reached to stop her as she brought the blade down.

The world lit as though lightning-struck and I was cast back against the column, where in the craze of pain I turned to see the axe-head buried into both the wood and my right arm. Bone revealed, blood bubbling at my chin from riven shoulder, unable to breathe; choking for air, I saw in that awful light the gray phantasm of my son, peering down at my wound for but a moment before he went toddling after his mother, who was running for her horse.

The workmen were upon me, prying me loose, unlashing belts to tie me off. One shouted she was getting away as others worked to force a length of leather between my jaws. It was then my breath returned and I howled. I gave out before they hauled me to their fireside, used their saw to hack my arm off clean. Awakening with the burning hell of their cook-pan pressed against my stump, the smell of my searing flesh, as only the damned should know. I didn't see her ride away. And neither would I, in all the time that followed, seek to find her.

Before this would come to pass, in Pinckneyville, I did follow her—out of our house, away from the sounds of rolling shot. In the yard our cart was ready, and at Randolph's Samuel was hurrying the widow up into the seat. Troubled, so it seemed, by my gift.

When I'd first presented it to him, announcing the name of the man they'd belonged to, Samuel had almost dropped it. Out in the yard that morning, he'd seen my hands and the blood they bore, took the jar quickly and slipped it in his coat. He looked about for if anyone was watching, then peeked inside to judge just what it held.

God, said Samuel, back to the old troubles.

It doesn't matter, I said. We're never coming back.

Thank Christ, he said, jostling the jar in his coat and looking about the yard, the dirt once churned with our struggle as we were bound and made captive, sown with our tears and blood. He shook his head. There'll be some repercussion. There always is.

Let Reuben deal with it. He can see what it's like to live his reputation.

God damn I'm glad to go.

And the tail of his words was finished in my mind: And be rid of you.

I wish I could say we're going on to better things, I said. But—

We had our time, he said. And God, how we used it.

If only I had known how much more time remained, the awful count of years, their endless and terrible advancement; and how I would advance with them—in age, in wealth, in sin. But I could only see so far ahead: to the cart, the road, the river, the sea and what it held for me.

In three weeks I would be standing on the shore at Last Island, salt air stinging at my eye as though across the Gulf a thousand wives of Lot had looked back in defiance of God and were in remnants borne upon the wind; there I'd consider the recent news from West Florida: Alexander Stirling, after hearing of Kneeland's fate, had rowed out to the center of a lake, refusing all aid and suffering cruel privations until he at last expired of disease. I prayed on this small satisfaction while Stephen White gave orders to our hands, a few mean boys of Berwick

Village who cared nothing for our crime so long as they were paid, putting bony shoulders to the paddles as we made down inlets and bayous from their town to the Atchafalaya Bay and then by cabotage along the coast to that final spit of sand and writhing root. The boats were sized for twenty souls between them, hard to manage for so few men. But soon we'd have the ballast—the weight of fortune in muscle and bone. And while we waited fishermen working turtle nets did pull ashore, and they scattered the sand with their catches, selecting punies for their supper, prying out the creatures' varicolored guts and drumming in gladness on their shells. I went and paid them to look away from our business soon to come and they took the coin with smiles and slime-slick hands, calling me a good man.

We'd been ready to camp there for a time if need be, pitch among the dunes and scrubby foliage for shelter; but in the evening, as the sky lit along its rim, there came masts extended in black spines, stabbing at the blood-bowed gut of Heaven.

The moon broke full and screaming in its bleakness to the tide. The fishermen brought out a pot for their meal, spooning mouthfuls of turtle gizzard even as it cooked over the lengths of broken driftwood gathered by the eager Berwick boys, with whom they shared. But they'd built their fire so near the water that the tide in its increase went inching ever nearer, threatening the meager flame, causing it to hiss at first, then drowning it entire to the laughter of them all. White by then had gone over to the feast, sharing their spoons, cussing that he'd burnt his tongue. I didn't move, ground my heels into the sand as a cloudbank overtook the moon, and I looked for the first time upon the night-black Gulf; in a breath I tasted it upon my tongue, unburnt for so long, and in that breath there came the last hissing gasp of the Lord's Word, which I would hear for a lifetime: The sky was light again and glutted Heaven hung there like a pustule; and I saw the mast-cross pierce the bloat of Paradise and the gore of all the souls I'd sent there spilling down in torrents on the ship. I saw the Negroes in their chains drowned in the blood of Heaven and set free. But I had come to know that my visions all were false, and that out there skiffs were put to oar, and that in them went people black as the night to come, shuddering against the waves and terribly afraid; as well they should, coming to a country such as this.

Acknowledgments

In the hope that I have done honor by their names, I give thanks to the following: my wife, Lauren, for love and endurance; my mother, for the language; my father, for the edge; Andrew Smith and Rachel Lane, for laughter in dark times; Catfish, for abiding kindness and a home away from home; Christopher Tusa and Michael Garriga, for taking in a stray and making him a brother; the students and staff of Seven Hills Academy in Tallahassee, Florida, for daily lessons in courage and humanity; Elisabeth Schmitz, for bringing me to tears; Gail Hochman, for steadfast advocacy; Josh McCall, for exquisite editing; Peter Blackstock and the staff of Grove/Atlantic, for tireless attention. I would like to give special thanks to the teachers, too numerous to name, who took interest in an often difficult student, and without whose guidance and encouragement none of this would be possible.

Above all, to white-bearded Anansi, benefactor and friend beyond compare, to whom no praise or thanks will do justice: I am forever in your debt.

Author's Note

Though I have strayed far from history in telling the story of Angel Woolsack, who did not exist, much of his world and those who inhabit it did. I am indebted to countless contemporary sources, the often contradictory facts of which I have embellished or obscured, but would be remiss to not acknowledge the modern scholars whose works served as inspiration and guide to this imagined history, namely: Stanley Clisby Arthur, *The Story of the Kemper Brothers* (1933) and *The Story of the West Florida Rebellion* (1935); William C. Davis, *The Rogue Republic* (2011); Ross Phares, *Reverend Devil: Master Criminal of the Old South* (1941); David A. Bice, *The Original Lone Star Republic* (2004); Andro Linklater, *An Artist in Treason: the Extraordinary Double Life of General James Wilkinson* (2009); Nancy Isenberg, *Fallen Founder: the Life of Aaron Burr* (2007).

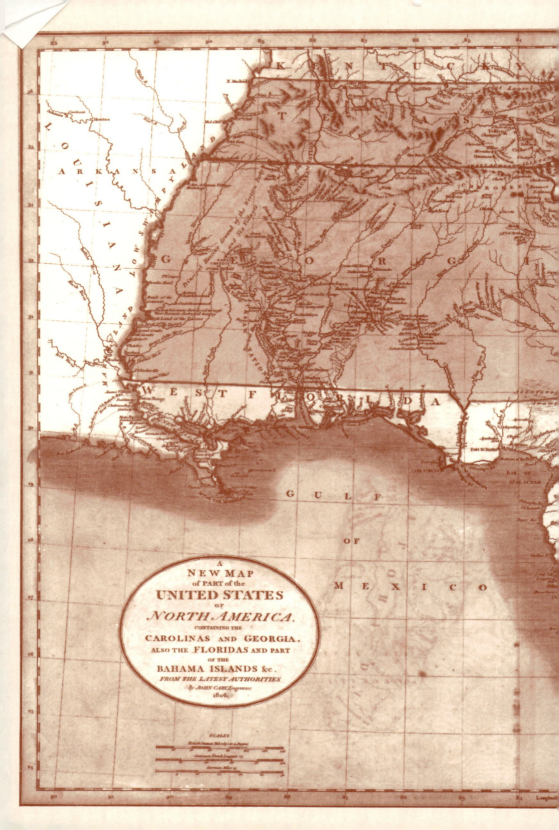

A
NEW MAP
of PART of the
UNITED STATES
OF
NORTH AMERICA,
CONTAINING THE
CAROLINAS AND GEORGIA,
ALSO THE FLORIDAS AND PART
OF THE
BAHAMA ISLANDS &c.
FROM THE LATEST AUTHORITIES
By JOHN CARY Engraver.
1806.